These Three Remain

A NOVEL OF

Fitzwilliam Darcy,

GENTLEMAN

PAMELA AIDAN

A TOUCHSTONE BOOK
Published by Simon & Schuster
New York   London   Toronto   Sydney

TOUCHSTONE
Rockefeller Center
1230 Avenue of the Americas
New York, NY 10020

TOUCHSTONE and colophon are registered trademarks of Simon & Schuster Inc.

This Touchstone Edition 2007

For information regarding special discounts for bulk purchases, please contact Simon & Schuster Special Sales at 1-800-456-6798 or business@simonandschuster.com.

Designed by Jan Pisciotta

Manufactured in the United States of America

10 9 8 7 6 5 4 3 2 1

Library of Congress Cataloging-in-Publication Data
Aidan, Pamela.
    These three remain : a novel of Fitzwilliam Darcy, gentleman / Pamela Aidan.
     p. cm. —(Fitzwilliam Darcy, gentleman ; 3)
     1. Darcy, Fitzwilliam (Fictitious character)—Fiction. 2. Bennet, Elizabeth (Fictitious character)—Fiction. 3. England—Fiction. I. Title.

PS3601.I33T47 2007
813'.6—dc22
                                            2006051420
ISBN-13: 978-0-7432-9137-8
ISBN-10:   0-7432-9137-9

To my husband,
Michael

Contents

And now these three remain: faith, hope and love.
But the greatest of these is love.

—*1 Corinthians 13:13*

These Three Remain

CHAPTER 1

Her Infinite Variety

*H*eigh-up, there!" James the coachman's voice rang out in its familiar timbre, urging the team pulling Darcy's traveling coach to put to in their harnesses and take them through the tollgate out of London and on to the road to Kent. Darcy relaxed into the green velvet squabs as the coach was pulled smoothly forward under James's expert whip. He flicked a glance at his cousin, who sat opposite him with his nose buried in the *Post*. The Peninsular War was heating up once more, with General Wellesley, now Earl of Wellington, again laying siege to Badajoz. This third siege of that crucial *ciudad* had commenced only a week before, and reports of the action were just arriving in London to fill the papers and the populace with new hopes and fears.

"Did you see this, Fitz?" Richard turned the paper over and vigorously poked a finger at one of the reports.

"Yes, one of the *many* articles I read while waiting for you to present yourself this morning." Darcy's lips twisted in sarcasm. Colonel Richard Fitzwilliam had arrived at Erewile House, Darcy's London home, the night before in order for them to get an early start on their yearly spring visit to their aunt, Lady Catherine de

Bourgh. But as chance would have it, his friend Dyfed Brougham had "dropped by," and the evening had stretched into the wee hours of the morning. Richard had been correspondingly late in arising, setting their journey back a considerable number of hours.

"Lie low, men. A jaw-me-dead is on the horizon . . ." Richard drew his hand across his brow as if to shield himself from the expected verbal ice shower.

"And you would deserve it," Darcy shot back with a snort.

"But I would then make plea to your kind and beneficent nature—" Richard continued. Darcy snorted again but couldn't suppress a smile. "—and place the blame entirely upon *your* friend."

Darcy laughed outright at that. "*My* friend? Dy hardly spoke to me once he saw you in the room."

"He *was* attentive; was he not?"

"Excessively!"

"An amiable gentleman, indeed, and well informed! I had always rated him a care-for-naught and a prime rattle. Never could understand your partiality for him, Fitz. Not your sort."

"He was not like that at university. Quite the opposite, in fact."

"So you say." Fitzwilliam shrugged his shoulders and settled back into the comfort of the coach's cushions. "And I can almost believe you after last night. Could not understand before why you gave him leave to call on Georgiana while we are on pilgrimage to Rosings; but it was a shrewd decision, I will grant you now."

Darcy nodded. "Yes, Brougham's approval will count for much when Georgiana makes her curtsy next year."

"Oh, that too, I'll be bound," Richard agreed. Darcy looked questioningly at his cousin, who in response, laid the newspaper down upon his lap. "You have not noticed how easy Georgiana is with Brougham? He makes her smile in a trice, and they can talk for hours, or would if propriety did not dictate otherwise. Aside from ourselves, I have never known Georgiana to be comfortable in male company, especially since—" Richard suddenly clamped his lips together. A moment of awkward silence passed. "But your friend has managed it, managed it quite well . . ." His voice trailed off at the frown that had begun to crease Darcy's brow. "Truly, you had not noticed?"

"Nothing untoward, Richard! Nothing that would be considered a particular notice of Georgiana on Brougham's part." Darcy bristled, assuring his cousin and himself in the same breath of the utter nonsense of the implications underlying Fitzwilliam's observations. "Nor, on Georgiana's part, an affection beyond that for a friend of the family."

"Of course 'nothing untoward,' Fitz! Good Lord!" Fitzwilliam made a strategic withdrawal back behind the *Post*. Darcy sighed lightly and closed his eyes. The last two months had not been the most agreeable of his life, and his preoccupations could easily have blinded him to what Fitzwilliam was intimating. But surely he was making much out of mere commonplaces! Dy had been kind to Georgiana, yes! More than kind, actually, with his silence on that matter of Georgiana's undue interest in Wilberforce's theological fusillade, which he had surprised her perusing the day of their reacquaintance and which she had, most unfortunately, dropped upon his foot. It was simply a matter of Dy's debt of friendship to himself and the fact of his irrepressible address and nice manners. If his sister had remained immune to Dy's engaging person, Darcy would have more cause for concern.

No, his concern had been with his own peace after returning from his ill-fated trip to Oxfordshire in search of "The Woman" who would serve as a proper wife. The events at Norwycke Castle had so disgusted and appalled him that upon his return to London he had forsworn any further ventures into the marriage mart in the foreseeable future. Instead, he had plunged himself into family and business concerns, as well as the more agreeable social obligations of an unattached male of his station. The first of those family concerns had been the highly disagreeable task of apprising his cousin D'Arcy of the behavior of his fiancée, Lady Felicia Lowden, at Norwycke. D'Arcy's face had gone black with rage, but to his credit and Darcy's relief, he had not demanded recompense from his messenger. Rather, he placed the blame where it lay and immediately consulted with his father, Lord Matlock, on how the engagement might be broken. Two weeks later a notice appeared in the *Post* in which Lady Felicia "regretfully" exercised her prerogative. The gossip was, of course, intolerable, but far better gossip now than the inevitable scandal later. The Darcy and Fitzwilliam families breathed a collective sigh of relief, while the de Bourgh branch contented itself with a long letter expressing satisfaction with the validation of previously unspoken doubts on the suitability of a connection in that quarter held from the beginning.

Georgiana, the dear girl, had refrained from pressing him for the details of his time at Lord Sayre's. She had made it her purpose to ensure his comfort at home and, with Brougham's connivance, to reinsert him into his usual social rounds. Within a fortnight of his return, Darcy was squiring her to concerts, recitals, and art exhibitions, while Dy dragged him to Jackson's Parlour, his fencing master's establishment, several assemblies, and a few nights before, a highly illegal prizefight. Between Dy's satirical humor and his unerring nose for the intriguing, and Georgiana's quietly expressed love, Darcy began to feel more himself. Occasional, dark prickings of his conscience did trouble him. The revelation of the true depths of his hatred for George Wickham, who had so nearly ruined his sister and poisoned Elizabeth against him was nearly as shocking to his understanding as was how close he had come to surrendering to Lady Sylvanie Sayre's passionately offered temptations. But as Richard had predicted, much of it seemed now only a bad dream, and he was finding it easier to excuse or ignore those uncomfortable memories.

Alas, that did not mean all was well. On the contrary, one of the problems he had hoped to have done with reared its head again almost upon his return to London; for he had not been in Town two days before his friend Charles Bingley ran him to ground. Bingley's joy at his return was so sincere, and his simple, unaffected nature such a wonderful contrast to those with whom Darcy had dealt the previous week, that an invitation to spend an evening dining *en famille* was accepted with alacrity. But Darcy and Georgiana had barely been relieved of their wraps and coats before Charles's sister Miss Caroline Bingley had swooped upon him to whisper in agonized tones that she could decently avoid a visit from Miss Jane Bennet no longer; and having committed to a visit on Saturday, she urgently requested any advice he might have for her in this distasteful matter.

Glancing a moment into her disingenuous eyes, he had replied that he could not imagine her requiring any direction of his and assured her of his confidence in her ability to depress the pretensions of so unsophisticated a young woman as Miss Bennet. Her love for Bingley he might doubt, but of Miss Bennet's understanding he was certain. Treated to an appearance of the imperious Caroline, she would know the acquaintance severed. But the damage had been done. He had spent the rest of the evening in frank discomfort, trying vainly to exorcise the bright and pleasing shade of Elizabeth Bennet that Miss Bingley's plea had conjured from his mind's eye and from among the company in which he had so often observed her.

And now Darcy and Fitzwilliam were on their way to Aunt Catherine's. The ritual visit had begun when Darcy was a child in the company of his parents and Richard, whose fractious nature mysteriously underwent an incomplete but notable transformation when he was in Mr. Darcy's company. Then it had been his father and Richard. Now, of course, he and his cousin had stepped into his father's role as adviser to Lady Catherine. It required both of them; and even then, Darcy was not confident that their suggestions were taken as seriously as his father's had been. No, his aunt's welcome had little to do with the maintenance or profitability of Rosings and more, much more, to do with her expectations of him in regard to her daughter, Anne. He very sincerely pitied his cousin Anne and wished her well in health and situation, but he did not so pity her that he was in any way willing to provide her a means of escape through an offer of marriage. Aunt Catherine might smile and hint until Doomsday, but—

"Darcy, what *is* that bit that you keep stroking at?"

"What!" Darcy brought his wandering mind back within the confines of the coach.

Fitzwilliam had laid aside the newspaper and now motioned toward his hand. "In your waistcoat pocket. And do not tell me it is nothing! I have noticed you fingering it lo, these several months, and it is driving me to distraction."

"This?" Darcy could feel the heat of the flush upon his face as he drew out the embroidery threads, now ragged and fragile from his repeated fondling. Blast Richard! How was he to explain them?

"You've taken up sewing?" Fitzwilliam teased upon seeing the coil. Darcy pulled a face at him and tucked them back into his waistcoat. "Come, come, Darcy! It is a lady's token, surely; and you must now tell me the particulars." He rubbed his hands together vigorously. "For Father Inquisitor will not rest until all is confessed. Shall I call for the thumbscrews?"

"Rogue!"

"Father Inquisitor Rogue to you." Fitzwilliam laughed but would not be dissuaded. Leaning forward, his elbows on his knees, he said, "From the beginning now."

Darcy leveled a look at his cousin calculated to freeze the blood in his veins. Inured to the familiar tactic, Richard quickly arranged his features, seeing his look and then raising it by the addition of a crooked eyebrow. "From the beginning," Richard intoned again and in a terrible voice reminiscent of his redoubtable father. "Quickly now, or I shall begin to think it is something serious!"

The color in Darcy's face heightened, and for a moment he felt something akin to sheer panic. *Serious?* A vision of those enticing curls caught up with ribbon rosettes and the remembered pleasure of her gloved hand in his coalesced in an instant, causing him to all but squirm in his seat. The irony was that he'd not been thinking of Elizabeth as he'd stroked the threads, but Richard's curiosity at them had taken him by surprise, animating thoughts and sensations that, he was near to confessing, had gained within him a life of their own. *Good Lord, not now!* he reprimanded himself as they washed over him, heedless of his consent. *Have some dignity, for pity's sake!* He glanced back at his cousin to find him gleefully watching his every shift.

"A complete triumph!" Fitzwilliam crowed, falling back into the seat. "I have finally discomposed you into blushing silence! Who *is* this singular lady?" Richard's all too accurate deduction lured Darcy toward the mortifying waters of Heated Denial, but his premature crow both stung Darcy out of his confusion and provided him with subject for a ruse.

"You are far off the mark if you think them a sign of a lady's favor." Darcy infused as much disinterest into his voice as he could command. That much, at least, was true; and its expression steadied him. The exercise of even that modicum of control began to sweep back the beguiling phantoms. "If I blush, it is with embarrassment at the recollection of an indiscretion on the part of a friend whose imprudence necessitated my involvement in a delicate matter—a rescue or intervention, if you will—before he committed a grave error of judgment."

The expression on Fitzwilliam's face declared he was not to be satisfied with so small a bone. "An error of judgment? But," he insisted, "there *was* a lady involved, was there not?"

"Yes, there was a lady involved." Darcy sighed. Richard would not be dissuaded if he scented a female at the bottom of a coil. He would have to give his cousin more. "My friend very nearly put himself in the position of being required to offer for a young woman of exceedingly unfortunate situation and family."

"Oh," Fitzwilliam responded thoughtfully, "that is trouble indeed." He paused and looked out the window as the coach shuddered over a rill in the road, then turned back to Darcy with a gleam in his eye. "But come, old man, was she beautiful?"

Darcy looked askance at his cousin. "Beautiful! Richard, can you think of aught else save if she was beautiful?" Fitzwilliam threw him a devilish grin and shrugged his shoulders. "Yes," Darcy said, exasperation evident in his tone, "if you must have it, she was a well-favored creature and sweet tempered, withal; but I swear she does not love him—leastways not near as much as his prospects." He tugged at his gloves, smoothing each in turn before delivering the coup de grâce. "Be that as it may, it was her family, not to mention a lack of fortune, to which every objection was raised."

"A man could suffer the family from a distance, surely, if the lady were otherwise desirable and fortune no impediment."

"Perhaps it could be overlooked," Darcy agreed hesitantly, "if it were proved that the lady was devoted to the gentleman. Such is not the case. I assure you, much more proof than was apparent would be required to negate the inconveniences attendant upon forging a connection with such a family as I observed."

"You make them sound a horror!" Fitzwilliam laughed.

"A family of reduced circumstances with any number of unmarried daughters allowed unbridled freedom to roam the countryside, impertinent as you please." He ticked off the points in a litany with which he had become quite familiar. "A father who will not be troubled to rule his family and a mother who looks on any new pair of breeches in the neighborhood as the property of one or other of her offspring."

"And did not you as well as your friend become her quarry?"

"I did not suit." Darcy looked down his nose at his cousin.

"I can well imagine." Fitzwilliam laughed at his ironic expression and then shook his head. "Your friend must have been besotted. Fallen 'violently in love,' then, was he?"

"In a word." Darcy seconded the description but then turned his attention to the passing scenery. Fitzwilliam was all too perceptive. It would not do to have him surmise too much. "But I believe he is now in a fair way to relinquishing that delusion."

"With your help, of course?"

"Yes," he responded brusquely and looked his inquisitor squarely in the eye. "With my help. I congratulate myself upon achieving it. It would have been a disastrous match. The bride's family would have made him the laughingstock of Polite Society."

Fitzwilliam breathed out a sobered sigh. "A laughingstock, eh? I hope your friend appreciates the service you have done him. He owes you his life or, at the least, his sanity. Well done, Fitz," he finished sincerely and reached for the *Post*.

Well done? Was it truly? Darcy frowned, his thoughts and emotions caught in a web of contention. His words to Fitzwilliam had not been hollow. Miss Bennet, he was still prepared to swear, did not suffer that most tender of emotions in regard to Bingley. Had he not observed her closely to discover just that? But neither, it was equally true, did she present the appearance of a fortune huntress. No, he would swear to that as well. Miss Bennet, quite frankly, was an enigma. An enigma that Bingley had pierced and he had not? Bingley had been adamant that she loved him! Darcy crossed his arms over his chest and stared out the coach window at the rolling hillocks and fields just come into their spring green. No, that chain of thought was unprofitable; the last link in the affair had been forged. He clenched his jaw as consternation seized him. That last link had been the one that bound him to Miss Bingley in a distasteful conspiracy of silence against his own friend. How he hated such disguise! How he despised the whispered fears of discovery Caroline Bingley never ceased to pour into his ear until Miss Bennet was safely gone from Town. However he might bow to its necessity or congratulate himself on Bingley's escape from the perils of such a family, the odium of the measures he had employed would remain a blot upon Darcy's conscience.

His conscience! Darcy closed his eyes against the cheery March sunlight slanting across the coach's seats. That staid organ of guidance and reproof had been of no comfort to him for quite some time. In his solitary moments, it churned up the dark anger he'd been forced to acknowledge at Norwycke, and it delivered him a sharp pang every time he surprised that expression on Bingley's face. Bingley was still pluck to the bone and ready with a smile, but behind it lay a shadow that Darcy had been confident would fade upon their return to Town and its many diversions. It had not, and Darcy knew his friend to be struggling to regain his former state by that private, reflective look of his, which spoke of the presence in his body of only half a heart. Bingley maintained his social life with determination but only a portion of his former eagerness. No lady's name had been associated with his own, although more than a few had been the recipient's of some small attention. Bingley read more and spoke less, exhibiting the reserve Darcy had formerly accused him of lacking, in the hope, Bingley once told him, of setting himself to rights again. It was likely a lost cause, for how did one regain innocence of heart or forget the sweetness of love? Darcy had been wrong about him. Miss Bennet's heart may not have been touched, but Bingley's truly had, and he would ever carry the wound. What other course had been open to him? None—and still act the part of a true friend and mentor. *But,* Darcy's conscience pressed him, *was it well done?*

Then there was Elizabeth. Had he done well with her? His characterization of her family had been unmercifully accurate, save for her and her elder sister. In that, he had done them a discourtesy in his recital to his cousin. Heaven forfend that she should ever hear of his words or that they should ever be associated with her. It was true that the unsuitable circumstances and temper of the Bennet family were impediments for Bingley. It was doubly so for himself. Although lack of fortune was not of paramount concern to Darcy, the insurmountable difficulty lay in the degradation of such a connection and the unending embarrassment the behavior of its members would invariably visit upon him and his family. ". . . surely, if the lady were otherwise desirable," Richard had opined, blithely multiplying the beneficial effects of distance. Although the lady was more than desirable, the moon was not distance enough to belie the difficulties! Yet did he not continue to rack himself with thoughts of her, dreams of her, and these blasted, entangling strands of silk that corded him up and bound him to her?

Darcy's fingers went unerringly to his waistcoat pocket, but a rustle of newspaper gave him pause. Looking up from under his brows, he watched his cousin, waiting for assurance that he was well engrossed in his reading. A disdainful snort and a "Well, I should hope so! Idiot!" proved Richard's attention to be engaged. Darcy slowly drew them out, the threads that had both served and tormented him. "Perhaps . . . if it were proved that the lady was devoted to the gentleman . . ." He had said that, traitorously holding out the exception to himself, knowing it impossible. She was in Hertfordshire; he was in Kent, or London, or Derbyshire—it did not matter where. They would never meet again unless he proposed it, nor should they. More than mere miles were involved. To attempt to engage her affection would be the act of a libertine, for nothing honorable could come of it. She would always be her mother's daughter; he would always be the son of his father—Darcy of Pemberley.

His fingers closed around the threads. Drawing himself up, he turned to the coach window and quickly released the catches, letting the upper pane slide down. It came to rest with a soft thud. The rattle of the harness chains and the sound of the horses' hooves upon the road were suddenly louder, catching Fitzwilliam's attention away from his paper. "Ah, fresh country air!" He grinned at Darcy and then went back to his reading. Darcy looked down into his gloved palm at the dulled, tattered silks. Then, closing his eyes against them, he leaned out the window and let them fall. Caught by a spring breeze, they drifted away, coming to rest by the side of the road.

"Who is that man, do you suppose, Darcy?" Fitzwilliam's face was full of amused incredulity. He cocked his head toward the window as the coach came up upon a short lane that led to a modest home. "By the look of him, he must be a clergyman; but a more queer bird I challenge you to find. Look at him!" Darcy roused himself to glance in the recommended direction and was brought up straight with a start of recognition. "He keeps bowing and . . . Here!" Fitzwilliam was out of his seat and had the window down and was now leaning out of it.

"For Heaven's sake, Richard, do not—"

"Greetings, my good man!" Fitzwilliam bellowed out the window as they passed and then sat down with a laugh. "Can that be our aunt's new clergyman, come to replace old Satherthwaite?"

"Mr. Collins," Darcy informed his cousin through gritted teeth. How could he have forgotten that that tedious little man, who on the merit of his collar had claimed such undue familiarity with him at Bingley's ball, would be here.

"Collins? You have met him, then?" Fitzwilliam asked in surprise.

Darcy nodded. "In Hertfordshire last autumn, when I accompanied Bingley on his ill-fated hunt for a suitable piece of property. Collins is related to one of the families in the neighborhood."

"How is he, then? As good at bowing and scraping as old Satherthwaite? Lord, what a sycophant he was! But it still made me cringe to see the way Her Ladyship led him about his own business."

"I suspect our aunt would have more of the same in any parson whose living depended upon her, but whether he meets or exceeds Satherthwaite, I cannot say. I *can* say this." Darcy's mouth twisted in wry humor. "I suspect that Mr. Collins is something of a bantam cock beneath his clerical collar." He paused, enjoying Fitzwilliam's incredulity. "He introduced himself to me at Bingley's ball."

"Introduced himself?" Fitzwilliam's astonishment was complete. "Why, the cheeky fellow! Aunt Catherine would not like to hear of that! I suppose when we meet I should expect to be greeted with my Christian name!"

Darcy snorted inelegantly in reply but lapsed into silence as memories of that occasion claimed him. The man had first intruded on his notice during his awkward attempt to lead Elizabeth through a country dance. Initially, Collins's ineptitude had seemed humorous, but the lady's mounting humiliation at her partner's want of skill and proper courtesy had nearly moved him to intervene. He had resisted the temptation and then, when Elizabeth's ruffled emotions had calmed, surprised her and the entirety of the room with the offer of his hand for the next set. What had followed had been of equal parts pleasure and pain. Like the threads he had finally put away from him. Like the memories he had not yet succeeded in sending after them.

The coach rolled on the short distance to Rosings, the seat of the de Bourgh family and home of their widowed Aunt Catherine. Darcy could see by a sudden display of restless attention to his neckcloth and the disposition of his coat and waistcoat that his cousin had begun marshaling his reserves of good humor and gallantry in final preparation for their reception and stay. Lady Catherine had terrified Richard when they were boys, but as he had matured and discovered the byways that led to female sensibilities, he had put that knowledge to good use with their aunt. For years now he'd turned her up sweet, as sweet as a woman of their aunt's disposition was ever likely to become; but it was an achievement, he always insisted, that required careful, yearly cultivation.

They passed the gates and began the sweep through the park. The horses under James's easy rein quickened their pace, scenting that their labors were nearly done. As they rounded a curve that took them near the open grove Sir Lewis de Bourgh's grandfather had cleared, Darcy's thoughts were interrupted by a flash of color, like that of a lady's gown or pelisse. Frowning slightly, he twisted about, trying to satisfy himself with what it might be, but the density of trees and the swiftness of the coach made it impossible.

"See something?" Fitzwilliam asked.

"Nothing . . . a servant on her way to the village, I suppose."

Darcy shrugged and then added with a teasing smile, "And no, I do not know whether she is beautiful."

"Darcy, you know I do not trifle with servant girls!" Fitzwilliam looked at him, affronted. "His Lordship would have nailed my hide to the stable door if I ever had and is perfectly capable of doing so still!" Fitzwilliam shuddered as he elaborated on the lengths to which he believed his parent capable of going in show of his disapprobation of such a pastime. "And Her Ladyship! Mater would hand him the nails!" The more heated his protestations became, the wider Darcy's grin spread until it finally caught Fitzwilliam's attention. Realizing he had been led on, he stopped short and glared at Darcy before he joined in his cousin's amusement.

By the time James had brought the coach beneath Rosings's portico, they were once more the sober gentlemen their aunt expected to descend from it. And expected they most certainly were. A retinue of servants lined the stairway to the door, all at exquisite attention, ready to unload the coach and conduct the visitors into Her Ladyship's presence.

"And so it begins." Fitzwilliam gave one more tug to his waistcoat and checked the line of his trousers. "If she complains that we are not in breeches, I shall hold you eternally responsible!" he assured Darcy as the coach stopped and the door immediately sprang open. The manservant at the door was the same long-suffering soul who had performed this office for as many years as Darcy could remember. He nodded to the man's "Welcome to Rosings, sir," and started up the stairs after him as soon as Fitzwilliam had descended from the coach. They both knew the way, of course, but Lady Catherine was a fiend when it came to observance of the proper formalities; therefore, both gentlemen followed sedately behind the slow-moving servant until they reached the doors of the Rose Salon.

"Darcy . . . Fitzwilliam. You are arrived at last!" The irritation in their aunt's penetrating voice was unmistakable. Doubtless, she had expected them hours earlier. Darcy gave his cousin a face that clearly communicated who was to take the blame for their late-ness. Fitzwilliam sighed; then, both of them advanced into the salon to make their bows to the lady who sat in regal command of all within her purview.

"Your Ladyship." Darcy bowed and kissed the hand his aunt extended. Fitzwilliam did likewise a moment later.

Lady Catherine sniffed as her eyes roamed up and down her two nephews. "Neither of you dressed properly! Breeches and stockings, sirs, are the correct attire for paying visits. I may lay this laxity at Fitzwilliam's door, I have no doubt."

Richard shot a murderous look at his cousin before beginning his campaign. "Your Ladyship, it was D—"

"Come," Lady Catherine interrupted him, "greet your cousin." Both men obediently turned to the pale creature on the settee at a right angle to Lady Catherine's and bowed. Anne de Bourgh's thin frame was completely obscured by the voluminous shawls deemed necessary to protect her health from the slightest inclemency. In most young women, this swaddling should have resulted in a com-plexion high with color, but Anne's wan face was mute testimony to her continued delicacy.

Darcy stepped forward and formally extended his hand. "Cousin," he murmured as Anne removed hers from beneath the shawls and placed it languidly in his. For all her wraps, his cousin's fingers remained cold; and as he raised them to his lips, he won-dered anew how she could support her life, caught as it was be-tween ill health and her mother's domineering officiousness.

"Cousin," she offered him listlessly in return. He stepped back in Fitzwilliam's favor and observed her as she received his cousin's attention and repeated her single-word greeting. There was no change in her pallid countenance, nor any spark of interest at their arrival in her eyes. Instead, she seemed relieved to have done with the formality, retreating inward as she slipped her hand once more beneath the shawls.

"Does not your cousin look in health?" Lady Catherine's question demanded their agreement, and neither of her nephews disappointed her. "We have engaged in a new regimen recommended me by one of the Regent's own doctors; therefore, it cannot but be beneficial. Within a year, I expect, Anne will be entirely able to take her rightful place." She turned a knowing smile upon Darcy. "An eventuality for which we have all waited with anticipation."

Only his careful reserve prevented Darcy from giving evidence of the contumacy that unexpectedly gripped him. Lady Catherine alluded, of course, to her expectation of nuptials between his cousin and himself. He flicked a glance at Anne, confirming his opinion that she believed in its "eventuality" no more than he did, and then looked away. It was an old theme, the tune of which he had long since learned to ignore without incurring open antagonism with Her Ladyship. But this time her insinuations had conjured up in him an exceedingly visceral response. Of a certainty, he wished his cousin any increase in vitality and health. Who would not? But no increase in those qualities would make her a fit wife for him. This, too, he had long known. Why, then, this tumbling of his equanimity? *You well know why*, his conscience intruded, but he pushed it away and concentrated on his next words to his aunt.

"All her relations will, indeed, rejoice, Ma'am."

Lady Catherine's smile hesitated at his response, but she did not press him, choosing instead to direct them to seat themselves and partake of some refreshment to relieve the depredations of their journey.

"You are inexcusably late, Nephews." She returned to her original subject when they had settled back into their chairs with their tea. "I expected you some hours ago and had prepared myself to hear of a serious accident. Since you are both in health, it must have been a problem with a horse or the coach."

"No, Ma'am," Darcy volunteered, deciding to spare Fitzwilliam his aunt's inevitable lecture. "We were late setting out."

"Late setting out! What could have prevented your leaving, I wonder. Surely that man of yours knows the clock!"

"Yes, Ma'am," Darcy replied carefully, "Fletcher is in nowise to blame."

Lady Catherine's piercing regard shifted to his cousin. Knowing he was about to be called to account, Fitzwilliam launched a flanking maneuver. "An old friend of Darcy's, the Earl of Westmarch, came by for a visit, Ma'am, and practically settled in for the night. We could not very well chuck him into the street—"

"The Earl of Westmarch?" Her Ladyship turned back to Darcy. "I am astonished that you should keep company with him, Darcy! I knew his father, you know; and what a disappointment his son would be to him if he were still alive. Now *there* was perfection in a gentleman. Twice I danced with him during my Season, and I do not deceive myself when I say that I would have been Lady Westmarch had not the scandal, which I am certain that woman started apurpose, forced him into marriage prematurely. I have heard only the most shocking things about the son and advise you to cut the connection or at least refuse to receive him at Erewile House when Georgiana is at home. You cannot be too circumspect in the care of young ladies. Their heads may be turned with the least attention by a practiced flirt. Her new governess keeps a close watch on her, I trust?"

Lady Catherine's trust was confirmed with a clipped "Yes, Ma'am" as Darcy rose from his seat and stalked to the tea table. His aunt's persistence in her delusion that he would take Anne to wife had sent him into a rebellious mood that was acerbated by the underlying truth that, if it were not Anne, it would be some other female equally equipped to defraud him of true companionship of heart and mind. His aunt's libel of Brougham and directions concerning his private conduct were not without years of precedent, but today they were fuel for the fire of Darcy's discontent. Perhaps it was wise that this year's visit be cut short.

"That is well, then," Lady Catherine called to him. "Although, if you had engaged the woman I advised, you would be sure to have nothing to worry about on that score!" His back still turned, Darcy gritted his teeth, set his cup down on the table, and reached for the teapot. "You may apply to Lady Metcalf on my eye for the proper governess. She declares Miss Pope 'a treasure,' which, I have not a doubt, she is. Steady and regular instruction is what young ladies require or there will be trouble, mark my words. I have only recently become acquainted with just such a situation and expect to hear of calamity any day. Five daughters and never a governess!"

Everything around Darcy seemed to still as his aunt's words echoed in his brain. Five daughters! His hand trembled slightly as he gripped the teapot's handle and poured another cup, causing the steaming brew to splash over the rim and into the saucer. Was it possible that Collins had apprised Her Ladyship of events in Hertfordshire?

"No governess, Ma'am? Extraordinary!" Fitzwilliam commented, as if such things were his daily concern. Darcy knew it to be a ploy, designed to keep their aunt's attention from once more focusing upon himself; but this time he was as desirous for more of the particulars as his aunt was to reveal them.

"Indeed!" replied Lady Catherine, nodding at Fitzwilliam approvingly, "and so I said. But, Nephew, that does not constitute the height of this family's folly. No, indeed!" Her Ladyship vigorously tapped her silver-handled walking stick on the floor. "Not only have they not had the benefit of a governess's discipline but they are all out before the elder ones are married! From the oldest to the youngest, who is a mere fifteen years of age! I have never heard of such foolishness, and so I informed Mrs. Collins's friend."

Darcy's cup rattled on its saucer so badly he was forced to stay it with his other hand. Mrs. Collins's friend? There had been no Mrs. Collins when he had taken his leave of Netherfield. Who was she, and who was her friend that Her Ladyship would hold forth upon Collins's relations? He took a deep, steadying breath and turned back to his relatives.

"Mrs. Collins?" Fitzwilliam queried. Darcy almost blessed him aloud.

"A modest, steady young woman my new rector recently took to wife, having met her during a visit I encouraged him to make to an estranged relative on his father's side. 'Come back with a wife, Mr. Collins,' I told him, 'and you come back with all you will need for a useful life.' I cannot say how often he has thanked me for that advice. She is exactly what I would have chosen for him. Not above herself, quiet, but with agreeable manners, as is her father, Sir William Lucas, who was lately here to visit them. I am informed that you have already made their acquaintance, Darcy."

Lucas! Darcy searched his memory for a name. Charlotte . . . Miss Charlotte Lucas, Elizabeth's close friend and confidante! How many times had he observed them tête-à-tête? Miss Lucas had married Collins? That could only mean . . . ! His fingers crept to the pocket of his waistcoat, but they found nothing. Where? Of course, he had left them upon the road! Looking up, he caught Richard regarding him curiously, his brow crooked at the disposition of his hand. Self-consciously, he smoothed down the waistcoat and essayed a response. "Yes, Ma'am. Last November in Hertfordshire. I . . . I had accompanied a friend who was in search of property in that neighborhood. In the course of that search, I met Sir William and his family."

Was fate to bring back into his life the reality of which those threads had been merely the shadow? He strained to know, to be certain who this friend could be, and yet, if it was Elizabeth, what should be his course?

"I am informed that you have also met Mrs. Collins's friend, Miss Elizabeth Bennet. It is quite annoying, Darcy, that I shall not have the pleasure of making a first introduction."

Elizabeth! It *was* Elizabeth! Darcy's heart began to pound, and his hands went cold as ice. How should he meet her? As indifferent acquaintances? As familiar antagonists? Had she completed her sketch of his character, or had she refrained as he had asked? And Wickham! With what other falsehoods had he plied her after Darcy had abandoned the field?

"Darcy?" Lady Catherine's voice brought him back to the present. "I was saying, I am much put out that I will not have the pleasure of making a first introduction, for Miss Bennet assured me that you were well acquainted. I find that she is rather close to impertinent on occasion, which might lead her to overstating the situation. Is this true that you are acquainted?"

"Quite true, Ma'am. The society in Hertfordshire was small, and we were thrown in each other's way rather often," he confessed.

"Is that so?" Richard pursed his lips, a wicked gleam lighting his eye. "Then perhaps we should pay Mr. *and* Mrs. Collins and Mrs. Collins's friend a visit tomorrow. What do you say, Darcy?"

A shiver of alarm passed through Darcy. Tomorrow? He gathered himself to discourage the project when a thought struck him. Would it not be better to have their first meeting away from the eyes of Lady Catherine? Although he would need to exercise caution where Richard was concerned, it was the perfect opportunity to test his own composure and discover how Elizabeth meant to go on.

"An excellent notion, Cousin," Darcy answered him. "I could not, in good conscience, deny you the felicity of becoming the object of Mr. Collins's admiration a moment longer than tomorrow."

Darcy gave the bell pull a quick, impatient tug. Finally permitted to excuse himself to prepare for dinner, he had almost fled his aunt's and cousins' company for the sanctuary of his bedchamber. Fletcher had not been there ready for him, a singular circumstance in and of itself and, at this juncture, a disconcerting one as well. Where was he? If he was dallying with . . . Darcy strode back across the great high-ceilinged bedchamber, his back stiff in agitated aggrievement with his valet's absence, but then stopped short. No, that could not be! Fletcher was now a man betrothed. Knowing his valet as he did, Darcy discounted his first, ungenerous impulse.

Fletcher held his simple sense of honor too close to trifle with his beloved's affection and trust. Perhaps a few more minutes of solitude would not be amiss if he was leaping to such unwarranted conclusions. Darcy strolled slowly to one of the great windows and stared out onto the green, rolling grounds that were Rosings Park. He must come to terms with himself and stop this ridiculous beating of his heart.

Elizabeth . . . here! It had taken all his power of will to keep the thought from himself as his aunt pontificated on the Bennet family, the new rector's wife, and all her latest projects in the village. But now, away from the scrutiny of his relations, the realization burst upon him like a flood. She was here! She had been in the very salon he had just left, and more than once, from the length of his aunt's discourse. She resided in the house at the end of the lane, just beyond the gate where Collins had stood greeting their arrival. She walked the lanes and paths of Rosings. That flash of color in the grove! Might it have been . . . ? The rush of blood through his body made the fine lawn of his shirt feel like rough linsey-woolsey and the collar tight and irritating. He turned to a mirror and hooked the fingers of both hands into the knot at his throat, pulling it apart in increasing frustration until it finally fell to the carpet at his feet. It was only then that he dared to look at his reflection, praying that he didn't look like . . . He groaned and turned away. Yes, he did . . . the veriest mooncalf!

To what had he pledged himself only just that morning? Had he not released those embroidery silks to the spring winds in solemn resolve to put from him all thought and desire of her? There was no possibility of avoiding the disturbing reality of those threads now, nor a voice whispered insistently, did he want to do so. Rather, he must needs master this irrational impulse that urged him to tear down to the parsonage immediately and insist on the privilege of drinking in all her remembered loveliness. He briefly imagined such a scene as he loosed the first two buttons of his shirt, but the memory of Elizabeth's challenging eye overarched by that expressively raised brow stayed his flight into fancy. No, such fashionable, violent adoration she neither expected nor craved. She would want the truth from him, as he, when the heat that now consumed him cooled, would want from her. And the truth was, nothing had changed. All the impediments remained, and he still would be guilty of trifling with her should he in any way indicate the tumult of his emotions and thus raise her expectations.

Darcy closed his eyes as he sat down heavily on the edge of his chamber's imposing bedstead, its grandeur as richly apparent as its lack of human comfort. He had never slept well at Rosings. Elizabeth. The conflictions of the previous autumn were returned now tenfold with her reentry into his life. The torments of his imaginings of her would be nothing compared with her actual presence. He shifted uncomfortably and unbuttoned his coat as he considered his dilemma. Were his desires merely manifestations of selfish willfulness, a lack of self-control? Or was it his duty and his beliefs, the code of conduct in which he had been raised, being shown inadequate? In four months he had not discovered the answer, but above the confusion, he did know this: beginning with the visit to the parsonage tomorrow and for the length of this reacquaintance, he must be careful—very, very careful.

The sound of hurried footsteps from the other side of the dressing room door brought Darcy up off the bed with a jerk. Fletcher! Quickly, he composed his features and turned to face the door as it swung smartly open.

"Your pardon, sir!" The valet bowed from the doorway. Darcy could see that he was panting slightly from his run. But from where?

"Fletcher!" Darcy's voice was more stern than he intended, but there was no other means of concealing his true state. "Where have you been while I have cooled my heels awaiting your attention? I would not have thought that you would find anything of overpowering interest at Rosings to cause such negligence!"

"That is true, Mr. Darcy. Nothing *precisely* at Rosings, sir, nothing at all. Precisely." Fletcher paused only a heartbeat before continuing. "May I help you with your coat, sir? Shall I have water for the bath sent up? It is ready and waiting." He pulled the kitchen bellrope then advanced upon his master. In a trice, Darcy's coat was down his arms and flung uncharacteristically upon the bed. "There. Your waistcoat now, sir?"

"Fletcher, where were you . . . *precisely*?" Darcy's brow lowered at the valet's busyness.

"Just now, sir?"

Darcy nodded.

"Why, in the kitchen, sir, testing the water that it—"

"Before that." Darcy cut him off.

Fletcher's mouth shut with a snap, and a curious look washed over his features. Then, lowering his eyes, he confessed. "I was at the parsonage, sir. But it was on your behalf, Mr. Darcy."

"On *my* behalf! At the parsonage?" Darcy sputtered in surprise and no little alarm.

"Yes, sir." Fletcher took a deep breath. "I heard that a lady you met and had much discourse with while we were in Hertfordshire was a guest there. Not content to hold with an idle rumor, I went to assure myself that it was, indeed, the same lady." He then raised his eyes and informed Darcy triumphantly. "I am happy to apprise you, sir, that it is the very same female, Miss Elizabeth Bennet."

Darcy regarded him darkly. " 'If this were play'd upon a stage—' "

"You would 'condemn it as an improbable fiction.' " Fletcher finished for him. "I assure you, sir, I was at the parsonage on just that errand—to determine if the lady was indeed Miss *Elizabeth* Bennet or no."

"Humph," Darcy responded, longing to know more, but to ask was impossible.

"The lady is in good health, sir," Fletcher murmured as he pulled Darcy's waistcoat from his shoulders.

"How do you know?" He couldn't stop himself from asking the question.

Fletcher bent to the task of dislodging Darcy's shirt buttons from the close-stitched holes. "The lady was just returned from one of her rambles when I arrived, and she looked very well. Mrs. Collins's housekeeper says she has never seen a young lady as often out and about the groves and pathways of Rosings Park as is Miss Elizabeth." The shirt joined the coat and waistcoat on the bed. The sound of water splashing into the bath in the dressing room distracted them both for a moment. "Unless the weather prevents her," Fletcher continued quietly, "it is her daily habit and delight."

"And you believed so strongly that I should know this that you went down to the parsonage yourself to ascertain the matter?" Darcy asked skeptically. "Why should I wish to know in what manner Miss Elizabeth cares to spend her time?"

"So that, at all costs, you may avoid her, sir!" Fletcher replied adamantly.

Darcy pursed his lips and looked narrowly at his valet, weighing their seven-, almost eight-year relationship, and the faithful part Fletcher had played in the terrible events at Norwycke Castle, against what they both knew to be his "improbable fiction." Fletcher must have had his reasons. Given his exceptional service, Darcy would press him no further, and he acknowledged to himself, he would probably have ample time to regret his generous motion later. Besides, the man had provided him with just the information he required.

The walking path from Rosings to the lane that passed by the parsonage of Hunsford was refulgent with the bold trumpets of spring and the softer colors of their more retiring bedfellows, but Darcy spared their beauty no more than an occasional glance as he followed behind his cousin and Mr. Collins. The good reverend had presented himself in Rosings's hall at the earliest possible hour that could not be considered an imposition and had immediately pled that Rosings's guests do him the honor of meeting his new wife. "We also may boast the felicity of guests." He preened under the Colonel's fascinated regard. "My wife's sister and a cousin on my father's side, whom Mr. Darcy has already had the pleasure of meeting, Miss Elizabeth Bennet of Hertfordshire."

"My nephews are already aware of Miss Elizabeth Bennet, Mr. Collins." Her Ladyship had cut in sharply as Fitzwilliam was accepting the invitation. "I informed them of her visit yesterday, almost upon their arrival, and of my disappointment in not having the joy of a first introduction. Now you deny me the joy of Fitzwilliam's introduction as well!" Mr. Collins had flinched visibly at her words and apologized profusely for his error. But the invitation had already been extended, and here they now were on the flower-bordered path to Hunsford.

Insensible to the lavish beauty freely bestowed by Providence, Darcy concentrated on catching the words of the one-sided conversation that drifted over the shoulders of the men before him. Fitzwilliam's keen sense of the ridiculous had recognized a fountainhead in Mr. Collins, and he was unabashedly monopolizing the man's conversation in their stroll to the parsonage in hopes that more of the same would gush forth. For this, Darcy was more than grateful. The emotions and apprehensions battling in his mind and disturbing the balance of his bodily humors rendered him in no fit frame to entertain Collins's absurdities; yet it was from the parson's studied speech that bits concerning Elizabeth might be gleaned in preparation for this, their first meeting since the ball at Netherfield. Darcy strained to hear what Collins was saying without giving the appearance of attention, but the odd tricks of the wind carried the man's words off willy-nilly into the grove, or his sentences so convoluted themselves that any sense of them was lost.

Giving up in a frustration exacerbated by the undisciplined tangent his emotions had taken, Darcy applied himself instead to shoring up the eroded edges of his composure. Although rather earlier than he had planned, they were to meet. Well, what matter the time? Morning or afternoon, soon or late? Had he not committed himself to a course of action when he released those embroidery threads to the winds? Those convictions, hard-won but held as firmly as his honor, would not be abandoned merely because the reality would soon stand before him! However, he was not a fool. The power his imagination had led him to allow her would be as nothing to the delight her actual person would bestow. His hand, he sternly reminded himself, was irrevocably withheld from her—there was no danger there—but his present discomposure was proof that his heart remained in danger. To that end, he must show her no favor, no attention, regardless of her temptations. *Remember who you are!* His father's oft-repeated admonition sprang to the fore. His back stiffened. There was Pemberley, Georgiana, family to consider. *Think on those!* he commanded himself. Resolute, he set his jaw.

They were now at the lane and, shortly, at the door. His face suffused with amusement, Fitzwilliam stepped back to join Darcy as their host rang the doorbell. "Ah, finally I am to meet *la Bennet* of the straitened society of Hertfordshire, whose previous introduction to you our aunt so laments!" Fitzwilliam murmured into his ear with a laugh. His satirical words caused the muscles of Darcy's stomach to bunch and twist. He looked at his cousin sharply. Did Richard suspect something? There was no time to consider the question, for Fitzwilliam was already halfway up the stairs to the parsonage's main floor, following close upon the heels of his latest amusement. Ahead of him, Darcy heard the door to the sitting room open and then the scraping of chairs and soft footsteps from within as its occupants rose to greet the newcomers. Fitzwilliam's broad shoulders disappeared into the room first; and before he could think, Darcy was face-to-face with Collins, who was already making his introduction to his wife. "Mrs. Collins." The rector addressed his helpmeet with formality. "Mr. Darcy, whom you will remember from his visit to Netherfield last autumn. My wife, sir, Mrs. Collins."

"Mrs. Collins, ma'am," Darcy replied. As he bowed to her

curtsy, the fresh scent of new lavender drifted over him, tickling his nostrils. Elizabeth! He forced his eyes not to wander from his hostess, though a host of emotions within immediately set up a clamor against such reserve, urging him to seek her out against all his fine resolve.

"Mr. Darcy, welcome," Mrs. Collins answered warmly. "How fortunate that you visit Rosings when Hunsford also entertains guests who are known to you; for my sister, Miss Lucas, and my dear friend, Miss Elizabeth Bennet, are also with us." A young woman whose features Darcy vaguely recalled from the Netherfield ball bobbed him a curtsy, which he solemnly acknowledged; and then he was before her.

In that moment, Darcy knew himself undone and all his fine resolve as substantial as smoke before the warm and luminous vision caught in the bright rays of the morning sun. Elizabeth! His heart exalted against all his precautions. Before he could bid it stay, her glorious eyes, deep pooled and fraught with intelligence, flashed up to him from under their fringed veil, meeting his—holding his—in such a bold manner that his breath caught in his chest, the questions contained in them rooting him to the very floor. The treacherous organ inside his chest bounded painfully against his ribs as those intriguing, maddening eyes changed in their expression; and alight now with a mysterious, womanly intuition, they narrowed upon him in curious study. For what did she search? More unnerving still, what had she already discovered? Did she so easily discern all those secret places within him that he'd dutifully, painfully locked and barred?

Helpless to look away, he could only await her conclusion. An eternity passed; the very air between them become charged and still. Then, her brow arched in that provoking manner that had so captivated him from the beginning. Her chin tilted up, and a sparkle of amusement illuminated her knowing gaze. The provocation of those enticing features caused the tightness in his chest to threaten to explode into a groan. Lord, how he had missed the challenge, the fascination, the uncertainty of her! How many times had he imagined her thus? All his defenses against her turned to ash as, like the rarest of wines, her effect upon him sped throughout his body, engaging every sense and nerve. It recalled him to the intoxication he had known those months ago in her presence and had carried within him, however he berated himself, ever since.

Part of my soul . . . Adam's words, his own words, spoken that long ago night broke over him; and his soul, comprehending what his reason could not, rushed to claim, to embrace that other half of itself with a joyful recognition that made him light-headed and tempted him to commit unforgivable liberties. He wanted to smile, he wanted to laugh, he wanted to take her hand in his and draw it up to his lips. He wanted the soft, sweet dreams of her that had tormented him, waking and sleeping, at last to find resolution. With dizzying speed his dreams gathered power until, for a terrifying moment, Darcy feared he had lost all command of himself. Clearly, he saw himself advance upon her and, without hesitation, sweep her into an unrestrained embrace of body and soul. But— please God!—he had not moved, had he? He struggled to regain a cognizance of his own limbs, but even now, her lavender scent teased him as his lips sought the soft warmth of her brow and he reveled in the intimate beating of her heart against his.

Elizabeth curtsied. Dimly perceived as it was, it still called forth his answering bow, and the performance caused a wave of relief to wash over him. His limbs had not betrayed him; he'd done nothing untoward! "Miss Elizabeth Bennet," he murmured tightly. His lips pressed firmly together, Darcy held his breath as he rose in order to catch her first syllables to him, but there were none to receive. Her curtsy was all that was proper. He felt her eyes flick over him, but he received no further greeting before she turned to acknowledge his cousin. Such propriety, Darcy knew, he should bless; for it allowed him to recover himself. Instead, he experienced a moment of swift, keen-edged regret. What would it have been like to see joy of his arrival in those wonderful eyes? He looked quickly away. Conjecture was a fruitless exercise. He was here to fulfill the claims of politeness, he reminded himself, nothing more.

"Mrs. Collins, ma'am." Fitzwilliam easily took the lead. "I can see you have been much at work in the short time of your marriage and residence. Hunsford never shone so under Rev. Satherthwaite's rule, I assure you! Do you not agree, Darcy?" He cocked his head at his cousin, silently urging him to pick up the conversation.

Darcy stared back at him in confusion. "I do not believe I was ever . . ." Richard's quick frown stopped him. "That is to say, I concur with Fitzwilliam, ma'am." He turned to his hostess. "The house is much improved since Lady Catherine's last rector resided here. The garden, particularly," he added on inspiration. Elizabeth's lips twitched at his compliment. What had he said that should arouse her to laughter, or was it scorn? He remembered their drawing room duels too well not to recognize her reaction as one or the other. Apparently, the ground was more uncertain than even he had supposed.

Giving up on his cousin, Fitzwilliam essayed again. "Hertfordshire is wonderful country, Miss Bennet. I am eager to know how you compare it with Kent."

Finally, Elizabeth smiled. "Comparisons are a difficult business, Colonel Fitzwilliam. How shall they be compared? In geography, in great estates, in magnificent views, picturesque villages? Or perhaps it is the hunting you wish compared?" Ah, there was the Elizabeth Darcy looked for, her eyes sparkling in mischief. But that they did so for his cousin he found intolerable!

"In any way that suits you, Miss Elizabeth," Fitzwilliam answered, "for I am convinced your opinion on any of those subjects is worth the hearing." He paused and then grinned. "Excepting, if you will pardon me, the hunting. I can apply to Darcy for all of that, you know."

"Do you 'apply' to him then too?" Her brow rose slightly. There it was again! That almost imperceptible lift of her shoulder, the fleeting purse of her lips. "But you are, of course, correct. I can compare hunting only by hearsay; whereas Mr. Darcy may do so with some authority. Of that, he has more share than most gentlemen." *More than my share?* Darcy's frustration increased.

"But that is merely due to appearances, Miss Elizabeth." Fitzwilliam's forehead had crinkled a bit at her words, but he was smiling gamely. "The taller a gentleman, the more authority he is accorded, whether he truly has it or no. Have you not found that to be true? And the Darcys"—he smirked down into her laughing eyes as he led her to a window—"are a tall race."

"Would you care to sit down?" Mrs. Collins's invitation recalled Darcy to his manners. He pulled his eyes away from Elizabeth and focused upon the calm, collected aspect of his hostess. But even as he nodded his acceptance, his eyes wandered back to Elizabeth. The light from the window was caressing her hair in a wonderful manner, bringing out warm, lustrous hues and highlighting those delicate tendrils at her neck that had escaped her combs. He swallowed hard, trying vainly to calm the skip and surge of his blood as he observed her and his cousin conversing so easily together.

"I thank you for your compliment of the gardens, sir." Mrs. Collins's low, clear voice brought him back to the business of choosing a seat. There were several arranged companionably about a low table upon which rested a china vase filled to bursting with narcissi and spring ferns. Although he did not discount his hostess's accomplishments, Darcy suspected it to be Elizabeth's handiwork. Surely she had gathered them that morning, likely on her return from a solitary ramble about the near edges of the park. What might she create if given the freedom of Pemberley's gardens? Something inside him smiled at the thought, and he moved to take the chair that put him in the best position to continue his observation.

The Collinses sat with him, looking at him expectantly. In a quandary as to what to say, he cast about for something other than the mundane but was spared the task by Mr. Collins, who was inspired to believe that he suffered an anxiety to know every plant, extant or potential, that lay in the beds surrounding the parsonage. Darcy settled in for the duration, but laughter from across the room brought his head up from the rector's interminable discourse to see Fitzwilliam grinning hugely as he leaned down to catch some further words from Elizabeth's lips. Richard was enchanted, of that there was no doubt. The unfeigned pleasure on his face clearly indicated that he was intrigued and delighted by his companion. How could he not be? Darcy's gaze traveled esuriently from the curls crowning her head to the pale green slippers that peeped from beneath the sway of her frock. Confound it! If ever he was to bring himself to order, he must adopt a more temperate approach.

Narrowing his regard to that of an indifferent acquaintance, he began again. She was handsome, no doubt, but no one would put her down as a great beauty. Although the sunlight did marvelous things with her hair, chestnut curls and velvety brown eyes were not in fashion. Her gown was of no great design nor was the fabric costly, but the gauzy translucence of the simple sprigged muslin did befit her so that, upon consideration, he would not have traded it for the world. Well, perhaps for silk, but only the lightest—Great Heavens, what was he thinking! He tore his eyes away in alarm at the direction his unruly thoughts had so easily taken. Another line was desperately needed. He turned back to the Collinses. Was the man still nattering on about the blasted flower beds?

When it could conceivably be argued that Collins had paused for breath, Darcy hastened to intervene. "How do you find Hunsford, Mrs. Collins? I recall some complaint from its previous occupant that the chimneys do not draw sufficiently. As Her Ladyship's adviser, I may make arrangements with Rosings's workmen directly on that score or any other lack you may have found." He measured his next words carefully. "Her Ladyship need not be troubled with the particulars. It would be my pleasure to see to the matter." There, if he must be the object of Collins's annoying flattery, at least let it be for some actual good he had done.

Collins's response to his offer was all he feared, but the look of relief in his wife's eyes was enough to confirm his suspicions that his aunt's cheese-paring ways in regard to her dependents had occasioned some discomfort in the parsonage. If Elizabeth were to visit her friend often, such could not continue. Darcy assured his host again that it was his pleasure and then fell silent. Elizabeth . . . here at Rosings. Would she come often? Would she be always here when he made his yearly visit? He stole another glance at her.

She was looking up into Fitzwilliam's face, considering whatever nonsense he was spouting to her with a pretended seriousness that failed to suppress the mirth tugging at her lips. Her cheeks were flush with pleasure as Richard valiantly attempted to keep pace with her wit, but Darcy guessed that her tally was the higher in their contest. Would she always be here? What an idiotic question! She would marry, soon or late. Darcy shifted uncomfortably, the thought so agitating he could barely sit still. He twisted his father's ruby signet ring unmercifully. It was inevitable! Soon or late, some fellow, favored of Heaven and with no obligations to anything save his future happiness, would whisk her to the altar and know in truth what Darcy could only dream of knowing.

The laughter Elizabeth had struggled to contain behind those invitingly pursed lips burst forth in sweet cascades of delight, and Darcy's heart faltered at the sound. That was the Elizabeth of the Meryton assembly, with the enigmatic smile and whispered laughter, the Elizabeth of the Netherfield ball, with her impudent curls and wistful gaze, the Elizabeth of Pemberley and Erewile House, whose imagined eyes spoke to him as he wandered the halls not quite alone. With growing irritation he watched Fitzwilliam bend to whisper something near her ear; and before Darcy could look away, she tilted her head, glancing over at him. Their eyes met, and he could no more pull away from their fascination than he could will his heart to stop beating. The answers to a thousand questions lay in the depths of those enchanting orbs, and he ached to ask them all. But even as the first one formed on his lips, her aspect sobered, the laughter fading to a curiously speculative regard of him before turning back to her companion.

What was she thinking? Why had she looked at him thus? Oh, this was intolerable! A faint voice as from a great distance protested that Fitzwilliam's behavior should be nothing to him, that his heart was in great danger should he engage with her, and that he had sworn only a half hour before to show her no attention or favor. Without thought and certainly beyond reason, he rose from the chair and in only a few swift strides was upon them. Both Elizabeth and his cousin looked at him with a surprise that was no less than his own at finding himself, in truth, across the room. *Speak!* his heart prompted.

"Your family, Miss Elizabeth, I trust they are well?" The question tripped more smoothly off his tongue than he had dared to hope, but Richard still appeared to wonder at his sudden intrusion. Little did Darcy care what his cousin thought of his manners, for at last her eyes were fully upon him. *Age cannot wither her, nor custom stale her infinite variety.* The Bard's consummate description of Egypt's legendary queen was Elizabeth to perfection. The pleasure of her was incalculable.

"I left them all in health, sir, and have since received assurances that they remain so. You are very kind to inquire." Her words were measured, polite, but her gaze withdrew from him almost before the end of her reply. Was that to be all? But, no! They flashed up at him again, exciting his anticipation. "My eldest sister has been in town these three months, Mr. Darcy. Have you never happened to see her there?"

A more unlooked-for dart she could not have loosed at him! How could he have forgotten? No, he had not seen her sister, but he had known of her, conspired against her. His conscience played havoc with him as she waited for his reply, her eyes strangely unreadable. Richard, too, looked at him curiously. He was a fool, a thousand times a fool, to have succumbed!

"No, Miss Elizabeth." He bowed in apology. "I regret to say that I was never so fortunate to meet your sister in London." She seemed to accept his word, but Darcy's conscience smote him so that he could not continue comfortably at her side. Without another word, he withdrew to the window and stared out into Mrs. Collins's garden. Let them think he was caught up in admiration of the blasted weeds! Anything other than the truth that he had nearly shown himself a fool in the teeth of his own convictions. Curse his weakness! It will not, *shall* not happen again, he vowed to himself.

CHAPTER 2

Too Dear for My Possessing

The noises that seeped out from under the dressing room door were unmistakable. Turning over heavily, Darcy burrowed into the pillows in one more futile attempt to find a comfortable position in the great bed before Fletcher—

"Good morning, sir!"

Too late! Darcy groaned into his pillow and then, with his customary resolve, slid his hands flat against the sheets and shoved against the bedding. In one fluid movement, he rolled off the instrument of his nightly torture and was on his feet.

"It is a lovely, bright Sunday morning, sir. Just as it should be for Easter." Fletcher reached up and twitched back the heavy damask curtains, which had, until that moment, held off the morning. He turned to his master, a smile pulling at the corners of his eyes. "Her Ladyship desires me to remind you that the barouche will leave at ten precisely and that breakfast will be served *en famille* at nine in the morning room."

"As they have been every Easter since I was four years old at least," Darcy groused under his breath while he stretched out the aching muscles of his back. A yawn overtook him as he ambled to the window to judge the accuracy of Fletcher's assessment of the coming day. Squinting fiercely, he peered out into the sun-drenched park. Yes, it would be a glorious day. The only clouds that troubled the expanse of blue sky were fleecy white and thoroughly benign in temperament. A slight breeze teased the leaves of the grove that separated Rosings Park from Hunsford village, their beckon causing him to wish that he had had his horse Nelson brought down and could meet the promise of such a day as it deserved.

"It is seven o'clock, Mr. Darcy." Fletcher's voice interrupted his vision of grassy hills and tree-lined lanes taken at a full gallop. "Shall I prepare . . ."

A hearty knock at the chamber door drowned out the valet's question, causing both men to look over in surprise as the door cracked open and Colonel Fitzwilliam's head appeared. "Oh, excellent, Fitz! You're up! But, Fletcher . . ." Fitzwilliam stepped into the room and closed the door behind him softly. "You have not got him shaved yet! It is seven, you know."

"Yes, sir, I was just about—"

"Well, go to it, man! Time marcheth on." He grinned at the valet, who bowed his acknowledgment of the orders of a superior officer and smartly took himself off to prepare the barbering gear. Richard turned back to his cousin. "Did I say 'marcheth'?" he asked wryly, then feigned a sigh. "Too long a soldier, I suppose. Soon I will not be at all fit for good company!"

Darcy snorted and turned back to his view of the park. "No fear of that! You seem to be doing quite well."

"Yes, actually, I am!" Fitzwilliam beamed. "And that is why I am here. I wish to hurry things along this morning so that I may perhaps have some pleasure of the parsonage females before services begin." He paused for his cousin's comment, but receiving none he pressed on. "I daresay, the delights of *la Bennet* will be more than adequate compensation for the irritation of Mr. Collins's sermonizing."

"Had a surfeit of him at last, have you? You have called at least twice this week," Darcy murmured, his gaze traveling the distance of the path through the grove. He could just see a corner of the church tower above the sway of leaves in the distance. The parsonage would lie just to the right, would it not?

"A surfeit and more, to be sure! But I would have braved his tiresome prattle more often than twice if it had been proper . . . if you had thrown over the accounts and accompanied me, Fitz, and kept old Collins occupied as a devoted cousin should! Dashed if *la Bennet* couldn't easily keep my attention for quite a— What?"

Darcy suddenly rounded on his cousin. "Is it possible that we might have a conversation without the subject of Miss Elizabeth Bennet continually figuring in it?"

Fitzwilliam regarded him wonderingly. "I imagine so, Cuz; but I never knew you to be averse to discussing a fine-looking young woman before. If that is what you wish—"

"I do so wish," Darcy interrupted emphatically and started for the dressing room. Surely Fletcher was ready for him by now, and if his shave would discourage Richard's line, so much the better.

Fitzwilliam shrugged his shoulders in compliance and crossed his arms, assuming an apologetic stance. "Very well, but then it comes about that I bear you ill tidings."

Darcy stopped at the doorway, his forehead creased in mounting annoyance. "What do you mean, Richard?"

"After you pled fatigue and left us last night, I suggested to our aunt that she invite the parsonage to tea this evening." He stopped, considering with amusement the curious look upon his cousin's face, then continued with an impish grin. "So not only will you be forced once more to bear Miss Elizabeth Bennet figuring in the conversation, you will have to bear Miss Elizabeth's figure—"

Darcy closed the dressing room door sharply upon his cousin and then leaned heavily against it, only to hear Fitzwilliam's laughter on the other side as he left the bedchamber. He glanced over his shoulder. The dressing room lay empty, and he was blessedly alone. Dropping his forehead lightly against the door, Darcy closed his eyes. The last five days had been some of the most afflicting in his experience, and the discomfort of his aunt's great guest bed only incidental to the troubled passage of the nights. Shaking his head at the vagaries of Providence that had brought Elizabeth once more into his circle, he pushed away from the door and dropped into the barbering chair. Leaning back, he cocked his head up and began a minute examination of the ceiling.

After the disastrous exchange with Elizabeth concerning her sister, Richard had seen that his cousin wished to be away from Hunsford and smoothly facilitated their departure. But the moment they were out of earshot of the parsonage and the occasional stray villager, he began to tease his cousin about his odd behavior. "Leave off, Richard!" Darcy warned curtly. Recognizing his tone, his cousin did his bidding. But if Richard was alive to the letter of the law, he was blithely indifferent to the spirit of it and had instead taken the tack of enumerating Elizabeth's manifold charms, calling upon Darcy for his agreement at every point until he had been ready to do his cousin an injury.

"Yes, she is all very well," Darcy agreed tersely from between clenched teeth, "but do you have a care, Richard. Her situation is open to me, and I warn you that she has very little in the way of expectation and exceedingly poor connections. You, my dear cousin, are much too expensive for her." He had stopped then in his long strides toward Rosings and turned a fierce scowl upon his cousin. "And she is a gentleman's daughter!"

Fitzwilliam had held up his hands in protest. "Of course, Fitz! Good Lord, you don't think I'd trifle with a woman right under the parson's roof, do you?" Darcy offered him only a piercing stare in reply and turned back to the path. "Well, you can have no objection to visiting!" his cousin declared, catching up with him. "Rosings is so deadly dull. It has been the same every year since we were boys. Now, finally, on its very doorstep, is a diversion charming and witty enough to make this interminable obligation pass more quickly."

"I cannot spare the time to make calls, Richard. There are accounts to overlook, the estate manager to interview, and the farms to inspect. I could use your help!" Darcy said.

"And you shall have it, Fitz," his cousin earnestly assured him, "but you won't need me all the time. I'm a damned nuisance when I've nothing to do, which you well know! So, in the interest of avoiding coming to blows, I'll toddle off and call at Hunsford when I'm not needed. Oh, I shall be careful!" he exclaimed at Darcy's narrowed regard. "The model of discretion and decorum!"

And so, while Darcy had buried himself in his aunt's affairs for the last four days in a determined effort to keep himself so busy that thoughts of Hunsford's guest did not intrude, Richard had been enjoying her company—twice! Both times he had come by Rosings's book room, which Darcy habitually commandeered for his yearly task, to ask if Darcy would care to accompany him to the parsonage. And both times Darcy had managed to look extremely busy and wave him off, only to watch jealously from the window as his cousin strode out of sight down the path leading to Hunsford . . . to Elizabeth. Then Darcy had returned to the table and the ledgers spread about on it and marked each minute until Richard returned. The blackguard cheerily hailed him from the doorway and informed him of the delightful time he had spent with "*la Bennet*," as he had christened her. How Darcy resented that appellation! Even though she had long been "Elizabeth" in his private thoughts, she ought to be "Miss Elizabeth Bennet" in public discourse; but if he should raise an objection, Richard would be upon him like a hawk.

Even so, his intense curiosity about all things that concerned her almost caused him to betray himself. It was maddening to hear Richard's bits and pieces dropped in conversations and not be free to pluck them up for closer examination. Just the previous evening, during their after-dinner brandy, his cousin had made reference to a book he had procured for her from their aunt's library. "Indeed!" Darcy replied, his eager interest apparent enough to cause Richard to stop in his discourse. He burned to ask the title, how his cousin came to know she desired it, how she received it; but instead he turned back to his brandy and silently cursed his tongue. He knew she read, she embroidered, she wrote, she walked; he'd known all that since Hertfordshire. What he wanted to know was what she read. Had she resumed Milton? What did she think about it? What pleasures did she find in her needlework and her rambles? What concerns were on her heart that set her applying pen to paper? He wanted to hear her voice and enjoy her smile and lose himself in her eyes . . .

A rapid staccato on the steps behind the serving entrance door alerted Darcy to Fletcher's imminent return. He straightened his posture as the valet entered, but with swift economy of movement, Fletcher soon had him leaning back in the chair again, a warm, damp towel softening his night's stubble. His valet's familiar ministrations . . . at least some things were not in turmoil!

"Mr. Darcy?" Fletcher's questioning voice penetrated through the comforting warmth. "I was thinking that the blue might do—the new one from Weston's, sir? And the cream nankeen breeches and waistcoat." Darcy had had the same in mind himself. It was Easter, after all! He pushed the thought that he would be certain to encounter Elizabeth again to the edge of his conscience.

"It is Easter, sir," the valet said when he did not respond.

"So it is. The blue it shall be, then." Darcy smiled to himself as he found a comfortable position and lifted his chin for the razor but then stayed his valet's hand in sudden caution. "You will take care this morning, Fletcher!"

"Of course, Mr. Darcy. If you will remain still!"

Lady Catherine's traditional Easter breakfast *en famille* proceeded in its grand manner as it had for over twenty years. The only difference Darcy noted that morning was his own impatience to have it done and be on their way to Hunsford Church. That

Richard also chafed to be gone was an unwelcome novelty that even Her Ladyship observed.

"Fitzwilliam!" Lady Catherine set a stern eye upon him. "I have an excellent digestion, equal to any in the kingdom, a fact in which I pride myself and encourage in young people; but if you will not cease fidgeting, I will be put off my breakfast entirely."

"My apologies, Ma'am." Fitzwilliam flushed and cast a beseeching glance at Darcy.

"I also understand that you arose this morning much earlier than is your wont," she continued. "Why is that, I wonder. I have never heard that you were a religious man, Fitzwilliam. Your mother's letters have long lamented your absence from the family pew. It cannot be that you have taken leave of your senses and become an 'enthusiast,' I trust! We shall have none of that nonsense in our family!"

"My dear aunt—" Richard began to protest.

"Then you can have no cause for impatience. Collins will wait! What else has he to do?" Having no answer, Richard lapsed into studied stillness until, being able to bear the inactivity no longer, he reached for another slice of toast and heaped it with an unconscionable amount of jam. With a look at his cousin that dared him to say anything, he thrust it into his mouth and began chewing on it as vigorously as possible without arousing his relative's ire once more. Darcy bit down on his lip, struck with unease and anger as Lady Catherine proceeded to declaim upon her next subject. It had been wise, after all then, that he had decided against Georgiana accompanying him to Kent. Regardless of his own reservations concerning her new interest in religion, he would not chance his sister's recovery to their aunt's crushing opinions. He stared at her as she continued her discoursing, wondering if he'd ever truly seen her before, and silently vowed never to allow Lady Catherine to bully his sister about that which had brought her back to herself and back to him.

The closer the hands of the Ormolu clock crept toward the

hour appointed for departure to Hunsford Church, the more needful it became to Darcy for some manner of activity to stave off his mounting impatience. Unable to countenance any longer the confinement of his aunt's table and conversation, he rose abruptly from his chair. To the astonishment of his relatives, he excused himself and, forestalling Richard from accompanying him with a frown, left the morning room for the air of Rosings's garden. Once beyond the doors, he stopped, filled his lungs with the sharp morning air, and then turned his attention to the garden and his own disordered emotions. The crunch of the white graveled path beneath his boots was the only sound that accompanied his thoughtful meander through the geometrical beds and hedges that Lady Catherine deemed correct in a polite garden. No suggestion of wildness, neither the veriest hint of the natural was tolerated here, only the mathematical order of sharp angles and precise beds. A formal, logical garden, Darcy mused, as he put as much distance between himself and Rosings Hall as the garden could afford. Would that the geometry of the garden might seep into his bones, discipline his unruly thoughts and emotions, and return them to the figures in which they had run before he'd ever heard of Netherfield. He slowed his stride; the path went no farther but divided right or left to circle the garden's perimeter. With a sigh, he turned back to face the manor house and the truth.

He was wild to see her; there was no denying the truth of it. But it was also true that he feared to see her. The memory of that moment in the parsonage, when her presence and his desire's imaginings had caused him to doubt his reason, had been a continual torment and tease. The scene had intruded on his every thought and accompanied his every action. One moment, the remembered delight would be such that he would give much to be caught up so again, and the next, when the reality of the situation reasserted itself, he swore that he would give anything not to be. Darcy clenched his fists. This mad swinging of his thoughts and desires was becoming intolerable! His resolve had melted in the candescence of her eyes. His self-physic of duty and busyness had been an utter failure. *Is there no means of quenching this fascination?*

The only response to his plea was the sudden, shrill call of one of the peacocks allowed to roam the park. On its heels followed a faint "Darcy!" from the house. Looking in that direction, Darcy spied Fitzwilliam at the opposite end of the garden, striding purposefully toward him. Come to plague him, most like. But as Richard advanced, something he had said earlier that morning teased Darcy's memory. What had it been? Something about having had a surfeit of Collins? Darcy seized upon the thought. Might that be the solution to his obsession with Elizabeth?

"Fitz! It is time to be off! What the devil are you doing out here?" Richard demanded querulously as he came upon him. "Why did you abandon me to the old she-dragon? Fitz!" He addressed him again when he got no reply. "And what the devil are you smiling at?"

It was indeed a fine Easter morning. So mild was the weather and so light the breeze that Lady Catherine consented to Darcy's request that the calash of the barouche be let down. The beauties of the Kent countryside, thus displayed in their full glory, were duly observed under the lady's express direction and commentary, but Darcy never heard her during the sojourn to Hunsford, nor he suspected, did his cousin. This was of no consequence, for an unfocused stare and an occasional nod were all Her Ladyship expected or desired from her nephews. Any more fervid a response would have given rise to a suspicion of "artistic" tendencies, which the lady deplored almost as much as "enthusiast" ones in men of rank.

The distance to Hunsford by carriage was not long, but it was obvious from the agitated demeanor of its rector as he fluttered about the threshold that they were late. Since Darcy's turn in Rosings's garden had hardly delayed their departure, it was plain that Lady Catherine's timetable had been designed with a grand entrance in mind. Members of the elevated strata of the local gentry stood with Mr. and Mrs. Collins outside the church doors in order to greet Her Ladyship and her distinguished nephews, but Elizabeth was not among them. Darcy tensed as the barouche swayed to a stop and it became apparent that neither was she to be seen within the threshold of the church. Chagrined, he glanced at Fitzwilliam, who was scowling with annoyance, first at his aunt and then at the crowd gathered on the church step.

"Too late!" Fitzwilliam grumbled under his breath as one of Rosings's scarlet-clad servants hurried to open the barouche's door. "And a bloody gauntlet to run as well!" Once the door was opened, he bounded out of the equipage, forgetting his duty to his aunt for the length of two strides before Darcy caught his arm. "Richard!" he hissed to him. Fitzwilliam stopped short, a question on his lips that Darcy answered with a silent cock of his head. "Oh, good Lord!" Fitzwilliam whispered fearfully and, pasting a smile on his face, stepped back to the carriage and offered his waiting aunt his hand down.

"I shall write to your mother, Fitzwilliam," Lady Catherine announced as she took his hand and descended from the barouche, her eye sharply inspecting his now blanching countenance, "and inform her of your unusual behavior. Further, I will advise that she read it to His Lordship."

"My Lady"—Fitzwilliam bridled—"I beg you to believe that I haven't turned Methodist."

"I should say not!" interrupted his aunt. "You were baptized in the Church of England, sir, of which fact I was a material witness, and there is an end to it! Now, no more of such nonsense!" She took his arm and nodded toward the church door. In seething obedience, Fitzwilliam escorted her forward.

Impatient to be past Richard's aptly labeled "gauntlet," Darcy turned to his female cousin and extended his hand. Anne's ephemeral touch drifted down upon his forearm for only a few seconds and, to his surprise, was quickly withdrawn when she gained the ground. He looked down at her curiously, but her gaze was averted from him, hidden by the brim and gathered flowers of her bonnet. It came to him suddenly then that she had not spoken a single word during their breakfast or sojourn, nor had he observed her attend to anything but the passing scenery or her own glove-clad hands, which had lain clasped in her lap. Even now she said nothing, merely stood like Lot's wife where she had alighted from the carriage, waiting.

"Shall we walk, Anne?" he asked evenly. The bonnet moved slowly up and down, and Darcy almost thought he heard a sigh as he once more offered his arm to his cousin. Two thin fingertips came to rest on his blue coat sleeve, but he knew so only by sight; their weight was undetectable. He started forward slowly, expecting a reticence from her that would require he coax her on, but she responded to his signal and walked in unison with him to the church door. Still without looking at him, she paused, anticipating his need to shift his walking stick to his other hand and remove his hat at the threshold. He nodded curtly to the assemblage there, forestalling any attempted conversation, and led her inside.

The sudden, cool dimness of the entryway beneath the bell tower was a welcome respite from the glare of public scrutiny, but Anne seemed to shrink even further within herself as a shiver caused the fingers pressed so lightly on his arm to tremble. He looked sharply down, maneuvering to catch a glimpse of her face, but the semidarkness and her bonnet still shielded her from him and for the first time Darcy felt some concern for his cousin. Something was wrong, that was very evident, but what could it be? Sudden shame flooded him as he realized that he could not possibly guess her trouble, for he had never taken even a passing interest in her concerns. She had always been merely Anne, his "unintended," his sickly, female cousin: a pitiable thing with which any healthy, young male would have had little to do. And, to his dishonor, he had not.

Hunsford Church was a respectable edifice. The structure it-

self was not a grand one, nor the nave a particularly long one.
But it might as well have been Westminister for the time it
seemed to require Darcy to escort his cousin to the de Bourgh
pew and Lady Catherine's side. Relieved at last to have completed
the promenade, he handed Anne into the box, and was free, so
he thought, to blend himself into the rest of the congregation as
he searched it for Elizabeth's profile. Doubtless, he thought as he
set aside his walking stick and hat, Richard had already found her
and he needed only determine in which direction the Rudesby
was gawking. But a surreptitious glance past Anne to Fitzwilliam
on her other side told Darcy that, far from engaging in a nave-
wide flirtation with Elizabeth, his cousin's habitual good humor
had quite fled. In all Darcy's past experience of Lady Catherine,
it was only his father who had ever been able to stand against her
and even bring her to some semblance of womanly reserve. Since
his passing, those more feminine aspects of her nature had been
overthrown completely by her imperious disregard of all but her
own opinions, of which Richard now suffered the brunt of her
latest rendition.

A flurry of movement and song from the rear of the sanctuary
brought the congregation to its feet. From habit, Darcy's limbs also
heeded the call, and he rose even while he discarded the puzzles of
his cousins to take up the more intriguing one of finding Elizabeth
in the crowd. Thankful again for his height, he began to search the
meadow of flowered and fruited bonnets for the one that sheltered
her glory from the casual eye, but at that moment the small boys'
choir began the processional, their voices—only occasionally on
key but earnest and clear—echoing against the ancient walls.
Darcy's gaze flicked down the aisle. Behind them, in stately stride,
came Mr. Collins, his white surplice starched to within an inch of
its life and his eyes cast reverently heavenward. So he proceeded
until he drew even with the de Bourgh pew, at which point he startled both Darcy and Fitzwilliam with a sharp turn in their direction and bowed deeply to each member of the family of his noble

patroness. It was just as the ridiculous man was rising from these embarrassing flatteries that Darcy saw behind him and across the aisle a flash of blue belonging to the ribbon of a straw bonnet decked with freshly picked lilies of the valley. As the brim came up, a pair of velvet brown eyes appeared above a pert nose and beguiling lips held back from exposing their owner's amusement by delicate, glove-clad fingertips. The sight was pure enchantment, and he was more than disposed to allow it to have its way.

Filled now with the sight of her cousin Mr. Collins, Elizabeth's lively eyes danced with the diversion. But not content with beholding his fawning attentions, her eyes swept up to observe his effect on others and, to Darcy's surprise, she began their examination with his own face. The expectancy in her eyes and the sweet curve of her lips shot through him like a bolt, pinning his senses to the moment, and in that eternal second he could only wait and watch for what would come. A puzzled frown lightly touched her countenance. Although it allowed him some respite, her bewildered regard excited his curiosity. What intrigued her?

The end of the morning's collect signaled that the assembled might resume their seats, giving Darcy only a few seconds to cast another surreptitious glance in Elizabeth's direction. The curiosity that had enlivened her face had been replaced by a thoughtful character focused on the intricacies of the stained-glass window, a gift of Sir Lewis's grandfather that hung majestically in the apse beyond the pulpit. It well became her, and he would have given much to know the nature of the thoughts that produced such an arresting display, but hard upon this observation was the guilty realization that he was once more engaged in a blatant invasion of her privacy. With reluctance, he withdrew from his secretive foray without catching her eye and gave his attention to Hunsford's unfortunate rector. Darcy's previous exposure to the presuming little man had not included a taste of his formal sermonizing; therefore it was, in a sense, the rector's "maiden speech." Darcy's expectations were not high, but as Mr. Collins arranged and rearranged his sheaf of notes upon the pulpit, the visitor was prepared to give him the benefit of a judgment reserved.

His papers finally arranged to his satisfaction, Mr. Collins turned to the family of his patroness and, to Darcy's consternation, bowed to them yet again, whereupon Lady Catherine nodded her permission to proceed. With growing apprehension, Darcy watched the rector arrange his face into the most solemn of lines and turn it upon his congregation. "My text this morning comes from the Epistle to the Colossians, chapter three: 'Set your affection on things above, not on things on the earth.' My subject for this Easter morn, my faithful congregation, is affection—or, more properly, what has been called Religious Affection. That is to say, I speak to you today in stern warning against the vulgar excesses of 'Enthusiasm!' "

"Oh no!" Fitzwilliam groaned as he shrank down in the pew, but Darcy came to a tense attention. This was his aunt's doing, he was sure of it.

"The text," continued Her Ladyship's mouthpiece, "directs us to set our affection on things above. This may not be construed as leave to indulge in flights of emotion. Heaven forbid! Religion is of a more steady nature; of a more sober, manly quality. She scornfully rejects the support of something so volatile, so trivial and useless as a lively imagination and the uncontrolled flow of, you will pardon the expression, 'animal spirits.' Such things find their home in the heated, disordered brain of the Enthusiast rather than in the dispassionate, rational understanding which the Supreme Being requires of the true man of religion."

Heated, disordered brain? Darcy crossed his arms over his chest and leveled a piercing stare at his aunt's minion.

"No, dear listeners." Collins brought his palm down upon the pulpit with a theatrical thwack. "True wisdom, true religion directs us to the reining in of passion and its disorders for the calm cultivation of moral virtues. Only fulfill the conditions on your part of duty and honor, become proficient in this lesson of the Gospel, and all will be well. *Self-reformation* is affection set on things above, not this vain, self-aggrandizing fervor."

Self-reformation! Darcy shifted, the pew having grown unrelenting in its discouragement of the slightest bodily comfort. Honor and duty were the air he'd breathed all his life, yet had he not been lately tempted to abandon them? How close had he trod to succumbing to the wiles of Lady Sylvanie, whose tragic madness had, nonetheless, shown him the shocking depths of hatred he harbored in his own heart? And what success had he found over these intervening months in rooting it out?

"I tell you, it is no more than the low canting of wild fanatics like that infamous Newton or Whitefield of the last century or Bunyan and Donne before them." Mr. Collins swept men his theological and literary superiors aside with a wave of his hand. "And I need not remind you where that led!" He paused dramatically, then spat out, "Regicide!"

Another groan arose from Fitzwilliam. "Dear God, now she'll write His Lordship that I'm planning to kill old George!"

Darcy's brows slanted dangerously, and his eyes narrowed into mere slits. If this reflected Lady Catherine's view, and he had little doubt that Collins's sermon had been written under her direction, she must never be permitted to stay two minutes alone with Georgiana!

"Trust, rather, in Reason, the Divine's handmaiden, and in your spiritual fathers—I am honored to be so appointed and advised by Her Ladyship, Lady Catherine de Bourgh—to prescribe to you what is proper affection, acceptable in the sight of Heaven. Thus endeth the lesson. Amen and amen."

After the benediction, the choirboys struck once more an attempt at their proper notes and began the recessional down the aisle, Mr. Collins in their wake. A small sigh near his shoulder recalled Darcy to the service of his cousin. Putting his displeasure aside, he quickly gathered up his hat and walking stick and reached for her prayer book, then glanced over at Elizabeth as he stepped out of the de Bourgh pew. If it were possible, she looked even more thoughtful, more lovely than before, and he profoundly wished that he might approach her, greet her at least, before he must leave. But duty and propriety demanded that he escort his cousin to the barouche. He must deny himself now, but this evening, he vowed, he would deny himself nothing of her that she would give.

"Cousin Anne." Darcy quietly addressed the apparitionlike figure beside him and offered her his arm.

The return journey to Rosings was accomplished in a weighty silence on the part of all in the barouche save its most noble occupant. Constrained by all of history and custom to keep silent within the walls of the church, Her Ladyship more than compensated for that charge of Scripture with an unending stream of commentary on her neighbors, their relatives, their servants, and their friends as the carriage wended its way down the lanes and up the drive of Rosings. Both Fitzwilliam and Darcy looked pointedly away during her considerable holding forth and gazed stonily out upon the countryside. Occasionally, Darcy would cast a glance at his cousin in the hope of discovering something about her person that would give him some insight into her troubles. She also gazed out upon the passing scene and never once looked in his direction that he could detect, the wide brim of her bonnet still acting as a shield against his inquiry and her thin hands clasped in a knot of gloves and the strings of her reticule. As worrisome as Anne's behavior might be, it was clear he could do nothing at present about it.

The deft motions of Fletcher's whisk across his shoulders ceased their brisk rhythm, signaling to Darcy that, according to the exacting standards of his valet, he was prepared to leave his rooms and present himself to his aunt. In terms of his apparel, this was undoubtedly so. Gone were the blue coat and cream breeches of the morning, and in their place, snugly buttoned to his frame, were an understated but expertly tailored black frock coat and trousers. Darcy regarded his reflection in the mirror as his valet, awaiting his opinion, stepped back. He stretched his chin up and away from Fletcher's knot, loosening it just enough to allow for some comfort. Truth be told, he had directed Fletcher to select trousers for the express purpose of setting Her Ladyship to moralizing upon his lack of proper evening dress and the lamentable casualness of young persons in this new century. Displeased with his appearance, perhaps she would be less attentive to his conversation, especially when he had opportunity to engage her rector's humble guest. But there was the rub! His exterior self was well accoutred, impervious to examination. But as his gaze traveled up from the elegant lines of his coat, past the exquisite knot of his neckcloth, to look into his own eyes, he saw in them the expectancy of pleasure and challenge that the evening would surely afford. It, in fact, ran rampant through his inner man, exciting pleasurable but disorderly sensations throughout his body. He closed his eyes and, beginning with *idiot*, silently applied to himself any number of epithets until the beat of the blood in his veins returned to a more steady rhythm.

"Mr. Darcy, is aught amiss?" Fletcher asked quietly from behind him.

"No, I am well pleased, Fletcher," he assured his valet as, with relief, he opened his eyes upon a visage more like his own self. Although it had taken an unusual degree of summoning, his habitual reserve had come to the fore and asserted itself. How long it would last in Elizabeth's presence was not something he wished, at the moment, to contemplate. He left the mirror and, pulling at his watch fob, strode to the door.

"It is six, sir," Fletcher offered. Darcy tucked the watch back into its pocket. They should arrive in a half hour, leaving enough time to settle Lady Catherine's complaints and engage in some calming, cousinly banter with Richard. Anne, as well, he remembered guiltily. She would not contribute to the conversation, he knew, but perhaps in her attention to their exchanges, he might observe something that would offer insight into her troubled sighs.

The servants were lighting the hall lamps as Darcy made his way to the stairs. Six and a few minutes, he calculated. In less than half an hour . . . He could not help but think on what it would be to see her here among his relations and in the stately apartments of Rosings. She would not be completely at disadvantage; he understood that she had been in Rosings's drawing room at least twice before, but the contrast in situation from that to which she was accustomed must affect her. If not situation then the temerity of Lady Catherine's invasive questions and imperious opinions coupled with her rank and station must dampen her vivacity. He tried to imagine Elizabeth, her magnificent eyes downcast, listening in quiet deference to his aunt's pronouncements; but the exercise only caused his mouth to arc into a smile. Well did he know from their conversations at Netherfield her fascination with the inconsistencies of human nature. Of such assorted follies, Lady Catherine was an abundant mistress. Was Miss Elizabeth Bennet diverted by them? Did she dare hold her own; and if so, how did she do it and continue to enjoy his aunt's favorable regard? The evening ahead was poised to be probably the most intriguing he had ever spent under his aunt's roof.

A loud click and a "Damn and blast, Fitz! Trousers!" alerted Darcy to his cousin's entrance into the hall. Fitzwilliam stood away from him, amazement causing his eyebrows to disappear beneath the fall of curls across his brow. "You know what Her Ladyship thinks of 'em, old man."

"Which is why I chose to sport them tonight, Richard, so that you"—Darcy paused and indicated his cousin's correct breeches, clocked stockings, and pumps—"will shine as an example of stability and manners in contrast."

"Oh." Fitzwilliam paused to consider the prospect, then smiled at his cousin. "Very decent of you, Cuz. Anything to stop the old she-dragon from going on about writing His Lordship. I can't fathom where she picked up the notion that I'd turned Ranter." He shook out the modest lace at his cuffs. "Sure I look the part, are you?" Darcy could not help laughing at his cousin's unwonted concern as he nodded his assurance. Wryly acknowledging his amusement, Fitzwilliam returned him a crooked grin. "Well, you would be anxious too, if it were you Her Ladyship had in her sights."

"So be your most charming self tonight and you'll soon be back in her good graces." Darcy grinned. "Shall we go down?"

On beholding their entrance, Lady Catherine's dry smile fell into a disapproving line, but she did no more than sniff deprecatingly at Darcy before commanding her nephews to sit on the settees that had been drawn up in a worshipful circle around her great chair. Anne and her companion Mrs. Jenkinson, were before them, seated across from Her Ladyship in their usual swirl of shawls, but tonight Anne was dressed in a particularly becoming gown that favored her pale coloring and slight figure. "Does not your cousin look charming tonight, Darcy?" Lady Catherine's question to him as he bowed to Anne froze the smile he had summoned up for his cousin before it reached his lips. The sincere compliment he had been about to offer would now appear only a command performance, emphasizing once again their strained relationship.

He rose from his bow to a much-distracted Anne, who was looking in every direction but his, her fingers clutching at her shawl. "Cousin Anne." Knowing he must succeed in commanding her attention, induce her to look into his face, he addressed her in the softened but earnest voice he used with Georgiana. "Anne," he repeated, and slowly she raised her eyes to his. "You, indeed, look well tonight." She blushed faintly at his words, and her eyes quickly dropped, but not before he detected a flash of gratitude and, perhaps, even a little pleasure in his compliment. So, he thought, Anne was not as indifferent to attention as she would have the world believe! But then, her world was admittedly very small, circumscribed as it was by her health and Her Ladyship's sensibilities and tastes. Honest, ingenuous compliments were, he was certain, a rarity.

Turning from Anne, Darcy eyed the settees that circled his aunt. None of them appeared sturdy enough to contain the anticipation coursing through him in currents that increased in force as the hands on the clock swept toward the appointed time. The need for a decision, however, was postponed by the sudden opening of the drawing room doors, causing Darcy's heart to lurch at the sound. "Traitor!" he murmured under his breath, attempting to shame it into submission even as his eyes were drawn inexorably to the doors.

First, of course, came Mr. Collins and his wife, the former with an aspect of abject deference. Mrs. Collins, however, improved her husband's standing by accompanying his excessive display with a more appropriate air and a simple curtsy of the correct degree. Miss Lucas followed immediately behind her sister, her frame trembling visibly as she caught Her Ladyship's eye, and then came Elizabeth. The bonnet and pelisse had been left with the footman, but her frock was the one of the morning. Delicate, creamy muslin flocked with flowers embroidered in blue and edged with lace, it flowed gracefully about her person, draping her figure in a most intriguing manner. He watched as her eyes swept the room and she awaited her turn to honor its occupants. She began with Her Ladyship, turned briefly to Anne and her companion, and brightened at Fitzwilliam. Then, she observed him. Their gazes locked, the avid expectancy in hers such a mirror of his own that Darcy's heart bounded violently in what felt like a mad attempt to unite with hers. Aghast, he pulled his eyes away, preempting her curtsy with his own stiff bow. Cure himself with a surfeit of her? How had he miscalculated so completely?

"Mr. Collins, pray be seated." Lady Catherine languidly beckoned her guests forward and indicated the seats to her left.

"Thank you, Your Ladyship." Mr. Collins bowed again before scuttling across the room in a manner that put Darcy strongly in mind of a quail he had disturbed while riding the previous morning. "You are all condescension, Ma'am, a fact widely known among all those—"

"Mrs. Collins, Miss Lucas." Her Ladyship interrupted his fulsome address. Mrs. Collins followed her husband to their assigned places, while her sister, Darcy noted, quickly sank into the seat that promised the best concealment from Lady Catherine's regard. But his eyes could not be long away from their desired object, and dangerous as it had proved to do so, he looked once again to her. She stood quite still, her aspect cool as her relations abased themselves to his aunt; but then, as he watched, he saw her lips twitch. A secretive smile began to tug at them, matched by a new brilliancy in her eyes. That familiar expression was soon followed by a deliberate pursing of her lips, a strategy he knew her to employ to gain control over her features, that they not betray her unseemly amusement. In beholding her delightful battle for mastery, Darcy pressed his own lips tightly together to forestall the grin that attempted to accompany his exaltation at one of his questions answered so quickly. Collins might quake and Her Ladyship's peers might tremble, but Elizabeth Bennet stood in no awe of Lady Catherine. "Miss Elizabeth Bennet." Lady Catherine nodded her acknowledgment. As Elizabeth walked with confident grace to take a seat, he marveled that she had sketched his aunt's character so handily in so short a time. Whatever would happen next?

Fitzwilliam answered his question by slipping round the guests and claiming the place next to Elizabeth on the settee. "Opportunist!" Darcy growled to him before lowering his frame into the last place available, that nearest his aunt and across from Elizabeth and his cousin. Swallowing his disappointment, he resolved instead to retrieve his situation by observing how she handled his cousin and what Fitzwilliam's behavior toward her might reveal. But almost immediately, Lady Catherine engaged him with some particulars of little consequence to anyone but herself. Long inured to her manner, he set himself to satisfy her demands while pursuing his own ends but found that the lady succeeded in irritating him more than she had ever done before. He could make nothing of the conversation opposite him, save that it was a lively one of earnest discourse punctuated by laughter on both sides. Fitzwilliam was delighted with Elizabeth; that was obvious. Darcy knew all his moods and their telltale signs. Richard might have begun in a flirtatious vein, but he was now captivated, and worse, intrigued, and not only by her person. The thoughtful expression on his face told Darcy that he was beginning to discover her mind as well. He shifted in his seat. It was inevitable, he conceded. Elizabeth did not simper, nor did she exude the fashionable *ennui* that one encountered in most females of the ton. No, her charm had a substance about it, a directness that a man could quickly appreciate with his mind as well as his senses. And Richard, deuce take him, was appreciating it quite enough!

"What is that you are saying, Fitzwilliam? What is it you are talking of?" Lady Catherine's querulous demand startled Darcy into the realization that he had not paid his aunt the least attention for several minutes. "What are you telling Miss Bennet? Let me hear what it is."

Yes, thought Darcy with an unholy satisfaction, *do tell us, Richard!*

"We are speaking of music, Madam," Fitzwilliam replied absently, his attention centered upon his companion to such a degree that he did not take his eyes from her for more than a moment in his answer.

"Of music! Then pray speak aloud. It is of all subjects my delight. I must have my share in the conversation, if you are speaking of music." Lady Catherine settled back into her chair, her captious impulses seemingly appeased by the latitude afforded by the topic. "There are few people in England, I suppose, who have more true enjoyment of music than myself, or a better natural taste."

Darcy looked sharply at his aunt, scarcely believing his ears. Could she really think that anyone with sense would accept such a ridiculous statement? Or was she engaged in a test of the credulity of her guests? Regardless of the answer, neither explanation spoke well of her.

"If I had ever learnt, I should have been a great proficient," continued Her Ladyship with assurance. "And so would Anne, if her health had allowed her to apply. I am confident that she would have performed delightfully." She paused to give her audience the opportunity to second her pronouncements, but unwilling to be long silent, she took up another, related subject in which to hold sway. Turning to her other nephew, she inquired, "How does Georgiana get on, Darcy?"

"Very well, Ma'am," he returned quickly. "Georgiana's music is a great joy to her and to those privileged to hear her, which is, alas, a small circle indeed." From the corner of his eye, Darcy could see that, at the mention of his sister's name, Elizabeth had withdrawn somewhat from Richard and was now attending to him. He pressed on in the same vein. "She will play only for family," he explained for Elizabeth's benefit, although he did not look to her. "But in the last several months she has made remarkable progress in her skill and expression."

"I am very glad to hear such a good account of her." Lady Catherine snatched at the reins of the conversation. "And pray tell her from me, that she cannot expect to excel, if she does not practice a great deal." Irritated by the gratuitous counsel, Darcy replied that his sister stood in no need of such advice and that she was very constant in her practice.

"So much the better. It cannot be done too much," Her Ladyship persisted, "and when I next write to her, I shall charge her not to neglect it on any account."

And I shall lay down instructions that any such letters be intercepted, Darcy resolved, his jaw tightening. Never had he allowed anyone who did not also command his own highest respect to interfere with Georgiana's education or peace. Lady Catherine's incessant advice he had always weighed judiciously and, save for matters of etiquette, usually found it wanting. In the past, he had marked this down to lack of occupation and, perhaps, excessive concern for family protocol. But the words that had fallen this morning from her clerical mouthpiece, today from her own lips, and during the course of this visit signaled to Darcy that she meant to insert herself into his life in a more direct manner. And that he would most certainly not allow.

"I often tell young ladies, that no excellence in music is to be acquired without constant practice," Lady Catherine grandly informed her audience as she pointedly turned to Elizabeth, the tense silence of the room only serving to encourage Her Ladyship in her discourse. "I have told Miss Bennet several times, that she will never play really well, unless she practices more." Darcy's eyes flew to Elizabeth's, certain that whatever would follow was sure to be officious if not insulting. How would she countenance it? How respond? "And though Mrs. Collins has no instrument, she is very welcome, as I have often told her, to come to Rosings every day, and play on the pianoforte in Mrs. Jenkinson's room. She would be in nobody's way, you know, in that part of the house."

Shame at his aunt's show of discourtesy so mortified Darcy that Elizabeth's reaction was lost in his confusion. Unable to look upon her or countenance his aunt's words, he rose from his place on the settee and took himself to one of the great windows, which commanded a view of the carriageway. Such improper behavior! Such disregard of what was due one's inferiors and guests! His jaw flexed harshly.

Voices, pitched low but animated, gradually reached his ears, and he turned back to the room to see Richard on his feet offering his hand to a gently amused Elizabeth. Well then, it appeared that she, at least, had acted the gentlewoman and had not allowed Lady Catherine's incivility to ruffle her. Nor, did it seem, was she daunted by her hostess's criticism, for Richard was even now leading her to the grand but disused pianoforte that stood in state in the corner of the room. She was to play! Drawn by his anticipation, Darcy approached only as close as the settee and, not trusting himself, resumed his seat. He watched closely as she laid her fingers upon the ivory of the keys, and as the lashes of her eyes swept her cheeks and her bosom gently swelled with breath for her song, he knew pleasure once again. But it was short-lived, for after listening to no more than half of Elizabeth's offering, Lady Catherine resumed her interview of all things pertaining to his recent activities and the welfare of Pemberley. He answered her vaguely, his replies terse, and looked pointedly away to the performer, but Lady Catherine was not to be deterred. If she did not cease, he told himself in growing vexation, he would miss Elizabeth's song entirely, and that, he determined, he would not be denied!

"You must excuse me, Ma'am." Darcy stood abruptly, cutting off Her Ladyship in midsentence, and with deliberation turned on his heel and strode toward the pair at the pianoforte. Once in motion, he could scarcely stop in the middle of the room, and so there was nothing for it but to join them. Reaching the instrument, he quietly took up a position that afforded him the best view of his fair tormentor and abandoned himself to the savoring of her performance.

"You mean to frighten me, Mr. Darcy, by coming in all this state to hear me." Elizabeth challenged him from under arched brows. "But I will not be alarmed though your sister *does* play so well. There is a stubbornness about me that never can bear to be frightened at the will of others. My courage always rises with every attempt to intimidate me."

Recognizing her tone from their duels of old, Darcy smiled but did not hesitate to meet her *en garde* with a parry and thrust of his own. "I shall not say that you are mistaken because you could not really believe me to entertain any design of alarming you." His smile widened as she pursed her lips at his reply. "And I have had the pleasure of your acquaintance long enough to know that you find great enjoyment in occasionally professing opinions which, in fact, are not your own." The joy of her laughter at his sally was reward in full for the discomforts of the evening.

"Your cousin will give you a very pretty notion of me." Elizabeth turned to Fitzwilliam. "He'll teach you not to believe a word I say." Richard shook his head in immediate denial and joined her in looking up at his cousin. "I am particularly unlucky in meeting with a person so well able to expose my real character, in a part of the world where I had hoped to pass myself off with some degree of credit," she continued. "Indeed, Mr. Darcy, it is very ungenerous in you to mention all that you knew to my disadvantage in Hertfordshire—and, give me leave to say, very impolitic too—for it is provoking me to retaliate, and such things may come out as will shock your relations to hear." A hoot of laughter from Richard greeted her assertion, but Darcy was not deterred. It was too delicious!

"I am not afraid of you," he said, smiling down at her.

"Pray let me hear what you have to accuse him of," cried his cousin. "I should like to know how he behaves among strangers."

"You shall hear then." She deftly accepted his counterchallenge. "But prepare yourself for something very dreadful. The first time of my ever seeing him in Hertfordshire, you must know, was at a ball—and at this ball, what do you think he did? He danced only four dances! I am sorry to pain you, but so it was. He danced only four dances, though gentlemen were scarce; and, to my certain knowledge, more than one young lady was sitting down in want of a partner. Mr. Darcy, you cannot deny the fact." She looked up at him with a sweet daring sparkling in her eyes. Perhaps he had been too hasty in agreeing to swords. Her accusation was all too true, her complaint of him all too valid. But, deuce take it, how was he to know that a stupid country dance among strangers would come to figure in his life to this degree?

"I had not at the time the honor of knowing any lady in the assembly beyond my own party," he offered.

"True. And nobody can ever be introduced in a ballroom." She dismissed him and his defense. "Well, Colonel Fitzwilliam, what do I play next? My fingers wait your orders."

Rankled by her reply, Darcy could not let it rest. "Perhaps I should have judged better had I sought an introduction; but I am ill qualified to recommend myself to strangers."

"Shall we ask your cousin the reason of this?" she inquired of Fitzwilliam, her eyes alight at Darcy's tactical feint. "Shall we ask him why a man of sense and education, and who has lived in the world, is ill qualified to recommend himself to strangers?"

"Oh, there is no difficulty in that," Fitzwilliam assured her. "I can answer your question without applying to him." He smirked up at Darcy. "It is because he will not give himself the trouble."

Just wait until you are in need of funds next quarter day, Darcy silently promised him. But what should he say? His only certainty was that he did not desire for things to stand in this manner. What would she do with the truth? Perhaps it was time to learn. He focused upon Elizabeth's face, willing her to understand. "I certainly have not the talent which some people possess of conversing easily with those I have never seen before," he confessed. "I cannot catch their tone of conversation, or appear interested in their concerns, as I often see done."

Returning his steady regard, Elizabeth took a breath. "My fingers do not move over this instrument in the masterly manner which I see so many women's do. They have not the same force or rapidity, and do not produce the same expression. But then I have always supposed it to be my own fault—because I would not take the trouble of practicing. It is not that I do not believe *my* fingers as capable as any other woman's of superior execution."

Darcy stood very still as she spoke, astounded by her words. She was perfectly correct; he knew that immediately. But it was more than the accuracy of her perception that was causing his heart to beat so erratically and the blood to skip and surge through his veins. Before him sat Diana and Minerva, courage and wisdom together, perched like an enchanting muse upon his aunt's piano bench! What a singular woman! Not only had she courageously taken apart his truth and shown him his self-delusion but she had done so with exquisite tact and grace. As he looked down into her magnificent, waiting eyes, he knew instinctively that any thought of control over his heart was a mere pretense and that he could no more suppress the smile that now spread over his face than he could deny her her due.

"You are perfectly right," he said. "You have employed your time much better." Then, looking as deeply as he dared into her eyes, he extended her metaphor. "No one admitted to the privilege of hearing you can think anything wanting. We neither of us perform to strangers."

That night, as Darcy lay in his aunt's disagreeable guest bed, he was grateful for the discomfort, for it allowed him time to rehearse the tumultuous events of the evening. He must settle his mind and come to terms with his feelings for Miss Elizabeth Bennet! The candle beside him flickered, sending shadows dancing across the canopy above his head as he stretched out and stared into the darkness, his fingers laced beneath his head. Here, in the silent reaches of night, he could think clearly, see her clearly, without distraction. There had been little exchanged between them after she rose from the pianoforte save what was polite and expected, but each glance, each word that fell from her lips, each courtesy in which they engaged was etched upon his memory. He could see her still as she sat at the instrument, the flames of the candles upon it playing in the brilliancy of her eyes. He reveled in each smile, each thoughtful pull of her brow, each song she had sung. In every way she had shown herself wholly possessed of the poise, intelligence, wit, and grace he had cataloged under Georgiana's insistent questioning. He knew Elizabeth Bennet to be compassionate and unfailingly loyal to those with the slightest claim upon her. To that, she had this night added forbearance and civility in the face of the unwarranted criticisms and insults of his aunt. And she had made him know himself.

What did he feel? Where did he ultimately stand in this agonizing tangle? The shadows flickered across the canopy, teasing him with the mystery of the effect this girl from Hertfordshire had exercised upon his life. It had been Georgiana, in her romantic innocence, who had first put it to him. Did he . . . love her? *I hardly know* had been his answer. At the time he had forestalled his sister and sought escape in abstractions upon the emotion, but now—! Now the truth was essential to his peace! Perhaps if he started from the beginning? He admired her, that was certain. He was impossibly attracted to her. Yes, every fiber in his body could testify to that. Her conversation and wit he found exciting, challenging, and intensely pleasurable. Fourthly, Darcy paused for a long moment. Fourthly? Laughter echoed in the silence of the bedchamber as he suddenly saw himself for the ridiculous man he was. What was he doing—acting the part of a miserly accountant, adding up the assets of his lady on one side of the ledger! *Admit it, man.* He watched the shadows dance to the flicker of his candle, giving himself just a little more time before committing himself to what would change his life forever. "You love her." He whispered the words quietly to himself so he could hear them from his own lips. "You love her." He spoke them again.

It was done. His life was never to be the same. How many months had he tormented himself, denying his feelings even as he imagined her at his side? What had he not done to cure himself of her, even going so far as to spend a horrifying visit at Sayre's in a dangerous search for a woman who could banish her from his mind and soul? The quest had been a farce from the beginning, for even as he had vowed to forget her in the arms of another woman, he had been unable to consign her silken threads to the flames or even leave them behind. Oh yes, he had finally found the strength to release those threads to the winds, but what had it profited him?

Immediately, the substance had slipped into their place, and he was entangled more firmly than before. He loved her and all the lovely things she was! And he wanted her. The sharpness of his desire for her soft comfort, her warm welcome, caused the breath to catch in his chest. Her presence at Hunsford and Rosings had given him a taste of the excitement that being daily near her would afford. The thought of returning to his previous existence, continuing to fight against this longing for her for the rest of his life, was insupportable! Greatly agitated, Darcy flung back the blankets and rolled out of the bed, his feet barely hitting the floor before he was striding back and forth across the room.

"There is a solution," he told the darkness. "Make her your wife!" Where before the answer had always been that such a thing was unthinkable, it was no longer so. "Why not!" he demanded aloud of the night. He knew how it would be. Had he not seen her by his side a thousand times as he walked Pemberley? She belonged there, her hand in his. He fell silent, letting the possibilities of a life with her thrill through him. They took his breath away. *Make her mistress of Pemberley, sister to your sister, mother of your children*, his heart pled with him. He stopped his pacing and sat down heavily upon the bed. Could he trust her with so much and his heart as well?

Let me not to the marriage of true minds admit impediments. The opening line of the Bard's sonnet recalled itself to him. "Impediments," he repeated, lying back again into the pillows. Enormous difficulties existed. Though his heart might desperately wish otherwise, his mind forced him to admit to them. He thought of Bingley. How he had worked to dissuade him from a connection with the very family that would become his! Then there was the degradation of his family, the diminishing of its honor, which he was sworn to uphold. He would be properly censured by his relations and, in particular, his mother's sister, Lady Catherine. Would they ever accept Elizabeth, or would she and Darcy both be cut off, their marriage and children forever strangers to their heritage? Finally, there was the reality of the indignities he had suffered at the hands of Elizabeth's family and the pervasive want of propriety they had so readily exhibited at Netherfield's ball as, one by one, they had exposed themselves to the contempt of their neighbors. Their behavior would attach to him, make him what he most feared, an object of derision by all of his society. The memory of the rest of that night assailed him, of Elizabeth's shamed eyes rising from the study of her gloves, sending a flush of heat through his chest. Dear God, he loved her! How he had wanted to protect her, comfort her, even then! The Bard's plea became a demand. *Let me not* . . . He wanted her at Pemberley. He wanted to revel in her warmth and liveliness, her heart and her mind. He wanted Georgiana's wish to know her to come wonderfully true. He wanted the sweetness that only life with her could give. He loved her. But, was it enough? The emotions warred to and fro in his chest, duty and desire—

A yawn suddenly overtook him. Darcy glanced at the mantel clock, his eyelids suddenly heavy. It was well past two, and despite the urgency of his heart, it was neither possible nor wise to make a decision tonight or even, he admitted, tomorrow. He lay again in the bed, grasped a pillow, and turning on his side, forced the mattress into a more submissive shape. There was time—he could easily prolong his visit—and he would use it to full advantage to observe her more closely, discover her mind on more specific issues, test the strength of his emotions against her reality. There was time. But he would decide, he vowed, before ever he left Rosings.

The doors of Rosings shut firmly behind him, Darcy grasped his favorite malacca by its gold griffin-head handle and, taking the steps two at a time, struck out in long strides across the park to the grove and the path that led to Hunsford. Despite his late-waged turmoil, he had awakened that morning curiously invigorated and eager for the day. Upon opening his eyes, he lay quite still, the memory of the confessions of the night rising to flow through him like a river of sweet, heady wine. Here and there, its currents swirled against the shores of his mind and emotions, bringing them exquisitely, wonderfully alive. Different—he felt so very different. How, exactly? Darcy felt his mouth curving into a smile at the utter predictability of his rational, logical self. What did it matter how? He felt so extraordinarily . . . alive!

The familiar sounds of Fletcher's preparations in the adjoining dressing room gently distracted him into another line of thought. Soon his valet would be coming through to inform him that all was in readiness for his morning ablutions. Darcy turned his head, regarding the empty pillow beside him. Fletcher's routine would certainly need to change when—No, he firmly took himself to task, he must not think of that now, for he could not allow such anticipation to color his thinking. First, he must put his hard-won decision into action, and to do that required that he take steps to be in Elizabeth's company, not lie abed daydreaming. He must see Elizabeth! This morning! "And without Richard," he firmly informed his heart. Flinging aside the bedclothes, he arose and opened the dressing room door, startling Fletcher with the information that he wished to begin the morning ritual immediately. Shaved and dressed in record time, he descended to a blessedly empty breakfast room, where he downed a cup of coffee between quick bites of coddled egg and toast. Now, finally, he was on his solitary way.

By Heaven, the day was glorious! Darcy slowed his pace as he entered the grove, the trees having taken him out of view of any chance observer at Rosings's windows. He left Fletcher with the information that he was going out on a walk should anyone inquire, but his destination he kept to himself. Now, under cover of the grove, he could strike off in any direction without being seen. The morning sun slanted through the branches above his head, gilding the motes of dust that filtered down before him as if offering him a faerie road to his heart's desire. *Faeries, indeed!* Darcy snorted at the foolish turn his thoughts had taken and shook his head, but the thought would not be banished, nor would the image that followed on its heels. Lady Sylvanie. He had once likened her to a faerie princess, and she had proved as dangerous. Her midnight tresses and stormy gray eyes invaded his reverie in the tempting guise to which he had so nearly succumbed in Norwycke's gallery. He shook his head again, this time to clear it. No, no faerie lay at the end of this path but a wonderfully real woman in whose heart lay no such darkness as had possessed the other.

The more pleasing vision of Elizabeth from the evening before, her brow arched above teasing eyes, slowed him further, until he no longer moved down the way but stood in the middle of the path, seized by a sudden disquiet. Yes, the real, human, unpredictable Elizabeth lay at the end; the Elizabeth who never failed to draw swords when they spoke. And he was proposing to visit her alone—without Richard. Save for that agonizing hour in which they had silently shared Netherfield's library, he had never been alone with her—without her family or friends present, without the support of his own friends or relatives. The uncommon usefulness of his cousin struck him forcefully. Perhaps he ought to go back, wait until Richard was up and about, and propose a visit to Hunsford. He almost turned when the import of his thoughts stopped him. She had challenged him to *practice*, had she not? Was he then to beg off at the first opportunity? Every emotion within him rose up in vociferous denial. Practice, then, he most certainly would! How better to further learn her mind and gauge the strength of his own feelings? Darcy started forward, his confidence increasing as he reminded himself that Mrs. Collins and her sister would be there. "And likely Collins as well. Depend upon it," he told himself. "Three ladies to one gentleman are conversational odds exceedingly in your favor, man!"

In short order, Darcy reached the end of the path and entered the main road of Hunsford village. The lane to the parsonage was hard by, and he turned into its narrow entrance, his boots brushing the closely bordered flowers as he walked in sure strides up to the door and rang the bell. The maidservant from his first visit opened the door. "Mr. Darcy, to see the ladies of the house," he informed the girl, who ducked him a curtsy and stepped aside. Taking off his beaver, he waited for her to relatch the door and take him up. The house seemed very quiet.

"This way, sir, if you please, sir," the girl gulped out and led him to the stairs. The sound of his boots upon the steps emphasized again to him the quietness of the place. No voices, no rattle of china or sound of steps masked his advance up the stairs and down the short hall. The maidservant stopped before the parlor door and, opening it, curtsied to the occupants. "Mr. Darcy, miss."

"Thank you," a hesitant voice from inside replied. Darcy stepped past the girl and into the room, upon which he immediately went cold. His heart's lady stood there in perfect loveliness and, Heaven help him, perfectly alone! Surely the others were about—somewhere! Darcy swallowed hard and did his courtesy, his eyes darting to the corners of the room as he rose. No, no one! He looked back to Elizabeth, whose eyes seemed to reflect his own discomposure. *Apologize, fool!*

"Miss Bennet," he began stiffly, "I must beg your pardon for intruding upon you. I had understood that all the ladies were at home."

As the door to Hunsford cottage shut and the latch fell into place behind him, Darcy paused briefly to settle his beaver firmly upon his head and look about him before setting off down the lane and back in the direction of Rosings. The unfamiliar elation that had threatened to turn him giddy in Hunsford's parlor was now somewhat abated, allowing him at last to think. He drew in a deep breath of the fragrant spring air and thanked Heaven for the renewed sense of control that his body, set in motion, bestowed. It was done, their first private interview! He had acted like a foolish schoolboy, of course, as unable to control his unruly emotions as the most callow youth suffering the pangs of a first love. *To where did the man who had "lived in the world" disappear,* he chided himself, *leaving that curst fool behind to babble on, revealing every nook and cranny of his heart?*

What had he said? He struggled to remember how it had begun. His brain seemed to have gone to sleep, for he was able to think of nothing intelligible to say. He replied to her inquiries with little grace and no originality. They discussed the Collinses, he seemed to recall, then the cottage, and something concerning Lady Catherine's efforts toward its improvement. Darcy fought a surprising rush of pleasure as he recalled sitting across from her, her eyes and attention on him alone. Elizabeth. So beautiful in her spring green gown, her distracting lips in a gentle curve that invited him to smile with her at her friend's practicality in marriage. Her hair—what would it be to see it down about her? "Gad, you are the veriest fool!" He cursed himself again as he battled against dwelling on the image his thoughts so easily created. This would not do! Darcy hefted his malacca into his palm and slashed at the bemused figure of himself he saw before him. His future could not be based on her hair or lips, or every objection and sneer he would later face would be richly deserved! *And*, he brought his thoughts to heel, *you must not forget what followed.*

He had meant it only as a passing observation, the business about fifty miles being "an easy distance" between Elizabeth's friend and her family, but it had excited such a vehement reaction that some devil in him decided to tease her with it. "It is a proof of your own attachment to Hertfordshire." He had smiled, prodding her. "Anything beyond the very neighborhood of Longbourn, I suppose, would appear far." Oh, how becomingly she had blushed at his sally! Darcy slowed his ground-eating stride and then stopped altogether. He had arrived at the end of the path unless he meant to walk on in the other direction. The sheltering grove lay behind him and the path descended from this point into an open field, then the formal park, with Rosings lying beyond. He could be seen, and he was unwilling, as yet, to expose himself to the possibility of an encounter until he had it thought out.

Stepping back into the shadows, he leaned against one of his aunt's trees and stared into space, re-creating that moment. Could that blush, so enhancing the creamy loveliness of her face and sending her magnificent eyes into a sweet confusion, have been the reason he had blundered on so recklessly? Or had it been her admission that she did not mean to say that a woman may not be settled too near her family? She hinted at her own feelings, did she not? That she was not bound to Hertfordshire, especially if fortune made the distance inconsequential? Had she not couched her protest in terms of her friend's attachment and not her own? The implications were obvious, even to such an addlepated idiot as he had been at the start of their interview. His delightful fencing partner was offering him her sword! Oh, not in every instance of their relationship, nor would he desire it; but in this, the most basic battle between the male and female of the race. Not only was she *aware* of his interest but she was signaling her *anticipation* of it!

Darcy closed his eyes, remembering the intoxicating thrill that had raced through every fiber of his being. Whatever Wickham's lies had encompassed, she was pleased with his attention. The blush had been wonderful to behold, but it had been her surrender that had taken hold of him and, yes, pushed his tongue past the careful guard his mind had always posted upon his emotions. He had said it then, had even drawn his chair closer to her to catch every word, every breath that would result. "*You* cannot have a right to such very strong local attachment. *You* cannot have been always at Longbourn."

As he pushed away from the tree, the alarm he had experienced at the import of his own words returned. He might as well have declared himself then and there; a more transparent intimation of a shared future was hardly possible! Darcy stalked back several yards down the path toward Hunsford and then returned, only to repeat the exercise. The look of surprise on her face had confirmed to him that she had, indeed, taken his meaning and that a retreat from the position his emotions had led him to was immediately necessary. It was too soon. He had not weighed things to his satisfaction as yet! At the same time, he dared not trifle with her feelings or expectations! So, what had he done to retrieve himself? He had plucked up a newspaper to mask his confusion and then asked her about being pleased with Kent!

Good Lord, what a blundering, caper-witted ass! Darcy stopped his pacing, a scowl upon his face, and rapped the malacca into his palm with stinging force. If the lady of the house and her sister had not returned soon after, there was no telling in what further ways he might have made a cake of himself! In self-disgust, he collapsed against a tree, but his gaze was drawn back down the path he had come. What, in the end, was the result of his morning's foray? *She is entirely receptive, open to your attentions. She may very well expect them to continue after your rash words!* It remained only that he come to the point for her to be his, for the sweetness he longed for to become truth. But, for the life of him, he could not as yet follow through. The social impediments remained; and they were mountainous, the familial ones hardly less so. All their claims fell upon him, and he felt keenly the justice of their reproaches. For what did he not owe to his name, his relations, and his posterity? Such an unequal match contracted merely to satisfy his appetites! Could the happiness it held out to him survive the opprobrium he would face the rest of his days? "No more!" Darcy groaned. He knew himself to be incapable of bringing peace to the warring parties within him. Both reason and emotion had failed him; there was nothing for it but to let fate run its course. "No more," he repeated, no longer a plea but this time a command. "Proceed as you have begun, and trust to God that fate will intervene, that something will happen to end this!"

"Fitz! Fitz, is something the matter?" Richard's voice echoed from among the trees in the direction opposite that which Darcy had taken to Hunsford. In moments Fitzwilliam was before him, his breath coming in puffs.

Coloring briefly, Darcy hastened to assure him, "Richard! No, nothing is amiss!"

"Then why the blazes were you yelling?" His cousin looked at him accusingly. "I thought you were being attacked or had fallen or something!" He looked to his coat and waistcoat, giving them a tug back into place.

"Nothing of the sort," Darcy answered, "but I thank you for the heroic charge to my defense. I fear that I was thinking aloud."

"Thinking! All that racket was thinking?"

"Aloud, yes."

"Thinking." Fitzwilliam's dubious regard almost put him to the blush again, but he stood firm. "Fletcher told me that you had gone out for a walk and was mum as the dead on where this walk was to take you. Now I know it was not in that direction." He pointed behind him. "For that is the way I took until it was obvious that you had not chosen it. Which leaves only that direction." He pointed beyond Darcy. "Unless you went blazing a new path." The Colonel eyed his cousin narrowly. "It appears to my admittedly simple military brain that you are dressed uncommonly fine to be cutting new paths through Her Ladyship's grove, leaving me to conclude that you have been to Hunsford already this morning!"

"Yes, that is true," Darcy confessed but said no more.

"And the ladies were at home and in good health this fine morning, Cuz?" Richard cocked a brow at him.

"Yes, all are in perfect health, I can assure you." Darcy smiled back innocently.

"Which prompted you to thinking—aloud, as it were?"

Darcy returned his cousin's questioning stare with a calmness of mind that he knew would infuriate him as little else could do.

"My dear Cuz," Fitzwilliam drawled, "it would give me no end of pleasure to plant you a facer for depriving me of a most agreeable visit this morning, and I would gladly do it if I did not fear spilling your blood over this new frockcoat of mine!" He tugged again at the front corners of the garment but then paused, a wicked smile slowly lighting up his face. "But I shall have my revenge for your taking leave this morning to visit without me! I have here"—Fitzwilliam patted his chest, surprising a rustling sound from underneath his coat—"a packet of letters that arrived express after you left. From London."

"Georgiana!" Darcy immediately regretted his teasing. "Here, Richard, you must give it me at once!"

"Oh, must I?" Fitzwilliam laughed, placing his hand protectively over the place where it lay.

"Richard!" Darcy breathed his name menacingly, then all of a moment threw down the malacca, sent his hat after it, and unbuttoned the first button of his frock coat. Suddenly, the idea of a brawl with his cousin was very appealing. It answered more than one sort of agitation he had suffered this morning.

"Fitz, what are you doing?" Fitzwilliam took a step backward.

"Obliging you, if you can get over my guard." The second button was undone as he spoke, and Darcy started on the third. "But I suggest that you follow my lead if you are concerned about blood!"

Darcy refolded the letters carefully and, without thinking, reached for the delicate ivory knob of the desk drawer before being brought up short by the sudden pain. Grimacing, he drew back slowly, a low groan whistling through his clenched teeth. Richard had a damned punishing right! The purplish bruise on his midsection would be a week in healing, but he discounted the annoyance as well worth the satisfaction of not only denying Fitzwilliam his "facer" but also prevailing so thoroughly in their contest that he had forced the surrender of the letters under the most favorable of terms. Darcy smiled at the memory of Richard's protests and petulant agreement to those terms, but it faded as his regard returned to the letters still in his hand. One, indeed, was from Georgiana. Her precise script had arrived once more wrapped in a letter from Dy Brougham, sent express by His Lordship. Although it was wise to open Dy's letter first, he had set it aside immediately, broken the seal on that of his sister, and settled in as comfortably as he might to give it his full attention. It opened with her best wishes for his health and that of their cousins and aunt, and continued on with an account of the extension of her studies beyond music.

> *My Lord Brougham has been so kind to suggest other books worthy of my perusal and has undertaken to better my understanding of art as well. To that end, we read together often and attend exhibitions and lectures of both historical and artistic subjects. You will also be happy to know, dear Brother, My Lord is not satisfied until I am able to ask intelligent questions of the subject at hand or I can answer his.*

"I am to be happy to know, am I?" Darcy frowned down into the delicate paper balanced between his fingers. "The deuced hedge-bird!" What was Dy up to? This was doing it far too brown. He'd asked him to watch over her, not live in her pocket! Darcy had almost decided to send off a pointed note to his overly conscientious friend when a name farther down Georgiana's letter caught his eye and sent a chill up his back.

> *Her Ladyship begged an introduction of D'Arcy, who obliged her and presented her to me as the new wife of a friend of yours from Cambridge, Viscount Monmouth. Lady Sylvanie Monmouth was most attentive, asking about my music and other interests. She particularly asked after you, Fitzwilliam, and was desirous of knowing when you would be returning to London. I was about to inform her when Lord Brougham, who*

had gone to procure some punch, came upon us and had the misfortune of spilling one of the glasses on Her Ladyship's gown, quite ruining it, I fear. Needless to say, Lady Monmouth was forced to retired to her carriage but promised to call upon me later this week.

"Sylvanie!" Darcy closed his eyes. "Good God!" He had hoped rather than believed that Tris would keep her at one of his estates for at least a half year before daring the gossips of London. Nothing of the events at Norwycke Castle had reached those itching ears, but the Viscount's hasty marriage was enough to set the London cats among the pigeons. More to the point, what did Sylvanie want with Georgiana? Why concern herself with an introduction to a girl who had not yet come out? That there was a purpose behind this contrived introduction, he had not a shred of doubt. Might she see Georgiana as a potential vehicle for her revenge for the death of her mother Lady Sayre? "Thank God, Dy was there!" Darcy blessed his friend, knowing better than to suppose the punch an accident, and reached for his letter.

Darcy,

Sending Miss Darcy's note express, old man, because something is up and I cannot like it. I wish you had confided to me what happened at Norwycke, for it would put me in a better position now to serve you. But enough. I have my own resources and will set about to discover what the new Lady Monmouth is about intruding upon Miss Darcy's notice. I swear, my friend, I left her for only a moment—you must thank your idiot cousin for the introduction, but what can one expect from a man who would offer for Lady Felicia? I succeeded in sending Her Ladyship packing before the conversation had progressed very far. Unfortunately, Lady Monmouth indicated that she intends to pay a call. Never fear; I will lay down instructions with your butler—maybe

Hinchcliffe as well—to say Miss Darcy is not at home. Now
there is a formidable fellow but very soft where your sister is
concerned! Good man, that! Of course, I shall also enlist the
excellent Mrs. Annesley, and I shall double my vigilance. My
friend, you may place full confidence in me with regard to this
matter, and I vow to keep you apprised. No need to toddle
back to town. All is in hand.

—Dy

Darcy eased his body forward and grasped the knob, pulling
the small drawer wide. Carefully, he placed the letters inside and
shut it. "All is in hand." As flighty as Dy appeared at times, Darcy
knew that his word on a matter made it as good as done. He could
not be pleased about the meeting of his sister and Lady Monmouth, but rushing back to London might be just what Sylvanie
desired by it. No, he would stay in Kent, for Kent was where his future was to be decided.

"Darcy? I say, Darcy!" It was the laughter in Fitzwilliam's voice
rather than his call that dragged Darcy's attention away from the
marvelous way the sunlight was playing among Elizabeth's luxurious curls. "I have never seen you behave so stupidly, Cousin! I
swear, madam." The Colonel turned to Mrs. Collins. "He is not
usually so boorish as to ignore his hostess completely! Why, I have
known him to string some half dozen words together at a go in a
most cogent manner."

"That, my dear Cousin, is because the military can rarely be
depended upon to retain the meaning of a communiqué composed of any more," Darcy shot back, now fully aware of his
cousin's amused gaze upon him. Impervious to the barb,
Fitzwilliam feigned a swoon, bringing the entire room to renewed
laughter. Blast Richard! But it was true. He had become distracted
and had been full of nothing save the woman sitting across from

him, haloed in the morning light from the nearby window. "I do beg your pardon, ma'am. Did you require something of me?"

" 'Twas nothing of great import, Mr. Darcy." Mrs. Collins's smile was sincere, but so was the curiosity that marked the rest of her features. He would have to exercise better care over his wandering attention. *No, not wandering,* he corrected himself. His problem was the reverse; it was so very focused . . . and entirely upon Elizabeth. Her face, her figure, her hair, the way her voice trilled up and down the scale so enchantingly, the delicacy of her hands as her sure fingers bent to her needlework. He dared not even consider her eyes and those lips that now curved up at his repartee with Richard—or was it at his distraction? Blast! Darcy turned his face away to the window. This was his third call at the parsonage this week, the second with Richard, and he was no further toward making a decision than he had been Sunday. The problem, he decided, was that there were too many other people about! Although from his late experience he knew private interviews to be fraught with dangers and difficulties, how else could he gain the answers he required? How was this to be accomplished? He could not depend on another happy accident, nor would he skulk about the shrubbery hoping to catch her alone.

"Oh, you must never think so!" Mrs. Collins's reply to something that Fitzwilliam had opined interrupted Darcy's bemusement with his conundrum. "Miss Bennet is a very hardy sort, as are many of Hertfordshire's young ladies. I have known her to walk from her home to Meryton and back twice in one day!"

Walk! Of course! How could he have forgotten? The memory of Elizabeth's wind-kissed cheeks and bright eyes when she had been ushered into the dining room at Netherfield returned with a disconcerting clarity. She walked often and alone there in Hertfordshire. Did she walk Rosings Park alone?

"Is it true, Darcy?" Fitzwilliam lifted a brow at him as he pulled him by force back into the conversation. "Is Miss Elizabeth

Bennet such an excellent walker as Mrs. Collins would have us believe?"

"Unquestionably," Darcy answered him, and then, suddenly, inspiration struck! If she did walk and alone would that not afford him the privacy with her he desired? "I can vouch for her personally in regard to her enterprise in Hertfordshire, but whether Miss Bennet finds Kent worthy of her rambles, she must confess."

"Ah then, does Kent tempt you, Miss Bennet?" Fitzwilliam smiled at his object. "Or perhaps I should ask, does Rosings Park? You must forget that we are Her Ladyship's relatives and tell the truth!"

Yes, she took great pleasure in her walks, and the fields and groves of Rosings Park were become as dear a ramble as any in Hertfordshire. Darcy smiled as the scene in the Hunsford cottage replayed itself in his mind. Elizabeth's confidential tone to Lady Catherine's relations had been one he knew to be sincere, and the satisfaction which came with the assurance that he knew her mind, could interpret her meaning, was deep and abiding. Her delight had been unfeigned. So, here he was traversing the park as soon as the dew had lifted in a welter of anticipation of meeting her . . . alone. The rapid beat of his heart had nothing to do with the length or pace of his stride and all to do with his hopes. That unruly organ had resisted every attempt to bridle it, rein it in to a more seemly rhythm, from the moment he had awakened this morning.

At the least, he had not startled Fletcher. His valet had been prepared for his early ring, receiving him into the barbering chair with no more comment than a "Good morning, sir." He had half expected some telling Shakespearean barb whose meaning he would be expected to ponder, but Fletcher had proceeded with quiet alacrity and sent him off expertly attired with only a wish of "Good fortune, Mr. Darcy." That had been a bit unusual! Darcy could not remember such a parting benediction ever falling from

Fletcher's lips before, but the sight of a flash of yellow through the trees ahead drove that curiosity from his mind and set his heart to beating an even faster tattoo. Gripping his malacca tightly, he quickened his pace. Then, as he rounded a curve of the path, there she was, a vision of cream and yellow drifting pensively among the lacy ferns and wild violets that carpeted the grove. Darcy slowed, making a last attempt at composing himself before she became aware of his presence, but it was for naught. Elizabeth's head came up from her study of nature just as he rounded upon her. Her eyes, wide with surprise, locked unerringly with his over the distance between them, in that moment unleashing so true a dart that Darcy felt it cleave clean through his chest to lodge deep inside and bring him to a complete stop.

"Mr. Darcy!" The surprise and uncertainty in Elizabeth's voice penetrated his awareness.

"Miss Bennet," he heard himself reply, and in so hearing, command of his limbs returned. He swept her a bow. Curiosity overruled the surprise in her eyes as he replaced his beaver and walked toward her. "Do you anticipate your walk this morning," he asked, his voice not at all as steady as he would wish, "or are you at the end of your ramble?"

"I was just about to turn back, sir," she informed him, her gaze now reaching beyond him down the path he had come. "Does Colonel Fitzwilliam not accompany you?"

"No, my cousin does not find the early morning light agreeable," he replied, anxious to have done with any talk of Richard. He forced himself to press on and take command of the conversation. "If you mean to turn back, Miss Bennet, may I offer you my escort?" Elizabeth's countenance again betrayed uncertainty. "It would be my pleasure," he added quietly and extended his arm. Slowly, she nodded her acquiescence and placed her hand upon his arm. Darcy could barely restrain himself from reaching over his other hand and covering it protectively. Instead, he motioned that they begin her return journey. "Shall we?"

"Yes, thank you, you are very kind," Elizabeth murmured.

"Not at all," Darcy replied absently, his concentration centered upon stilling the clangorous din of his heart while at the same time enjoying every sensation her closeness afforded.

"Mr. Darcy." Elizabeth tilted her face up to his. "There are any number of walking paths in Rosings Park, are there not?"

"Yes, I believe that is so," he replied and then quickly looked away down the path in order to hide the smile that threatened to appear on his face. Gad, this was going to be impossible! How could he not grin like a fool with Heaven poised there on his arm?

"As I thought." Elizabeth's self-congratulation on this seemingly elementary deduction puzzled him, but the mystery was soon rendered clear when she continued. "Although I have not walked all the paths of Rosings, I do beg leave to inform you that this particular path I find to be quite efficacious for quieting the spirit and for solitary reflection."

"Indeed!" Darcy looked away, desperate to prevent the grin that again threatened to spread over his face. Thank Heaven that his height and bearing concealed it from her view! It would not do to be too obvious, to reveal openly the extent of his pleasure in what she had so delicately conveyed to him. It was settled, then! He was to meet her here if he wished to further his designs for private conversation and mutual understanding.

"You favor solitary walks, then, Miss Bennet? Do you not wish for companionship?"

"Oh, at times! The right companion can make all the difference in the pleasure a ramble affords. But if that companion may not be had, I prefer my own company, sir, and quiet."

"We are of the same mind in this regard as well then." He nodded. The *right companion*—ah, better and better!

Elizabeth looked up at him, a puzzled frown creasing her brow. "I do not catch your meaning, Mr. Darcy."

"It was you who noticed it first, I am sure." The puzzled crease remained, and as he could not bear that that should be so, he explained. "You told me once that you saw a great similarity in the turn of our minds. I beg to remain silent on your particular observations that evening, but in general, I believe your assessment to be correct."

"Indeed!" exclaimed Elizabeth, whose turn it now was to look away. The remainder of their way back to Hunsford was accomplished in a silence that seemed to Darcy a companionable one, which neither side broke until they reached the gate of the pales opposite the parsonage. This he opened with his free hand, and only then did he succumb to the temptation to clasp in his own the hand that rested on his arm. Taking it, he held it as he did his courtesy. Then, releasing it quickly, he stepped back.

"Good day, Miss Bennet," he said softly.

"And to you, Mr. Darcy," she responded. He returned her a quizzical smile as her eyes once more curiously probed his, then with a tip of his hat, he turned back to Rosings Park. Once more in the shelter of the trees, Darcy smacked the malacca smartly into his left palm. This was progress! By Heaven, he could hardly wait until tomorrow!

The next morning it rained, and although the landowner in Darcy was grateful for it, the rest of him was reduced to pacing the halls of Rosings and growling at his cousin for little or no reason. Finally, when Richard could take no more of his bad humor, Darcy retreated behind a book in a corner of his aunt's well-stocked but little used library. Doubtless she would have read them all if she had been a great proficient, Darcy thought wickedly and then chastised himself for his lack of charity. What was wrong with him? He knew what was wrong with him! He wanted to be in the grove with Elizabeth, her hand again on his arm, her closeness filling his senses.

Letting out a great sigh, he turned back to the book he had carelessly selected and tried to concentrate on the printed words before him, but a soft click of the bolt in the doorknob brought his head up out of it with a start. Was Richard trying to sneak up on him, the nod cock! The door swung open only inches before revealing the hand behind such stealth. Darcy's eyes widened in surprise. Anne! The slight form of his cousin slipped inside the library and hastily, though softly, closed the door behind her. But no Mrs. Jenkinson! Darcy's brow crooked in surprise. This was likely the first time he had ever seen Anne without her companion hovering over her. Not pausing to look about her, Anne walked straight to the shelves between the north-facing windows and began an anxious scan of them, book by book. The rigidity of her figure and the small sighs of frustration which carried across the room made it clear to Darcy that she was not meeting with success in her search of the lower shelves and would soon require the library stairs. His sympathy now bound to his curiosity, he rose from his chair.

"May I be—" He got no further. Upon hearing him, Anne cried out in alarm and whirled about to face him with such a look of fright upon her pale countenance that Darcy feared she would faint on the spot. For a moment both of them stood motionless, staring at each other until Anne's eyes shifted away and she seemed, to Darcy, to shrink in upon herself.

"Cousin." He began again, his voice pitched low. "May I be of some assistance? Tell me what you are looking for that I may help you search." Anne looked up at him then, seeming to measure his sincerity. "Anne?" he pressed her gently.

"Wordsworth," she whispered finally. "The first volume of his poems. Mrs. Jenkinson took it away before—Mamá does not approve . . ." She stopped and blushed. "Please, I must find it."

"Certainly," Darcy assured her and turned to the shelves she had been searching. "Do you have reason to believe it here?"

"Mrs. Jenkinson always puts the books I have read here. Mamá then knows what I have been reading."

"I begin to understand!" Darcy smiled down at her before stepping closer to the shelves. "The book shall be found, Cousin." The look of relief and gratitude Anne cast upon him was sad to see, and it tugged at Darcy that until this visit he had little considered how her life must be. The least he could do was find her book, and he set about it with a will.

"Aha! Found it!" Darcy plucked his quarry from between the two books where it had been wedged on a shelf above even his head. "Anne, here it is!" he cried and held it out to her. His cousin reached up, but he released it too quickly, and the volume fluttered to the floor, pages scattering everywhere. "Anne! Forgive me." Darcy immediately bent to retrieve the pages.

"No! Do not concern yourself!" His cousin bent to the ruin of her book, but Darcy was before her. Turning over the volume, he saw that not a single page was missing. Puzzled, he took up several of the sheets of paper that lay around them.

"No! Please, give them to me," Anne begged him. "Darcy!"

He rose then from the scatter and stepped away, his eyes traveling between the sheets he held in his hand and his cousin's distraught countenance. Although he had spared them only a glance, he knew what they were. "Anne, allow me to look at them."

"You will laugh at me!" she charged him.

"I promise, I shall not laugh," he countered, looking straight into her fearful eyes. Taking the downward cast of her eyes as reluctant agreement to his request, he walked with them over to the window and began his perusal. He could feel Anne's eyes upon him as he did so, her anxiety an almost physical thing occupying the distance between them, but he read on, unhurried. Several minutes passed until, turning over the last sheet, he looked to his cousin.

"These are quite good, you know. I especially like this one." He handed her the top sheet.

"You do . . . truly?" Anne looked up at him uncertainly.

"Yes, truly. How long have you been writing poetry, Cousin?"

A hint of pleasure shone in Anne's face at his words. "Almost a year now."

"And have you shown these to no one?"

Anne shook her head. "No one, not even Mrs. Jenkinson. Mamá does not approve of poetry, and Mrs. Jenkinson must answer to her. It is best if she does not know. I was working on these today and was surprised by her while I was consulting Wordsworth and so secreted my poems in its leaves."

"But, Anne," Darcy protested, "you cannot keep this forever to yourself! Share them with your family, at the least!" He sat down next to her and took her hands in his. For the first time, she did not flinch or pull away. "Anne?"

"You need not fear being saddled with me as your wife, Cousin. I know Mamá wishes you to believe that I am becoming well, but I fear she is deluding herself. I am not better, Cousin, and I have come to the conviction that I will never be healthy enough to marry anyone."

"Anne! My dear girl!" Darcy held her hands tighter.

"That was when I began to write," she whispered near his shoulder. "I wanted finally to say something, create something . . . something beautiful, perhaps . . . without Mamá's interference or her criticism." She paused, her breath catching in her throat. "I know people think little of me; and I do not blame them, for there is little to see or admire. But, I feel things, Cousin, deeply; and when I became convinced of my future, those feelings seemed to gather and burst through to paper." She looked up at him, only a hint of a tear shining in her eyes. "I will never marry, never have children. These are my legacy, poor as they are. And I am not yet finished, not finished feeling, not finished writing what I feel. I could not bear Her Ladyship's scorn nor, should she change her opinion, that she puff me about. Can you understand, Cousin? Will you keep my secrets?"

"Dear God, Anne!" Darcy stared at his cousin, then at their clasped hands as helplessness consumed him. Of course he would remain silent, but what did that signify in the face of her confession? "Can you be mistaken?" he finally managed.

"There is no mistake, Cousin." Anne looked at him with the compassion he should have been offering up to her.

He looked down at her small hand resting in supplication upon his sleeve. There must be more comfort he could give than his vow. "I promise. Your secrets are safe, Anne. I would that there were more than my mere silence to merit your gratitude. I have avoided and ignored you shamefully, and I am heartily sorry for it."

Anne gently disengaged her hand from his clasp and rose from the settee. "Do not berate yourself, Cousin. It was a game Her Ladyship forced upon us. Whereas I had not the strength or courage to gainsay her, you have handled her brilliantly. For that, you have my thanks." A weary sigh escaped her lips, causing Darcy to rise in concern. "No, I am just a little tired. Please, I must return to my room. I am supposed to be resting." She cast him a rueful smile. "It has been good finally to tell someone, Darcy. Strange that it should be you." And with a curtsy, she was gone from the library, its door shutting softly behind her, leaving Darcy to the contemplation of the rain spattering against the great windows.

Anne did not appear at dinner that evening. Mrs. Jenkinson arrived late in the salon outside the dining room with her charge's plea that she be excused due to a sick headache and fatigue. Dinner was, therefore, a desultory affair, for which the inclement weather was held accountable and for which an evening of billiards was prescribed as the most promising means of relief by an emboldened and fidgety Richard. His hopes were to be dashed, at least temporarily, by a demand from his aunt that he and his cousin undertake to relieve her boredom by presenting themselves at the card table in the drawing room immediately after their brandy.

"Will you be in humor to play after Her Ladyship retires?" Fitzwilliam looked at his cousin from under gathered brows before tossing down the remainder of his glass and motioning to Darcy to refill it. "Cards with the she-dragon and Mrs. Jenkinson is rather not my idea of the way to retrieve a day characterized chiefly by its deadly dullness." He took another sip. "Lord, I wish the parsonage had been able to come! Then we should have had some fun!"

"Although I cannot supply you the fascination, I will endeavor to answer your need for entertainment," Darcy responded drily as he filled Fitzwilliam's glass and set down the decanter, bridling as he did so at Richard's allusion to Elizabeth. He could not like the easy manner in which his cousin spoke of her, and he determined to bring it to an immediate halt. "Or is it that quarter day is too distant a prospect?"

"No, my pockets are not to let quite yet, Darcy." Fitzwilliam's chin came up at his cousin's ungracious jab. "And you are off the mark on the other as well. I have found you to be excessively fascinating on this visit to Kent."

The brandy in Darcy's glass sloshed back and forth. "Then the military life must not be as demanding a profession as is claimed," he retorted, meeting Richard's sharp-eyed regard, but almost immediately he regretted it. This tack would only encourage his cousin's curiosity, and his accusation was more than provocative! "Your pardon, Richard, that was uncalled for." He leaned back in the chair. If only he could retreat to the library or his rooms! The tension between the demands of his heart and his name, coupled with the intensity of his disappointment in not seeing Elizabeth that day, were causing him to act like a prize gudgeon.

"My apologies as well, Fitz." Richard sat down heavily and motioned out the nearby window. "It must be this damned, drizzly rain. Has us both up in the boughs. Pax, old man?" He raised his glass.

Darcy nodded and tipped his glass up in response. "Pax." They both took long, slow swallows. "Do you think we dare test this peace of ours and indulge in a few racks later?" He noted to his cousin then, with a motion of his hand, that the brandy was causing a reddish flush to spread over Richard's cheeks.

Fitzwilliam rubbed at his jaw and laughed. "Perhaps we had better examine our tempers and our sobriety after Her Ladyship has tried them at the card table. We may both be ready to commit mayhem by the time the last card is played!"

The tedium of Lady Catherine's card play and its accompanying monologue drove both men to seek the sanctuary of their rooms rather than hazard their tempers at the billiard table. It was undoubtedly one of the wiser decisions he and Richard had made recently, Darcy thought as he passed through the bedchamber door and was quietly greeted by his valet. The day's revelations and disappointments could only make Darcy receive with relief Fletcher's quick promise of hot water and a soothing concoction of his father's recipe the moment he had divested him of his evening attire. Later, his ablutions completed and seated before the bedchamber's low fire wrapped in his dressing gown, Darcy made a halfhearted attempt to collect his thoughts. But the hour, the fire, the warmth of the drink sliding smoothly down his throat all conspired to send them straightway down the path, through the grove, and past the pales to a certain residence where eyes alight with a welcoming smile waited to comfort the ache in his heart at their too-long absence.

"Oh!" The single exclamation was more than enough to bring Darcy round from his study of some insect-wrought damage to several of the trees, which he had noticed while awaiting Elizabeth's appearance. The trees were still sturdy enough, but if something were not done, they would eventually be reduced to hollow shells and become a danger to any who passed by. He had just finished his assessment and made a mental note to send for Lady Catherine's forester when Elizabeth had come upon him as he rounded one of the damaged trees.

"Miss Bennet." He bowed, his entire being coming suddenly alive with pleasure at the sight of her as well as relief that he had not missed her. Further, judging from the direction she had come, she was at the fore of her walk, which meant that he would have her company for the greater part of an hour. Excellent!

"Mr. Darcy." Elizabeth ducked him an awkward curtsy. Was that a frown upon her face? Darcy waited impatiently for her to raise her head, but when she did, her expression was all that a well-bred young female's should be on such a meeting. The tense muscles surrounding his stomach relaxed somewhat, and he stepped forward.

"You are just beginning your walk, I gather," he began quickly, too ebullient to pause for her to either confirm or deny it. "Rosings Park has been the work of generations. It was, as well, a haunt of my youth; therefore"—his voice dropped—"I know it rather intimately." At the last word he regarded her earnestly. "It would be my pleasure to act as your guide and begin to acquaint you with some of its lesser-known beauties."

Elizabeth blinked up at him, seemingly a little stunned by his offer. "You are most generous, sir, but I could not ask for so much of your time. It must be an imposition."

Her appropriate concern pleased him. "Not at all! I am at your disposal, Miss Bennet." He offered her his arm, and as the other day, her hesitant acceptance of it delighted him with its delicacy of manner and eschewal of expectation. "Of course, we may only make a start of it today. A complete exploration would not be possible even during the entirety of this, your first visit. I promise you, it will be quite some time before you will have seen all that Rosings Park has to offer." This observation seemed to impress her, for her only reply was a faint "Indeed!" as he indicated the direction in which they were to go.

They walked on in silence, Darcy in a quandary as to what sort of topic he should introduce now that her company had been secured. Really, he was quite satisfied, for the present, with her nearness and the exciting pressure of her hand upon his arm; but convention and consideration required they converse. And he would, upon reflection, be very happy to receive so close to his ear whatever observations or opinions on most any subject that she might entertain. Learning more of her was, after all, the reason he had given his conscience for these almost clandestine meetings.

"Do you enjoy your stay at Hunsford, Miss Bennet?" He finally broke the quiet with a safe, mundane inquiry.

"Yes, yes I do," Elizabeth answered him with feeling. "Charlotte—Mrs. Collins—is a dear and longstanding friend who knows my disposition very well and is quite comfortable to leave me to my own devices."

Just so! Darcy luxuriated in Elizabeth's assurance that this and future encounters would not be endangered by Mrs. Collins's unexpected presence. Further, and as he had suspected, the rector's wife had some inkling of how things stood and had signaled to Elizabeth her cooperation in the matter. He looked down upon the straw bonnet that bobbed at his shoulder, a sense of contentment overtaking him. Would not this be what it would be like, this sweetness, this sense of completeness arising from her presence beside him in mutual support, mutual pursuit of a fully shared life? If only the din raised by his duty could be silenced!

They had reached the first bypath, barely discernible even to his familiar eye, and he gently turned her in to it, smiling reassuringly at her questioning brow. "Patience!" was the sum of the explanation he offered her. Carefully pushing aside the occasional wand that had grown across the way since his last visit to this particular place five years before, Darcy ushered Elizabeth down the faint trail. For the most part, it proceeded straightforwardly, not winding save around the odd great rock or tree jutting from the earth; for it was one that he and Richard had blazed as boys whose object it was to arrive at their destination as quickly as possible rather than to excite pleasure in the going. Within minutes, they reached it, the glade that had been so many places to him in his boyhood—Crusoe's desert island, a wilderness fortress under the gallant Wolfe in America, a castle to be defended alongside Arthur—and he turned to see her reception of it. Elizabeth's exclamation of delight was all he had hoped for.

"Fitzwilliam and I found this place the summer I was ten years of age, despite some forceful dissuasion from Her Ladyship's forester." She turned from him, then, and he watched silently as she explored, confident that she understood what had now become his first gift to her.

Someday he would tell her the rest, how Lady Catherine's forester had tried to keep Richard and him from roaming the wood that long ago spring with tales of a fearfully wild boar that inhabited it. Of course, such stories were all they had needed, and they had taken off like a shot to find the creature. How, by the time they had reached the main path through the grove, they had so thoroughly scared each other with imagined sounds of snorting in the brush that they had fallen as much as run down the small hill with not the least idea which direction they were heading and so stumbled upon this hidden glade. Someday he would tell her . . . but not today. Today what he wished was to share with her that mysterious, magical spirit he had always felt possessed by this patch of wood.

"Thank you, Mr. Darcy. It is quite lovely." Elizabeth rejoined him after several minutes, gratitude resting lightly upon her face. "I would never have found this place on my own."

"It is my pleasure, Miss Bennet," he returned as she stepped away from him and began threading her way back to the path by which they had come. Darcy acknowledged the wisdom of her unspoken message; they should not stay longer here in the glade alone. Giving his old haven a grateful nod for doing well by him, he turned to start after her. The rustling sound of leaves mixed with the clicking of branches gave warning that spring winds were stirring overhead. From long acquaintance, Darcy knew they would soon rush down into the glade. Instinctively, he grasped the brim of his hat and looked to Elizabeth to call a warning, but the words caught in his throat as the winds swirled about her in teasing, intimate play with her bonnet and frock.

At that entrancing sight, everything within him suddenly urged him after her, strenuously assuring him that all he wanted would be answered if he would just this very moment enfold her in his arms and bring her within their shelter, if he could caress her cheek and search out the soft reaches of her lips! He started forward, the contentment he had felt now displaced by desire, oversetting him so that it was not until he was almost upon her that his rational mind succeeded in bringing himself to order.

The sound portion of his mind which still remained warned him that the struggle to attend to rationality was becoming increasingly desperate in anything touching upon Elizabeth. That much was too obvious to ignore any longer, and the sudden realization of this lessening of his self-command cooled his ardor as no indignation on Elizabeth's part ever could have done. He slowed his pace, keeping his distance as they walked up to the main path of the park. It was not that desire was gone; he still knew that ache, but he was more himself and able to think with some degree of collection.

"Mr. Darcy, I think I should return to Hunsford." Elizabeth greeted him with her decision as he joined her on the upper path. Darcy could only thank God for her announcement. His equanimity alone in her presence had been tested enough for one day. "Mrs. Collins mentioned she would have need of me, and I should think she is well ready for my help by this hour."

"Of course, you must go to the aid of your friend," he replied solemnly. But despite the danger that still remained, he could not prevent himself from adding, "Allow me, I beg you, the peace of mind seeing you to her door would afford." Her brow rose at that; nonetheless, she accepted his proffered arm, and together they turned back to the village.

Again, only silence and the path were shared between them. Now and then he would steal glances at her as they wended back to Hunsford, but he could make nothing of her steady, calm features. Occasionally, he thought he detected the frown he had suspected earlier, but Elizabeth's diffidence prevented confirmation, and he set it down to a lapse by her into thought. They walked on, but try as he might, Darcy could not recapture that sense of contentment he had experienced earlier on the path. He was still too much aware of her, he ruefully concluded, and wondered whether marriage might temper the emotions tumbling about within him and direct them into more happy channels. There was a question! Would marriage, after all, make him happier? It was fervently to be hoped, although he could not say that he had observed it to be true in his married friends. Rather, their marriages, arranged for reasons of family, connections, or fortune, had so little to do with his own situation that he could have no point of reference. Of the happiness of wives, he had even less idea, save for the disconcerting evidence supplied him by the many lures matrons of various ages had cast to him since his majority. Perhaps the answer lay in some other direction.

"Miss Bennet," Darcy began and then fell silent, no longer certain how to broach his question, but he was spared the embarrassment, for it appeared that she had not heard him. He began again.

"Miss Bennet, what, may I ask, is your opinion of the happiness of Mr. and Mrs. Collins?" Elizabeth's stride faltered for a moment, almost dislodging her hand from his arm.

"How do you mean, sir?" She turned his question back, her voice curiously tight.

"Your friend, Mrs. Collins." He narrowed his inquiry. "Would you say that she is happier in the married state and with Mr. Collins than before becoming so?"

"Happiness, as with distance, Mr. Darcy, is a relative term." She left his question hang, her eyes searching out the path ahead of them, but then she relented. Without looking at him, she answered, "Yes, she is happy, sir, as hard as it is for me to admit that something I could not at first rejoice over has redounded to her benefit. Given Charlotte's nature, expectations, and understanding, she considers herself perfectly happy in her marriage, and I must agree with her."

"So, you would posit a couple's happiness in marriage with the agreement of their natures, their expectations of life, and the mutuality of their understanding?"

Her silence at his question was such that he feared she again had not heard him. Finally, her answer came so softly that he had to bend to hear her. "It is a beginning, at least. Without them, I believe the chances for happiness are quite remote." She glanced up at him briefly, then looked away; but Darcy was well satisfied. Had she not, in her attempt to sketch his character, compared their dispositions and remarked on their similarity? Her ready wit and intelligence, her understanding, were well and delightfully established with him. What of her expectations of life? She could not be mistaken in his interest, yet she behaved with a restraint and a modesty that excited his intense admiration and gratitude. Contemplation of how this would stand her in good stead as his wife, as mistress of Pemberley, and as a leading figure in Society occupied him as pleasantly as did that of her profile until they passed the pales and came upon the parsonage gate.

"We have arrived, Mr. Darcy." Elizabeth's voice, low and hesitant, recalled him from his thoughts.

"We have, indeed, Miss Bennet," he answered earnestly, and as before, he possessed himself of the hand upon his arm and raised it to his lips. "Good day, Miss Bennet." He bowed.

"Good day, Mr. Darcy." She curtsied quickly and left him standing among the flowers at the parsonage lane's entrance.

He did not turn back until she was safely inside, and even then, he lingered. Despite her family, her lack of fortune and connection, he saw now that he would always be proud of her, could always put his trust in her because she understood him, she was like him . . . and he loved her. "Part of my soul, I seek thee," the lines from Milton returned to seize him again with their power and veracity, "and thee claim, my other half."

CHAPTER 3

As a Dream Doth Flatter

*I*t had taken but little persuasion, in fact none at all, to convince Her Ladyship of the benefits of issuing an invitation to the parsonage for Thursday evening. A word or two about the amiable effect of music on the passage of an evening and the entertainment to be had with more hands at the card table, and it was done. Richard had said nothing as he led Her Ladyship to the desired conclusion, but that very fact put Darcy on his guard. With the summons penned and a humble acceptance received, he could look to the next day's necessary deprivation of Elizabeth's company with an admirable calm.

Tomorrow! Tomorrow would witness the climax of months of desire, denial, and debate. His future would be settled and in a manner most satisfactory to his hopes: a union the like of which he had observed between his parents, both sympathetic of mind and warm of heart. Wrapped in his dressing gown, with a glass of good port before the bedchamber fire, Darcy allowed his fancy full play, composing for himself a heady picture of Elizabeth by his side as he introduced her to Pemberley. It would be daunting for her at first, he had no doubt; but he was equally certain that she would soon take command of his home the way she had his heart. He could see her among his mother's flowers making Eden her own, in the music room filling it softly with song, and in the library sharing a book or merely each other's company through a long winter's evening. In truth, he could envision her gracing every room of Pemberley with her lively, delightful presence. Days spent in sweet companionship followed by nights . . . He stopped that thought with a sigh. And the servants would adore her, of course: the Reynoldses at Pemberley, the Witchers in London. Lord, she will probably have Hinchcliffe eating out of her hand in less than a fortnight! He grinned to himself. And Georgiana! Darcy's smile deepened. Ah, there lay the one consideration in this matter that placed second only after his own happiness! Georgiana would at last have a sister—a friend—to love and confide in, one who had his full confidence and would take her best interests to heart.

Although, he checked the pleasurable flight of his fancy, her exposure to Elizabeth's family would have to be judiciously limited. Darcy sipped at his port as a picture of the Bennet family formed uneasily in his mind. Naturally, Elizabeth would wish to see them, at least occasionally. There would be those times, he supposed, when he would send her off to visit them; but he did not yet like to think of their being parted. That very reasonable unwillingness gave rise to the foreboding thought that he would then be obliged to accompany her on these visits. He took another sip of the port. A week or two with his Bennet in-laws? No, that was simply not possible! They would have to come to Pemberley . . . when he had no other guests nor was in expectation of any. The thought of the nobility and gentry of Derbyshire, or even his Matlock relations, in the same room with Elizabeth's family was more in the nature of a nightmare than a dream! He could well envision the astonishment on his aunt's face should he require his aunt Lady Matlock to spend an afternoon or evening in the company of Mrs. Bennet and her younger daughters. His Lordship would simply stare him out of all countenance at the mere suggestion! That is, he reminded himself, if he was even on speaking terms with them after his undistinguished marriage! Slowly, thoughtfully, he finished off the port and set the small glass down on the side table. Was he really going to do this? Was he, in truth, going to dare his family, his world, to accept a woman of no distinguished birth, without even fortune to recommend her, as one of them?

"Mr. Darcy, sir?" Fletcher's low-pitched inquiry brought him up out of the bog of unpleasant realities in which he had become mired. "Is there anything more you wish tonight, sir?"

Darcy looked at the clock; it was very late. He should have dismissed his valet long ago. "No, Fletcher. Good Heavens, man, you should have reminded me of your attendance an hour ago!"

"Not at all, sir." Fletcher bowed but made no motion to leave. "Are you certain, sir? Your pardon, but you seem"—he paused and appeared to be searching for the right word—"unsettled, sir. Is there nothing you might wish to better prepare yourself for rest?"

Darcy tapped the edge of his empty glass. "You have well supplied me. No, I wish nothing more to drink."

"A book, then, sir? Something from your shelf or, perhaps, the library?" Fletcher cocked his head toward the door.

"No, I think not." Darcy yawned. "I could not concentrate long enough to make a good beginning. Good night, Fletcher." He dismissed the valet firmly but then relented in the face of his concern. "All is well; I promise you."

"Good night, then, sir." Fletcher bowed again.

The dressing room door clicked softly behind him as Darcy turned slowly back to the fire. *Unsettled*. His perceptive valet had described him perfectly. The formidable task of reconciling all the relevant parties in his proposed marriage loomed larger with every tick of the clock toward that hour. He knew how it would be. Lady Catherine would be outraged, Lord and Lady Matlock stunned and severe in their disapproval, and all of them would importune him with every objection known to man. His friends would be shocked, his enemies would snigger, and Bingley would never forgive him for doing himself what he had so strongly advised him against.

"Plague seize it!" Darcy's jaw set. He would make his offer and the Devil take the hindmost! Which, knowing his relations and peers, he most certainly would—and with pleasure! Darcy closed his eyes and rubbed at his temples, where the eddy of a headache was beginning to swirl. He must redirect his thoughts, or any hope of rest this night was lost. A book, as Fletcher had suggested? No, something shorter—poetry! Arming himself with a branch of candles, he stepped to his shelf and drew out the slim volume of sonnets Fletcher had packed. Taking the book over to the bed, he set the branch down on the table and, casting aside his dressing gown, made himself as comfortable as possible among the pillows and bedclothes. Which one was it? He quickly leafed through the pages, scanning the lines until he found the one that had, the other day, brought Elizabeth so forcefully to his mind that it seemed written for her. Ah, yes! He settled back and allowed the words their nourishing sway.

"If I could write the beauty of your eyes . . ."

"Darcy! Darcy, do you come?" Fitzwilliam's voice echoed through the upper corridors of Rosings outside Darcy's suite and penetrated through the mahogany door. Fitzwilliam's person soon followed his voice as Darcy's door was flung open to reveal his cousin elegantly clad for a walk. Darcy's brow hitched up as he took in the vision before him. "What?" demanded Fitzwilliam, his self-possession fading somewhat under his silent scrutiny.

"I am honored." Darcy sketched him a mocking bow. "Such refinement disposed upon a mere walk with your cousin in a country park! I would have thought to see you in buckskin, not breeches and a coat fine enough for London! And, good Lord, is that a striped waistcoat?"

"I would have you know it is not in the least outré." Fitzwilliam bridled under his tone. "Even if you did set Beau Brummell about his business with that fancy cravat knot of Fletcher's! Besides," he continued indifferently as he sauntered into the room, "I thought we might continue on and drop in at the parsonage when we were finished. After tonight, you know, there will be no more *la Bennet*." He looked at Darcy from the corners of his eyes. "And I, for one, shall miss her."

"Humph!" had been all he had deigned Richard's first remark worthy of, but the second was quite another matter. "Shall you really?" he drawled with just enough skepticism in his tone to bring up his cousin's chin.

"Yes, really, Fitz! Miss Bennet is quite enchanting!"

"A description you have bestowed upon every woman who has caught your fancy," Darcy challenged him. How did Richard truly regard Elizabeth? "What woman have you not squired about whom you did not find 'enchanting' at one time or another, only to be bored within a month?"

"Low hit, old man," Fitzwilliam returned with a frown.

"Bang on the mark!" Darcy shot back, then relented. "And I have no quarrel with you there. Doubtless, you are justified in your final assessment."

"It is my initial opinion, then, that you hold in so little regard?" Fitzwilliam cocked his brow at him. "I see." He turned away for a moment, then faced his cousin again. "Since we both likely agree that I have the greater experience in these matters, having been so often 'enchanted' and then disappointed," he proposed sardonically, "we might also posit that I have learnt something along the way."

Darcy inclined his head in agreement to the supposition. "We might."

Fitzwilliam nodded back. "Well then, from my vast experience, let me assure you that Miss Bennet is something out of the ordinary. Of course, she is lovely to look upon. Her modest style, in contrast to the expensive drapery we are accustomed to, only enhances her person. Oh, she lacks a bit of Town bronze for having been immersed in the country. She cannot speak of all the little inconsequentialities attendant upon life in London, nor take a part in the latest *on-dits*, but that is part of her charm. Those things compose the greater part of the conversation, so called, of most young ladies of our acquaintance. It is such a pleasure to converse with a woman of honest opinion on interesting subjects and to come away feeling still that you have been well entertained."

"That is as may be here, in the country, with no other females about to offer competition," Darcy countered. "What if there were, or you had met her at some assembly in London? Better yet, what if she were to come to London with no more to recommend her than you have seen here in Kent; would you seek her out, introduce her to your parents?"

"Would I pay a call? Unquestionably! Take her to the park or the theater? It would be a pleasure! But as to the other, I doubt that Miss Bennet would receive an invitation to any event hosted by the *ton*, and it would take more credit than mine to bring her to their notice. I hate to think of how she would fare among the cats and pigeons with so little, in their estimation, to support her."

"Your parents, though, would you introduce her?" Darcy pressed him.

"I don't know." Fitzwilliam paused. "When could they meet? I suppose I could wring an invitation to tea from Mater, but that would appear damned odd of me unless I had very particular interests in that direction." He looked curiously at his cousin. "Which I do not, or rather, cannot. Is that what you are hinting at, that I should be more circumspect? I know my situation, Fitz. More's the pity!" He sighed. "I believe if her situation were different, they would be as enchanted as I, but then, it is not I who must hold up the family name. That task belongs to D'Arcy, and that privilege of first birth I gladly accord him!" He laughed. "But come, Cousin, are you ready? The dew is lifted and the grounds await!"

"I must beg your pardon, Richard." Darcy shook his head. "Unless I am to postpone our departure yet again, I find that there are some matters that require my attention."

"More 'matters,' Fitz!" Fitzwilliam whistled under his breath. "By all means, look to them, for I do not think that I can support another rapturous display from Her Ladyship. I believe that next spring I shall make arrangements to be unavailable. Would you hold a posting to Spain to engage Napoleon sufficient excuse? Yes, well, I thought not." He grinned at Darcy's snort of laughter. "Get about your 'matters,' then, while I enjoy the day. If I leave you to them now, will you be finished before Saturday?"

"I hope to have them well in hand by tonight, certainly by tomorrow," he assured him. "Off with you!"

"Yes, sir!" Fitzwilliam saluted him with a tap of his walking stick against his brow. "And if I should meet the enchanting Miss Bennet, do you have any orders, sir?"

"Do not let your admiration run away with you!" Unable to prevent his voice from taking an edge, Darcy looked away but, after a calming breath, continued, "and extend to her my best wishes for her day."

"Done and done, old man." Fitzwilliam seemed not to have taken offense. "I shall make report of her reply when I am come back," he called over his shoulder as he headed out the door. "Good luck with your 'matters,' Fitz, and good hunting to me!"

Darcy moved to the door Fitzwilliam had blithely neglected to pull shut and listened as the eager beat of his cousin's boots faded into the reaches of the house. Minutes later, a heavy door slammed, and he knew that Richard was finally, safely gone. Lady Catherine had left earlier with Anne and her companion on a mission of beneficent interference in the lives of her neighbors, and he had Rosings more or less to himself, as he had hoped. A rising excitement gripped him. It was *only* a matter of hours! It was a mat-

ter of *hours*! Both perspectives contained equal portions of anticipation and dread, and preyed upon him in their turn. Richard's
words also had been of dual encouragement and warning as he
had acknowledged Elizabeth's superiority but tempered his regard
with the realities of their world. It was possible his cousin might
support him, but Darcy had no illusions that it would be without
reservation. *Why must this be so difficult?* he importuned Heaven.
Stopping before the French doors that opened into the garden, he
stared out into it unseeing. He had been a creature of duty all his
life and had met its demands without thought or complaint. It was
only here, in this one, desperately important instance that he
wished a reprieve. He wanted happiness—he wanted love. He
wanted . . . Elizabeth! Instantly her image was before him, smiling
in that maddeningly distracting manner, filling his mind's eye and
the deepest reaches of his heart.

"I am that sorry, Fitz! It clean escaped my mind." Fitzwilliam
pulled a penitent face at Darcy's annoyance that he had spent an
hour in Elizabeth's company and still failed to offer her his greeting. "But we did speak of you, which is very like, is it not?" he offered in apology as they made their way to the stairs.

"Idiotish wretch! It is nothing 'like' in the least!" Darcy replied.

"Better a whisker than an outright Canterbury tale." Richard
grinned at him. "Oh, come round, Fitz! *La Bennet* will be here
soon, and you can do all your wishing in person. Take warning,
though; it will absolutely require you to open your mouth." Darcy
gave his cousin a withering look and proceeded down the stairs,
his pace quickening as he went. She had spoken of him? He fairly
burned with curiosity about what she could have said to Richard,
but he dared not ask, not at this juncture. If Richard caught the
least hint of what he intended this evening, he would have an audience for his every move.

It had been sufficiently unnerving under Fletcher's anxious

eye as his valet dressed him for the evening. Neither of them had spoken, an unusual enough state of affairs, but then every piece of clothing had been tugged and buttoned against his body with the utmost precision. His dark gray trousers fit smoothly tight, as did his subdued but elegant pearl-colored waistcoat. He had firmly refused another appearance of the Roquet, but the knot Fletcher had devised in its place seemed no less uncomfortable a work of art. The valet had then presented him his frock coat, easing it up his arms and over his shoulders with the utmost care to prevent a crease in the fine, jet-black fabric. Then down it had been drawn and the double breast buttoned snugly against his chest until he could barely breathe! Fletcher had passed him his watch and fobs, observing his every positioning of those accoutrements, and followed them with not one but two handkerchiefs.

"Two, Fletcher?" he had asked, breaking the unearthly silence.

"Yes, sir," the man had replied diffidently. "One for you, sir, and one for the lady, should she require it." Darcy had taken the holland squares without another word and quickly stuffed them into his breast pocket, wondering as he did so how on earth Fletcher knew of such things. When he was ready at last, his valet had escorted him to the door, and opening it, he had bowed him out with "My very best wishes this evening, Mr. Darcy, sir!"

"Thank you, Fletcher," he had replied solemnly, and only then had the valet looked him briefly in the eye. "Your servant, sir," Fletcher returned softly and, at Darcy's grave nod, had closed the door.

Darcy reached the bottom of the stairs two steps ahead of his cousin and turned smartly to the right into the hall and then the drawing room. It was nearly time! Lady Catherine was already present, seated in her great chair at the end of the room, as were Anne and Mrs. Jenkinson on the settee nearby.

"Darcy," called his aunt as soon as she saw him, "you must hear this, though you will hardly credit it, I am sure!"

"Your Ladyship?" He made his courtesy but did not take the seat to which she had waved him.

"One of the cottagers—Fitzwilliam, you must hear this as well—one of my cottagers has taken it into his head to apply to the parish! It is already common knowledge in Hunsford, evidently, that he has done so!"

"The poor man must be destitute!" Fitzwilliam exclaimed, only to receive a freezing glare from Her Ladyship.

"He cannot be destitute!" Lady Catherine passed judgment. "He is one of my cottagers, and therefore, it is impossible that he be in want. I told him as much last quarter, when my steward presented me the man's petition to be forgiven his rents. 'It is want of industry, not charity,' I told him, 'that finds you in this predicament. If I forgive you this quarter's rents, I have no doubt I shall receive a petition for the next.' "

"I saw no petition, nor did your steward inform me that any had been presented," Darcy interposed, his voice tight with displeasure. If such things were kept from his oversight, he could hardly move to relieve them before the situation of his aunt's more precarious tenants became desperate.

"Of course you did not! Shall I suffer such a blot upon the name of de Bourgh for one man's laziness? I shall not!" Lady Catherine pronounced heatedly.

"But it has now become unavoidable, Your Ladyship," Darcy returned in tones of strong disapproval. "The man has been forced to apply to the parish, and it is, as you say, 'common knowledge.' Who is the man?"

For a full thirty seconds, as Richard was to inform him later, Darcy silently held Her Ladyship's eye in a demand of the answer that was broken only by a cry from Mrs. Jenkinson that Miss Anne "not distress yourself and lie back a moment, miss." At her words, Lady Catherine broke from the contest and looked to her daughter, saying tersely as she passed him, "Broadbelt, Rosings Hill," before demanding an account from her daughter's companion.

Concern for Anne drew Darcy over to the settee; but as he bent to inquire if he could be of any service, his cousin looked full up into his face and, to his astonishment, cast him a quick wink. Momentarily startled, he quickly covered his reaction with an air of sobriety and nodded his understanding. Evidently there was even more to his cousin than she had yet disclosed during this extraordinary visit to Kent.

"More 'matters' for you, I fear." Fitzwilliam joined him at a goodly distance from the anxious group at the settee.

"Without question," he returned. "I suspected of whom she spoke. The poor man has the worst land on the estate and, to complicate matters, a large family and equally large ambitions for them. He is trying to send to school as many of his sons as show promise, which makes for tired scholars and weary laborers."

"And less income." Fitzwilliam shook his head. "He shall have to keep them home."

"He does, Richard. They school only out of season, but he keeps them to it on their own at night. It is his parcel. The land is truly wretched."

"What is to be done?"

Darcy sighed. "I shall speak to the steward tomorrow." The Sunday tenant visits Georgiana had wheedled him into this winter came to mind. He could not help but smile at the thought of the turn her more feminine Darcy sense of outrage would take at such a state of affairs. From observation of her ministrations at Pemberley, he could fairly guess what she would deem appropriate succor. He would see to it tomorrow.

The sound of the drawing room door opening behind him brought Darcy up straight, a mixture of excitement and panic jolting up his spine. Elizabeth! The knot of his neckcloth became suddenly unbearably tight, and he reached up to pull at it as he swung around to greet the arrivals. The old footman announced Her Ladyship's guests in the overloud voice of one who was losing his hearing.

"The Reverend Mister Collins and Mrs. Collins, Your Ladyship." The Collinses made their bows to the room, but Darcy only nodded perfunctorily, his eyes searching the darkened entrance for Elizabeth.

"Miss Lucas, Your Ladyship." Little Miss Lucas, hesitant as always, made her brief curtsy and moved aside. The door closed behind her.

Where was Elizabeth! Darcy looked at the closed door in disbelief. She had not come? How—why could she not have come? For a moment he could not move but only stare at the offending portal.

"Fitz?" Richard's questioning voice broke his trance. Ignoring his cousin, Darcy strode over to the knot of visitors and hosts with every intention of pulling Collins aside to charge him with an explanation when Lady Catherine unknowingly anticipated him.

"Mr. Collins," she demanded stridently, "where is Miss Elizabeth Bennet!"

"Your pardon, Your Ladyship, Miss Bennet is quite distraught to be denied the honor of accepting your most gracious invitation this evening. It was with the greatest disappointment that—"

"Why, Mr. Collins, why is she not here!" Lady Catherine cut him off.

"Miss Bennet suffers a sick headache, Your Ladyship." Mrs. Collins curtsied her interruption into the conversation. "She begs you will excuse her this evening."

"A sick headache!" The rest of Lady Catherine's opinion on sick headaches was lost to Darcy as he turned away in confusion. She was ill! This was an exigency for which he had not accounted. Ill? Richard had said nothing about her appearing ill this afternoon.

"Damned unlucky turn of events." His cousin joined him at the window. "Instead of enjoying *la Bennet* we must suffer *le Collins*! Odd, though . . . she did not seem ill this afternoon."

"How did she seem?" Darcy could not stop himself from asking the question.

"Thoughtful, a bit pensive perhaps," he replied. Then he laughed. "We did speak of you, after all."

Richard's attempt at humor brought Darcy's thoughts to a focus. She had spoken of him! She also knew there lacked but one day before he was to depart Kent. Could she have become uneasy in his delay? Or could she, in feigning illness, be offering him an opportunity? The idea was not an improbable one. It could very well be. On the other hand, she might truly be ill. He thought of her alone, waiting in expectation or resignation, and his course was determined. In either case, it was impossible for him not to go to her . . . and immediately!

Without a word, he wheeled abruptly about and strode away from the window. Intent upon the door, he ignored Fitzwilliam, who finally stepped in front of him and then took him by the arm. "Fitz! Where are you going?" he hissed at him. "You cannot just walk out!"

"Stand away," Darcy shot back, his voice low-pitched but commanding. He would brook no further delay or debate.

"Fitz! Think what you are doing!"

"I have! I know what I am doing!" He shook off Richard's detaining hand. "Make my apologies to Her Ladyship and the Collinses—or do as you wish! I am past caring what she thinks of my manners!" Darcy challenged his cousin, his eyes mirroring the implacable set of his jaw.

Fitzwilliam's hand dropped from his arm, his face a study in apprehension. "Do as you desire then, and Heaven help you, Cousin!"

Responding only with a clipped nod, Darcy walked past Fitzwilliam, opened the door, and with hurried strides passed through the hall. He took the stairs in twos and threes, hitting the corridor that led to his rooms at nearly a run. Fletcher must have heard him coming, for the door to his chambers was unceremoniously yanked open a second before his arrival.

"Mr. Darcy!" the valet exclaimed, his eyes wide at his master's almost wild appearance.

"Fletcher, my coat and hat—immediately, man!"

Fletcher said not a word as he hurried back to the dressing room to gather the demanded items, leaving Darcy to the quiet orderliness of his rooms. She had not come! He strode the length of the room and back. The more he considered that singular fact, the more plain its meaning grew. She had prevented him from making the mistake of declaring himself in an unseemly setting, and then what had he done but withhold himself from her, incommunicado, for an entire day! She probably had been expecting him, and his absence instead had confused her—or decided her. It would be just like Elizabeth to act to bring matters between them to culmination. Their sparring at Netherfield and, lately, at Rosings should, of all things, have taught him that!

Fletcher's footsteps brought Darcy around. "Sir." His gray coat was held out for his arms. Catching his sleeves, he plunged his arms into the sleeves and pulled the garment up over his shoulders before the valet could assist him. "Your gloves, sir." Darcy pulled them on and reached for his hat, plucking it from Fletcher's grasp and tucking it under an arm as he made for the door.

"Fletcher." He stopped short at the portal and turned to his valet. "If anyone should inquire . . ."

"You were urgently needed elsewhere, sir," Fletcher supplied smoothly. "And you will not be back—?"

Darcy nodded appreciatively at his valet's astuteness. "An hour." He considered the possibilities. "Several hours," he amended as he smoothed his gloves. "Perhaps longer."

"Very good, sir," he replied, his confident, professional air a steadying calm upon Darcy's churning thoughts. His long stride ate up the length of the hall, but at the top of the stairs Darcy halted. If he used the main staircase and doors, he risked being waylaid by Richard or spied by one of Her Ladyship's servants sent to inquire after him. Turning on his heel, he retraced his steps to come to a stand before the door to the servants' halls. Not since he was a boy had he traversed the small, dark corridors used by the staff in their unobtrusive service to the household, but surely he could remember the way!

"Darcy?" Fitzwilliam's voice echoed up the stairs. He had no choice. In a moment he was on the other side of the door and making his way to the servants' stairs and down, dodging several maids overburdened with armloads of sheets and toweling on their way up to the bedchambers. The servants' hall was deserted, and Darcy stepped down into the long, low room, searching for a door to the outside. Finding none, he crossed the room to discover a short hallway, a step up on the other side, and the desired exit.

After putting some distance between himself and Rosings, he stopped and looked back at the manor house he had left in so precipitous a manner. Richard must be questioning his sanity! His cousin had guessed where he was going and had been alarmed at first. But he had wished him Heaven's blessings then, had he not? When the time came, when he brought Elizabeth back on his arm his affianced wife, Richard would support him. Her Ladyship, now . . . Her Ladyship presented an immediate and highly volatile hurdle, her absurd notion of his being pledged to Anne only the first volley she would fire at him. The outrage she would marshal against his choice would be voluminous and well fueled by the bitter disappointment of her long-held designs. He thought better of his desire to bring Elizabeth back to Rosings this evening. It would be best not to expose her to his aunt's wrath until Lady Catherine could be brought to silence on his choice of wife. His wife! The hard edge of urgency that had impelled him from Rosings softened at the joy that thought bestowed. Darcy turned and set his face toward Hunsford. There lay his future, his well-being, the comfort of all who were Pemberley. It was time to secure it!

He set off determinedly and soon covered the distance to the grove. The air among the trees was cool as he strode beneath their shelter, the memory of his walks there with Elizabeth bringing a secret smile to his lips. Soon . . . soon she would be his! The thought warmed him as he sojourned through the grove, but as the path began its descent toward the village, Darcy's pace slowed. In order to obtain the devoutly desired lady, the offer must still be posed. Although Darcy knew he could depend upon her excellent understanding, he knew also that he must still say the proper words. The address he had composed for the familiar grandeur of Rosings had been worthy of its setting. Now those phrases and the sentiments to which they alluded appeared to him too large and studied to fit into the humble parsonage parlor. He did not wish to appear the fool in this most solemn occasion of his life.

You can still turn back! the voice of duty was quick to offer as he approached Hunsford village, but Darcy knew it for the lie it was. He could no more turn back now than fly. But the lid he had thought sealed on the multitude of objections to his course flew wide at the warning, and accusations of bringing disgrace to his name and family, of which he would rightly be charged, flew at him with the vehemence of repressed furies. The events of the Netherfield ball, the insults and impertinences to which he had been subject, the appalling behavior and lack of propriety he had witnessed—all returned to present their claims. The enormity of what he was about to do gripped him even as he approached the parsonage gate. He put his hand to the latch and paused. Here, only days ago, he had known his heart to be decided and had finally confessed to himself the illusion of completeness without her. He looked to the door at the end of the lane. Everything he desired, all that he most desired, was before him.

"Miss Elizabeth Bennet," he instructed the wide-eyed maid who answered his ring. He was admitted into the front hall hurriedly and with an absence of ceremony, the maid ducking him an awkward curtsy and mumbling something about the parlor abovestairs. Taking her to mean that that was where he would find Elizabeth, he nodded and stepped back to give her passage. The sound of their shoes upon the stairs was overloud in his ears, much as it had been the day he had surprised her alone. This time, of course, he knew her to be alone, but the silence of the house struck him as akin to a breath held against the arrival of long-awaited news. The rattle of dishes, the closing of a door, any domestic sound would have been a welcome distraction to the beating of his heart and the plaguing doubts that were hammering at his brain. He came to the parlor door, pausing a moment to pull off his gloves and make a futile attempt to collect himself as the maid knocked and announced him. Then, with his beaver under one arm and his heart pumping violently in his chest, he stepped into the room.

Their eyes met immediately he crossed the threshold. "Mr. Darcy!" Elizabeth dropped into a curtsy. Eager as he was to drink in the sight of her after almost two days, his bow was of the briefest sort. She motioned distantly to indicate he should choose a seat.

"You are not ill, then," he affirmed hurriedly, stepping toward her. "They said you were ill; so I came to . . . I wished to hear myself that you were better."

"As you see, sir, I am." She returned his solicitude coolly, adding "I thank you" at the last, just before taking her seat.

He stepped away and lay aside his things before sitting down in a chair opposite the one she had chosen, his heart working madly as he considered the woman before him. Beautiful! So beautiful! Insistent, ardent impulses arose within his breast and trampled rationality underfoot, further muddling his thoughts. He wanted her; oh, how he wanted her! Her brow arched at his silence. Caught in open admiration, he looked quickly away. She said not a word, but the sound of his heart, his very breath, roared in his ears so that he could not think.

He must clear his head, regain command of his emotions! He stood and began pacing the room. Against wisdom's counsel, he glanced over at her. *Speak!* his heart demanded. He stopped and turned to her, his address forming in his mind. *Miss Elizabeth Bennet, would you do me the honor—* The full weight of the word descended upon him in a rush. *Honor?* The honor in this affair was all his, and he was preparing to put it wholly to shame in a way that the whole world would see and disparage! The icy displeasure of his family for the low connections he would bring into their midst, the cold embarrassment of his friends and peers when he was again among them, the derision of his enemies—all worked on him. He turned away to the window to stare unseeing into the early evening. But an hour before it had been so clear to him, and now he was back in the morass of doubt and indecision. His fingers slipped into his waistcoat pocket before he realized what he was doing. Nothing! Darcy's lip curled in disgust with himself. Of course the silken threads were not there! He had given them to the winds. He turned back to the room, only to be immediately lost in Elizabeth's lovely profile. Should *caution* follow them?

Beautiful, intelligent, graceful—she was all those things. Her voice thrilled him, her skill at the pianoforte soothed him, her disdain for artifice answered his own, her compassion was genuine, her mind delightful, her courage in carrying her point, even against him, excited his deepest admiration and desire. To have this embodiment of all the Graces as his own! Swelling pride at the idea of possessing her brought him away from the window. He must have her! He opened his mouth to speak, but the room seemed suddenly full of all her relations: her scheming mother, the wild younger sisters, her indifferent and tactless father, and the shadowy aunts and uncles in trade ranged themselves about her, rendering him mute. He fell back, feeling the eyes of all his own family upon his back, waiting in silent plea that he not do this thing. Near to choking with helpless frustration, he took back that step, then took another into the center of the room; and in that moment she looked up at him, her dark, magnificent eyes large and questioning.

Sweet Heaven, Elizabeth! Darcy's heart rose in his throat, forcing the words out before it in an unstemmable tide. "In vain have I struggled. It will not do. My feelings will not be repressed." Hardly pausing, he gasped in a draft of air, his voice thick with overpowering emotion. "You must allow me to tell you how ardently I admire and love you." If it were possible, her eyes opened even wider at his words, and a deep blush colored her features. For his own part, the relief of confessing his feelings at last gave rise to such light-headed elation as might be afforded by a glass of strong wine. "Almost from the moment of our acquaintance I have felt a deep, passionate affection for you that has overridden all my efforts to the contrary." His heart beat excitedly but now in a more steady rhythm, his words flowed freely. "It was not long before I knew myself to be enchanted by you, inexorably drawn and captivated. You have been in my mind and heart for months, Miss Bennet! I have gone nowhere, seen no one, and you are not there with me."

He stepped closer and looked deeply into her eyes, wishing she would rise and meet his ardor. "Of the difficulties presented by the differences in our stations, the numerous obstacles presented by the inferiority of your family, I am only too aware. They are of such a nature that, indeed, no rational man may disregard their weight. I have struggled with them all and from the beginning, measuring inclination against my own better judgment and the knowledge that all of Society and my closest family will look upon our union as a degradation. It has been just these heavy impediments which have kept me silent until now upon the subject of my regard. They cannot be helped; neither can my sincere attachment to you, though I have done all in my power to conquer it." He stopped for a moment and gathered himself before presenting the offer that would secure his future. "I am convinced that you are and will always be mistress of my heart, that our futures are entwined as threads and, like them, will be stronger for their being woven together as one. To that end, I pray and hope you will reward my long and arduous struggle with acceptance of my hand in marriage and consent to become my wife." There! it was done! Let the world go to the Devil; he would be happy! His breath coming in short pants, Darcy leaned against the Collinses' mantelpiece and looked to Elizabeth for the words that would secure at once that happiness he so desired and the disgrace he most feared.

A delicate blush had spread over her countenance during his declaration, but by its end, the blush was transformed to high color. She averted her eyes from his, looking instead at hands now clasped tightly together in her lap. Why did she not speak? Was she overcome? Had he expressed himself too ardently?

"In such cases as this, it is, I believe, the established mode to express a sense of obligation for the sentiments avowed, however unequally they may be returned."

What? He could not have heard her aright! Darcy straightened from his position, confusion seizing him and making her words of no meaning.

"It is natural that obligation should be felt, and if I could *feel* gratitude, I would now thank you. But I cannot—I have never desired your good opinion, and you have certainly bestowed it most unwillingly." Her eyes flashed up at him. "I am sorry to have occasioned pain to anyone. It has been most unconsciously done, however, and I hope will be of short duration. The feelings which you tell me have long prevented the acknowledgment of your regard can have little difficulty in overcoming it after this explanation."

A flood of emotions at her easy dismissal of his months of struggle and the denial of all his hopes swept through Darcy in quick, powerful succession: numb disbelief, shock, acute embarrassment, and finally, an anger so searing that he could not trust himself to speak. In a pale fury, he stood at the hearth in pitched battle with his outraged sensibilities. He, who had forsworn so much to offer her the world and his heart, to be treated in such a careless manner! Who was she to spurn him so! His mind raced in circles, unable to settle into an ordered stream. *Why?* The question screamed in his brain. He looked back at her, but she seemed to have done with him. *Oh, no, my girl! You are not done with me yet!*

"And this is all the reply which I am to have the honor of expecting!" he demanded in a cold rage. "I might, perhaps, wish to be informed why, with so little *endeavor* at civility, I am thus rejected." He adopted a sardonic tone. "But it is of small importance."

Elizabeth rose from her seat at his words, her face a shocking mirror of his own. "I might as well inquire why, with so evident a design of offending and insulting me, you chose to tell me that you like me against your will, against your reason, and even against your character?" She laid a hand on the table between them as if in need of its support. "Was not this some excuse for incivility, if I *was* uncivil?" The fire in her eyes was no less hot than the blood that rose to Darcy's face at her next accusation. "But I have other provocations. You know I have. Had not my own feelings decided against you, had they been indifferent, or had they even been favorable, do you think that any consideration would tempt me to accept the man who has been the means of ruining, perhaps forever, the happiness of a most beloved sister?"

She knew! How? Richard—damn and blast! Darcy held his fire, knowing it would be useless to interrupt her.

"Can you deny that you have done it?" she demanded of him.

"I have no wish of denying that I did everything in my power to separate my friend from your sister," he answered with an air of tranquil superiority, "or that I rejoice in my success. Toward *him*," he emphasized, "I have been kinder than toward myself."

Elizabeth appeared to bridle at his insinuation but abandoned the affront to launch against him again. "But it is not merely this affair on which my dislike is founded. Long before it had taken place, my opinion of you was decided. Your character was unfolded in the recital which I received many months ago from Mr. Wickham . . . "

Wickham! Cold, implacable hatred, easily distinguishable from that hot indignation which had previously engulfed him, rose to peer at Elizabeth from behind hardened eyes. "You take an eager interest in that gentleman's concerns!"

"Who that knows what his misfortunes have been can help feeling an interest in him?" she countered.

"His misfortunes!" Darcy spat out the word contemptuously, his emotions rising dangerously at the intrusion of that hated name between himself and one he loved yet again. "Yes, his misfortunes have been great indeed."

"And of your infliction," Elizabeth cried. "You have reduced him to his present state of poverty—comparative poverty. You have withheld the advantages which you must know to have been designed for him . . . "

What tale had that devil told her? In what way had his name and character been abused that Wickham should so poison her, the woman he loved, against him? If ever the blackguard had dreamed of revenge, he had now surely achieved it, destroying Darcy's deepest hopes and injuring him in the most intimate manner possible!

". . . You have done all this! And yet you can treat the mention of his misfortunes with contempt and ridicule."

Enough! Pushing away from the mantelpiece, Darcy strode quickly across the room. "And this is your opinion of me!" he thundered. "This is the estimation in which you hold me! I thank you for explaining it so fully. My faults, according to this calculation, are heavy indeed." He checked in midstride and turned back to her, suspicion writ large upon his features. "But, perhaps, these offenses might have been overlooked, had not your pride been hurt by my honest confession of the scruples that had long prevented my forming any serious design. These bitter accusations might have been suppressed," he continued acrimoniously, "had I, with greater policy, concealed my struggles, and flattered you into the belief of my being impelled by unqualified, unalloyed inclination; by reason, by reflection, by everything." She stood so still under his barrage, still and defiant of him yet. "But disguise of every sort is my abhorrence. Nor am I ashamed of the feelings I related. They were natural and just." He stepped back from her and angrily gathered up his gloves, hat, and stick. "Could you expect me to rejoice in the inferiority of your connections? To congratulate myself on the hope of relations whose condition in life is so decidedly beneath my own?"

Elizabeth's voice was eerily composed. "You are mistaken, Mr. Darcy, if you suppose that the mode of your declaration affected me in any other way than as it spared me the concern which I might have felt in refusing you, had you behaved in a more gentlemanlike manner." Darcy started at her words. She might as well have slapped him across his face as presented him with such a charge. "You could not have made me the offer of your hand in any possible way that would have tempted me to accept it."

He looked down at her in mute astonishment, his incredulity at her words vying with the creeping heat of mortification that was fast gaining ascendancy over his conviction of the justice of his position.

"From the very beginning, from the first moment, I may almost say, of my acquaintance with you, your manners impressing me with the fullest belief of your arrogance, your conceit, and your selfish disdain of the feelings of others, were such as to form that groundwork of disapprobation, on which succeeding events have built so immovable a dislike." Elizabeth's voice rose. "And I had not known you a month before I felt that you were the last man in the world whom I could ever be prevailed on to marry."

She was lost to him—utterly, irretrievably lost! Darcy's head reeled. *Dear God—Elizabeth!* The pain in his chest was growing intolerable. He must leave, get away. It was too much! "You have said quite enough, madam," he managed to reply. "I perfectly comprehend your feelings, and have now only to be ashamed of what my own have been." He bowed and backed away to the door. Laying a hand on the latch, he stopped, his head bowed, then turned to her, looking deeply into her eyes one last time. "Forgive me for having taken up so much of your time," he said in a strangled voice, "and accept my best wishes for your health and happiness." Without waiting for her curtsy or a reply, Darcy pulled at the latch and hastily left the room. He took the stairs at no slower a pace, and in bare moments he was outside, the door shut solidly, irrevocably behind him.

The meadow was little more than a blur as Darcy turned from the parsonage door and set his face for Rosings. By the time he gained the path through the grove, he was able to marvel that his legs should continue to carry him onward without his conscious direction, that his body was, to all outward appearance, still whole and hale with life. But appearances, had he not just so bitterly been taught, were not to be trusted. He pushed blindly on, his shoulders hunched against the racking pain in his chest while his mind spun in tight, shocked circles like a child's top, unable to fasten onto anything other than the soul-wrenching truth that she was lost to him. Not only lost to him, but never his from the start. *From the very beginning* she had taken him into dislike, before Wickham had defamed him, before even he had moved to detach Bingley from her sister. *The last man in the world whom I could ever be prevailed on to marry.* Her words repeated themselves again and again in his brain, knelling the death of all the hopes for happiness he had cherished. Would he ever be able to wipe from memory his parting sight of her, his lovely Elizabeth, so fiercely adamant in her utter rejection of him? "Oh, God!" The pain drove deep, obliterating thought and mercilessly flaying his emotions, rendering his chest so tight that he could barely breathe. *Elizabeth . . .* all his being groaned.

The tiny stones of the manor's graveled lane went scattering when Darcy struck the path in a driven gait, but it was not until the steps of Rosings confronted him that he even comprehended where he was. He slowed to a halt, confused to find himself so soon arrived. Looking up at the cold reality of the marble steps leading to the manor house's imposing façade, he was at last brought to himself. Thoughts of self-preservation surfaced, warning him that he must rise above his anguish, keep his head, if he was to gain his rooms without incident. His stomach lurched at the prospect if he did not. Rapidly mounting the stairs, Darcy passed swiftly across the threshold, so intent upon avoiding delay or discovery in the public rooms that he neglected his usual nod to the old manservant at the door. In moments, he was across the hall and bounding up the stairs, but at the first landing and turn, his flight was arrested.

"Darcy!" Richard's call to him was too clear to be ignored. He stopped and looked vaguely down upon his cousin, whose untimely appearance could only mean that he had been lying in wait for his return. "Fitz?" Fitzwilliam looked up at him warily, a note of uncertainty in his voice. "Is it well?"

"Well?" he repeated, unable at first to attach any relationship between the word and his condition; then he almost laughed at the irony. Good God, would he ever be truly well again? "Well enough, but you must excuse me." He turned away from the balustrade and continued up the stairs before anything more was offered. The humiliation of Richard's condolences would be one more burning coal lodged in the pit of his stomach; he would rather put a gun to his head!

The corridor to his rooms was empty, and in a breath, he was at his door and then safely behind it. Closing his eyes, he leaned back against the solid mahogany, his limbs threatening to give way at last to the anguish that was consuming him. *You could not have made me the offer of your hand in any possible way.* Darcy bit his lip against the moan that welled in his chest. No one, no one, must see him like this! He listened for any sound of occupation from his dressing room; all was silent save the ticking of the mantel clock. Pushing away from the door, he went to stand before the ornate timepiece. Was it possible? He glared disbelievingly into its face. Could it be that little more than an hour had passed since he had quit these rooms in a fever of expectation? He threw his stick and coat into a chair, his hat and gloves following soon thereafter. An hour! He snorted bitterly. More than enough time to lay waste to a man's dreams.

Abruptly he turned his back on the clock and stalked into the bedchamber, his fingers plucking at his coat buttons and then the knot of his neckcloth. Pulling at it savagely, he unwound the length, dropping it on a table as he slowed to a stand in the middle of the room. *What was he to do?* he demanded to know. He looked about at the cold, aloof orderliness that was his life as if the answer lay there waiting to be discovered. A wave of revulsion washed over him. This grand sterility! It had sedulously fed his pretensions even as it had revealed the shameful exhaustion of a once honorable resolve, and he wanted nothing so much now as to be clear of it! He advanced upon the bell pull with the express intent of summoning Fletcher to begin packing when the absurdity of such an action struck him. It was dusk; the sun was already below the horizon. Such an obvious testimony to flight would in nowise support the indifferent façade he must, at all costs, maintain before the world.

Indifferent? A tremor rippled through him, setting him down hard on the edge of the bed, his head sinking into his hands. Indifferent to such a loss? Indifferent to the echoing hollowness within his heart? How could he continue, pretend that Elizabeth did not exist for him, when she had come to define his hope for the future? Darcy slumped back upon the unyielding bed, the stiff brocade of its covering harsh against his cheek, and stared at the canopy stretched above his head. What was he to do? What did life hold for him now?

Your arrogance! He flinched, Elizabeth's charge cracking across his memory like a whip. *Your conceit!* He shook his head. How could it be? He had always abhorred such displays, yet this was

Elizabeth's opinion of him. She had despised him, had faulted everything about him from the start! *Unjust . . . ungenerous*—her litany would not cease—*The man who has been the means of ruining the happiness of a most beloved sister.*

"No! Not so!" The denial exploded from his lips, the force of his indignation bringing him upright, his conscience bristling at the injustice of Elizabeth's indictment. As if it were his habit to make sport of the dignity and hopes of others, and especially those beneath his station! He should have answered her back, laid out the matter of her sister as he had so rigorously observed it, before her. He had had good and sufficient reasons to dissuade Bingley from his perilous course, reasons that had been based upon an impartial conviction, not whim or interest. Why had he not risen above the paltry syllables offered by his wounded pride?

Pushing himself from the bed, Darcy stalked to the window and leaned against the casing. Why? Because her attack upon him had left him almost speechless, first with shock and then with an anger that even now was seething dangerously in his vitals. Ungenerous! And what had she been? Every action of his was attributed to either malice or caprice! "Good God!" Darcy smacked the heel of his hand against the casing with such force that the pane rattled in its frame. Turning away, he strode over to the delicate crystal decanter, seized it by its throat, and wrenched out the stopper. The amber liquor sloshed into the ornate etched glass, spilling over the sides to spread in a pool on the table. Jamming the stopper home, he swooped the glass up to his lips as he resumed his strident gait.

Arrogant and conceited was he? What did she know of Society? Precious little! She could not have the slightest idea of what his life was like or what his position, his relations, and his peers demanded of him. Her country social circles and modest background bore not the slightest comparison to the milieu into which he had been born! He brought the glass up again, and then, wiping the back of his hand across his mouth, he slammed it down. And what had been her behavior toward him? She had bantered and fenced with him, accepted his attentions, encouraged in every way his belief that she but awaited his declaration, only to throw the true heart and immeasurable consequence he had offered to her back in his face! Darcy burned with the humiliation of it. He leaned back against the wall, his face aflame. A Darcy of Pemberley, to be dismissed like a damned tinker with only a basketful of shoddy goods to his credit when he had been prepared to entrust her with all that he was! Who was she to treat him thus, to hold him so cheaply? By what right did she accuse him of a whole catalog of ignoble offenses! The answer was not long in coming.

Your character was unfolded in the recital which I received many months ago from Mr. Wickham.

"Wickham!" The hated name resonated through every part of his body, finally emerging in a growl of rage that brought Darcy's helplessly disordered thoughts into a focus and propelled his fist straight into the wall. Wickham! *Who that knows what his misfortunes have been . . .* Darcy held the thought in a crushing grip as it set him again to churning up the carpets with his agitated pacing. *Who that knows!* Whatever the "misfortune" Wickham had manufactured for her ears and then laid at Darcy's door, it had done inestimable damage to his name. His character had been grossly maligned, and for what? So that Wickham might tickle the ears of an obscure village and garner for himself a few sympathetic rounds of ale? What devil had prompted him to spin his deceit around Elizabeth?

"Mr. Darcy?" Darcy spun around at the untoward intrusion and delivered his valet a ferocious glare of displeasure.

"Fletcher! What do you here?" he demanded harshly. "I did not summon you."

His valet glanced up at him, shocked surprise showing pale against the concern on his face. "Your pardon, sir, I thought—that is, I only just learned of your return and—"

"Spare me your thoughts, if you please!" Darcy angrily bit off each word. "Your services are not required tonight. Leave me!"

Fletcher's face went ashen. "Y-yes, sir," he choked out as he bowed and stumbled back in haste to the dressing room, but Darcy had already turned away, his mind again fastened upon the one indictment in this excruciating debacle of which he knew himself entirely innocent.

It must not stand! his honor declared hotly. If there were anything this day about which he was certain, it was that George Wickham's lies impugning his character must be exposed and his name vindicated. Due pride might prevent him from answering all Elizabeth's charges, but those based upon Wickham's falsehoods and insinuations must, in justice to himself, be confronted and shown as the slander they were.

But how was it to be accomplished? He reached out and caught hold of the brandy glass as he passed. A private interview was not likely to be granted after what had passed between them, nor did he relish the idea. As he drained the glass, his gaze traveled over the room, resting at last upon the secretary and the precise stack of stationery that lay there. A letter! But would not propriety require that he place it privately in her hand himself? He wrapped an arm around one of the bedposts, his heart quickening. A letter of vindication, personally delivered . . .

Relinquishing his hold, Darcy walked over to the secretary and dropped into the seat as he drew a sheet of foolscap before him. Flicking open the inkwell, he rifled through the quills and pens until he found one to his liking and dipped it into the ink. He wrote her name with a flourish across the top of the sheet, then paused and leaned back in his chair. What he was about to do he would have considered unthinkable only hours before. In truth, he had never thought to put anything of his dealings with Wickham to paper, but now he proposed to do so and, further, do so for the eyes of a woman who had no connection to his family or share in their concerns!

Darcy set the pen down, the enormity of what he contemplated at war with the indignation of his soul. His honor required—no, demanded—that he prove his innocence to her, but to do so would require that he trust Elizabeth with that person dearest to his heart after herself. Georgiana! Darcy's heart contracted with pain at the danger in which he would be placing her. A mere recital of Wickham's habitual conduct would not serve his purposes, nor would a vaguely worded account of his entrapment of a nameless young woman. Such a tale could only be regarded as hearsay. No, it would have to be the entire, painful truth and his cousin offered in corroboration of it. By his own hand, she, who had misjudged him so severely, would be possessed of that damning knowledge whose discovery he had so assiduously protected from the world.

Closing his eyes against the world, Darcy searched his heart. Earlier today he had been entirely prepared to entrust Elizabeth with all: his heart, his home, his people, his honor—all. Now, despite everything, did he trust her still? Leaning forward, his eyes gently traced her name at the head of the sheet. Then, with a deep, resolute breath, he retrieved his pen and dipped it into the inkwell once more.

Darcy stared dully at the bright red sealing wax dripping onto his aunt's fine stationery and thought it might as well be his blood that dripped onto that ivory sheet . . . . *the last man in the world whom I could ever be prevailed on to marry.* The words echoed with merciless clarity through his brain and then, like a dagger, plunged unerringly to his very heart. He removed his personal seal from his writing kit and, in like manner, stamped the crest of the Darcy family into the soft, red wax. It was done! The letter, which had cost him a night of agony, was ready to be placed into the hand of the woman who had so decidedly refused his.

Pushing back from the writing desk with a groan, he glanced out the window at the approaching dawn before rubbing at his dry, smarting eyes. Wearily, he picked up the packet and read the name written so carefully in his own hand. Miss Elizabeth Bennet. He did not have to wait long for the pain to surge through him again. How could he have supposed that these emotions, awakened against his leave, were ever his to control? Had he not acknowledged that lack to himself and to Elizabeth as well, only a few hours ago, when he made his offer of marriage? He had hoped that writing his defense against her bitter accusations would restore him to mastery, but he now knew the exercise to be only one more vain hope in a long line of self-deceptions. Rising quickly, as if to shed himself of such naïveté, Darcy put out the guttering desk candle with his thumb, welcoming the small, quick burning sensation. He looked again at the letter lying in his hand, his rendering of her name flowing across the stark paper field. Yes, it was done! It remained only to deliver this last excuse for contact with the woman whom he had so unwillingly come to love and begin to put the pain and humiliation of yesterday behind him.

Laying the letter aside, Darcy walked to the silver ewer on the table and poured water into the bowl. He rolled up the wrinkled sleeves of his fine lawn shirt and bent over, splashing his face. Just as he began to towel off the dripping water, he caught the reflection of his face in the mirror above the bowl and almost started at the image. Slowly, he dropped the towel and, with one hand bracing him against the wall, leaned forward, willing himself to look into the mirror again. The face that looked back at him was one he had never seen before. His eyes were red-rimmed with weariness—nothing unusual in that. He had certainly spent enough nights studying at university to recognize sleep deprivation in his reflection. No, there was more . . . a certain helplessness that seemed to stare back at him from behind his eyes and a new grimness about his mouth that had changed his entire visage from the confident one he had always worn to greet the world.

Confident! What he had cultivated as confidence, Elizabeth had damned as arrogance. Darcy's anger and wounded pride from the previous evening swelled anew as he pushed away from the wall and strode across the room. The accusations did not sting so much, but they continued to anger him. Arrogance and conceit! Those two qualities were held in abundance by most of his peers. They were almost prerequisites for acceptance into Society! He had always looked with disdain on those who led Society in affecting a boredom with life relieved only by the scandal sheets and games of social intrigue. Rather, he had worked diligently to attain a real superiority of understanding, which had earned him, so he believed, a respected place in the world. All this, only to be accused of the very things he abhorred and then painted as the coldhearted persecutor of certainly the most wicked man of his acquaintance!

Darcy stopped at the window and leaned against the casing. Dawn had come. The light of the sun glanced through the park, shyly promising an unusually beautiful day. As the delicate morning rays fanned his cheek, Darcy relaxed, his anger and its tension suddenly forgotten. In their stead stole the quiet knowledge that Elizabeth was certain to be sharing this dawn. She would be out early, walking the park in that sure and easy stride that did not apologize for its country origins.

Darcy smiled, taking pleasure in the picture his mind created as he imagined her traversing her favorite route. He remembered the first time he'd seen her come in from walking, her hair delightfully windblown, her eyes bright and unwearied, undaunted after a three-mile trek to nurse her sister. He had thought, at first, that her sister's illness had been merely an excuse to insert herself into the Bingley household. He'd even flattered himself to think that he might be the reason she had come. It would not have been the first time a hopeful young woman had plotted to gain his notice. But Elizabeth had truly been concerned about her sister and had spent little time with Bingley's entourage of relatives and guests. Her devotion to her sibling had been unmistakable, and he had added that devotion to a growing list of talents and graces that continued to draw him to the woman whom he had earlier dismissed as not handsome enough to tempt him.

The more he had looked, the more intrigued he had become. Every encounter with her began as a cautious dance and ended in verbal swordplay that often left him in doubt of her intent but never of her intelligence. Sometimes she had angered him with a challenging verbal thrust delivered with rough skill but uncomfortable accuracy. Other times, she had been so wide of the mark in her assertions concerning his character that he could only contain his frustration with her by putting some distance, either real or social, between them. No, Elizabeth had not been afraid of him as a man or awed by his position in the world. It was true; she had not, as she so strongly asserted, ever sought his good opinion. She was so different from every other female he had ever met, and he had found her irresistibly enchanting. Darcy remembered rising expectantly every morning last autumn at Netherfield wondering what direction their next verbal engagement would take.

The dawn was now well on its way to becoming morning, and Darcy turned quickly from the window. He must not miss her! The only quiet way to get the letter to her was to deliver it himself, but how was he to approach her after having been rejected so summarily? Such bitter words as had passed between them made the task almost impossible. Darcy tugged at his shirt as he walked toward his dressing room to look for his best walking clothes. He pulled on the fashionable waistcoat and polished boots with the solemnity of a knight arming for battle. He must plan the encounter carefully. He must not bungle the affair as he had yesterday. He would politely approach her, hand her the letter, and then—Darcy sighed as he slowed and came to a halt in his preparations—then he would disappear from her life and the loneliness, the cold duty that was all he had known before Elizabeth would return and swallow him up.

Darcy reached for a freshly starched neckcloth and returned to the mirror to begin the meticulous task of creating an acceptable knot without Fletcher's assistance. He would not tamely accept such a future! There must be something to which he could devote the awakened energies of his heart, someone who would not damn him for being who he was. A much-cherished face wreathed in welcoming smiles appeared in the mirror beside his reflection. Georgiana! So much lay before her! Soon she would make her bow in Society. Her presentation at Court would occur within the year. It was imperative that he consult closely with his Aunt Matlock concerning her debut and then, when Georgiana was presented, begin the task of sorting out the fortune hunters from the acceptable admirers who were sure to descend upon an heiress. Darcy's heart softened with the love he bore for his sister. He had much to learn about the young woman she was fast becoming. He had hoped that she and Elizabeth— No, he had to stop thinking about his hopes, about Elizabeth.

Darcy shrugged into his coat, walked back to the writing desk, and picked up the letter. "Miss Elizabeth Bennet." He had so many memories of her: her smile for her friends, her brow sweetly wrinkled in concentration, her eyes wide with curiosity or rolled up in laughter. He had seen those eyes soft with love and affection as she gazed unobserved at her family. How he had wanted to be the object of that loving gaze, to feel the warmth of that smile directed at him! Unable to account for it, he brought up his hand to a wetness upon his cheek. He hurriedly brushed it away but then stopped and, to confirm his suspicion, looked down. The tear glistened brightly on his fingertip in the soft morning light.

The air was clean-edged, in keeping with the new spring, whose verdure was still endeavoring to blur the outlines of winter past. As Darcy once again slipped out the door of the servants' hall, he paused to breathe in its cleansing freshness while he pulled on his gloves, but it was of no avail. The finality of the letter, written with firm detachment even in its salutation, continued to weigh heavily in his hand. Slowly, he let the useless breath escape back into the air. It would all be over soon, all but the cold emptiness that even now began to lay claim to that place within that had been suffused with first a warm expectancy and, lately, a scorching indignation. He swallowed hard at the thought and set out, eager to escape the notice of anyone connected with Rosings.

It was habit, rather than intent, that took him across the park and set him on the path through the grove, his weary mind refusing to grapple with anything more difficult than keeping his body in motion. But as the exercise sent his blood pumping through his veins, he became more sensible of his surroundings. Here they had walked; here he had courted her. Had any scene been witness to a more thorough deception than this plantation had been? Every tree stood in testimony to his humiliation. Had Elizabeth been that artful, or had he been that blind? He, whom the brightest of Diamonds gracing the most exclusive of drawing rooms had failed to entrap, to have been brought so completely to heel by a country-bred girl of no family, only to be spurned, suffer abuse of his character, and have his just scruples thrown in his teeth! The knot at his throat grew tight as the hot blood surged up into his face. Good God, what could have possessed him! *Desire,* his mind sardonically provided him. Desire had made a fool of him, and loneliness, the longing for intimate, feminine companionship, had fanned the fire of it into a blaze and left his pride in ashes. His pride. Would the ashes be stirred yet more by the inherent difficulties of the interview at hand? Darcy thought ahead to the inevitable moment toward which he was striding. Would Elizabeth receive him, or would she retreat from his intrusion upon her privacy? If she did consent to speak to him, would she accept the letter, and accepting it, would she read it? Bringing the letter up before him, he gazed upon her name written in his own hand. A careful, written defense had seemed of such necessity last night. Morning's light now threatened to cast his long night of labor into as vain an exercise as his hopes had been the day before. With a shake of his head, he lengthened his stride. There was nothing for it but to continue as he had begun and hope that Providence or feminine curiosity would persuade Elizabeth to read his letter. It was not in his hands to effect anything more between them than a courteous salute and a dignified withdrawal. He hoped he was capable, at least, of that.

He was almost to Hunsford before he stopped to appraise his situation. Elizabeth was yet to be seen, and he had no desire to mount the steps to her very door in search of her. Shifting his malacca under his arm, he pulled at his watch fob and flicked open the lid. It was yet early; he could not have missed her, surely! It must be that she had yet to set out upon her daily walk, and he was to have the pleasure of walking an anxious, uncertain picket until she did so. Darcy tucked his watch back into his waistcoat pocket and turned off in an oblique direction onto one of several paths that led through the plantation from Hunsford village. He walked until he could no longer see the high path, then turned about and strolled slowly back. He did this several times, choosing various trails that converged at his watch point.

When he had exhausted them all, he stopped and stared down toward the parsonage, but the only movement he detected was that of a servant scattering grain or crumbs to the chickens. Then instead of returning to the house, the woman laid down the basket, dusted off her hands, and pulled forward a straw bonnet that had dangled unseen on its ribbons down her back. Elizabeth? Darcy narrowed his gaze on the distant figure as she tied the ribbons under her chin and, after casting a look over her shoulder to the parsonage, advanced to its gate and skipped quickly through to the meadow below him. Yes, Elizabeth! His blood ran warm and tingling, then suddenly cold. He took a step backward into the trees. The sight of her still affected him, his heart's habit still urging him toward her; but then that other voice intruded, strongly maintaining that she must not spy him here tamely awaiting her as if he were dancing hopeful attendance upon her like some mooncalf.

He retreated even farther, until he lost sight of her altogether and leaned up against a great tree by the path to await her. Now that their meeting was at hand, it was imperative that he gather himself, ensure that he come away from the encounter with the credit and dignity due his name. A creaking of branches stirred by the spring breezes caught and distracted Darcy's straining attention from the path to the tree under which he had taken up his post. By chance, it was the one he had noted the other day whose interior decay he had reported to his aunt's forester. Evidently the man had come immediately at his word, for upon closer examination, Darcy saw there were charcoal marks indicating that the tree was to be cut down. With a grim turn of countenance, he looked up into the branches. The groan of limb against limb seemed a perfect echo of the nameless emotions that swirled painfully inside his chest. *No, not nameless,* his conscience prompted. *Perhaps,* retorted his heart, *but certainly inadmissible.*

A flurry of birds taking flight alerted him, and straightening from his pose against the tree, he pulled at his coat and waistcoat. Then, setting his jaw into lines that the assembly rooms at Meryton would recognize instantly, he strolled forward to meet her. But even though he retraced his steps to his former watch point, she was nowhere to be seen. Where in the world—! Vexed both that he had not waited to assure himself of her direction and that Elizabeth had perversely chosen another than her usual route through the park, Darcy stepped over to each divergent path in the hope of spying a flash of color. Nothing! He stopped in the midst of the last one, his jaw clenched in frustration as he considered his situation. Where had she gone? He had almost resolved to turn back to Rosings when, suddenly, she appeared. Evidently she had avoided the park entirely and had chosen instead a lane that ran for some distance alongside its boundary. In minutes, he quickly noted, she would pass by a gate. Coming out from among the trees, he determined to intercept her there.

Darcy knew the moment she saw him, for though some distance still separated them, he could almost feel her start of recognition and the quick beat of her heart when she turned away from his approach. "Miss Bennet!" He lengthened his stride, her name out of his mouth before thought could decide how to proceed. She stopped and, after a moment of hesitation, turned to await him. His relief that she did so was short-lived, for immediately upon his approach he was struck with the ease with which even now her person excited warm memories and desires within him. Then, as he neared her, his gaze came to focus upon her pale, strained countenance and withdrawn eyes. The reality of their situation quickly asserted itself. His jaw tightened. He brought forward his letter.

"I have been walking in the grove some time, in the hope of meeting you." His voice fell cold even upon his own ears. "Will you do me the honor of reading that letter?" Wordlessly, Elizabeth's hand came up. He strongly suspected it did so most unwillingly, but he placed the letter in her grasp and watched her fingers close around it. Done. It was finished! His brief flight into hope was at an end, and he would never look upon her again. The truth of it smote him to his soul. Darcy clamped down forcefully upon his jaw lest any sound should escape and, bowing slightly, turned back to the plantation and park and strode away. Even when he was sure that she could not possibly see him, he strictly overruled the impulse to stop or look back. Instead, he quickened his gait, refusing to think as well as feel. *Survive . . . just survive but the rest of this infernal day*, he told himself, *and then you may leave. Yes, by Heaven, leave!*

"Well, here you are at last!" Darcy spun around sharply at the disembodied voice arising from behind one of his suite's hearthside chairs.

"Richard!" The scraping of boots against the floor was soon followed by his cousin's lanky form struggling up out of the deeply cushioned chair. Darcy quickly closed the door, advanced to face his intruder, and demanded, "What are you doing here?"

"Lying in wait for Napoleon!" Fitzwilliam answered him sarcastically. "Looking for you, old man; and don't raise a breeze! You have been damned elusive, Fitz. Not like you." He folded his arms across his chest. "You have even Fletcher worried. I've never seen him look so Friday-faced! What?" Fitzwilliam demanded at Darcy's quick grimace.

"Nothing of your concern, I assure you." Darcy shifted his gaze away from his cousin's intense examination. "I have called for the carriage to be at the door by nine tomorrow. Can you be ready?"

"We do leave tomorrow then?" Darcy raised a sardonic brow at his cousin before turning to divest himself of his coat and gloves. "You have changed your plans once already without bothering to consult me," Fitzwilliam protested to his cousin's turned back.

"We leave tomorrow at nine. There will be no change of plans." He turned and faced Fitzwilliam. "I find myself quite desirous of getting back to London as soon as may be possible. I have left Georgiana to Lord Brougham's care long enough," he offered.

"I cannot disagree with you there," Fitzwilliam relented. He threw his hands up at the frown on Darcy's face, then cocked a brow at him. "It will not do, you know. You cannot intimidate me with that frown of yours. Oh, it is an excellent fierce one, I assure you; but you forget that you are dealing with the Highly Disappointing Issue of His Lordship, the Earl of Matlock. Not even in the same race as Pater, Fitz." He returned to the hearth chair and fell back into it. "So pack it away, and tell your old Father Confessor. What is it, Cousin?"

"I am sure that I have not the slightest idea . . ."

"Damn and blast, Fitz," Richard cut him off, "do not poker up at me like a missish old maid. Here." He leaned forward on his elbows and looked at him earnestly. "It has to do with Miss Bennet, does it not?"

A thrill of apprehension coursed up Darcy's spine, stiffening his jaw and adding coolness to his reply. "Miss Bennet?" Richard's answering grimace and exaggerated sigh clearly displayed his disappointment. Knowing his cousin to be capable of a ferocious tenacity when his interest was piqued, Darcy cast about in his mind for some means of diverting him. Richard could not know how far he had carried his foolishness with Eliza—Miss Bennet. And, Darcy determined, he never should; but he did need Richard's help. Should she ever apply to him for the truth of his letter, Richard would die rather than reveal anything that touched upon Georgiana. Darcy quickly laid hold of the bone that would answer for both of them. "Yes, Miss Bennet," he repeated slowly and paused, eyeing Richard's alerted countenance. "I find myself in need of your assistance."

"Yes," his cousin replied encouragingly, "go on."

"You may have noticed that Miss Bennet and I have a tendency to quarrel," he began tentatively.

"Ha!" Richard snorted. Darcy glared him into an embarrassed cough and an "I beg your pardon; continue, Fitz."

"Miss Bennet and I have, unfortunately, stumbled into a tangle of misunderstanding that could be resolved with honor on both sides only by the revelation of our family's past dealings with George Wickham."

"Wickham! Good Lord, you do not mean . . ." Fitzwilliam looked at him in shocked disbelief.

"Yes, Georgiana." Darcy allowed his revelation to sink in.

"I knew she was angry with you." Richard shook his head slowly. "But . . . Georgiana?"

"What!" It was Darcy's turn to be surprised. "She told you she was angry with me?"

"Yes, well, in so many words. Yesterday, when I was touring the park, I encountered her by chance; and in the course of conversation, it became apparent that you were not in her good books. I tried to warn you." So, Darcy thought, she had been overset before he had even left from Rosings, and probably by the rendition of his efforts on Bingley's behalf he had suspected was courtesy of Richard. "But what does Georgiana have to do with it?"

"Nothing directly!" Darcy sighed and rubbed at the insistent pain centered between his brows before continuing. "Richard, it is all a veritable Gordian knot; and you must believe that only a matter of vile slander would induce me to breathe a word concerning Georgiana." He walked to the mantel and, grasping its edge, leaned down to stare into the embers glowing upon the grate.

"I know, Fitz," his cousin quietly granted him. "In what way do you wish my help?"

Darcy solemnly looked up at his cousin. "Should Miss Bennet ever apply to you for the truth of what happened last summer, you are to tell her. In your own words and with nothing held back, tell her."

Fitzwilliam's eyes did not waver from his cousin's. "You trust her that much?"

"I do," he answered him, withdrawing his gaze.

Fitzwilliam turned away, paced the room in thought for a moment, and then looked back. "And it will restore your honor in Miss Bennet's eyes?"

"Perhaps," Darcy answered quietly, his eyes glancing up from the glowing embers, "your testimony and time will prove the just mind I believe her to possess."

"Then do not fear, Cousin." Fitzwilliam advanced upon him and thrust out his hand. "She shall have my word on it—today!" The firm assurance of Richard's clasp was like balm to Darcy's wounds, the first indication that survival of the soul-wrenching events of the last twenty-four hours was more than a dream.

At his cousin's insistence, Darcy retrieved his coat and gloves, and once Fitzwilliam's were procured, the two set off for Hunsford. The distance was traversed in a companionable silence. Darcy, though dreading a second meeting and the proof it would likely afford of the ineffectual nature of his written words, kept pace with the determined gait of his cousin, whose face was almost beatific in its focus on the knight errantry upon which he was set. Sooner than Darcy would have believed, they were mounting the steps at the parsonage door. Fitzwilliam, in the advance, gave him a bracing grin as he pulled at the bell.

"It shall be all right and tight, Fitz. I promise you!" he assured him. "Should I say anything further on your behalf?"

"I pray you, do not," Darcy answered him quickly, "else this errand will have been for naught!"

Fitzwilliam shrugged and turned back to the door, which was now opening. "Good day!" he greeted the serving maid. "Colonel Fitzwilliam and Mr. Darcy to see the ladies and Mr. Collins."

"It shall be done, Your Ladyship." Darcy bowed over his aunt's hand, bussing it with his lips before stepping back to allow Fitzwilliam the same honor. He was desperate to be gone, but Lady Catherine was in no temper for their expedient removal. A vast and varied number of remembrances to other family members had been pressed upon him literally at the last moment. Commentary and recommendation had followed on any aspect of their imminent travel that might delay the departure Her Ladyship so lamented and Darcy so keenly desired. There had been nothing for it but to take matters quite actually "in hand" and grasp Lady Catherine's extended fingers with a curt promise to do as she bid him. It was now Richard's turn, and Darcy stepped away to allow him his full opportunity as object of Her Ladyship's concerns, messages, and lectures.

The day, to this point, had seemed to tick forward at half its usual pace. From Fletcher's call this morning through breakfast and the packing of the carriages, everything and everyone had seemed determined to draw out the process of departure when, in contrast, his every motion and thought had been performed to the beat of an insistent, internal drum call to leave. Darcy's forbearance was wearing perilously thin. Looking out the window while Richard suffered their aunt's instruction, he saw the first carriage swing onto the drive, the horses already in unison as they pulled away from Rosings for London. Fletcher and Fitzwilliam's batman, Sergeant Barrow, both well versed in the requirements of their gentlemen, had seen to its packing with a military precision and were now on their way. But even Fletcher had seemed to move through his duties at a dull pace. "Friday-faced" had been Richard's accurate description of his usually confident and pre-scient valet. Although Richard could not know why Fletcher looked so, Darcy did; for his own failure to secure Miss Bennet's hand had doomed his valet's hopes for matrimony as well. Fletcher's fiancée had been quite adamant, it seemed. Until her mistress Miss Bennet was happily married, she would not be parted from her, despite all Fletcher's considerable skill in persua-sion. Darcy had, of course, spoken not a word to his valet on the subject of his interview with Miss Bennet, nor had Fletcher al-luded to the fever that had overtaken Darcy this last week or its sudden demise. Aside from such a thing being the height of imper-tinence, there had been no need. Fletcher had surmised the truth almost immediately, and it had taken the heart right out of the man. Excepting the days surrounding the death of his father, the last thirty-six hours had been the most silent in their nearly eight-year relationship.

"Thank you, Ma'am; His Lordship shall be delighted to hear it! Incredulous, but delighted." Darcy turned back to the room and his cousin's last bow over Lady Catherine's hand. Evidently, their aunt had called a truce of some sort. She usually did so after hav-ing amused herself with tormenting her Matlock nephew for the entirety of their visit. Darcy suspected that her condescension had more to do with securing their annual return for the relief of her frightful loneliness than with any real conciliatory motions on her part.

"Farewell, then." Lady Catherine conceded the ceremony to be at an end. "I look to see you in the autumn. Anne is so wonderfully improved that I venture to say we shall attempt to join you at Pemberley!" At this she looked meaningfully at her daughter and then back to Darcy. He briefly glanced over at his cousin. Her aspect continued leaden and withdrawn, but he knew it now for the subterfuge it was. He had waited on her earlier to tender his good-byes, knowing that nothing of the true state of their understanding could be expressed at his formal leave-taking. Anne might be frail, but beneath the façade beat a heart filled with passionate, beautiful words the world would never have suspected. If any good had come of this visit, it was this revelation.

"You are welcome at Pemberley any time, Ma'am," Darcy returned. "Fitzwilliam?" he queried Richard, who cheerfully nodded his readiness.

"Ma'am, Anne." Fitzwilliam bowed quickly in his cousin's direction, and they were finally away.

"Heigh-up!" James the coachman flicked his whip, snapping the end just above the leader's ear. The carriage jerked forward once, twice, and then settled into a rhythmic sway as the horses brought their efforts into accord. Darcy swallowed hard and set his eyes straight ahead. He was leaving, finally leaving this scene of the worst humiliation of his pride and the deepest wound to his heart he had ever thought to experience. In minutes, they had swept down Rosings's drive and now were slowing briefly to take the turn into the road that skirted Hunsford village. In moments they would pass the parsonage. Darcy's heart began pounding loudly in his chest. He would not look, by God, he would not!

"Look, Fitz! It appears we shall end as we began!" Richard's bark of laughter forced him to look up.

"What is it? What do you mean?" Darcy leaned over, reluctantly following his cousin's gaze out of the window.

"Old Collins, waving like mad from the parsonage gate. Now I call that a proper sendoff! I only wish . . ." Fitzwilliam's voice fell silent as the carriage whisked them past their aunt's ducking and waving clergyman.

Darcy leaned back against the squabs. "You 'only wish' what?"

Fitzwilliam colored. "My curst tongue!" he castigated himself and then looked over apologetically to his cousin. "I only wish I could have done you the service you requested of me and spoken to Miss Bennet yesterday. Had she been home, I would have, at once! I am that sorry, Fitz!"

"Do not be hard upon yourself." Darcy shook his head. "In the end, it likely will matter little." He looked away then, his gaze ostensibly upon the passing scenery. "I doubt I shall ever have occasion to encounter her again."

CHAPTER 4

A Hell of Time

"Fitzwilliam?" Georgiana's voice, lifted in soft query, drifted across the wide expanse of the breakfast room table of Erewile House, mounted the hurdle of the *Morning Post* Darcy had erected between himself and his sister, and settled with tentative, questioning grace squarely on the page before him. The concern he detected in it was very like the look that had shaded her face the night before as they had once again dined in a silence dictated by the distraction of his thoughts. He was home, but his journey, rather than a return to London, had taken on the nature of a flight from Kent; and Darcy had mounted his own steps more with relief at sanctuary found than with joy at family and friends rejoined. In truth, since that humiliating evening in Hunsford's parsonage, he desired nothing more than to be left alone. Not even Georgiana's gentle presence, or her quiet efforts to make him comfortable, could he tolerate for long. His anger with himself for holding his duty so cheaply and his indignation with Elizabeth for doing the same with his honor seethed continually within his brain and held his chest in a steel band. No, the anguish of it was for him to bear alone; it was certainly not for the ears of a much younger sister!

Perhaps, if he considered his reply long enough, she would take the hint and press him no further.

"Brother?" her voice gently probed again.

Reluctantly, Darcy lowered the paper and looked cautiously into the sweetly deferential but determined countenance at his right hand. This particular dual aspect of Georgiana was appearing with an increased frequency since his homecoming. Darcy had no difficulty in putting it down to Brougham's doubtful influence while he had been away in Kent, for it had been "Lord Brougham this" and "His Lordship that" ever since Darcy had descended from the carriage Saturday evening. It was now Wednesday. He was heartily sick of it.

"Yes, Georgiana?" The tight irritation in his voice did not go unnoticed, and he would gladly have strangled himself to prevent the wilt and withdrawal that now shadowed his sister's eyes. Darcy carefully laid the paper aside and reached deliberately for her hand. "Forgive me!" He sighed. "I fear I have not been myself." He was answered with a wry little smile and the delicate squeeze of her fingers.

"No, dear brother, you have not." Georgiana regarded him with pitying curiosity. "Was Aunt Catherine *very* difficult this year?"

"Her Ladyship was . . . herself . . ." Darcy shifted uneasily as he released her hand and leaned back in the chair. "Or, perhaps, a little more 'herself' than usual. It was well that you did not accompany us," he added and then fell silent as another's face crossed his vision. Rigid with anger, Elizabeth's contemptuous eyes slashed at him. *"Your arrogance, your conceit, your selfish disdain . . . "* Good God, how many times had he relived that galling litany? He closed his eyes. Thank Heaven, Georgiana had not been witness to it! The thought alone made his stomach turn. Now, for the first time, he experienced the burning self-reproach with which his sister had had to contend after she was made to understand Wickham's betrayal. At least Georgiana could plead naïveté; whereas he—how had she put it?—a man of sense and education, and who had lived in the world, had no such luxury! How could he have been so be-sotted, so taken in? No, he had not been, nor was he yet, himself; and Darcy was in nowise confident that he would ever know that particular state again.

"Fitzwilliam?" Her deepening concern, now painfully evident in Georgiana's voice, almost made him wince. Her solicitude he knew to be tender and unquestionably prompted by love, but that his demeanor had exposed him, given her cause to pity him, mor-tified him to the bone. Sorely tempted to ward off her solicitude with another ungenerous reply, Darcy abruptly pushed away from the table. Clearly, he was not fit company for anyone today!

"I beg you will excuse me," he said over his shoulder as he made for the door.

"But, Mr. Lawrence!" Georgiana's reminder stopped him just as the servant opened the door. Blast! They were to make a final ex-amination of Georgiana's portrait today. The appointment had been set before he had gone into Kent. He turned back.

"Two o'clock, is it not?" Darcy returned her affirmative reply with a curt nod. "I shall wait upon you at one-fifteen." Signaling the end of their conversation with a bow, he escaped her unwanted pity for the sanctuary of his study, where he could entertain his brooding anger in peace.

As he drew near the study door, a furious scrabbling fol-lowed by a galloping patter forewarned Darcy of an imminent assault upon his person. This soon? He had instructed Hinch-cliffe to send the summons only days ago! Slowing, he cau-tiously approached the threshold and peered within. But instead of a brown, black, and white cannonball launched in wild greet-ing, there just within the door, sat Trafalgar at perfect attention save for a foolish grin upon his canine jowls. "So, you have ar-rived; have you!" The first real smile to touch Darcy's face for al-most a week slid across his features as master and hound beheld each other with satisfaction. "And whence come these pretty manners, Monster?" Trafalgar's hindquarters wriggled but managed to stay, for the most part, on point. Darcy lifted an amused brow at this almost Herculean effort, provoking an undignified whine deep within the hound's chest. The wriggle became more pronounced.

"For pity's sake, pet the beast!" Darcy started up, his hand inches from Trafalgar's broad, silky ears, to behold Brougham leaning comfortably against the study's mantelpiece.

"Dy!" Darcy straightened, an accusatory tone in his voice. How had his friend gotten past Witcher and entered unannounced? Following Darcy's look, Trafalgar glanced briefly over his shoulder but then looked back to his master with wide, beseeching eyes. The whine grew louder.

Brougham straightened as well and motioned toward the hound. "No wonder he'd such disreputable manners. You tease him unmercifully, Darcy. It took our entire journey down to bring him to some semblance of order!"

"*You* brought him down?" Darcy stared at his friend in surprise, but recovering, he added, "And I do not tease him!" Trafalgar's whine threatened to escalate into an unpardonable bark.

"Then do pet the poor creature before he disgraces himself!" Brougham drawled and, without invitation, made himself comfortable in one of the study's well-upholstered chairs.

Shooting his friend a glance fraught with irritation, Darcy bent and caressed Trafalgar's soft crown and then twisted his silky ears between his fingers. "Monster!" he addressed the dog affectionately and was answered with a shuddering sigh and a languorous lick of his hand. Laughing, Darcy rose and, followed closely by his hound, took a chair opposite Brougham. When he was seated, Trafalgar positioned himself as near to Darcy's boot as was seemly and raised his head to regard his late traveling companion with something akin to triumphal disdain.

"Ha!" Brougham marked his charge's betrayal. "I am now put in my proper place, I see: airily dismissed from polite company like a governess whose students are called upon to perform for their papa!" Brougham's "For shame!" was answered with a sniff and his "Ingrate!" with a wide-mouthed yawn as Trafalgar settled in closer to Darcy's leg.

"*You* brought him down from Pemberley?" Darcy repeated stiffly, interrupting the trade of insults. "Why ever did you take upon yourself such an office?"

"It seemed the thing to do." Brougham's gaze flitted up from Trafalgar to rest upon Darcy. "I knew from your letter to Miss Darcy that you would make your return on Saturday and suspected that you would wish a private homecoming. Having been forced to cut short a jaunt to Scotland that I had planned before *you* postponed your departure from Kent"—he tipped a curious brow at Darcy, to which Darcy declined to respond—"I decided to take my leave just before your return and asked your sister if there was any service I might do either of you during my short sojourn. Miss Darcy mentioned that you would likely send for your animal upon your return. So, with her help, I obtained your man Hinchcliffe's authorization and a promise to keep mum about my surprise, then delayed in Derbyshire on my way back from Scotland long enough to retrieve young Master Trafalgar." Brougham leaned back into the chair. "We enjoyed a most *instructive* drive down together. I would have you know, Darcy, 'Monster' is a name not wide of the mark. Due to your undisciplined beast's execrable behavior, my credit at the Hart and Swan on the North Road is thoroughly destroyed."

Darcy bit down on his lip, his hand twitching to bestow an approving pat on Trafalgar's unrepentant head, but there was a more pressing debt to settle and a warning to serve. "I must thank you for your watchful care of my sister. You have discharged my request with astonishingly dutiful care, it would seem, for Georgiana has spoken of little else but you since my return."

"Ah," Brougham replied, "I see." Resting his elbows on the

chair's arms, he templed his fingers beneath his chin, regarding Darcy steadily. "You object to my attention to Miss Darcy? I had thought that you welcomed what I could do for her in Society."

"I would be a fool not to," Darcy returned evenly, "but she is very young, Dy, and you play the gallant extremely well."

Brougham's face suddenly darkened. "Do you accuse me of making a game of Miss Darcy's favor?"

"I do not." Darcy regarded his friend piercingly. "I only make mention of her youth and remind you how easily a young girl might be led to imagine herself in love." At that, Brougham rose from his chair and, in visible agitation, walked the length of the room. Darcy looked on him with wonder. Dy stood for a moment, his back to Darcy, then turned, his face relaxed now into the careless lines Darcy saw when they were in company.

"Of course, it is proper and right for you to warn me, Darcy! It is hereby noted, and I shall endeavor that Miss Darcy not be cozened into believing any such thing. I assure you, she is safe *with* and *from* me; and here is my hand on it!" Dy extended his hand, which after rising, Darcy grasped with relief. "But I find it incumbent upon me to advise you of something as well, old friend," Brougham added.

"Yes?" Darcy answered cautiously.

"Miss Darcy is many admirable things. She is, indeed, a credit to your care and liberality; but, my friend, she is a girl no longer. Beware you treat her so, or underestimate her understanding, for there is a strength in her which you have yet to see."

"So." Darcy drew up haughtily. "Do you now presume to teach me as you have my sister and my hound?" At the word *hound* and his master's inclination toward him, Trafalgar rose as well and, stationing himself at Darcy's side, looked up with equal hauteur at their guest.

"Wouldn't dream of it, old man!" Dy laughed. "No future in it!" The study clock struck the hour, drawing all three pair of eyes to it. "You are to view Miss Darcy's finished portrait today, are you not?" he inquired when the echo had faded. "I would count it an honor if you would allow me to accompany you, for I confess, I would very much like to see it."

At last, he was alone! Poised at the closed dressing room door, Darcy listened as Fletcher completed his preparations for the next morning and finally departed for his quarters. With the click of the servants' door, Darcy relinquished his hold on the guard he had vowed to maintain with the relief of a man who had been unburdened of his commission to hold back the wind. The rush of its sudden release flowed through his frame, and for a moment, the tightness in his chest was diminished. For a moment, he could take a deep breath and believe it was a night like any other. Then thoughts of her came as they had come every night since his return as soon as he was decently alone; and the virulent admixture of anger and anguish in his heart, suppressed during the day, could be read plainly in his every feature.

Wrapping his dressing gown tightly about him, Darcy moved to the hearth and took the chair closest to the glowing embers. It was a cool April, necessitating a fire still be laid at night, and he stretched out his slipper-clad feet to take advantage of its warmth. God knew, Darcy snorted, he had none in himself. No, according to Miss Elizabeth Bennet he was a coldhearted miscreant who rejoiced in ruining deserving young men and blighting the hopes of maidens wherever his disdainful gaze happened to alight! He looked at the chair across the hearth rug and knew that, if he closed his eyes, he would be able to see her there. Smiling grimly, he slowly shook his head. "No, Miss Bennet, I do not wish you here to catalog my many shortcomings."

Darcy's gaze shifted to the brandy decanter at his side. No, the potential for warmth in that quarter was tempting, the haziness it would afford even more so; but he would be damned if he would allow her to drive him to drink and turn his life into a common

Cheltenham tragedy! His life! His life had been well enough until Charles Bingley had taken it into his head to let a country house and then induced Darcy into overseeing his transformation into a member of the landed gentry. Why ever had he agreed to it? Pity? Boredom? If only he had not succumbed to Bingley's entreaties, he would not even have entered Hertfordshire last autumn. He would not have met . . . her. The thought brought a sharp pang to his chest. Even now, would he never have wanted to know Elizabeth, the first and perhaps the only woman who could draw him both body and soul, who could merrily stand against him on a point of contention and yet excite both his admiration and desire?

"Elizabeth," Darcy groaned, cradling his brow in his hands. She had given every appearance of receiving him in Kent. Her visits to Rosings had been lively and her behavior toward him amiable. Yes, she had teased him at times, but he knew that to be her way. His observation that she delighted in expressing opinions not strictly her own she had greeted with scandalized laughter but not denial. He had seen the acknowledgment of a "hit" in the knowing arch of her eyebrows. Their walks had been conducted almost formally. Little had been said, it was true; but it was his actions that he meant her to read, and she had given him no reason to believe himself mistaken in his advances.

Darcy fell back against the chair, rubbing at his eyes and raking a hand through his hair, his mind struggling to fit together all the pieces of this puzzle that was Elizabeth Bennet. At least she could no longer hold Wickham's story against him. His letter *must* have laid those charges to rest. If she could not abide him, there was a degree of comfort and vindication to be found in that, was there not? He leaned forward, his elbows on his knees, and looked searchingly into the fire. If Elizabeth had known the truth about Wickham, had read aright his wordless apology for slighting her on their first meeting, would it have changed her belief that he was the last man in the world whom she could ever be prevailed on to marry? Good God, those words still cut him like a knife! To her, he was the *last* man; for him, she seemed the *only* woman. Could fate have fashioned a more perfect twist or held him in any more derision?

Darcy rose from the chair. The embers were dying as were the coals in the warming pan that heated the sheets. If he did not go to bed soon, he would not find sleep before the chill returned. Casting aside the dressing gown, he removed the pan and slid between the bedclothes. Would it have made any difference if Elizabeth had known the truth? Darcy closed his eyes against the question, only to see her there armed with her other accusation. No, it would have made no difference; for had he not "ruined the happiness" of the sister she loved? Darcy groaned and, turning on his side, grasped a pillow and buried his face in it. No more . . . no more tonight! His only relief lay in dreamless sleep, but a ragged night of fitful, dream-curst sleep was all Providence saw fit to give him.

When Fletcher came in the next morning to pull back the curtains, Darcy was torn between a desire to curse him roundly for awakening him and the urge to thank him for putting a point to the disturbing phantasmagoria that had plagued his night. Eschewing both for an uncharacteristic lack of resolve, he struggled upright and swung his legs out of bed, his eyes smarting from the morning light that poured in through the window. How could there be so much sun? He was in London, was he not? Grimacing, he looked at the devastation wrought upon his bedstead by his restless night. The chambermaids would have a fine time of it, for it looked as if he'd engaged in mortal combat. Darcy looked up to see Fletcher staring openmouthed at the upheaval.

"I-I beg your pardon, sir," he stammered when he realized Darcy's eyes were upon him. "Should you want your barbering now, sir?" He carefully looked away from the bed.

Darcy heaved a sigh. "Yes, I suppose . . ." His voice trailed off as he thought of the day ahead. The first test of his uncertain disposition would be breakfast with Georgiana. Supper the previous evening had been yet again an exceedingly uncomfortable exercise, his preoccupation interfering at every turn. Georgiana had sat very straight and still, casting him glances well seasoned with worry throughout a meal that he had barely tasted. Frankly, he did not care to repeat the performance. "Fletcher," he recalled his valet from the dressing room, "send down for a tray. I shall breakfast in my chambers this morning."

"Very good, sir" came the formal reply, but Darcy knew that his valet's curiosity at this directive would be multiplied by every member in his household and received with dismay by his sister. Better, though, that he should disappoint her from a distance than chance hurting her feelings close at hand. He shambled into the dressing room and settled back in his shaving chair, determining that for the next quarter hour he would do nothing but surrender himself to Fletcher's ministrations. The unvarying ritual required no thought, only submission to his valet's murmured instructions. The soothing effects of warmed, fragrant towels on his newly shorn face would not be amiss, either. Lord, he felt absolutely terrible! Darcy closed his eyes awaiting Fletcher's return. Unsettled, lethargic, disinterested—he felt a specter in his own house, drifting from room to room, unable to feel at home in any of them. He could not read, he could not write, he could not even enjoy his sister's music without falling into fruitless reflection. "With what I most enjoy contented least," he murmured to himself.

"Your pardon, Mr. Darcy?" Fletcher had returned. How could he have been so careless as to repeat the phrase aloud and within his valet's hearing!

"Shakespeare, Fletcher. Surely you have heard of him," Darcy drawled sardonically, raising his chin for the lathering brush.

"Yes, sir. The Twenty-ninth Sonnet, I believe," Fletcher replied smoothly and began his expert application of shaving soap to his master's face and neck. Darcy closed his eyes again, eager that the familiar motions should preoccupy Fletcher and lull himself into a state of thoughtless oblivion.

" 'Yet—' " The single word hung in the air with no further support. Opening an eye, Darcy beheld his valet, razor in one hand, reaching for the strop.

"Yet?" he repeated curiously as Fletcher set the slide and snick of the razor into a rhythm upon the strop.

" 'Yet,' " Fletcher replied with feeling. "The next line, sir." With a light touch, he lifted Darcy's chin another fraction, turned it and made the first pass. " 'Yet!' followed most auspiciously by 'Haply.' Taken together, they make all the difference, sir. Most comforting."

Able to do no more than make a noncommittal grunt in answer to Fletcher's enigmatic observation, Darcy looked at the ceiling. What should he do with himself today? Yesterday, Hinchcliffe had somberly directed his attention to a stack of correspondence that still remained discreetly ensconced in the portfolio on his desk. He had tried to deal with it several times in the past few days, but try as he might, he could not focus his mind on the facts contained therein, nor find it in himself to care overmuch about their contents. He could drop in at Boodle's; he'd not shown his face there since before he'd left for— No, the effort to appear interested in the goings-on of his club was simply beyond him. What he really needed was a hard, bruising ride over challenging terrain that would take his mind and body to the brink of exhaustion. Then see if Miss Elizabeth Bennet haunted his dreams! But there was no such place in London, and Nelson—too much of a handful for Town—was enjoying his stable of mares in Derbyshire. That avenue for his temper, it seemed, was closed to him as well. Was there nothing he could put his hand to that would rid him of this, this— What? From what, exactly, was he suffering?

When, in disgrace with Fortune and men's eyes. The words of the sonnet returned to revolve inside his brain. *I all alone beweep my outcast state . . . Disgrace?* he asked himself, testing the thought for a moment before hardening against it. Well may he have been in disgrace in Elizabeth's eyes, but be it in hers or any man's eyes, that did not make it so! There was, after all, an innumerable host of men in the world who were the greatest fools, and their opinion counted for nothing. Yet— Darcy paused at Fletcher's word and flicked an eye toward his valet. Yet, Elizabeth's charge lay heavy against his conscience. "Had you behaved in a more gentlemanlike manner." To be in disgrace with one who mattered; further, with the woman with whom one had thought to spend one's life; whether just or no, *such* disgrace was a crushing blow indeed.

Full apprehension of the next line came hard on the heels of his admission. *Outcast state . . .* Yes! that was how he felt: cast out, bereft of any prospect of contentment or joy, rejected by Fortune. *Wishing me like to one more rich in hope . . .* Nothing in the present was of interest to him; nothing in the future offered him hope that this situation would change. Darcy closed his eyes against the silent groan that began deep in his chest and traveled inexorably throughout his frame. *Hope*—the word, so rich and full, pregnant with sound and meaning—mocked him. From where was hope to come? His cousin had but to wait for the next pretty face to ease his disappointment. The idea of venturing out into the marriage mart for a replacement to install in his heart was, to Darcy, too appalling. Such an exercise could not possibly be done, not by him. Elizabeth was irreplaceable. He'd learned that quite well enough at Norwycke Castle. *More* rich in hope? He derided himself. He was destitute of it.

"The towel, sir?" Fletcher had finished shaving him.

Darcy nodded but arrested his valet as he turned, his curiosity at Fletcher's words getting the better of his judgment. At this point, any straw would do. " 'Yet'? What did you mean by it, Fletcher?"

" 'Yet' *and* 'Haply,' sir." Fletcher carefully averted his eyes from Darcy's and set about rearranging the shaving equipment on the tray. " 'Yet' turns the point of the sonnet. All is hopeless before it; then, in the very midst of the poet's self-abasement, 'yet' suddenly appears, a word suggesting that hope may still exist, that all is not truly lost."

"Humph." Darcy snorted his dissatisfaction. "Hope against

hope: a poet's romantic solution to what the rest of the world knows as the unyielding *nuda veritas* of life."

"You would be entirely correct in that, sir," Fletcher replied, "save for the presence of 'haply.' "

"Haply? By chance?" Darcy frowned.

"By *Fortune*, if we follow the Bard's metaphor," Fletcher amended. "Hope reborn begins with no more than a thought; but that thought is able to move the poet from misery to joy. 'Haply I think on thee,' and then 'bootless cries' are turned into 'hymns at heaven's gate.' " His voice fell almost to a sigh.

"All this with a thought," Darcy interrupted, discontent and skepticism hard-edging his words.

"No, sir, not *a* thought—Fortune's thought. Would you like the towel now, sir?" Fletcher cocked his head toward the steamy article whose comforting fragrance was beginning to tickle Darcy's nose. Nodding, he sat back again in the chair, closing his eyes against the towel's imminent application. It landed suddenly in a hot and unceremonious heap upon his face as, in a shocked voice, his valet exclaimed, "Miss Darcy!"

In a single, swift movement, Darcy flung the towel from him and shot bolt upright. "Georgiana!" Never had his sister entered his chambers uninvited! He could not even think when her last visit had been; certainly, she had never seen its walls before he was properly dressed.

"I-I beg your pardon, Fitzwilliam," she stuttered to his incredulous gaze. Although she was obviously nervous, she returned his regard steadily, breaking only to slide a glance at Fletcher, who had remained next to his chair in slack-mouthed surprise.

"Is, ah, is something the matter?" Darcy's brain did not seem to be working at all properly.

"Breakfast" was her simple reply. The revelation of her purpose for appearing in his chambers was no less surprising than her actual presence there. He had known she would not receive the news with anything less than disappointment. Evidently, she had received it with a great deal more and had bravely determined to beard the recalcitrant lion in his den. Darcy passed a hand over his freshly shorn cheeks as he took in her straight, dignified carriage, yet softly tender eyes. Quite suddenly, he was put in mind of their mother. *So be it,* he sighed to himself. How could he refuse in the face of such a revealing glimpse at the woman that his sister was becoming?

"I shall be pleased to join you as soon as I am dressed," he conceded. "Tell the servants to lay my place."

"I would prefer to breakfast with you here, please . . . in your chambers." She was clearly pressing the advantage of his surprise. Her voice had trembled a bit but had, in the end, held firm. Even so, she was not finished. "I have already instructed that both our breakfasts be brought up."

"Indeed?" Darcy looked upon his sister with new appreciation. She was becoming something more than what she had been. Was this further evidence of Dy's influence or proof of his contention that she was a girl no longer? If he was to discover which, Darcy would have to submit to her arrangements. He inclined his head in formal acquiescence to her wishes. "Then I shall be pleased to join you even sooner, as I am dressed."

Her smile was a delight. "Thank you, Fitzwilliam." She curtsied, and after glancing curiously once more at Fletcher, whose dazed attention had not abated during the entirety of the interview, she departed his dressing room, closing the door behind her. For a full minute, neither Darcy nor Fletcher moved or spoke, both of them caught up in a contemplation of the closed door.

Finally, Darcy cleared his throat. "Well, it appears that we have received our orders, Fletcher."

Now properly attired, Darcy hesitantly emerged from behind his dressing room door. He had, throughout his valet's ministrations, been occupied exclusively with the thought of what he would find on the other side of the door. As interesting as was this new confidence Georgiana exhibited, it did not bode well for his desire to tend to his wounds in private. She would want an accounting for his behavior. How would she approach the matter, he wondered, and how would he avoid it?

Georgiana stood behind one of two chairs drawn up to the small gateleg table, now opened to its fullest extent and laden with covered dishes. Even covered, the savory aromas of the viands tucked beneath were seeping into every corner of the room. Against his will, Darcy's stomach growled.

"Oh, good, you *are* hungry then!" his sister greeted him. She signaled the servants to uncover the dishes, and as Darcy seated her, they bore the covers out the door.

They were alone. Darcy took his seat opposite and drew it up to the table, while casting her an uncertain smile. This was all so very strange; he felt off balance. He looked down at the dishes. The most tempting of choices lay before him, and really, the smells wafting up from them were entirely irresistible. The knot that had been his stomach relaxed somewhat as he reached for a plate. Georgiana's smile widened as he filled it, but she said nothing about his awakened appetite, merely setting about her own meal with a precise grace. Stiff with caution, the muscles in Darcy's back gradually released. Perhaps she would be satisfied with the return of his appetite and desire no more of him for the present.

"Fitzwilliam?" Her address, with its implied question, came when he had finished pouring his first cup of coffee. "Must we have a formal unveiling of my portrait?"

Prepared for a question in quite another vein, Darcy looked at his sister with surprise. "You do not wish it?"

"No, I do not," she replied diffidently. "It is not that I dislike the portrait; it is very nice. It is just that . . ." She stopped. Seeing that she was searching for the right words, Darcy held his peace and lifted his cup to his lips. Was she retreating into shyness again? It was expected that a young lady on the verge of coming out had her portrait painted. The Unveiling was the first step in that vital process. She began again. "How did you feel when your portrait was painted?"

She referred, of course, to the one hanging in Pemberley's gallery, painted upon his twenty-first birthday. He recalled feeling mightily embarrassed by it, and to this day, he avoided looking at it when he traversed the hall. He much preferred to gaze upon his forebears' faces, particularly that of their father, painted at the same age, and one of both their parents painted when he was ten.

"I remember disliking the attention and fuss and thinking that the fellow in the painting could not possibly be me," he admitted.

"Yes!" Georgiana leaned toward him eagerly. "How not you?"

"Oh, older, I suppose, better. Certainly wiser than I could claim at the time." *Or even now,* Darcy thought ruefully.

"The ideal of you, rather than the you that you knew yourself to be," she supplied him, then smiled. "Although, I have always thought your portrait captured you exactly."

Darcy accepted her compliment with a bow of his head. "The proper perspective for a younger sister to take, to be sure." He smiled back. "But how is this to the purpose? It is expected that it will be unveiled. Lawrence would have reason to take offense if it were not. He would consider it a commentary upon his skill." He could see from the look upon her face that the last troubled her. "It need not be a grand affair. Only family and close friends," he offered. "It is a perfectly lovely portrait, Georgiana."

At his description, her eyes fell; but when she raised them he saw a serenity in them but a serenity not untouched by the world. "Yes, 'perfectly' lovely." She leaned closer still and reached for him, her fingers lightly grazing the top of his hand. "Fitzwilliam, it is not I! I am not that 'perfectly lovely' girl in the painting, and I have no wish to take part in the deception, to stand beside it and pretend that everything it depicts is true."

"Would you have Lawrence add some spots, a wart or two, perhaps?" he teased, but in truth, he was uneasy, confounded by her reticence. "Georgiana, there is nothing amiss with your portrait!"

"Nothing but honesty about who I truly am." She sat back in her chair and breathed a sigh. "Fitzwilliam, when you first saw your own portrait, the idealized you, what else did you feel? What did you think?"

Closing his eyes briefly against her intense scrutiny, Darcy breathed out heavily as he flexed his jaw. What did she want from him? *The truth,* he heard the answer clearly, *only the truth.*

He opened his eyes again and answered, "I hoped to God that one day I would be the man in the painting—better, wiser—that I would not be a disappointment to my station, my name, . . . or myself," he added as he turned his gaze from her searching one. But he *had* disappointed himself. Norwycke had shown him the dark depths in his heart he had been unable to remedy. He continued, but he could feel his confidence fading. "That I would . . . in every way . . . truly be the gentleman . . ." He stopped, choking at the one word Elizabeth had flung at him that had, during their interview, most made him flinch.

Rising abruptly from his chair, he left the table; but there seemed no place to go, no place to escape what was now become the damning truth. Even were it true that he played the gentleman in all other venues of his life, he had utterly failed in the eyes of the one he most desired to believe him admirable. If he had been found so severely wanting in Elizabeth's small world, did he even know himself? Sylvanie's taunts took on new meaning. Had she recognized this in him and played upon it? With that revelation came the suspicion of the truth of Elizabeth's other epithets: *arrogant, conceited, disdainful of the feelings of others.* They had seemed to depict the character of a monstrosity that he had thought born of her anger, and he had summarily dismissed the whole as having any relation to himself. Yet had he not brooded angrily over those words for days now, resentful of Elizabeth's ungenerous attachment of them to him? Why had her words not caused him to hate her? For, despite all his anger and resentment, he literally ached with the loss of her. His stride had taken him to the window, and spreading his arms, he grasped either side of its frame and stared out against the sunlight pouring through it. Hate Elizabeth? How could he? How could he hate the woman he loved for demanding of him the man he had always desired to be?

The light pressure of a hand on his arm brought him back. He looked down into brimming eyes full of compassion as his sister gently pulled on his sleeve. Helpless to deny her, he bent and received the benediction of her kiss upon his cheek. "*Dear* Brother, tell me," Georgiana whispered. "Tell me what happened at Rosings."

At Georgiana's plea, Darcy looked down into his sister's face, his heart stilled in his chest, before he turned away to stare once more out his window. Georgiana's loving appeal and gentle kiss pierced him to the quick, tempting him to lay before her all the crushing pain of Elizabeth's determined rejection and the bitter knowledge of himself that he had gained from it; but there was in her eyes something that made his tongue cleave to the roof of his mouth with a sudden, irascible stubbornness. Was it possible that she could understand his pain? Yes, he might grant that what she had experienced at Wickham's hands had been similarly devastating before working such unexpected changes in her and bringing the singular sort of maturity she now exhibited. But while he continued grateful for the solace she had found in religion, he could not, in the cold economy of Heaven that was his own experience, find anything, not even the compassionate solicitude in Georgiana's eyes, to draw him in that direction. It had always made him uncomfortable, and now, in all he had lately undergone at the behest of Providence, he was become decidedly inured against it.

"Fitzwilliam?" The catch in Georgiana's voice warned him that his demeanor had betrayed something of what had passed within him. Whatever that had been, and he could not put a name to it as yet, he knew it was not something for her tender sensibilities. Working to settle his features into softer lines, he turned back to her, grabbed for her hand, and brought it up to his lips.

"It was nothing, sweetling. You must not worry." He stroked her hand with his thumb but could not look into her eyes. Suddenly, his room, indeed all of Erewile House, felt oppressive and confining. He must get out, it was impressed upon him, or suffocate! He released Georgiana's hand. "I thank you for breakfast and your company, but I must leave you now." He walked quickly to the bell pull and gave it a quick tug.

"Leave?" Georgiana's brows slanted down in puzzlement. "Where must you go?"

"Out, my dear," Darcy returned almost curtly. The urgency to escape from his sister's keen observation felt like an intolerable weight hung large within his chest.

"B-but . . . we have not finished discussing the Unveiling," she stammered, her eyes pleading with him to remain.

"The Unveiling," he repeated absently, unwilling to meet her gaze. "I believe it cannot be avoided."

"Fitzwilliam, please—" she remonstrated, but he cut her off.

"You must reconcile yourself, Georgiana, and proceed in the expected manner with as good grace as you can. I will grant you that the guest list may be pared down to only family and our closest friends, but the Unveiling must proceed." He dared then to glance at her, but he saw with relief that she had turned away from him. A click at the dressing room door claimed his attention.

"Mr. Darcy, sir?" The formality of Fletcher's bow revealed that he had not, as yet, accustomed himself to the fact of Miss Darcy's unusual presence in the master's rooms.

"My coat, Fletcher. I am going out."

"Out, sir? But where, sir?" the valet asked, puzzled at the stark order. "Do you require your walking coat, your driving—"

"Out!" Darcy repeated, his irritation growing as he cast about for a destination that would satisfy both his inquisitors and his own requirement for relief. The solution came to him with sudden clarity. "Out—fencing!"

"Very good, sir." Fletcher bowed low again, but his delicacy was for naught; for, despite its softness, the sound of the bedchamber door closing behind Miss Darcy's skirts echoed clearly through the room.

"Yes." Darcy looked about him approvingly before beginning his warming exercises. He had made the right choice. The atmosphere of the fencing rooms was just what he required to exorcise the demons of mind and the cramp of his body that had plagued him since That Day. He threw back his shoulders and began tracing the slow arcs and easing into stretches that would loosen the muscles in his back, arms, and limbs, readying them for the demands which he would soon place upon them. It had been rather a long time since he had held sword or foil, and though the weight felt good in his hand and the urge to immediate action was great, he knew it behooved him to commence his reacquaintance slowly. Yes, this was exactly what he needed. No one here would think of demanding of him anything more than common decency, fair play, and style in his swordsmanship. Of those, he was quite as capable as any gentleman and more so; for the first two lay in his blood and, as to the last, he knew his swordplay was generally considered both powerful and elegant.

From the corner of his eye, Darcy spied Genuardi, the fencing master, who acknowledged his presence with a salute and a bow. Pausing in his regime, he returned the courtesy, ignoring the wistful or jealous glances cast him by lesser blades who dreamed of such attention, and then returned to his study. The blood in his veins began to flow faster; his sinews and muscles warmed. The stiffness fell away from his limbs. His movements increased in their speed and fluidity until, finally, he felt that rush of power, of such control over his body that he knew it would do all he asked of it. God, it felt good! He slowed his movements, his heart pounding only moderately, then stopped to wipe the sheen of perspiration from his brow and survey the room for an opponent. He heard the step behind him only a second before feeling the tap on his shoulder.

"Darcy, old man! Where have you been?" Surprised at the voice, Darcy pivoted to face Lord Tristram Monmouth, who gestured carelessly with his foil. "Care for a go?" Tris's brow lifted lazily, but there was in his old university roommate's manner a certain nervous tension for which Darcy could not account. That Monmouth was here at all was strange enough. He could not remember seeing him in the fencing rooms any time over the last two years. Perhaps his wife, Lady Sylvanie, had lost her fascination.

"Monmouth," Darcy returned, nodding his assent, and walked away to claim a position on the floor. Tension was good. It made one's opponent too careful or too reckless, and either could be used to advantage. Centering his feet upon the mark, Darcy looked up to observe his challenger and decided that, in Monmouth's case, it would be too reckless. Why, he could not assay, for Tris's *"En garde!"* had already sounded loud in his ears. They met. Within seconds, Darcy knew he had been right. Tris's swordsmanship in their university days had been admirable, but he had not, evidently, advanced his form much beyond that.

Their engagement was not a long one, its duration more a result of his permission than of Tris's skill, but in the course of it, he found himself, not once but twice, forced to block an illegal thrust. The first he put down to the heat of the moment; the second time, he was not so certain and quickly put an end to their play, scoring his *touchés* in the remaining bouts with precision and speed. Stunned by Monmouth's actions, he searched his face as they exchanged the formal ending salute, but Tris only smiled back at him, seemingly unaware that anything untoward had occurred. Was it possible he had just been carried away or, perhaps, forgotten proper form over the years?

Still smiling, his old mate advanced upon him, his hand out-stretched. "Better than university days! Damn me, Darcy, if you are not!"

"I have kept at it." He grasped Monmouth's hand briefly.

"In a word!" Monmouth snorted. "After your demonstration at Say——, the last time we met, Manning wagered that you could take any or all of the rest of us in under ten minutes. Well, old man, you know how I cannot resist a sporting wager!"

"I hope that I have not done you significant harm," Darcy offered, relieved to have an explanation for Monmouth's actions.

"No, no! I am in good funds, thanks to My Lady." He winked at him. "Who, by the by, would be *very* pleased if you would accept her invitation sent you this week to dine with us and a select number of friends." Monmouth paused for Darcy's reply but must have sensed the polite decline that hovered on his lips, for he then continued hurriedly, "I can promise you an interesting evening, Darcy, not the usual set at all. 'Tell him he will not be bored or hunted!' she said, and I swear, 'struth! Sylvanie likes fascinating people around her: artists, thinkers, writers—deep uns like you. Allow me to convey My Lady your acceptance, there's a good fellow!"

"Acceptance! What are you accepting now, 'good fellow' Darcy?" Both men looked up in surprise to see Lord Brougham propped against one of the pillars that marched along that side of the room. Monmouth stiffened visibly at the voice, but when he saw that it was only Brougham, Darcy could sense the relief that swept through him. His own surprise remained at the fore. He had never seen Dy in Genuardi's fencing rooms or heard of his membership in any other. What could have tempted him today? Or could Georgiana have sent him?

"An invitation to dine with a collection of jaw-me-deads. Nothing in your line of interest, Brougham, I assure you," Monmouth drawled as his gaze traveled pointedly over His Lordship's elegant, unruffled figure. "No gaming—well, there's a pity—only a little music and a great deal of conversation. Philosophy and politics, that sort of thing."

"Brougham," Darcy interrupted, stepping toward his friend, "Georgiana?"

"In a manner of speaking, but do not trouble yourself—as yet." Dy held up a restraining hand and then turned a supercilious gaze upon their companion. "Philosophy and politics, eh, Monmouth? Both in one evening? I should say, it *will* be select and, you are correct, quite beyond my poor brain. But, tell me, My Lord, who will *you* talk to all evening?"

Monmouth's sword arm tensed briefly but relaxed when Darcy swiftly interposed himself between them. "His Lordship and I have unfinished business to discuss!" He deflected Dy's question and shot him a dark frown. Then, looking back at Monmouth, he continued, "Please convey to Lady Monmouth that I accept her invitation."

At his promise, a look of satisfaction replaced the anger in Monmouth's face, and with a smirk at Brougham, he turned to Darcy. "Her Ladyship will be very pleased to hear it. Tomorrow at eight, then? Good! Your servant, Darcy." He bowed. "Brougham." He barely paused to nod in his direction before sauntering toward the dressing rooms.

"You cannot truly mean to go, Fitz!" Brougham's lip curled in disgust as they watched Monmouth walk away.

"You would not have me go back on my word, would you?" Darcy rounded on him.

"In this particular case, I would, and with great urgency," Brougham replied. "One does not owe one's word to the Devil!"

"Coming it rather strong, are you not?" Darcy bristled. "And I would not have given it if you had refrained from antagonizing him. Good Lord, Dy, you all but called the man an idiot to his face!"

"I beg your pardon, Fitz; I was under the distinct impression that I had! But that is neither here nor there." Brougham dismissed the topic of His Lordship. "What I wish to know is why, after I have taken great pains to avoid an acquaintance springing up between Miss Darcy and Lady Monmouth, you are now increasing its likelihood?"

"I have never seen you here before today." Darcy met the uncomfortable question with one of his own. "Have you come to fence, or did Georgiana . . . ?"

"Oh, to fence, my friend; and it appears that we have begun already, although I am not yet undressed for it!" Brougham began to unbutton his frock coat. "I was distracted, you see, by your magnificent display of forbearance on the floor. You know, he fouled you twice."

"That does not make him the Devil!"

"True, Fitz, very true; Monmouth is only a serpent, and a very lowly one at that, running the Devil's errands." Just then, one of the room's attendants appeared to relieve Brougham of his coat and waistcoat, and both men fell silent. Darcy watched closely while his friend divested himself of the restraining garments of their station and then stepped back as Dy accepted the protective waistcoat and foil the servant offered and began his own regime of limbering stretches.

Shaking his head, Darcy let out a heavy breath. Dy had succeeded yet again in piquing his curiosity with his enigmatic speech. Questioning him further or issuing a demand for an explanation he knew to be useless. His old friend would merely return him a shrug of his shoulders and a ridiculously vacant, puzzled look with the reply that he had quite forgotten whatever silly thing had come out of his mouth and that Darcy should not regard it. Besides, Dy knew that his friend's appearance in Genuardi's fencing rooms was not accidental but related in some way to Georgiana; and that concerned him more than his opinion of the company Monmouth kept. After only a few minutes at his exercise, Dy dropped his sword arm and looked back to him with a curt "Ready?"

"That is all the preparation you require?" Darcy looked dubiously at his friend. "How long has it been, Dy? Have you done anything since university? You can hardly have warmed sufficiently—"

"Afraid I shall disappoint you, Fitz?" Dy cut him off. "Have no fear, my friend. My blood is quite up and has been for the last half hour or more." He walked off then to an empty position on the floor, leaving Darcy little choice but to follow him, his eyes narrowing in perplexity. What was this uncharacteristic behavior about? If, out of concern, Georgiana had sent Dy after him, why fence with him? It was much more his old friend's way to suggest billiards at their club or some sporting event to "banish that tedious set of your jaw," as he called Darcy's jealous protection of his privacy. Save for the rigors of the field, Darcy could not recall observing Dy in a sweat in all of the two years since he had returned to Town. He took his place opposite Dy and, after their salute, settled into the *en garde* from which their engagement would begin.

"My Lord! Mr. Darcy! *Scusatemi!*" Signore Genuardi called out urgently as he quickly strode across the hall toward them. "*Perdono*, signori, are you knowing one the other? *Prodigioso!*" He beamed at them with the fondness of a master for his prize students. Darcy looked to Brougham uncertainly, a suspicion beginning to form. "*Per cortesia*," the fencing master continued, "allow me the pleasure. I will judge." He then motioned them back into position and in a ringing voice that echoed above the murmur of the now attentive hall proclaimed, "*En garde!*"

"We have an audience, it would seem." Dy matched Darcy's advance but made no motion to offer the attack. "I had not anticipated such interest. Unfortunate, that!"

"You know Genuardi?" Darcy flexed his wrist, causing the tip of his foil to trace out tight circles in the air between them.

"Everyone knows Genuardi."

Oh, how he hated it when Dy played his obtuse games with him! The irritation decided him. Springing to the attack, he took first priority, pressing Dy back several steps before being blocked and parried. Brougham's riposte was effective but unremarkable, exactly what Darcy had expected from a good swordsman who had been away from the sport for several years. He blocked Dy's thrust, parried, and pressed his attack back upon him, but this time he did not force him back as far before being blocked. Brougham's parry was nicely done, and the first part of his attack was a move they had learned and practiced together in their university days. He deflected it easily but was met with it again, this time accompanied by a new twist of Dy's wrist and body that greatly increased its effectiveness. He avoided it by a hairsbreadth and fell back one, then two steps.

"*Touché!*" the fencing master declared. "To His Lordship!"

Brougham drew back from his victory immediately and saluted him. "You are underestimating me, Fitz! I expect it from others, but not from you. I should not have gotten that one."

"You will not get it again, I promise you," Darcy bit out and returned to position.

"*En garde!*" Genuardi called them back together. This time, Darcy waited, intent upon observing everything possible about Dy's stance and style, but his opponent offered no clues, merely smiling and holding his foil up before him in a desultory fashion. Darcy grimaced back, then lunged into first with a ferocity that swept them both into a display of arm that elicited shouts of admiration from the onlookers as they swiftly traded right-of-way, lunge, and parry.

"*Touché!* To Signore Darcy!" The blood was singing through his veins as he gave Dy back his salute. They were excellently matched, and it felt . . . good!

"Up to your weight that time?" Dy threw at him before returning to position.

"More what I expected of you, yes. Quite good." His smile remained as ever, but as Dy turned away, Darcy had the sudden, uncomfortable feeling that more than his swordsmanship was being measured. It was a deuced curious sensation that he had felt more than once in the two years since their friendship had been re-sumed. He turned at position and looked back into Dy's face, only to meet eyes that were focused upon him with a piercing intensity. Darcy brought up his foil.

"*En garde!*" Their third bout was like the previous one: swift, powerful, elegant. Darcy found that his friend answered him stroke for stroke, and the allotted time was almost gone before the tip of Dy's foil caught him just under his heart. "*Touché! To His Lordship!*" The entire school and club were gathered at the side-lines now, and the response was deafening.

As they exchanged salutes, Darcy leaned toward his friend. "And where have you been training and not breathing a word of it? If that had been swords and serious—"

"You would still be whole and hale," Brougham interrupted, the smile gone. His eyes bore into Darcy's. "A man must *have* a heart to be slain by that stroke."

"What?" Darcy's brows shot up in surprise, but the fire he had seen in his friend's eyes had already been replaced with his habit-ual nonchalance.

"You must forgive me, my friend, but I can spare you only one more bout. A pressing prior engagement, you understand. This lit-tle *tête-à-tête*"—he sighed—"was not on my calendar for today." He offered him a small bow and sauntered back to position, leav-ing Darcy to stare after him in dawning comprehension. Dy was angry with him! He returned to his mark in some confusion, his mind casting about for an explanation. Why? And what was this about having no heart? Turning back to face him, Darcy went into position immediately. The noise of the onlookers quieted now that it could be seen that both of them were ready. He took a deep breath. No manners, no conscience, and, now no heart! *See what you have begun, Miss Elizabeth Bennet?* He snorted bitterly. *All that remains now is a Greek chorus!*

"*En garde!*" Signore Genuardi's command cracked through the now silent hall. This time, Dy did not wait for Darcy to decide whether to take first opportunity but came at him directly with force and speed. Not only he but those gathered to watch as well could see that Brougham's sword work was in earnest, and Darcy had never felt so hammered. *If that was the way of it, then so be it!* he resolved as he parried Dy's lunge, taking the right-of-way from him and setting to. He put every move, every feint, every twist of body or wrist that was at his command into his attack and had the satisfaction of driving Dy back almost to his mark. The exhilarating sense of his body as a finely tuned and responsive instrument returned, along with an exquisite timing that seemed to send every thrust exactly where he wished it to go. Although Dy had successfully avoided the tip of his foil thus far, he knew that he was forcing from him the employment of every shred of knowledge and skill he possessed. Back and forth they worked, and the onlookers could contain their appreciation no longer. Shouts of encouragement mixed with those of astonishment as the time ticked forward with neither man scoring a hit amid the dazzling display. But Darcy, wholly focused on his goal, neither saw nor heard the uproar. Suddenly, there was an opening.

"*Touché!*" Genuardi could barely be heard, but those around him took up the cry. "To Signore Darcy!" The hall seemed in chaos, but the two men on whom the excitement had centered stood apart from it, their breaths coming in gasping unison as, with an awkward caution, they eyed each other. Slowly, a reluctant smile spread across Dy's features, and he brought his foil up in salute. "Well done, old sod! You might make a swordsman yet!"

"Ha!" Darcy laughed, returning the gesture. "And I might say the same of you! Two to each of us—not a decisive outcome!" Then he turned a sober regard upon his friend. "Are you going to tell me what this was all about?"

Dy looked away. *Which one will it be who answers the friend or the fool?* Darcy wondered.

Darcy wondered, "I stopped in at Erewile House this morning to see whether you had recovered from your jaunt in Kent," the friend replied, turning to look him full in the face, "only to find Miss Darcy alone and in very low spirits." He paused and took a deep breath. "Whatever it was happened in Kent, Fitz, I beg you will not give Miss Darcy the grief of it! She is all concern for you, while you behave with her in a shabby, patronizing manner nursing your Kentish grievances."

"Brougham!" Darcy growled. *Who was he to—*

Ignoring his interruption, Dy continued, his voice low but exceedingly clear. "*She* will say nothing against you, nor would she even if she felt herself misused, she respects you so well." He shook his head slightly. "But I am under no such compunction and take leave to tell you that, as much as you are my friend, there is more swordplay where this display came from should you continue to behave toward Miss Darcy in a manner so careless of her feelings!"

"You take much upon yourself!" Darcy drew himself back. "You step beyond the bounds, Brougham, and are quite out of your—"

"Am I, Fitz?" Brougham looked searchingly into his face. "Then knowing me as you do, p'rhaps you ought to ask yourself why I have taken such an uncharacteristically fatiguing step on your behalf!" With that, Dy threw the foil to a waiting servant and left the hall.

"The fox crying sour grapes, Darcy?" Monmouth appeared, stepping ahead of the crowd coming to congratulate the swordsmen, and cocked his head toward Brougham's retreating figure.

"No," Darcy replied absently, staring after his friend. "More like a Greek chorus."

In a pique of equal parts irritation and curiosity, Darcy followed after Brougham a quarter hour later when he had acknowledged those who had taken his part in the contest and retrieved his clothing. Dy had left the hall immediately, it appeared, without stopping to freshen or resume his usual impeccably garbed state.

Where would he have taken himself? Hurriedly buttoning his coat after tying his neckcloth into something presentable, Darcy left the fencing hall and hailed a cab.

"Boodle's," he called up to the driver as he leapt into the vehicle. If the story of a prior engagement had been merely the tale he suspected it to be, it was likely that Brougham would have withdrawn to their club, expecting that Darcy would follow. If not, well, he had no intention of chasing after his friend all over London. He would take his leisure among the gentlemen of his club and wait for a more opportune time to corner Dy. More to the point, he admitted to himself, he was still in nowise ready to return home.

The ride to the address was not a long one, hardly providing him time enough to consider the meaning behind his friend's provocative words. It was clear that Brougham did not approve of the manner in which he was keeping himself from Georgiana, causing her distress over his behavior and concern for his health and the well-being, he supposed, of his soul. But what the Devil business was it of his! Dy's actions were suspiciously like those of a lover! Darcy shifted uneasily, dismayed that the thought should arise once more. Had Dy not taken his hand and sworn that he was no danger to his friend's sister? And then there was the matter of the differences in their ages and temperaments . . . "No, it could not be!" he assured himself aloud. There had to be another reason. It must be that Dy had come to regard Georgiana as the sister he never had while he had the charge of her. His friend was warning Darcy that his behavior toward her was not what Brougham, in his severely limited experience, considered "brotherly." Darcy leaned back into the cushions. Yes, that *must* be it!

Free now to turn his attention from the messenger to the message, he could only concede that Brougham was right; and he had known that immediately. He *should* have more care for Georgiana's tender feelings—had he not always done so?—but at present, he found himself reluctant to act on the admission. That unwillingness, as so many other thoughts and emotions he had experienced this week, struck him as curiously unlike himself. Smothering the thought quickly, Darcy looked out on the exclusive shops and clubs of fashionable London. Things would come about . . . in time, and when he had gotten himself to rights again and Miss Elizabeth Bennet was a distant memory, they could all return to the way it had been, to the life he had planned before he had lost his senses in the parlor at Hunsford's parsonage.

Once inside Boodle's hallowed halls, he crossed the black-and-white marble-tiled entrance and hurried up one of the broad staircases to the clubrooms beyond. A quick survey revealed that Brougham was not among their denizens, although others of Darcy's acquaintance were there, and he was hailed with enthusiasm by more than one gentleman as he made his way through the rooms.

"Darcy." Sir Hugh Goforth nodded to him as he passed through one of the billiard rooms. "That friend of yours was looking for you."

"Sir Hugh." Darcy stopped and bowed. "Brougham, was it?"

"No, no—have not seen Brougham for an age. Bingley, I think the name was. Said he was taking his sister over to see your sister, or something like. Was hoping you would be about, I gather."

Darcy almost flushed with the ire that seized him as he thanked Sir Hugh for the information. Bingley—whose headlong flight into love had started the whole miserable affair and whose chestnuts he had drawn out of the fire only to be thoroughly burnt himself! Darcy let out a heavy breath. Well and so, it appeared that Bingley and his sister had returned from their annual trip to Yorkshire and were once again in Town. If he had bothered to look at the stack of calling cards Hinchcliffe always laid so precisely upon his desk, he might already have been in possession of the knowledge and sent round a note forestalling any thoughts Charles might have entertained of an imminent visit. As it was . . .

"I say, Darcy!" Sir Hugh called from the other side of the billiard table. "Devereaux's horse is running, and he must as well. Care for a game?"

He ought to go home. He ought to go home, ask Georgiana's forgiveness, and welcome Bingley and his sister back to Town. He ought to be there this very moment discharging the mountain of papers awaiting his attention on his desk, as had always been his custom.

Darcy turned back and reached for a cue. "As many as you like, Goforth. I have all afternoon."

The Bingleys' visit could not be staved off forever, and though Darcy had arranged to avoid it the previous day, Charles's card appeared once again the next morning. Resigned to it, Darcy met his sister in the drawing room to await their entrance. He had spoken to Georgiana only briefly the night before, his curiosity about what she knew of Brougham's behavior driving him to seek her out after having shunned their home most of the day. She replied innocently enough that, yes, Lord Brougham had come by to see him, but that they had spoken very little after His Lordship knew he had gone out.

"And what 'very little' did you discuss, Georgiana?" he had asked her in an offhanded manner as he examined a piece of her embroidery lying on the small tambour table. Her work was, as everything she did, exquisite and precise. The silks were fair on their way to portraying a scene from Eden, their mother's conservatory garden at Pemberley. A collection of differing colors strewn alongside it caught his eye, and without thinking he reached for them.

"He asked how you had been keeping yourself since returning from Kent, as he had not seen you about since bringing Trafalgar to us. Then, he kindly inquired about the Unveiling."

"Nothing more?" He fingered the strands, their cool silkiness sliding so familiarly between his fingers.

"We spoke a little of a book he had sent and encouraged me to read. I recall nothing more; although, for a moment . . ." She hesitated and then looked at him curiously. He followed her bemused gaze to his hand and flushed to see he had unconsciously entwined the silk threads about his fingers. As indifferently but rapidly as he could, he unwound them and laid them back on the table. "Oh, you may have them to add to your others, if you wish," she assured him with a small, quick smile.

"For a moment . . . ?" he prompted her and turned his back on the wretched temptation.

"For a moment"—Georgiana's young brow wrinkled in perplexity—"he appeared unwell . . . but not ill, precisely. I cannot say; it happened so quickly. You know him so well." She looked up at him. "What could it have meant?"

"Humph," he snorted. "It meant that he had determined to embark upon an errand he knew to be officious and impertinent." He looked away then in some exasperation, confounded with the inexplicable workings of Dyfed Brougham's mind. Did Darcy really "know him so well"? He leaned down and bussed his sister's forehead. "Good night, my dear."

"And to you as well, Brother." Her smile for him was shaded with uncertainty.

He left her to spend a restless night knocking about his chambers, at once unable to sleep and distrustful of the dreams sleep might bring. The morning had been a loss, for try though he might to deal with the backlog Hinchcliffe had laid before him, he could wade through little of it before drifting into a reverie or dozing off to sleep. Giving up, he had stretched out on the divan in his study and recouped an uncomfortable but dreamless hour before Witcher's diffident knock had awakened him to the arrival of Bingley's card.

The look of constrained relief on Georgiana's face at his appearance in the drawing room gave him pause, and as he took her hand to kiss, he could feel an unwonted tension about her. "Georgiana?" he murmured, keeping an eye on the door that would shortly open upon their visitors.

"It is nothing, Brother." She flushed, withdrawing her hand from his grasp.

"Nonsense!" Darcy returned, but gently. "Give over; what is it?"

Her flush deepened. "Miss Bingley," she confessed ashamedly. "I—" The drawing room door opened at that moment, revealing the subject of his sister's confusion. No more could be said.

Darcy stepped forward. "Miss Bingley." He offered her his bow and then turned to her brother and put out his hand, "Charles! So, you are returned."

"Darcy! Yes!" Bingley took his hand and shook it vigorously. "London, or rather, the Season called, and Yorkshire was no place for us, you may believe! Miss Darcy." He turned and bowed to Georgiana. "It will be our very great pleasure to attend your Unveiling next week."

"Charles! Miss Darcy's *portrait's* Unveiling, if you please." Miss Bingley rolled her eyes. "We are all anticipation, Miss Darcy." She turned an indulgent smile upon her object. "It will be the most brilliant Unveiling of the Season. Do I understand aright that Lawrence himself attends?" Not waiting for an answer, she looked to Darcy. "Why, that is the greatest of good fortune, is it not, Mr. Darcy? Your sister's introduction to Society is already a Subject; Lawrence's presence will guarantee the Unveiling's success. I predict Erewile House will be inundated with well-wishers!"

Darcy felt rather than saw Georgiana's tremor of dismay at Miss Bingley's fulsome compliment. Incredible that the woman who professed to love her so well had not the slightest notion of his sister's true nature! She took her up as one might a pretty doll and with no more care than that for her mind or feelings! He drew back from Miss Bingley and turned to her brother.

"You are, of course, most welcome, but it will not be as well attended as you might expect. We have lately decided that only close friends and family will receive invitations."

"Oh, you cannot mean it!" Miss Bingley claimed his attention with a shrill gasp as she took his offered chair. "Miss Darcy—" she appealed to Georgiana.

"But I do," Darcy broke in, regarding her in arched irritation. Damn and blast if he would allow her to tease Georgiana any further about it! "It was Georgiana's wish."

"Would you care to take some refreshment, Miss Bingley, Mr. Bingley?" Georgiana interposed with a smooth, firm voice. Bestowing upon her a surprised but approving smile, Darcy seconded the suggestion. "Yes, you must want for some tea. I have no doubt Mrs. Witcher has it and more already prepared." He motioned Bingley to a seat and pulled at the bell cord. "Now, Charles, you must tell us how you occupied yourself these weeks in Yorkshire."

As Darcy buttoned on his waistcoat before his mirror that evening, he could not decide if he was glad Brougham had not come by that day or if he was out of humor with him for staying away. Dy was a will-o'-the-wisp, it was true; but to come at him as he had on the fencing floor and later in regard to Georgiana, and then to disappear? It was the outside of enough! Still, if he had come, what might have transpired? Likely a disagreement distasteful to them both and an estrangement of their friendship, for Darcy was at this very moment preparing for the Monmouths' select gathering, and nothing Dy would have said would have dissuaded him.

In point of fact, he was already experiencing enough disapproval of his prospective evening from his valet without Brougham's to add to it. On Darcy's first informing Fletcher the night before that he was going out to a formal affair, his valet had brightened considerably and set about surveying his wardrobe with something like his customary enthusiasm. Today, though, his spirit for the project of presenting his master in the height of fashion had flagged decidedly. "His Lordship and Lady Monmouth's did you say, sir?" he had repeated in some disbelief upon discovery of his master's hosts for the evening. "Are you *quite* sure, sir?" his valet had queried him as he shaved him for the second time that day.

"Yes, Fletcher." He had looked up at him ironically. "I am quite sure that is who extended me the invitation." Knowing there was more, he ventured, "Why?"

"In a word, Norwycke Castle, Mr. Darcy!" Fletcher had grimaced in disgust. "And since then, His Lordship and, most especially, Her Ladyship have been observed to be traveling with a rather, ahem, *diverse* company, sir."

"So Monmouth told me. 'Philosophy and politics' was his description. Hardly akin to what lurked in the shadows of Norwycke, Fletcher!" To this observation, his valet had ventured a skeptical sniff. " 'One may smile, and smile,' sir," he had replied and returned to the plying of his razor. Nothing more was said, but each piece of Darcy's evening clothing had been handed to him with an air of reluctance, and the knot at his throat was nothing of particular note or elegance.

Later, as the hansom took Darcy to Monmouth's town house, the combined effect of Fletcher's and Brougham's disapproval worked to produce in him a species of regret that he had accepted the invitation. But it was of a weak sort, for he also found himself curious about how the former Lady Sylvanie Sayre had gotten on after the horrific events at Norwycke Castle and also not a little intrigued by what the temper of the intellectuals and artists who had gathered around her might be. Such company gave the evening an air of piquancy, and piquancy or danger outright was infinitely preferable to what consumed him now, twisting his vitals ever and again into their familiar, painful knot. If he was to . . . If Elizabeth were to . . . The door to Monmouth's town house opened, candlelight and the murmur of a dozen conversations spilling out into the street. Desperate to escape the pain, Darcy laid hold of the invitation before him to think and feel something other than the wretched chasm of his loss and followed the beckoning from inside.

"Darcy, welcome!" Lord Monmouth greeted him from the top of the grand staircase that dominated the hall. "Do not dally down there!" he commanded as Darcy gave his hat and coat to the footman. "Come up, man! Her Ladyship is most anxious to see you!"

Darcy wound his way through the crowded hall and gained the steps, but his progress was impeded by the number of guests on the stairs, some going up or down, others holding intense conversations or serious flirtations on the risers. Monmouth still awaited him at the top, a broad smile yet upon his face. Tris always had liked crowds of people around him, and judging from the number here, Sylvanie had succeeded in making her social mark as a successful hostess. His Lordship should have been quite pleased. It still seemed strange to Darcy that Sylvanie would desire to resume their acquaintance. His refusal of her sensual offers at Norwycke and his undeniable part in the discovery and ultimate suicide of her mother must surely have made any contact between them painful or, at the least, exceedingly uncomfortable. Yet she had pursued an acquaintance with Georgiana that had required Dy's intervention to discourage, and now she desired above all things to see him.

"Tris." Darcy bowed and then gripped the hand Monmouth held out to him. "Amazing number of people you have here for a 'select group' of philosophers and politicians!"

"Oh, these." Monmouth waved dismissively. "These are mere window wares, my friend. The important ones are in the Green Room, where Sylvanie holds court. Come!" Monmouth drew him along, threading a way for them through the hallway toward a pair of great double-hung doors. "A moment!" He smiled when they had arrived and then rapped on one of the doors. The handle began a slow revolution, and the door cracked open. Quickly, His Lordship put a hand upon it and pushed in, surprising the servant on the other side into taking a hasty step backward. "Fool!" Monmouth growled as he ushered Darcy into the room. "Lord, how I hate dealing with day-hired servants; they never seem to grasp the smallest bit of instruction or even recognize those who pay their wage! But here we are, the inner circle!" He stopped another servant and, lifting two glasses off his tray, handed one to Darcy. "Some refreshment, old man, and then Her Ladyship. Cheers!" He lifted his glass in salute and downed half the punch before Darcy had even responded. Making a perfunctory motion with his glass, Darcy brought it up to his lips and was struck immediately by the strong smell of whiskey. Drawing back, he looked at his friend.

"A whiskey punch, Monmouth?"

"An *Irish* whiskey punch," replied a brogue-laced voice from behind him. One of Darcy's brows hitched up as he turned to discover the identity of his informant.

"Ah, O'Reilly." Monmouth acknowledged him. "Allow me to introduce you to a very old friend. Mr. Fitzwilliam Darcy of the Darcys of Pemberley in Derbyshire. Darcy, Sir John O'Reilly of County ———, Ireland."

"Your servant, sir." Darcy bowed.

"And yours, sir," Sir John responded, his demeanor warming slightly. "So, Darcy. Come to talk politics or philosophy?"

"I have not yet decided, Sir John, as I am a newcomer to Monmouth's 'select' gatherings," he confessed with a wry tilt of his chin toward his host. "I believe it would be the wiser course to listen and learn before giving my opinion on either subject."

"You must not possess a drop of Irish blood if that is your way." Sir John laughed. "Lack of familiarity never stopped one o' my race from holdin' forth on a subject. Not knowin' what he is talkin' about only encourages an Irishman to wax more eloquent upon it."

"I do not know whether I should agree with you, sir, or not." Darcy joined in the laughter Sir John's witticism had provoked in those immediately around them. "But I expect if I am careful to listen, I shall learn that as well."

"Very politic of you, Mr. Darcy." Sir John nodded at him. "You'll do. If you will excuse me? Monmouth." He winked at His Lordship and then melted into the crowd.

"Drink up, Darcy." Monmouth indicated his still untasted punch. "Sylvanie awaits." Darcy raised a brow at his glass and then sampled its contents under His Lordship's amused regard. It took all his willpower to suppress the choke and gasp his throat demanded of him. As it was, irrepressible tears sprang to his eyes. "Ha!" Monmouth clapped him on the back. "Not a whiskey drinker, I see!"

"No, not usually," he managed to reply as he wiped at his eyes. A servant appeared at his elbow.

"May I take that, sir?" he asked, bowing and then producing an empty tray.

"Yes, here." Darcy put down the unfinished glass.

"Very good, sir." The servant bowed again and whisked it away.

"Humph," observed Monmouth, "a day-hire who actually knows what he is about! Well, then." He grinned. "Now you are 'baptized,' you may wander freely, old man. Oh, yes!" Monmouth responded to his look of surprise. "Without the smell of 'water of life' on your breath, you would be held in suspicion. All is right and tight now! But, My Lady first." With that His Lordship took Darcy's arm in a firm grip and set off with purpose for the other end of the drawing room. It was just as well, for the whiskey had, by this juncture, reached Darcy's head, and for the moment, the room appeared somewhat confusing. They passed the servant who had taken his glass, and something about him struck Darcy as so curious that he halted their progress to stare after him. "What is it, Darcy?" Monmouth asked.

"The servant, the one who took my glass."

"Yes?" His Lordship prompted impatiently.

"For a moment . . . he seemed familiar," he finished lamely.

"Likely you have seen him in service at other houses; as I said, he *is* a day-hire."

A rustling sound replaced that of the conversations around them. A path between them and their destination opened to reveal Lady Sylvanie Monmouth rising from her seat surrounded by a coterie of men and women, all of whom exuded an intensity of passion for whatever subject had just been suspended. They all turned curious, glittering eyes upon him as Her Ladyship smiled and held out her hand to him. If he had called her a faerie princess before, it had been a weak metaphor. No, it was the Queen of Faerie who smiled upon him. Her luxurious black hair tumbled in ringlets about her creamy white shoulders, and as she moved toward him, her diaphanous emerald gown revealed more than any man but her husband should have known. The memory of what she had offered him at Norwycke raced through his frame.

"Mr. Darcy, welcome!" Her voice fell warm and intimate upon his senses. "How we have longed to see you again!"

Darcy could not be certain whether it was Sylvanie or the whiskey which had kindled the warmth that was now spreading throughout his frame, but the curst tight knot that had taken up residence in his chest a week before seemed to come loose. The welcome in her every movement as she approached him soothed his battered pride, then excited in him an appreciative anticipation. He smiled back at her and bowed, said, "Lady Monmouth," and rose to a face made even lovelier by a light of gentle amusement.

"So formal, *Mr.* Darcy?" she returned with a low-pitched laugh. "But we are more intimately acquainted than that, are we not?" She nodded to Monmouth, who bowed his leave with a smirk and took himself off to another part of the room. "We are not so careful to observe all the old proprieties here." Lady Monmouth took his arm, drawing him back to where she had been seated. "The world is changing and ablaze with new ideas that have no patience for that which is past." She glanced up at him, gauging his reaction, he supposed, but the delicious warmth suffusing him from within and caressing his senses from without overrode any impulse he might have had to take issue with her words. "Here, I am simply Sylvanie to your Darcy." Lady Monmouth resumed her seat on the divan and indicated to Darcy the space beside her.

As he took the place next to her, her admirers, who had drifted away at her desertion of them, strolled back, their eyes lighting upon him with a keen interest. Among them, though, were some who regarded him with a troubled uncertainty, while others cast upon him looks that bordered on hostility. One in particular, an intense-looking gentleman whose stance seemed to indicate resentment of Darcy's favored status, leaned near her ear and murmured something as she signaled a servant for more refreshments to be brought. "My dear Bellingham," she replied smoothly in undertone, "all is well!" She turned a wry smile upon Darcy. "They are all eager to know you! Will you allow me the introductions?"

Nodding his uneasy permission, Darcy reached for a glass of wine from the tray that appeared at his elbow. True to her word, all noble titles were abjured, and Sylvanie made her introductions by surname only. Nonetheless, Darcy recognized several who were titled lords or ladies, though minor ones. Those with a claim to some little fame for their art or writing were introduced as such, those with political aspirations with the names of their connections. As he had anticipated, they were a diverse lot, although *radical* might have been a better epithet, he decided. Further, many of them, as was his first new acquaintance of the evening, were Irish. Even as Darcy hoped he harbored no prejudice toward that fractious population, he could not have been unaware of the problems the radicals among them had been presenting to the government as it sought to prosecute a united effort against Napoleon. An indifferent Tory by birth, he had delved no more deeply into modern political philosophy than with an appreciative reading of Burke. Content as he was in the careful observance of his personal creed of responsible obligation to King on the one hand and to his own lands, tenants, and people on the other, the "Irish Question" had never intruded on his consciousness. If he read this gathering aright, it was about to do so.

" *'What have you got in your hand,'* Darcy?" Bellingham demanded of him, his eyes narrowly focused on his face. Darcy stared back at him, a brow raised in warning.

"Bellingham!" Sylvanie responded sharply but then continued in a more conciliatory voice. "All is *well.*"

"It is a simple enough question." Bellingham ignored her, his gaze intent upon Darcy. "What have you got in your hand?"

"It appears to resemble a glass of wine." Darcy brought the glass to his lips and drained half of it, all the while holding Bellingham's eyes with his own. "Yes, definitely wine! But pray, enlighten me, sir, if you deem it otherwise." He held the glass out to him.

Bellingham drew back at the offer, a look of supreme disdain upon his countenance. "I thought as much." He sneered and then turned to his hostess. " 'All is well,' Sylvanie?" he questioned her. "Not bloody likely!" Then, with the briefest of nods, he stalked away.

Darcy stared after him in wonder, but when his gaze returned to those about him, he immediately sensed that his welcome among them was dissipating as quickly as Bellingham's stride was taking him to the door. What had he said? He quickly downed the rest of the contents of his glass.

"You must take no notice of Bellingham." Sylvanie leaned against his arm and, reaching across him, took the glass from his hand. The scent of her perfume drifted over him, the smell of new roses and rain-drenched moss. "He is a strange man at best, and tonight he is more than a little preoccupied." She smiled up at Darcy from under shapely black brows. "Do not let him spoil the evening." Darcy found he could not help returning her smile and inclined his head in agreement. "Excellent." She laughed in pleasure with him and then rose from her seat, placing the glass on a table. "Come then; there are those here who, I daresay, you will enjoy meeting." Rising, he stepped up at her invitation, and once again, she tucked her hand inside his arm. "As your hostess, I must ensure your comfort," she murmured intimately, "and as I must leave you in a few minutes, I would have you well provided for until I return."

"You must leave?" Darcy asked, loathe to be left to his own devices in a room of strangers. He found too that he liked the caress in Sylvanie's voice and the warm pressure of her on his arm.

"Only long enough to sing a few songs for my guests. Tonight is rather special," she whispered conspiratorially as they made their way across the room. "Monmouth has secured Tom Moore for this evening! He consented to sing but only on the condition that we perform a duet and that I play for him."

"An honor, indeed," Darcy acknowledged, much impressed. He had heard the widely popular Irish tenor perform on more than one occasion and in highly prestigious company. That Sylvanie had obtained him for her soiree was, in itself, a social triumph of the first order. Moore's desire that she sing and play for him was a supreme compliment.

"Sylvanie, darlin'!" Sir John O'Reilly's exclamation brought them to a halt. "What would you be doin' with Darcy here? Keepin' him ta yerself all evenin'?"

"O'Reilly!" Sylvanie brightened. "Have you already met, then?"

"Didn't Monmouth himself introduce us when he first come in the door?" He paused and bussed her cheek. "I've the distinct honor o' bein' his oldest new friend here! Is that not the truth, m'fine lad?" O'Reilly winked at him again from under bushy, grizzled brows. If Sylvanie were Faerie Queen, O'Reilly was one of the wee folk writ large, although Darcy suspected his treasure lay in his silver tongue rather than in buried gold.

Sylvanie laughed. "Then perhaps you would not object to taking charge of his further introduction, for I must see to Moore and the entertainment. But I expect you to take good care of him," she warned, "for I shall return and demand him of you when I am finished." She nodded to them both but bestowed upon Darcy a lin-

gering caress of her fingers before removing her hand and threading her way gracefully through the knots of guests.

"I suppose that means she'll be wantin' you back sober, more's
the pity." Sir John sighed dramatically. "Ah well, what can no' be
mended must be endured. Here!" He stopped a servant and, lifting
two whiskeys from the tray, handed one to Darcy. "To endurin'!"
He toasted him and tossed it back.

"To endurance." Darcy repeated and lifted his glass as well. It
had been some time since he had tossed back any appreciable
amount of whiskey, and that which was served here was potent.
The liquor scorched a trail down his throat, but at least this time it
did not bring tears to his eyes. He brought the glass down to behold a smiling Sir John.

"There now, better this time, eh?" He then motioned round the
room with his glass, the remainder of his whiskey sloshing dangerously as he did so. "Know many of the others here?"

"Almost no one," Darcy replied. "Monmouth is a friend from
university. I met Syl— Lady Monmouth while visiting her brothers
in Oxfordshire last January. Moore I have heard sing before, of
course, but have not met."

"Would you be wantin' to meet anyone in particular?" Sir John
finished his glass and cast about him for a place to lay it.

"I am not certain." Darcy hesitated, surveying the crowd a moment before recalling the curious incident that had happened earlier. "Yes, Bellingham." Darcy looked down at Sir John and then
stayed him as he began to search the room. "He has already gone,
but perhaps you would explain something he said."

"Somethin' he said now?" O'Reilly's tone cooled. "Bellingham
says all too much, I'm thinking."

"It was a question, actually, which I apparently did not understand; for he took great offense at my reply."

" 'What have you got in your hand?' Would that be the question?" At Darcy's surprised nod, O'Reilly looked away and swore
under his breath. "And what did you answer him?"

"That I held a glass of wine . . ." O'Reilly almost choked at his answer. "Which was the truth; but he was listening for something else, was he not?"

"Oh, aye!" O'Reilly raised his eyes to Heaven, then shook his head. "You'll have observed, bright lad that you are, that most of these present at Sylvanie's gatherin' are of Irish descent or persuasion. He was testin' your sympathies to see where they might lie, and 'a glass of wine' was no the right answer!"

"Yes, he made that quite clear!" Darcy agreed. "But—"

"Ah, there's the darlin' and Moore beside her!" Sir John interrupted him, turning Darcy's attention to the door. Indeed, Sylvanie was there, posed enchantingly with her harp in her arms and the great Moore at her elbow. The crowd parted to allow them into the center of the room, applause rising as they passed. "Here, Darcy." Sir John deposited his glass, snagged another pair of tumblers from a tray, and handed him one. Looking about him, he saw that all the servants were busily engaged in distributing identical glasses to everyone present and that all were getting to their feet. "Wait for the toast now, lad!" Sir John nudged his arm and nodded his head toward their hostess and her famous guest as all grew quiet.

Holding her harp loosely in the crook of one arm, Sylvanie tossed back the curls that tumbled in rampant luxury over her shoulder and accepted with Moore a glass from a servant. The expectancy that gripped the room laid hold upon Darcy as well as all attention centered upon them. Suddenly, Sylvanie raised her glass. *"What have you got in your hand?"* she asked.

"A green bough!" those in the room thundered back, raising their glasses in turn.

"Where did it first grow?" Moore stepped up and raised his glass to the room.

"In America!" came the unison reply. Darcy looked down into the glass in his hand with consternation, at a loss as to what he should do. He felt he ought to know, he ought to decide and then act upon it; but how to begin such an enterprise eluded him.

"*Where did it bud?*" Beside him, Sir John bellowed out the question.

"*In France!*" The answer sliced through the air, then all once more grew silent as every eye returned to their hostess.

Sylvania let her gray-eyed gaze travel slowly over the room. They were entirely with her, of that Darcy had no doubt. She held them delicately but with surety in the palm of her hand as she stood in fierce beauty before them. A look of exaltation washed slowly over her face, recalling to Darcy memories of their conversations at Norwycke Castle. *Power,* she had said when last he had seen that look, *the power of riding the crest of passion, is life worth the living.* Had she proven it so? As she thrust her glass again high in the air, Sylvanie's voice rang out, a sudden clarion in the silence. "*Where are you going to plant it?*"

"*In the crown of Great Britain!*" The roar circled the room, and a hundred glasses of Irish whiskey were drained in an instant.

"Now, lad, now!" O'Reilly urged him as he wiped his lips with the back of his hand. "Ah, a glorious sight, isn't she?"

Darcy nodded. "Yes, she is." He brought the glass up and tipped it toward her. *To you, Sylvanie,* he toasted her silently, *and your passion for life.* At that moment a servant stepped up to Sir John with a tray on which he thankfully deposited his empty glass. Seeing it, Darcy brought the toast to his lips, only to have the man turn sharply toward him, knocking the glass out of his hand. With a startled exclamation from all three men, the heavy glass tumbler hit the floor with a dull thud.

"Your pardon, sir!" The servant ducked his head as he apologized and then went down on the floor to retrieve the glass. Darcy frowned at the man's broad back as he blotted at the carpet, recognizing him as the one who had arrested his attention earlier that evening. The man's face was properly averted from his betters, but there continued something about him—his movements, perhaps—that seemed so familiar. He rose then and, with his back to Darcy, proceeded to attend to Sir John, who was flicking at the droplets of whiskey that had been flung upon his waistcoat.

"Have a care, man!" Sir John bit out angrily, displeased by the man's futile attempts at remedy.

"Yes, sir," the servant responded, then more loudly, "*Excellent advice*, sir!"

"What?" Sir John demanded in surprise at the man's impertinence, but the servant was already bowing and thereafter whisked himself and the tray quickly into the crowd. "Cheeky blighter!" O'Reilly commented to Darcy, who stood frozen for a moment staring after the man in disbelief. That voice! It could not possibly be . . . ! He stretched to attention, trying to follow the servant's path through the room, but even his superior height could not afford him a clear view of his quarry.

"You must excuse me, O'Reilly! Your pardon!" he blurted out and stepped round him, but Sir John laid a strong hand upon his arm.

"Where are you off to, lad? Sylvanie will want to know," he demanded of him.

"I do not know." Darcy looked desperately after the servant. "You must excuse me!" Pulling away, he hurried in the direction the man had gone, dodging the servants and guests strolling the drawing room. Finally, he gained the door and slipped out into the still crowded corridor. Peering over and around the heads of the throng, he caught a glimpse of his prey entering a doorway farther down the hall. The man hesitated and then, as if come to a decision, turned to look him full in the face. Confirmed! Darcy did not know whether to give in to triumph, anger, or curiosity, for all three vied for the upper hand as he made his way down the hall to the last door. When finally free from the crowd, he quickened his stride, more so as his object appeared to urge him to hurry.

"What the—" he began, but the erstwhile servant frowned heavily at him and pulled him through the doorway, closing the door softly behind them. Darcy strode several paces into the room and then, rounding quickly upon his quarry, demanded, "What in God's name are you doing here posing as a servant, Dy?"

"Will you keep your voice down? You are bellowing like a blasted ox!" Brougham frowned at him again, causing Darcy to cross his arms tightly over his chest and return him the same. His Lordship ignored him, checking again at the door that none should overhear or disturb them.

"You are following me!" Darcy accused him. "Of all the—"

"No, I am *not* following you," Dy quickly shot back, then retracting his statement, added, "Not exactly. It happens that I was already engaged to come here tonight before you allowed Monmouth to goad you into accepting his invitation; although the idea of assigning you a keeper does have a certain merit to it! Good Heavens, Darcy, I warned you to stay away, and you walk right into it!"

"Into what? You talk in circles, Brougham!" Darcy returned, his temper rising. "And if you were invited, why warn me away? You make no sense!" He dropped his arms and, gesturing toward his costume, peered at his friend intently. "And why are you dressed as a servant? Is this some sort of odd start, Dy, some sort of prank?"

"No, Fitz." His Lordship sighed and looked to Heaven before returning his inspection. "But it *is* rather a long story, too long to relate under this roof."

Darcy nodded curtly. "I would imagine so. Come round tomorrow and tell me. Perhaps by then I shall be able to see the humor in it." He made to leave, but Brougham stepped in his path.

"You cannot go back!" He laid ahold of Darcy's shoulders. "Fitz, do you not realize what is going on back there? It is treason, old man—" Darcy's dismissive snort interrupted him. "Or the next thing to it, and you should not be seen among them!"

"Dy!" he warned him, "do you seriously expect me to believe that Monmouth invited me here to entertain me with a show of treason?"

Brougham held the breath he had taken in preparation to answer him back and, instead, looked at him with such piercing intensity that Darcy almost began to doubt himself. When finally he spoke, Dy dropped his hold of him and stepped back. "No, not to entertain you, Fitz, to blackmail you."

"That is preposterous!" Darcy burst out.

"Indeed? You were to be made drunk or, failing that, drugged and then 'discovered' in Her Ladyship's bedchamber by the 'outraged' husband and other suitable witnesses." Dy's voice tightened with loathing, then shaking his head at him, he continued with exasperation. "And from what I saw of you and Lady Monmouth tonight, such an eventuality would hardly be questioned. You were playing right into her hands!"

"*Her* hands?" Darcy repeated, now listening with more attention.

"Oh, Fitz! You cannot for a moment think that Monmouth concocted all this! I told you he was only an errand boy and a ham-handed one at that! Regardless"—Brougham dismissed His Lordship—"you would have then been assured of their silence in exchange for regular donations into a certain charity for the relief of orphaned Irish children." He laughed bitterly. "Of course, the true beneficiaries would be Irish revolutionaries, for that is Her Ladyship's driving passion. You were the perfect target, old man! Rich, in charge of your own fortune, and with a younger sister to protect. Then, to add spice to this evil brew, you are also someone with whom Her Ladyship has a score to settle."

"Lady Sayre." Darcy sighed heavily.

"Yes, Lady Sayre," Dy confirmed. "Lady Monmouth holds you responsible for her mother's death." He paused and looked searchingly at his friend. "Do you believe me now, Fitz, or would you like to see the glass I knocked out of your hand?" Dy picked up the tumbler from the tray and held it up to a branch of candles, where the smallest of specks could be seen still clinging to the bottom.

"O'Reilly?" Darcy asked, knowing the answer. Dy nodded. "Good God!" The closeness with which he had come to disaster took his breath away.

"Well, so He was this time, although you hardly deserve it," Dy observed drily. "Now, are you going to leave this nest of villains or must I arrange your kidnapping? Lady Monmouth is probably looking for you as we speak."

"But how did you know?" Darcy looked at his oldest friend in confusion. "What are you—?"

"Too long a story," he said over his shoulder as he turned back to the door. "You must leave . . . now!" Opening it, Dy peered out. "Good, there is still much activity in the hall and down to the door. Do you know the Fox and Drake on Portman Road?" Darcy nodded. "Meet me there in an hour, my friend, and I will answer your questions." For the first time that evening, he smiled, though wryly. "Well, some of them! Now get yourself out of here!" Clapping him on the shoulder, Dy then pushed his old friend out the door. "And be quick about it!" he whispered urgently and closed it behind him.

Although the corridor still teemed with Sylvanie's guests, Darcy at first felt suddenly, horribly alone and, then, like the world's greatest fool. Gathering himself together, he began to thread his way back through the throng to the head of the stairs. If he could leave without notice, it would be the greatest of good fortune, and nothing more would come from this night than a much-needed opening of his eyes to the political realities of a country at war, from both within and without. That, and an entirely tumbled-over understanding of one of his oldest friends! He still reeled from the sudden reappearance, despite the servant's clothing, of the Dy Brougham he had known in university, but that puzzle would have to wait for the Fox and Drake. His first task was to get out of Monmouth's town house and, as Dy had so succinctly recommended, be quick about it!

"Darcy!" The shout came from behind him. He knew it could only be Monmouth, probably sent by O'Reilly to hunt him down. Darcy hesitated, for a moment his breeding holding him hostage to convention, but Monmouth's second shout of his name propelled him toward the stairs. He had reached them, the post at the head of the stairs under his hand, when a grip closed about his arm from behind. "Darcy!" Monmouth breathed heavily. "The evening has only begun! You cannot be leaving?"

Monmouth's touch made his skin want to crawl, but he controlled the urge to pull away and turned back to his old hall mate with a remarkable calm. "Yes, I fear I must; another engagement, you must understand, which I ignore at my peril."

"But Sylvanie is to sing in only a few moments! Surely your appointment will allow for that!" Momouth urged him. "And she will be extremely disappointed if you do not stay and hear her. A song and a drink, what do you say, old man?" An undercurrent of panic colored the reasonable words of his request and the wary look upon his face, putting a period to any doubts Darcy may have had about Dy's veracity.

"Impossible, Monmouth," he replied firmly. "I am behind the time already and beg you will excuse me."

"You made no mention of another engagement when you arrived," His Lordship persisted. "Come, if something has offended, allow me to make amends. For old times' sake, Darcy."

"Old times' sake, Tris?" Darcy could no longer mask his disgust. "How could you?" he demanded of him and pulled away. Monmouth's protests were met by his back as he stalked down the stairs and requested his things from the footman. A flurry of activity warned Darcy that the plans for his entrapment had not yet been given over by all the participants. As he placed his beaver atop his head and took his walking stick from the footman, Lady Monmouth appeared at the head of the stairs.

"Darcy!" Her voice, low and entreating, called to him. Propriety and good breeding, he very well knew, demanded he acknowledge her, but right now his feeling about social niceties were that they could be damned! Taking his stick into a ferocious grip, he turned pointedly to the door, causing the doorman to spring for the handle and wrench it open.

"Another time, then," Sylvanie promised with a scornful laugh, "when you are less easily frightened by the world that is coming." Those in the hall and on the steps around her tittered appreciatively.

Darcy stood motionless, beyond measure angered and stung by her mockery and the public humiliation she had dealt him. Summoning every ounce of hauteur he possessed, he turned on his heel and raised cold eyes to her beautiful, taunting countenance.

"Never, madam," he answered her, biting off each word in solemn vow, "never on your life!" Not deigning to wait for a reply, Darcy swung back to the door and, with broad stride, walked out into the cool night air.

"The Fox and Drake, Portman Road," he instructed the driver of the first conveyance that pulled to a stop at the curb.

"Righto, guv'nah." The cabbie laid a finger to his brim, saluting him.

It was only after he'd been sitting back in the hansom's dark interior for a few blocks that the anger-wrought tension began to loosen its grip on Darcy and allow him to think. *Think!* He wrested the privilege of mocking himself from Sylvanie's duplicitous hands. *How have you fallen into the role of the world's greatest fool? That you have been deceived for years by one of your oldest friends and twice entered willingly into the orbit of a woman bent on using you for God knows what nefarious purposes? That the woman you love . . .* He looked out the window. The streets of London were alive yet with the city's more exalted citizenry and would continue so until the small hours of the morning. Ladies leaned on their gentlemen's arms, laughing and excited, eager for the glitter and whirl of gatherings within the lofty halls of the many ballrooms and drawing rooms promised by row upon row of stately homes.

Darcy closed his eyes against the sights, the yearning slicing through him, painful as a cut to the heart. Yes, the world's *greatest* fool! And what the world's greatest fool needed now was a drink!

The hansom pulled to a stop. Darcy climbed down and threw the fare up to the driver, who caught it handily. "G'night, gov'nah!" He nodded as he pocketed the coin.

"That remains to be seen," Darcy responded. The driver laughed and commanded his horse to walk on, leaving Darcy to inspect the front of the public house. Its sign hung brightly illuminated in lamplight, showing a strong young fox exuding a wide grin while a fat drake dangled from its jaws. "Almost," Darcy addressed the fox, which he had no doubt was a vixen. "But tonight the drake got away." He bent and opened the pub's door. Immediately, he was welcomed by its owner.

"What will it be, sir? I have a room available," the man offered cheerily.

"No, no room, just a table in a corner," he answered him. "Are you well stocked?"

"Why, yes, sir!"

"Good! Bring me your best brandy." The man's smile grew broader as he put a glass on a tray in front of him and began to open a bottle. "No, you misunderstand me." Darcy stopped him. "Not just a glass. Leave the bottle as well."

It was curious, Darcy reflected as he cradled the remains of his second glass of brandy, how every time his thoughts managed to fight their way up into the realm of his control, when he could begin to hope to direct them into rational avenues, they fell down again into a ghastly, maudlin tangle. He sat back and stared for a moment at the glinting amber liquid captured in the glass in his hand, then downed what remained of it. Where was Dy, anyway? If he would only come, the blasted sneaksby, the scoundrel! Acting like a positive coxcomb all these years! Laying the glass aside, he pulled out his pocket watch. Its hands danced wantonly but were not so wayward that he could not in the end verify that, indeed, an hour and more had passed without Brougham showing his face. He shoved the ill-behaved mechanism back into his waistcoat pocket. Well, when Dy did arrive, Darcy would tell him exactly what he thought of him! Yes, the delivery of a good dressing-down would serve admirably in putting a stop to this infernal brooding!

As if to pledge himself to his design, Darcy snagged the brandy bottle and poured himself another, but he missed the snifter's rim by a hairsbreadth, the liquid fire flowing instead down its side and puddling around its base. With an oath, he moved the glass. That he had fallen into distemper was the conclusion he came to as he sat in a corner of the Fox and Drake and finished his second glass of brandy. Try as hard as he might to argue otherwise, he was forced to concede that he had not yet spent any significant time without Elizabeth Bennet occupying the uppermost place in his thoughts. Nothing had served to dismiss her completely: not his anger at her accusations, his indignation at her opinion of him, or the monumental shock at her rejection of his suit. He imagined her wiping her hands of him, crowing her triumph in bringing him to his knees. Did she and that friend of hers, that Mrs. Collins, laugh together over his humiliation? Darcy's jaw hardened as he again picked up the bottle, this time finding the glass without mishap. Nothing helped relieve or even mitigate his disconsolation. Solitude betrayed him, sleep fled him, sport offered only a temporary reprieve, and Society—well, look at what his venture into Society had almost done to him! And now, here he was alone, in a strange public house, on his third glass, and with not even the comfort of a friend to keep him from getting ape-drunk. How had he come to such a pass? He retrieved the brandy glass and raised it in toast to himself. "To the World's Greatest Fool!"

"Oh, I would hazard you have rather heavy competition for that title, old man!" Dy sat down heavily in the chair across from him, his face drawn and tired.

"Where did you come from?" Darcy demanded without looking up and then downed a significant portion.

"The back door," Dy replied casually. "I know the owner. He

told me you have been drinking this." He placed a new bottle of brandy on the table. "But I did not realize that he meant by the bottle. Let me call for some ale or, better yet, some coffee—"

"This will do very well." Darcy cut him off and took up the bottle, placing it next to his original before pouring his friend a glass.

Dy eyed him speculatively. "I believe the last time we did something like this was the first time we met."

"I believe you are right." Darcy held up his glass.

"To old friends." Dy tipped his glass against Darcy's and joined him, then sank back into the chair with a sigh.

"Well, 'old friend.'" Darcy nursed his glass, watching the brandy swirl. "Are you finished playing footman for the night, or must you toddle off soon to play next as my lady's maid?"

"I suppose I deserve that, but I had hoped better from you, Fitz," Dy returned steadily. "I had also thought to find you sober enough to hear my explanation," he added as his friend took another drink.

Darcy raised a brow at him. "I'm sober enough to hear your miserable excuses for deceiving me . . . deceiving me into thinking you had abandoned your reason in favor of . . . of what? I never could fathom it, but I still counted you as friend." To emphasize the point, he replenished their glasses and, picking up his, lifted it to Brougham. "To old friends."

"We already drank to that," Dy drawled, a wry smile relaxing the tension in his face. He tipped his glass to Darcy's all the same and closed his eyes as the liquor warmed his senses. "Oh, what a night!" He shook his head and then leaned forward, his elbows on the table, and studied his friend. "And now I have you to contend with. Were you in charge of your faculties, I might know what to do; but three sheets—"

"Two," Darcy interrupted. "Haven't reached three . . . yet."

"Every bit of three sheets to the wind," Brougham insisted with a snort. "I do not think I have seen you bosky since that first meeting at university! It was over women then, and we both forswore them at the time, if I recall." At the remembrance, he suddenly sat up straighter, a look of alarm upon his face. "This is not about Lady Monmouth, I hope!" He gestured to the half empty bottle.

"Sylvanie?" Darcy peered intently at Brougham's face, the better to bring it into focus. "You must be mad!"

"You are not the first to think so!" His Lordship lapsed into thought. "You seemed rather taken with her tonight, and it naturally occurred—"

"Nothing 'natural' about Sylvanie, I assure you." Darcy laughed bitterly. Then, in a more pensive tone, he continued. "Nor any female, come to that! Not to be trusted, not a one of them— from first to last!"

"That is quite a sweeping condemnation!" Brougham sat back and folded his arms across his chest.

"But true, nonetheless." Darcy leaned forward and set down his glass. "In their girlhood they learn how to twist men about their fingers, beginning with their fathers, then . . ." He stabbed at the table with a finger. "Then, they start working their wiles on every honest-hearted man that crosses their path, turning him into a beef-witted Jack Pudding before he knows what he's about!"

"Indeed?" Brougham's eyebrows rose.

"Indeed!" Darcy returned and took another drink. He hardly tasted it now, but the fiery liquor seemed to flow into the gaping fissures of his wounds. "Ungrateful, teasing creatures!" he continued as his friend made himself comfortable, "designed by Nature to drive a man mad. They look up at you with eyes that leave you breathless and then steal your soul!" His voice lowered almost to a whisper. "Beautiful eyes that promise a paradise you alone may explore." He placed his glass down carefully on the table.

"And then?" His Lordship asked quietly after several minutes had passed in silence.

"Then, when a man's guard is down and his hand is out, they turn on him."

"*Touché?*" Brougham quizzed him.

"*Touché* and the whole damned engagement!" Darcy slumped back into his chair and rubbed at his temples. "Deceitful, Maygaming wenches, the lot of them!"

"Undoubtedly you are right," His Lordship agreed indifferently. "Perhaps Benedick's course is the wisest after all, and every man should do himself 'the right to trust none.' "

"Hear, hear." Darcy, raised his glass, the brandy sloshing dangerously.

Brougham lifted his as well. "To the forswearing of all the race of Deceitful Women . . . especially those of Kent!"

Darcy lowered his arm in flushed confusion. "Kent? Who said anything of Kent?"

His Lordship looked at him quizzically. "Why, you did; did you not?"

"Did I?" Darcy's brows lowered in perplexity with his faltering grasp on the conversation. "No, no, the trap was merely set there . . . in the park."

"In the park?" Brougham questioned, then his face cleared with recollection. "Oh, yes, Rosings Park! Your aunt's estate. Well then, it must be the Deceitful Women of London Who Visit in Kent that we are forswearing. And Heaven knows, I heartily agree with you there! To the Deceitful— No?" He stopped his toast as Darcy began to shake his head.

"Hertfordshire!"

"Oh, Hertfordshire!" he expressed with surprise. "Cannot say that I know much about the women of Hertfordshire, not enough to forswear them, I'm sure! You must enlighten me first, my friend."

A look of supreme distaste crossed Darcy's face. "They breed them like rabbits in Hertfordshire, at least five to a family! They have tabby cat mothers who do nothing but lie in wait for a likely gentleman to pounce upon and leg-shackle to their daughters, all of whom scamper as they please like hoydens about the country-side running after red coats!"

"In Hertfordshire?" Brougham returned with amazement. "I had no idea it was such an interesting place!"

"Interesting!" Darcy set his glass down with such force that the contents sloshed out, soaking the ruffle of his cuff and sleeve. "Blast!" He pushed away from the table, but not before some had dripped onto a leg of his trousers. His outburst caught the attention of the pub's young serving wench, who hurried over with a piece of toweling, but upon closer examination of her patrons, she also drew out the clean handkerchief that had served her as bodice lace.

"Here, dearie," she cozened Darcy as she dabbed the frilly square of cheaply scented holland about his sleeve. "None the worse!"

Withdrawing from her ministrations, he commandeered the piece of cloth with a tersely polite "Thank you, miss," and bent unsteadily to employ it upon his trouser leg.

"Yer welcome, I'm sure!" she simpered back to him, but as he did not immediately look up from his endeavor, she flounced away to more appreciative customers.

When he carefully sat back up, it was to behold Brougham's amused countenance. "Certainly you were in no danger in this disreputable shire; your way with women must surely have insulated you against any such encroaching or shocking females as you have described!" He paused as Darcy returned him a scowl. "Or perhaps not all were so shockingly behaved or enamored of red coats and gold shoulder braid?"

"Ha!" Darcy snorted, absently tucking the handkerchief into his coat pocket. "Dress the blackest villain in a red coat and he is instantly a saint whose whispered lies are more to be believed than another man's entire life and character!"

"Ah, a Serpent in the Hertfordshire garden!" His listener nodded sagely as Darcy took up his glass again and, noting that most of the brandy had spilled out, reached for the bottle. Brougham's hand forestalled him. "Here, Fitz, allow me," he drawled and poured him short. "Enough for our vow," he explained to Darcy's displeased frown, "which I take us to be offering up against your Hertfordshire Eve. Yes . . ." His Lordship waxed eloquent as Darcy looked on him in growing confusion. "A highly appropriate metaphor when one thinks on it. Serpent in the garden, Eve in the park—which is really nothing more than a large Garden, you un-derstand—whispers in her ear, Eve figuratively 'bites' and then serves you—our Adam—the core of bitter fruit. Yes, the symmetry is near perfect!"

Darcy's glass hit the table again. "What the Devil are you talk-ing about? I have never been in a garden with a woman named Eve!"

"Then of whom are we speaking?" Brougham asked inno-cently.

"Elizabeth, you idiotish wretch!" Darcy ground back at him. "Elizabeth!"

"Oh, is that the deceitful wench's name! Elizabeth!" Brougham looked relieved. "Then I may now in all good conscience offer the vow." He stood and lifted his glass as his companion fumbled for his own. "To the forswearing of Elizabeth, Ungrateful, Deceitful Wench . . ."

Darcy brought his arm back down, his mind a muddle. For-swear Elizabeth? She would never be his, he knew that well enough, but to vow against her? Curse even the memory of her? It was not even remotely possible!

". . . an Unworthy Creature of the lowest order . . ."

Darcy stared hard at his friend. Lowest order! Elizabeth? What did he mean by that? "No, not-not low," he mumbled as a vision of Elizabeth easily, graciously holding her own against his aunt's im-perious demands flashed through his mind.

". . . Despoiler of the Hopes of honest men . . ."

"No, not low," he argued a bit louder against the laughter that Brougham's oration was provoking across the room. His speech had by now attracted the attention of the pub's other patrons, who being already primed for any sort of mill, regarded a show provided by the gentry as especially entertaining.

". . . and, let us not forget, Tease, who after having led them on an intoxicating chase down the garden, or rather, park path . . ."

"No!" Darcy bellowed as he attempted to stand. The room swayed and howled with mirth, refusing to come clearly into focus.

"A Disgrace to— Pardon me?" Brougham inquired loftily. "I believe I was in the midst of—"

"How dare you, sir!" Finally, Darcy had found his feet and rose, belligerently intent upon putting an end to Dy's slanderous speech. "How dare you bandy about Elizabeth's name in a public house and in such an infamous manner!"

"Darcy." Dy began in a conciliatory tone, but his companion would have none of it.

"You are speaking of a lady, sir!" He was interrupted by jeers from across the room. "A lady," he insisted passionately over their calls, "of incomparable worth!"

"Darcy." Stepping between his friend and the pub's raucous patrons, Brougham laid an earnest hand upon his arm. "I would be honored to drink to such a lady . . . providing you sit down, my friend."

Eyeing him at first with some suspicion, Darcy slowly resumed his seat as Brougham did the same. For a time, they sat in silence as Darcy tried to read his friend's face through his self-inflicted haze but, he concluded, Dy was such a changeling to begin with that his state of inebriation was hardly a factor in the effort. With as much acuity as he was able to bring to bear, he searched Dy's face, and what he saw in his old rival and friend's countenance was a sincerity of concern and a warmth of sympathy that were impossible to discount as mere playacting. No, the playacting had been the ridiculous toast, the posing as a servant, maybe even the whole frivolous persona he had presented to the world for the last seven years! But here, now, was his truest friend in the world come back from a very long journey, and the timing of his return was impeccable.

Brougham broke their silence with a sigh and then, with a wry smile, leaned his elbows once more upon the table and looked Darcy square in the eye. "I think you had better tell me about her, old man," he prescribed, his voice compassionate but firm. "She must, indeed, be of incomparable worth if she has so won your heart."

From habit, Darcy bridled at Dy's quiet request that he lower his defenses; but the old reserve, the shield between himself and the world, had already been rent by a young woman from Hertfordshire. Why should he hold it up against his oldest friend? He would not reveal all; it was too much, and the details were unimportant now. But he would tell him something of it, enough to understand.

"Her name is Elizabeth," he began, looking past Dy's shoulder the better to maintain the shreds of something akin to dignity, "and I am the last man in the world that she could ever be prevailed on to marry."

CHAPTER 5

Though Thou Art Forsworn

"*D*arcy!" Brougham's agitated whisper pierced through Darcy's senses like the crack of a rifle as they struggled to navigate the front steps of Erewile House. He winced at the pain that reverberated through his head and tried again to put one foot in front of the other and still stay upright. To be perfectly honest, Dy was in charge of navigation and had been since they had departed the Fox and Drake a half hour before. The cool night air outside the public house had done nothing to revive Darcy's brandy-disordered faculties, so it had become Dy's unwelcome task to see him home and into Fletcher's capable hands. If Darcy were not already flushed from drink, he would have been from the supreme embarrassment he ought to have been feeling. He had no doubt that, come morning, he would feel every drop of mortification that he ought.

Gaining the top step, Brougham steadied his friend against the door with his shoulder and tried the knob. "It's locked!" he hissed to him, "which is as it should be, but it is a cursed inconvenience for us! Do you have a key?" Darcy fumbled beneath his coat in his waistcoat pocket and, after several tense seconds, produced his key to the obvious relief of his navigator. "Thank the Lord! Now, if we can manage not to raise a hue and cry once we are inside . . ." He bent to the keyhole and swiftly released the lock, but the door was still against them. "Another lock?" Dy looked up at him.

Darcy groaned. "Yes . . . forgot. Ordered before I left . . . for Kent."

"And have you also forgotten to acquire the key?" Brougham asked in exasperation. Sighing at Darcy's grunt of admission, he straightened and began a search of his own coat pockets. A soft "aha!" told Darcy that he had found what he searched for, and Dy once more bent to the lock plate of the front door. In a breath, the second lock was released, and the door of Erewile House swung back a few inches.

Darcy stared down in befuddled astonishment. "How did you manage that?"

"Practice," Dy answered. Dawn was only beginning to invade London's streets, but there was enough light for Darcy to make out his friend's bitter smile. "I shall tell you about it later," he whispered, "when you are sober and your head is not splitting. But now we must get you inside and, Lord help us, upstairs to your bedchamber without bringing your entire household down upon us."

"Georgiana," Darcy muttered, nodding his head in agreement and then wishing he had not. The movement started the pain inside his skull careening from one side to the other.

"Yes, Miss Darcy." Brougham reiterated the identity of the person they both most wished to avoid in Darcy's present state and offered him his shoulder. "Now, in you go!" Gratefully leaning on the proffered support, Darcy lifted one foot and hesitantly set it down upon the threshold as Dy pushed wide the door. With another push and a grunt, they were both inside and stood for a moment like errant schoolboys surveying the silent, empty hall. "All clear! There's a mercy!" Brougham looked about them and then steered Darcy toward the stairs. "Come on, then, old man," he encouraged, but Darcy could only grimace as each step's change in altitude caused another painful explosion in his brain.

When they had finally reached the top, he was soaked with perspiration from the effort and was forced to lean heavily upon his friend's shoulder merely to stay vertical. Fortunately, Dy knew his way quite well around Erewile House, and Darcy was spared the necessity of directing him to his chamber. Still, he barely restrained himself from groaning out a desperate thanksgiving when they finally stood before his door. "Almost there, my friend!" His Lordship gripped the knob and slowly twisted it, the click of the latch barely audible. "There's a candle, Fitz!" he warned, but Darcy had already jerked back and shut his eyes against the flame.

"Fletcher," he whispered, not yet daring to open his eyes beyond the merest slits. "He will likely be asleep in the dressing room. Get me to a chair. I *must* sit down!" He groaned, but Brougham made no further move into the room. "Dy?"

"That may present some difficulty," His Lordship returned drily. "Good morning, Miss Darcy."

"Georgiana!" Darcy's eyes flew open as he lifted his head in surprise. "Ahhh," he groaned as the light from the branch of candles in his sister's hand invaded his sight.

"Fitzwilliam!" He sensed the fear in her voice and not only heard but felt the thump of the silver candleholder as it hit the table next to the chair. "My Lord," she addressed Brougham, "is he hurt? Oh, Fitzwilliam!" She returned to him, her hands reaching for him and coming to rest lightly on his arms. "Set him down here, in the chair!" she instructed Brougham. "Or should he lie down? My Lord?"

"Yes, please." Darcy could only sigh, closing his eyes once more. That Georgiana should see him like this!

"The chair, I think, Miss Darcy," His Lordship decided. "His man can handle getting him to bed." Dy stiff-marched him over to the chair where his sister had awaited his homecoming. He helped

Darcy into the chair, sparing him the indignity of falling down into it as he probably deserved. Immediately, Georgiana was on her knees before him, her hands seeking his.

"But is he hurt, My Lord? Shall I call for a surgeon?" She looked over him anxiously. Darcy chanced opening his eyes just at the moment that her anxiety was replaced with a questioning frown, which in turn gave way to shocked surprise. The mortification that swept him was worse than he possibly could have imagined. "But he is—! Fitzwilliam cannot be—!" She looked up at Brougham with a face that begged him to deny it as Darcy flushed in guilt. Fumbling in his pocket for something to wipe the sweat from his brow, his hand closed on a handkerchief; but his efforts to bring himself to a semblance of order were met with a sharp, shocked "Oh!" from his sister and a rueful snort of laughter from Dy.

"What is it?" he asked, looking from one face to the other, baffled at their reactions. Dy motioned to his hand, from which drooped a very lacy bit of holland cloth. Darcy's countenance went crimson as he hurriedly stuffed it back into his pocket.

"I fear you are correct, although in only your first surmise, Miss Darcy," His Lordship returned gently, "but I beg you will take it in stride as I know you are able. Your brother has been through deep waters of late, and tonight was, I believe, an aberration, the nature of which he will be very loath to repeat."

Georgiana gripped her brother's hands tightly and, with more compassion than he had any right to, smiled encouragingly at him through misted eyes. "Yes, I understand, My Lord, better than you know."

"Well, then." Brougham sighed as he stepped away. "I shall rouse Fletcher, who will know exactly what to do, I have no doubt, and leave you both to your ministrations. May I call on you and Miss Darcy this evening?" he addressed a much subdued Darcy.

"Yes," Darcy answered with gratitude, "whenever you wish. Dy—"

"I know, my friend," His Lordship assured him. "And there is also the confidence that I owe to you for which we never found the time or the right circumstances. Tonight then." He bowed low. "Miss Darcy, Fitz." He let himself out through the dressing room door.

"A true friend," Darcy murmured as the door clicked shut. Hesitantly, he looked to his sister.

"Yes, he is," she agreed and turned a soft, wistful countenance upon him. "And he desires only your good. That I know." Her softness assumed an air of puzzled dismay. "But I would never have dreamed that he—that *you*—! Oh, what has happened to you, Fitzwilliam? Can you not tell me?"

"Ahem!" From the dressing room door came the extraordinarily loud sound of a throat being cleared, and precisely ten seconds later Fletcher's head cautiously appeared at its border. Darcy almost sighed with relief.

"Later," he promised his sister, his head pounding, "I will recount what is fitting; but at this moment and, I fear, for some hours to come, I will be suffering the consequences of every man fool enough to look for solace in a bottle. Please." He winced at the pain his efforts to rise from the chair were inflicting. "Go to bed, dearest, and let Fletcher assist me to mine."

"As you wish," Georgiana responded, her brave smile not quite erasing the concern that shaded her tired face, "but you will remain in my thoughts and prayers, Brother, until then." Reaching up, she quickly kissed his cheek and, with a look to him that spoke all her love, left him to his valet's care.

"Fletcher, your shoulder, man!" Darcy gasped as soon as the door behind his sister had clicked shut.

"Sir!" His valet set something down and was at his side in a moment.

"I believe I am about to be sick."

"Stand firm, sir!" Fletcher maneuvered him to the bed, where Darcy gratefully sank down, only to have a glass of some vile concoction thrust into his hands. "Drink this, Mr. Darcy! It will settle your stomach and go far toward clearing your head, sir."

"Or put me out of my misery entirely." Darcy looked into the glass with dubious distaste. "Where did you get it?"

"It is a recipe that even His Majesty the Prince has found effective." Fletcher looked suddenly abashed. "Although, I hasten to add, there is no comparison implied, sir."

Darcy managed to raise a brow. "I should hope not!" Sniffing it tentatively, he drew back with a grimace.

"It will help you sleep," his valet added and then stifled a yawn.

Stop acting like a child and take your medicine, Darcy reproved himself. *You deserve no such sympathy or relief as you have met with tonight!* He gulped down the liquid, which was every bit as vile as he had suspected.

"There, sir." Fletcher took the glass. Setting it down, he began peeling away Darcy's coat and waistcoat, then unbuttoned his shirt. "Lie down, then." Darcy let himself sink back onto the pillows and slowly brought his legs up onto the bed. Deftly removing his shoes, Fletcher set them with the rest of his clothing and returned to throw a blanket over his supine form.

"Thank you, Fletcher," Darcy breathed out, his eyes closed. "I'll ring for you when I am able."

"Very good, sir." His valet gathered up the discarded clothing and made for the door.

"Fletcher!"

"Yes, sir?"

"In my coat pocket."

"Yes, sir?"

"Did you find something?"

"Yes, sir." Fletcher's even-voiced professionalism betrayed nothing concerning the nature of his discovery.

"When it is laundered, please have it sent to the Fox and Drake along with half a crown."

"Very good, sir. Good night, sir."

Darcy heard the door shut but little more as a blessedly deep, dreamless sleep claimed him for the first time in weeks.

The magnitude of the headache that greeted Darcy the next day was less than he had feared it would be, and even that would soon be soothed by the powders that Fletcher had carefully left beside his water glass sometime during the morning. Leaning on his elbow, he reached over from the bed, poured the medicine into the water, and watched as the early afternoon sun caught and reflected the particles as they drifted and dissolved on their way down the column of liquid. Drifting and dissolving . . . not unlike himself, he reflected. He drank it in one swallow and then sank back against the pillows, closing his eyes again. He had done all that his society and breeding expected and more. He had, after his sire's death, set himself to be like him—the best man he could be in all his deal-ings, whether as landlord, master, brother, or friend. He held him-self to scrupulous honesty in his business concerns and exercised unfailing caution in his social affairs. Yet in all the upright princi-ples he imbibed and all their attendant expectations in whose pre-cise fulfillment he took pride, he saw now that he was a mere observer of life, a creature of convention and propriety. Never had he allowed the world beyond his immediate family any claim upon him. In point of fact, he was bred and nurtured to that view. Like a chess master, he had ordered his life according to his own unbri-dled prejudices and the conceits of his class, congratulating him-self on his adherence to them and dismissing all that did not conform to them as unworthy of his consideration . . . until Eliza-beth.

Darcy's heart turned over in his chest as her name brought home to him every knot of frustration and ache of longing he had ever had of her. Elizabeth, the contradiction of all his expectations. How could he ever have anticipated that on that one fateful night in a hedgerow village in Hertfordshire, amid the most undistinguished company he had ever been called upon to suffer, he would meet both his Nemesis and his Eve, that the dissolution of his carefully contrived existence was begun? Ending, he reminded himself with a groan, in a nest of political and social intrigue and the bottom of a brandy bottle in a strange public house. He flushed with embarrassment and disgust as he remembered his behavior of the evening before. Thank God, Dy had been there! Because of his friend's peculiar eccentricities, he had succeeded only in making an ass of himself. It could have been very much worse, but that did not dilute the hot shame and repugnance he felt at his weaknesses displayed them.

He opened his eyes and stared up at the ceiling. He must rise and face the day and reflect carefully upon what all that had happened revealed about his character. It was not a pleasant prospect. Already he knew himself to be much diminished in his own estimation. How, then, must he appear in the eyes of his beloved sister? Had his drunken display lost him her respect? Would his confessions of weakness today sink him even further in her regard? The possibility sent a stab of fear through his body. How was he to exert his care and guidance of his sister if he no longer commanded her respect, if every decision he issued was received not with confidence but with dubious hesitancy? For that matter, how confident did he remain in himself? Putting away that fearful thought, Darcy slowly pulled himself upright, pausing to test his equilibrium before swinging his legs over the edge of his bed. The resulting pain in his head was a dull one thanks to Fletcher's powders and, possibly, that witch's brew he'd downed. At least he had slept.

The clock on his mantel struck three, announcing the fact that the day was fast waning and his interview with Dy would soon be upon him. Darcy was more than curious about what Brougham would confide concerning his strange behavior and turn of personality over the years since university, but he also entertained a maddening uncertainty about what Dy had made of his drink-induced confession of the previous evening; and, worse, what he might do with it. He drew up short at the thought. Exactly what *had* he confessed? Darcy strained to remember how the evening had played out after he and Dy had resumed their seats at the Fox and Drake.

"You had better tell me." Dy had pinned him with a compassionate air containing not a trace of pity but rather the heartfelt regard of an old friend. Slowly, finally, Darcy opened his mouth, and what had been his most private concern seemed to rush out of him: his initial interest, his resistance and caution, and then his eventual fascination, desire, and love.

" 'Thy likeness, thy fit help, thy other self, Thy wish exactly to thy heart's desire,' " Dy quoted absently to himself after Darcy had finished, then whistled under his breath. "Good heavens, Fitz, I know you well, my friend; and having said that, I must say that your Elizabeth must be an extraordinary young woman to have tied you into such excruciating knots!"

"She is not *my* Elizabeth, but you are correct"—he sighed— "she is an extraordinary young woman."

"So you have said. Pardon me, but I take it from your opening salvo that, despite your manifold reservations and doubts, you *did* offer marriage."

"Yes," he stated. "After I had committed myself to forgetting her, we were thrown together in Kent. Her closest friend had wed my aunt's parson several months before, and Elizabeth had come for a visit not knowing that I would be attending Lady Catherine during that same time. You can imagine my shock to find her there, neatly lodged on the edge of my aunt's park and already quite Her Ladyship's favorite."

"Shock! I would say panic as well! You were in a hopeless position! In love against your better judgment, only recently committed to putting her out of your mind, and there she is!" Brougham shook his head. "And so easily to hand!"

There was a long silence then, but not an awkward one. Dy

merely nodded his head in commiseration and then looked away, the tired lines of his face growing deeper as he seemed to withdraw into private contemplations. In time he rose and called to the serving girl for a pot of strong coffee and cups, then taking his seat, he turned again to his friend with a single word. "Then?"

Darcy took a deep breath. "Then, after nights of wrestling with what I owe to my name and station, the prospect of the justifiable disapprobation of my family and Society, and the consequences of allying myself and Georgiana with a family of questionable propriety, I succumbed. Life, a future without her seemed an impossibility. 'Part of my soul' since we are quoting Milton." Dy nodded. "I began to court her, or at least I thought that was what I was doing. At the time, I thought her subdued responses were due to modesty and her consciousness of the disparity in our stations; but in that, as in so much else, I was completely mistaken." He laughed grimly. "I had made up my mind to ask for her hand, you understand, but found it difficult to finally come to the point. Eventually, an opportunity presented itself, and I leapt upon it. She was alone at the parsonage; I went to her."

The coffee arrived, delivered by the pub's owner himself, who cast a questioning glance at Dy as he laid out the cups. Brougham responded with a weary smile. "I will close up for you." Waving the publican away, he then poured them both deep cups. By this time, they were almost alone, closing time having past. "You went to her," Dy prodded.

"And she refused me," Darcy responded grimly.

"There is more to the story than that!" Dy returned.

Darcy closed his eyes, his jaw working as the scene, so oft remembered, sprang easily into even his inebriated consciousness. "More? Oh, yes, there is more," he answered bitterly. "I professed my love in the strongest terms and, with even more vigor, gave her to know all the struggles I had overcome before appearing at her door to tell her so."

"Your struggles," Dy repeated slowly. "Pardon me, but did I

hear you aright? You gave her to know all the reasons you should *not* be making her an offer of marriage?" Setting down his coffee, Brougham regarded his old friend in fascination. But after a moment's reflection, the corners of his mouth hinted at an upward turn and he began to nod his head in agreement. "Yes, yes, that would be the Darcy approach, wouldn't it? No need to pander to the lady's sensibilities now, is there?" he offered in tart sarcasm. "Her attractions had prevailed over the inflexible Darcy canon, and what was more natural than that she be made to know her extreme good fortune and how little she deserved it!" Laughing humorlessly into the dangerously narrowed eyes Darcy set upon him, he smacked the table, setting the coffee to dancing. "Yes, only you, my friend, would make the lady's general unfitness the leading topic in a proposal of marriage. Pray, enlighten me! Which of your scruples led you into such a confession?"

"Honesty . . . honor . . . pride—call it what you will!" he bit back angrily.

"To be sure, it was one of them, but it is for you to call, not I!" Dy retrieved his cup and settled back. "Please, continue. How did the lady respond?"

Darcy hesitated, fallen as he was under Brougham's satirical eye, but the conviction that relating the painful events would release him from the tangled confusion that gripped him body and soul propelled him on. "She sat in utter silence." He closed his eyes as he spoke, the scene vividly alive in his mind. "Her color high, neither looking at me nor replying to my suit. I was stunned at such a response," he continued, looking up at the smoky beams of the pub's ceiling. "It was hardly what I expected. Perhaps she did not believe me, I thought, or perhaps the prospect was too much for her." His gaze returned to meet his friend's. "I pressed my suit, desiring her to know that I had considered our proposed union from every conceivable angle for months, that my offer of marriage was not the result of a schoolboy's infatuation but a well-considered proposal that took into account our relative situations in life."

Whistling low, Brougham shook his head. "Why, I would venture there is scarcely a woman in all England who would refuse you an offer to become mistress of Pemberley no matter how pompously you came or how insensitively the offer was made! With all that before her, within her very grasp, yet she was silent! Extraordinary!" He paused, allowing them both time to ponder it before concluding, "And then, despite the immeasurable advantages she and her family would gain, she refused you! She had taken a very great offense, I imagine?"

Darcy laughed grimly. "She took not only offense but the offensive as well! My character was called into blackest question due to Wickham's lies to her months before and then—"

"Wickham! The son of your father's steward Wickham?" Dy asked in surprise. "Odd that he should turn up after all this time and in Hertfordshire! Is he the red coat—but of course, he is. In the military now, is he?" Darcy nodded and drank a bit of the coffee. "Go on," Dy encouraged.

"Then she laid into me about her sister and Bingley."

"Ah, so this is where Bingley comes in! The Unsuitable Hertfordshire Miss about whom you enlisted my help at Lady Melbourne's is your Elizabeth's sister?" Darcy had nodded again and then waited for Brougham's laugh. It did not come.

"She blames you for her sister's disappointed hopes," he stated flatly.

"And she is right to do so, although I had considerable help from Bingley's own sisters. They did not want any Hertfordshire relations of that sort, and I could not but agree . . . at the time."

"I remember," Brougham replied, then sitting up straighter, he continued. "It is most unfortunate that she discovered your hand in the matter. The death knell of your hopes, I suppose?"

"Death of them? Hardly!" Darcy cried. "She gave me to know in what light she had held me from our very first encounter, which had convinced her that, of all men, I exhibited the epitome of arrogance and conceit. This charming sketch of my character furnished her primary objection to me and laid the ground for her later summation: I am an unfeeling monster who ruins men at whim and dashes the hopes of virtuous maidens."

"Such animosity! And you never suspected?" Dy's brows furrowed deeply.

"No, fool that I am!" Darcy slumped back into the chair. "As I was saying when you came in, 'the World's Greatest Fool.' "

"Well . . . well," Brougham repeated with a sigh. "I believe that is enough for tonight. You need to go home. *I* need to go home! It has been a very long day and night, my friend, and ranks among the most interesting in my experience. But you need to go home," he emphasized again. Darcy could not but agree. Struggling up out of the chair, he swayed and blinked until Brougham reached out and steadied him. He managed to walk to the door, but while he waited for his friend to close up the pub for its owner, the night air hit him like a blow to the head, and his stomach heaved.

"Now, this *does* recall university days," Dy remarked wryly before stepping out from the shadows to hail a passing cab.

"Where to, gov'nah?" the cabbie called down, then added, "Is yer friend there all right? It'll be extra if'n I got ta clean up after you!"

"He'll do," Dy called back as he piloted Darcy toward the step up into the cab. "Grosvenor Square. Take the turns with care, though, and I will double your fee!"

Slowly and with deliberation, Darcy tucked his pocket watch into his waistcoat pocket and adjusted the fob as Fletcher took a whisk across the shoulders of his frock coat. They, both of them, stood silently before the mirror in his dressing room as they had countless times in the past, about the daily business of preparing him to meet the world as a gentleman. Everything was in place: his pocket watch, his seal, a handkerchief—his own, this time—sequestered neatly in his coat. His clothing fitted perfectly to his frame, a modest but artistic knot lay about his neck, his shoes shone, his chin was smooth. He appeared every inch as he should have until he dared look at the face in the dressing mirror, which with its drawn lineaments and bloodshot eyes, declared his pose a fraud. Quickly, he looked away, but not before glimpsing Fletcher's carefully bland countenance reflected at his shoulder. There had been no impertinences this day, no quotations from the Bard concerning his state of the previous night, just quiet service performed with a minimum of display and an almost complete absence of noise. Although Darcy found himself grateful for the consideration, it also represented to him the cautious uncertainty into which he had cast his household with his unprecedented departure from his usual habits.

It was now half past four, or so had said his pocket watch. He could hardly believe it; he had never before arisen so late in the day. It was an altogether disorienting experience to go about the movements of early morning in the late afternoon. That, along with the queer sensations in his stomach and the slow ordering of his mind, gave the present moment a strange, fantastical air. He did not like it at all.

"Mr. Darcy?" Darcy looked over to his valet, his expression inviting him to continue. "Is there aught else you desire, sir?"

"Oh, a multitude of things!" A smile pulled briefly at his lips at the return of humor to Fletcher's eyes his wry tone had evoked, but he continued somberly, "But most of all the recovery of the last twenty-four hours so that I could spend them more profitably. I should have heeded your advice."

Coloring at the praise, his valet looked away. Darcy pulled at his cuffs and then at his waistcoat. "Am I ready for Miss Darcy?"

"Assuredly, sir." Fletcher bowed and left at his master's nod.

Strolling back into his bedchamber, Darcy was greeted by a bored and yawning Trafalgar. Although the dressing room door was no obstacle to him, the hound had acquired a healthy respect for his master's valet and that man's active opinion of the presence of animals within his artistic realm. Therefore, as fascinating as all his master's activities in that most sacrosanct of rooms were, Trafalgar exercised a rare discretion where it was concerned and waited without the door for Darcy to emerge. Seeing him come at last, he scrambled to his feet, his eyes fixed in hope upon his master's face.

"No, not today, Monster!" Darcy was forced to dash Trafalgar's simple canine hopes. "I must see Miss Darcy . . ." The hound's ears wilted even as Darcy reached down to scratch them, and with a sharp snort, he stalked over to the door, nosed it open, and left Darcy staring after him in dismay. Even to his hound, it appeared, he was a sad disappointment!

Following in Trafalgar's offended wake, Darcy strode down the hall and then the steps of an Erewile House frozen in silence. The clatter of his shoes upon the stairs so sullied the unnatural quiet that the sound brought Witcher out into the hall with a harsh reprimand upon his lips before he realized who it was that had transgressed his orders.

"Oh! It is you, sir! I beg your pardon, sir." The elderly butler's eyes widened in embarrassment at nearly ringing a peal over his master. In both their younger days, such peals had occasionally been rung, but that had been many a year ago. Witcher's stolid demeanor reasserted itself as he bowed and held himself in readiness for his master's orders for what remained of this very strange day.

Darcy gestured in dismissal of the offense. "You would do me a courtesy by lifting the ban, Witcher, and relieve the staff as well, I imagine." He cast about then for something, anything, that smacked of his normal course. The more quickly his household fell back into its accustomed patterns, the sooner this aberration would be forgotten. "And send coffee to the Small Parlor, please," he ordered.

"Yes, sir. At once," his butler answered, but then continued. "Mr. Darcy, sir, Lord Brougham called earlier and left his card for you with instructions that you read his note. I placed it on your desk, sir."

"When did he call?" Darcy asked in surprise. Come and gone already, had he?

"Two o'clock, sir. Miss Darcy passed by the hall and spoke to him briefly, but he stayed no more than ten minutes, sir, as was proper."

"Thank you, Witcher." Darcy turned in the direction of his study, his curiosity awakened. "And send round that coffee, if you will."

"Very good, sir."

Free to satisfy the mystery of Dy's early visit, Darcy entered his study, and striding past Georgiana's portrait, which sat there on an easel until Unveiling Day, he went directly to his desk, where an elegant, gilt-edged calling card rested in a silver tray. Snatching it up, he sank into his chair and flicked it over.

> *Fitz,*
>
> *Will call again later and for dinner as Miss Darcy has invited me to dine tonight! I strongly advise you to stay home today. Trust your sister to receive the truth aright. She, also, is an exceptional young woman!*
>
> *Dy*

Darcy grimaced at the message, a hot flush creeping up the back of his neck. "An exceptional young woman!" Yes, he had bled quite freely in the pub last night, there was no question. By turns, Dy's wit and sympathy had teased everything of consequence out of him save the dangerous knowledge of Elizabeth's identity. Sighing, he tossed the card onto the desk and then sat back, his fingers working at his temples. He had felt such a relief at the time finally to tell aloud the entire chronicle of the wretched affair, but the discordance of his own perception of the tale as he told it and the memories of his friend's responses to it preyed on his mind.

Yes, yes, that would be the Darcy approach, wouldn't it? Dy had skewered him with sarcasm. *Only you, my friend, would make the*

lady's general unfitness the leading topic in a proposal of marriage!
Darcy winced. Was that what he had done? His memory ranged
over the first minutes of that awful interview once more. What had
he said in that ill-fated suit so undesired by its object? Good Lord!
He remembered it so plainly now! He had plunged straightway
into an examination of the injurious deficiencies of station and
consequence her family represented. He had spoken of degradation and social censure, following it with a warm description of
the certain wounds to his family that would be incurred as a result
of his surrender to inclination. In short, he had talked only of
himself, his family, his consequence, and her "unfitness," then
claimed a fastidious abhorrence of disguise as his justification!
Darcy sucked in his breath. He had insulted her abominably, then
excused the recitation of his vaunted scruples on the grounds that
they were natural and just! He closed his eyes and saw again how
her eyes had flashed as she had rejected his insolent proposal.

Natural and just? Had he ever considered her feelings? No! He
raked a hand through his hair and then dropped his head into his
hands. Despite all her early signs to the contrary, despite all the wit
and vivacious honesty about her that had attracted him, despite
even his own deeply held desire for a marriage characterized by
love and friendship, he had treated her with a reprehensible condescension and insensitivity. Why? Why had he done so? *Pray, enlighten me!* Dy had jibbed at him. *Which of your scruples led you
into such a confession?* His disguise was finally rendered transparent. It was family pride—his pride—that all his life had invariably
set at naught those outside his circle and tempted him to think
meanly of the sense and worth of the rest of the world. Elizabeth
had felt it, called it what anyone outside his concern would agree it
to be, what even Dy had seen it to be: *pride* attested by an arrogance of mind, a conceit of class, and a self-absorption that disdained to acknowledge the rightful feelings of others.

Darcy's chin sank to his chest as the truth fell like hammer
blows upon his faltering conscience. Pride, not a refined set of

scruples, had been his master in this enterprise from beginning to end! He struck his fist on the desk and, pushing away, threw himself into an agitated pacing of the room. What had he ever said or done that had not been tempered by it or could not be traced back to it? He turned, his eyes coming to rest upon Georgiana's portrait. Slowly advancing on her beautifully posed image, he halted before it, examining it with new perspective. Yes, his sister had unwittingly given him the key that morning she had questioned him concerning his portrait. She had expressed her discomfort with the untruths she claimed her own presented. *I hoped to God that one day I would* be *the man in the painting,* he had answered her while the keen edge of his failure in Elizabeth's eyes had flayed away at his estimation of progress toward that goal.

That he was not yet the man in the painting he had that day freely admitted to himself with some pain; but now, as he thought again of that portrait, Elizabeth's charge came against him with new clarity. *Had you behaved in a more gentlemanlike manner . . .* Seething with anger and self-pity since it was delivered, he had retreated into irascibility, yet he had not been able to bring himself to curse her memory for the simple truth that, with those words, she had demanded of him the man depicted in his portrait. His lack in that regard, he now saw with horror, had been not merely in degree, in isolated specifics, or only where Elizabeth was concerned, but in essentials that reached into the core of who he believed himself to be.

An appalling certainty broke upon him that the very path on which he had embarked toward his goal had been, from the beginning, terribly flawed, tainting and distorting everything that had followed. Pride was not a weakness, he had loftily instructed Elizabeth, when under the good regulation of a superior mind. Good God, what arrogance! But it did explain all: his aloofness from others, his reputation in Society, his suffocating hatred of Wickham, his attraction to Sylvanie, his interference in Bingley's happiness, and most devastatingly, his struggle against his own starkly human need and love for a certain extraordinary gentlewoman of diminished consequence. The pervasiveness of it threatened to overwhelm him. An abhorrence of disguise, had he? Indeed, he was a master of it, having deceived himself utterly!

Ten difficult and humiliating minutes of self-reproof later, Darcy entered the Small Parlor of Erewile House to find his sister curled comfortably on a divan, bent over a book, with the remains of tea lying on the low table in front of her. At the sound of his footstep, she looked up, her face filling with relief that he had at last arrived. "Fitzwilliam!" she exclaimed. Then tempering it with a return of uncertainty, she apologized. "I am sorry; you have missed tea, or rather it has grown cold and stale! Shall I ring for new?"

"No, thank you, Witcher is bringing coffee." He smiled at her and then, sweeping her feet off the divan, sat down beside her. "But first, I have something I wish to say."

"Yes, Brother?" Georgiana sat very straight, her countenance solemn.

"My girl . . ." He reached for her hands and, holding them to his chest with one hand, nudged up her chin with the other. "I have not behaved toward you as an elder brother should and, in so doing, have caused you pain and denied you what is your due." He breathed in shakily. "I cannot reveal everything that has occasioned my ill behavior, for it involves others; but what is due you, I will." Bowing his head, he grasped her hands tightly. "I have come to beg your forgiveness, Georgiana, and beg I must; for I have done nothing that would recommend myself to your mercy."

A tear slipped quickly from his sister's lashes and traced a path down her cheek to fall upon his hand at her chin. "Dearest Brother." She gave a small gasp. "Freely and with all my heart!"

"As quickly as that!" He bit his lip, looking down upon her glossy tresses. "Do you ask no penance?"

"No deeds, no penance," she answered, shaking her head.

"Mercy requires neither." Georgiana's smile was pure joy. "I would rather tell you a story. Will you hear it?"

"I will listen, dearest, and carefully." A knock at the door signaled the arrival of his coffee. After Georgiana had poured and he had supplied himself with the first solid food in almost an entire day, he settled back as comfortably as was possible on the divan. "Now, your story," he prompted, "after which, I beg you will permit me to explain a little concerning my behavior of late and what you saw last night. Is that agreeable?"

"Yes, above all things." Georgiana nodded, tucking her hand intimately against his arm. She allowed him to pull her head comfortably against his shoulder before drawing a deep, tremulous breath. "There once was a foolish young girl who, save for the mercy of God, nearly ruined her family and her beloved elder brother by putting herself into the power of a wicked man . . ."

It would have been impossible to keep an account of how many times during her narrative Darcy went hot, then deadly cold. Wickham's treachery, his smooth and unscrupulous seduction of his generous benefactor's daughter, Darcy's own innocent sister, stirred into flames the fury that had lain smoldering in his breast for almost a year. As Georgiana spoke of their meetings under the complacent eye of her companion, Mrs. Younge, anger and guilt very nearly choked him. What he said, what he did when she had finished, he knew to be of the utmost importance. If he had learned anything in the last weeks, it was that he might no longer entertain a careless confidence in his ability to deal rightly with his fellow man. But when his sister related how she had succumbed to the blackguard's urgent plea that they elope, her words of self-recrimination forced them from him.

"No, Georgiana! Dearest girl!" he remonstrated, holding her close. "What chance did you have against him?" He stroked the curls that tumbled against his shoulder. "You have been too gener-

ous with me, for the *world* can see that it is I who am to blame!
You had no defenses against him, for neither was I with you to
shield you nor have I any credible reason for my absence. I should
have taken you to Ramsgate or wherever you desired to go!" Releasing her, he rose and walked blindly to the hearth. Leaning his
head against the cool marble, he took a deep, shuddering breath. "I
neglected you. And for what? Nothing! Nothing half as important
as your well-being. God and you forgive me!"

"No, Fitzwilliam." Georgiana's negation vibrated delicately in
the air between them. "I lacked nothing in the way of true defenses
against his blandishments. Credit me at least with knowing what
was right and what was due my family!" She rose and came to him,
laying a hand upon his back. "What I lacked was the character to
reject his appeals. He played to my sympathy and romantic
dreams, yes, but he also encouraged my vanity and fed my discontent with countless pointed insinuations."

Darcy shook his head and turned away.

"Brother, I have always been encouraged to think so well of
myself. Insulated by wealth and rank from any serious demand
upon my character, I had little experience of its worth. I have since
learned that in those more important things I am poor, helpless,
and needy. It was the most important lesson I have in this life to
learn.

"So, you see, Fitzwilliam." She laid earnest hold of his arms.
"You may not take upon yourself the entire blame. But for what
blame you do hold in it, dear Brother, I forgive you with all my
heart."

Darcy looked down at the young woman, anxiety for his receipt of her absolution troubling her features. He had gotten what
he had hoped for in this part of his confession, but it seemed altogether too easy.

"I was unforgivably selfish, Georgiana!"

"Brother." Georgiana tried to stem his confessional flow.

"I should have done—"

"Fitzwilliam! I know you are selfish!" she exclaimed and then laughed at his affronted expression. "You are usually the most kind and generous of brothers, but with others, and also at times with me, you *do* look to your own concerns first. Oh!" she cried, "please, do not frown so when I merely agree with what you have confessed! Did I not forgive you already? More and I will suspect you of taking pride in your confession!"

The blush that colored his face he would have wished due more to contrition than to the embarrassment and chagrin he truly felt. It seemed he could not even confess his faults without a display of pride. "Well, ahem, I thank you, then." He cast about, unable to look his sister in the eye. "You are very kind."

"No, not 'very' kind, for now"—she turned and, resuming her seat on the divan, indicated the place next to her—"it is your turn, and I hold you to your promise."

His turn! How was he to begin? Ignoring her invitation, he circled behind her and across the room. The rustle of her gown informed him that his progress was being followed. His bid for time to collect himself denied, he turned back and, with a sigh, sat down beside her.

He closed his eyes and leaned back. "You will remember my letter from Hertfordshire about a certain young woman. We spoke of her at Christmas, I believe."

"Yes, Miss Elizabeth Bennet."

Darcy opened one eye to peer down at her. "You remember her name?"

"Oh, yes." Georgiana's gaze was wide with expectancy. "I could not easily forget the name of a woman who had caught your interest and approval so well as she had."

"Yes, well." Darcy sighed. Then he began, in a fashion, to acquaint his sister with all that had occurred, the memories crowding upon him too swiftly, too poignantly to offer a precise chronology.

"At Rosings, I found my attraction to her growing stronger each day. I came to the point that, despite the manifold obstacles, I decided I could not live without her. I began to court her, at once eager to conclude the matter and ashamed of what I regarded as the sure consequences of my choice. My ambivalence was so complete that my object had not the slightest suspicion she was being so singled out. When finally I could deny my desire no longer and went to her, she greeted the offer of my hand with cool dismissal, professing herself surprised that I had held her in such regard."

"She refused you!" Georgiana looked up at him, incredulous. "No, it cannot be! There was a mistake, some misunderstanding—"

Darcy took her hand between his, quieting her. "Yes, there was a mistake and a misunderstanding." He shook his head at the hope that began to light her eyes. "It was my mistaken conceit that intervened between Elizabeth's sister and Charles. Elizabeth had only that morning discovered my hand in her sister's unhappiness and justly tasked me with it. The misunderstanding . . ." He paused. Must he reveal to her Wickham's reappearance? "The misunderstanding concerned a malicious rumor about me that Elizabeth had no reason not to believe given my ill behavior toward her earlier. Of course, once she knew of my interference in the former, she was disposed to believe me perfectly capable of the meanest injustice."

"But you explained this, surely!" Georgiana protested. "I know you must have been sorry for what you had done!"

He gripped her hand more tightly. "I am sorry to say, I was not. Her rejection so pained and humiliated me that I justified myself to her at every turn." He sighed. "We exchanged words that I will regret to the end of my life. Later, I wrote her a letter explaining my actions in regard to her sister, for which she will never, I believe, forgive me. As for the misunderstanding, I have hopes of being acquitted in that quarter, but none so strong as to support a rapprochement. Her opinion of me and my faults, she made quite clear. No, she does not, nor can she ever, love me, my dear." His voice dropped.

"Dear Brother!" Georgiana's pity was sweeter than he had ever suspected pity could be.

"I raged against the crushing of my heart and the advent of a joyless future. I blamed her for deceiving me, fate for toying with me, everyone and everything save myself. As you said, we have been brought up to think well of ourselves, perhaps too well. Since my return from Kent, I have meanly thrashed about in my pain without a thought for those who care for my well-being. Last night, despite good counsel, I plunged into dangerous company for no better reasons than an appeal to my pride and the flattery of my person. It took Lord Brougham's intervention to bring me to my senses, yet I rewarded his trouble with drunkenness. In my pride and conceit I have behaved abominably, foolishly. I stand shamed." He swallowed hard. "I am not the man I had thought to become, before the memory of our father. Further, I have given you pain, Georgiana, most selfishly," he concluded, "and I am heartily sorry for it." He released her hand and waited, steeling himself for whatever should come.

"Brother," she gasped, putting fingers to her lips to force back the sob in her voice. "Such pain, Fitzwilliam! I knew your anger, your isolation came from hurt of something, but this! To love so and receive . . ." Emotion caught her up again, preventing her from continuing.

"My pain . . ." He reached into his coat pocket and brought out his handkerchief to daub at her cheeks. "My pain is not sufficient excuse for my actions even if I had not brought its cause upon myself."

"What a sorry pair we make." She looked up at him as he did her his gentle service. "We have, both of us, been given to see ourselves and have responded like children, unwilling to be taught and resentful of our discipline."

"But *you* are reconciled, I think." He looked at her closely. "Whereas I am only resigned."

Gently, her head came to rest upon his shoulder, and her hand was shyly laid over his heart. "I know," she whispered. "But it is a step away from the angry pain you have been suffering so cruelly and alone. Pray, do not continue so, Fitzwilliam!"

Slipping his arms around her, Darcy held her close and placed a kiss upon her curls. "Shall you be my Portia, pleading my case before the bar?" He laid his cheek upon the place he had kissed.

Georgiana sighed as she burrowed deeper into his shoulder. "Not I alone, dear Brother; but yes, ever your Portia."

What remained of the day, Darcy spent in his study working at his neglected affairs under the benevolent observation of his hound. Trafalgar had forgiven him also, it seemed, appearing unexpectedly at his usual place by the desk when once Darcy had turned his back to the door. Erewile House still lay hushed, but it was no longer silent as the servants brought it to order for that evening's dinner and guest. From the other side of his door, footsteps softly clicked down the hall, doors opened and closed on the clink of china and silver, and murmured orders were passed along to underlings, all creating an undertone reminiscent of normalcy.

More than once during the early evening, Darcy's gaze strayed from his papers to his sister's portrait, and he wondered again at their extraordinary interview. She knew now all that was needful. His character had been laid quite bare, his devastating misadventure into love revealed, and the result had been not an estrangement but rather a new closeness built upon who rather than what they were to each other. Rising from his desk, he looked more carefully at her image and, after his study, determined that she had seen better than he. Lawrence had gotten her entirely wrong. It was a fine painting, no mistaking that, but Georgiana was correct. Although she had put it in quite different terms, he now saw that it had not captured the essential humanity of the remarkable young woman who was his sister. No, he would not insist on a public unveiling, he decided. Let the family come to view it if they wished and the thing be sent on to Pemberley.

A knock at the door brought his head around, and Trafalgar's came up as the door opened to reveal Witcher's smiling mien. "Excuse me, Mr. Darcy; Lord Brougham is here to see you, sir."

Darcy looked past his butler but saw no sign of his supposed visitor. "Lord Brougham, Witcher? And where might he be?" A sound of footsteps signaled the approach of his erstwhile dinner guest, who appeared a trifle breathless at his study door. "Ah, yes. You are correct; it is Brougham. A bit early for dinner, are you not? Or is it late for tea?"

"You were to give me a few moments, Witcher!" Brougham cast the servant a look of exasperation. "It was meant figuratively, man! Never expected you would be precise to a pin!" He turned back to Darcy as the unrepentant butler bowed and closed the door. "The man is inestimable, Fitz, but remarkably obtuse at the most significant moments."

"Meaning that you have yet to discover a way around him." Darcy's laugh was tempered by an acute unease at the arrival of his friend. After a day's reflection on his foolish actions and sodden confessions, how might Dy regard him now? "Inestimable, indeed! But you are rather early. We did not expect you for another hour."

"I could wait no longer to satisfy myself as to the condition of your head, old man! Or the rest of you, for that matter. I have no doubt that it has been quite some time since last you had that much to drink."

Declining to answer, Darcy instead offered him a tight smile and sketched a bow. "Here you see me! Judge for yourself."

Taking his invitation with irksome literalness, Brougham circled him round in precise imitation of the examination Brummell had given him the night of Lady Melbourne's soiree. "Rather the worse for wear, my friend," he concluded, shaking his head. "Dare I ask how you feel?"

"Not as bad as I might thanks to Fletcher's vile potion, but bad enough to entertain the thought of going Methodist."

Brougham looked at him sharply. "What do you mean?"

"Only that I believe I shall abstain from drink for a time." He returned his friend's regard cautiously. "What should you think I meant by it?"

In his typical fashion, Brougham ignored the question in favor of another of his own. "You have explained last night to Miss Darcy?" he asked, strolling over to the bookshelf.

"Yes, yes, I did." Darcy watched as Dy's fingers lazily caressed the ranked, leather-clad volumes.

"In detail?" Brougham asked as he perused the titles.

"No, of course not!" he replied. "Georgiana knows only that I fell in with some questionable company and you helped me to see how impolitic it was to remain." He paused before adding, "I told her about Hertfordshire and then . . . and then about Kent."

"Ah." Brougham pulled out one of the company upon the shelf and gingerly opened it. "She knows about the lady, then, and the rest." His gaze traveled steadily to and fro across the pages, nor did he lift it to ask, "How did she respond?"

"She forgave me," Darcy replied simply.

"Well, she would have to now, would she not?" Dy looked up at him briefly and then fell to a study of the book once more. "Religious as she is."

Darcy stiffened at his tone. What did he mean to imply? "I believe she truly forgave me," he replied in hauteur, "and from her heart."

"I see." Dy looked over at him, his eyebrow crooked in that infuriating way Darcy had known since university, indicating that he saw no such thing, or that the speaker's words were a pile of rubbish. "Very comforting, that—choosing your truth. Makes life quite tolerable when lived on such terms, does it not? Well, at least for a bit." He shrugged. "Until one brushes up against another's truth whose fur does not lie in the same direction."

"A fine one you are to be lecturing on the nature of truth," Darcy retorted, stung by his friend's carelessly leveled skepticism.

"I did read philosophy, old man!" Brougham protested mildly as he turned another page.

"As did I." Frustration gave way to anger. "But that is not my meaning, and well you know it! This charade of yours, this concealing of a first-rate mind behind the mask of a cork-brained rattle with more hair than wit, has grown exceedingly tiresome! What is the truth there, my fine friend?" Dy looked up from the page at his sharp tone, but his appreciative grin for his friend's verbal thrust only angered Darcy further. "And last night at Monmouth's! Posing as a servant, for God's sake! Closing for innkeepers! And my door." He suddenly remembered. "The lock! I may have been drunk, but I remember the lock!"

"I had hoped you would have forgotten that." Brougham shook his head. "Pity you did not!" He set the book aside and regarded him meditatively. "But I did promise you an explanation, and an explanation, of sorts, you shall have." He held up a hand to forestall the expression of dissatisfaction that sprang to Darcy's lips. "I owe it to you for more reasons than one, and for the sake of our friendship and future relations, I will tell you all that I am able." He sighed, his face creasing in rueful lines. "It is a rather complicated affair, though, I warn you."

"I would not expect otherwise!" Darcy folded his arms and leaned against the edge of his desk. "You have been seven years at this game, man!" The thin line that was Brougham's mouth plainly spoke his discomfort, causing Darcy to prompt, "By all means, proceed!"

"It began in the middle of our last term at university." Brougham turned away and strolled to the window to peer down into the street below. "We were competing for the Mathematics Prize; do you remember?"

"Yes," Darcy recalled. "I did not see you for days at a time during the preparation of our papers for the committee."

"Yes, well . . . I was not at work on my paper; not the entire time. I was not even in Cambridge but here in London."

"In London!"

His friend nodded but continued to stare out the window. "One evening while I was at work on my thesis, some men appeared in my rooms and whisked me off to a very private meeting, one which I was not permitted to refuse. My work in the relation of mathematics to linguistics had gained the notice, it seemed, of certain officials in the government who wished me to apply it to ciphers being passed here in England. Being young and impressionable, I agreed at once!" He stopped and looked back at Darcy. "No, that is not the absolute truth. I agreed because it was, at last, an opportunity to exorcise a personal demon. I have never told you of my father, Darcy. Have you never been curious as to why?"

"Naturally, I was." Darcy straightened, surprised at the turn of Dy's explanation but intrigued with its direction. "That you do not go by your title, Westmarch, but prefer Brougham was always curious. But early on you had made it clear that anything to do with your family was a private matter."

"My family!" Brougham snorted. "Yes, I suppose you could call it that! My father, the Earl of Westmarch, was said to be a brilliant man; and perhaps at one time, he was. I have no notion of his intellect save in the inventive ways he studied to persecute my mother and humiliate me. He also had the Devil's own temper, was a quick hand with his riding crop, and had a passion for gaming. The fortune my mother brought to the marriage was quickly dissipated, and after my birth, he had no more use for her, preferring, as he did, to graze in fields elsewhere."

"Good God, Dy!"

Brougham shrugged his shoulders. "It is a common enough tale among our class, Fitz. You understand why I practically begged to spend that summer after our first year with your family at Pemberley? Even though the earl was dead and I had nothing to fear going home, I hungered to experience what a real family was. Your father was such a revelation! I am honored to have known him and confess that he has always been my ideal of what a husband and father should be."

Darcy nodded, acknowledging the tribute. Both of them swallowed hard and looked away.

"Pardon my digression." Brougham broke their silence. "My own father's need for money became desperate after my mother's death, for her income from her family's holdings now devolved upon me, and my uncles had made certain that he could not lay his hands upon it. It was then that he turned to intrigue."

"Intrigue?" Darcy frowned. "With whom?"

"Anyone!" Brougham threw up his hands. "Anyone with coin: French, Irish, Prussian, the Barbary pirates for all I know! Westmarch Castle became a tollhouse for anything or anyone that wished to elude the notice of the government."

"A traitor!" The condemnation burst from him.

"Yes, a traitor." Dy's face hardened. "And not even for a cause, a belief, but merely for money. When he was finally caught by the authorities, he put a bullet through his brain before they could take him. Since his suicide had saved the Home Office the cost of a scandal, it was all hushed up. An accident while cleaning his pistol, or some such tale. But I knew, Fitz, I knew!" He turned away, his head and shoulders stiff. "So, you can see that I viewed this offer as a means of redeeming my name. Translating ciphers was also a fascinating challenge. The pitting of one's mind and imagination against that of an unknown enemy was exhilarating. I finished out our last year at University dividing my time between my thesis and my work for the Home Office."

"And still managed to win several prizes!" Darcy shook his head in chagrin.

Smirking, Brougham faced him. "You have not quite forgiven me that, I believe!"

"No!" Darcy answered. "But I can hardly begrudge you them after this. Go on." He brought his old friend back to his subject.

"For I do not see how this explains these last seven years or these mysterious pranks of yours."

"Ah, but I have set the stage, as it were." The steady, concentrated gaze reappeared. "It became obvious from their content and complexity that the ciphers were originating in the upper classes of British society, circulating within them before finally being sent to France. With Napoleon's forces gathered at Boulogne in '04 for a proposed invasion, the Home and Foreign Offices went into a panic. The plans for Pitt's coastal fortifications in Sussex and Kent were discovered in a packet bound for Holland. I saw them myself and deciphered the note that accompanied it; a very elegant, inventive one I might add." He smiled wryly at the memory.

"Well done, Dy, but the problem remained!" Darcy was caught in his friend's narrative. "It was the men themselves who needed to be apprehended!"

"Precisely!" Brougham replied. "But how to discover them? They moved in the first circles of Society. They were highly intelligent and possibly powerful men. They might even have been part of the government itself! The introduction of an agent would prove useless, for he would never be accepted, let alone trusted. It remained, therefore—"

"It had to be one of their own!" Darcy looked at his friend in wonder and some apprehension. "Someone they would accept without question but who was their equal in cunning and resourcefulness. Good Lord, Dy! You turned spy?" Brougham offered him a confirming bow. "All this time! Your pose as a rattle and nod cock?"

"Unfortunately, yes." He sighed. "It was rather depressing how quickly I was accepted as such, but there it is! For King and Country, you know!"

"But did you catch them?" Darcy persisted. This was too incredible! His best friend a spy!

"Oh, yes, I caught him." A strained look appeared upon Brougham's face. He veiled his eyes. "But I cannot reveal his name or those of others I have exposed. They are dealt with by others and quietly while the Rattle continues on his rounds of dancing and hunting, gaming and playing Society's fool. I swear, Fitz, you do not want to know what is revealed to a fool about those of our set."

"Or to a servant?" he asked quietly. It may have begun as a noble quest to redeem his family's name and an exciting challenge to his active intellect, but now the chase was taking its toll upon his friend. Darcy could see it in every line.

"Yes, when I do not have the right connections, such as those that would gain me entrée to the fanatics who surround Lady Monmouth. She has no use for the likes of me, much too devoted a lady to want my sort of fool. Would you offer me something to drink, old man?" he asked abruptly. "Dry work, this confessing! Almost envy you your way!"

"Getting drunk, do you mean?" Darcy groaned. "I do not recommend it. Besides, you may say something you ought not." He strode over to a cabinet and opened it upon an assortment of spirits. "Wine or brandy?"

"Wine! We dine with your sister in a few moments, and I do not wish to have anything stronger lingering about my person."

Darcy poured him a glass and then put the bottle away. No wine until supper for him! "And your familiarity with innkeepers and wonderful ability with locks?"

"Tools of the trade, Fitz." He almost drained the glass in the first swallow. "In this business it is not enough to know the powerful. One must follow treason behind locked doors, through the streets, and into the gutter as well. There are parts of our fair city you would not believe existed even were I to swear on my honor to it. But gutter or town house, the stench is the same, and few are what they seem. I was even beginning to worry about you, old man!"

"Me?" Darcy stared at him, surprised and affronted.

"Oh, not that you were disloyal! Heavens, man, do not poker

up so!" Brougham chided. "But I was worried about the company you were keeping. Sayre and Trenholme were always dubious pieces of work, not your sort at all! Then, it seemed that you were taken with Lady Sylvanie, now Monmouth, who has become a rather dangerous woman with whom to be connected. Recently, your behavior had become so unusual, especially in regard to Miss Darcy and since your return from Kent, that I did not know what to think. When you insisted on accepting Monmouth's invitation, I feared for your reputation and tried to discourage you." Dy skewered the area over his heart with a finger. "But you ignored even my 'pointed' advice."

"I thought that display was concerning Georgiana," Darcy responded, only partially mollified, "which is another subject we must discuss before we join her."

"Must we?" Brougham's jaw hardened. "I would rather not." He downed the last of his wine.

"I believe we must." Darcy tensed at his friend's reluctance. "You were quite correct about her, and your reproofs to me were more than warranted. I thank you for both. I see now that I have lately given into your keeping responsibilities that were rightly only my own and that I must ask you to relinquish." Abruptly, Brougham turned and walked back to the window, leaving Darcy to frown after his frame outlined against the gathering dusk. "Dy?"

"Do you have any idea what an extraordinary and precious young woman you have in your sister, Fitz?" Brougham leaned against the window frame. "I doubt that I have met her like in any female of our class, or at least in any that my public character has been allowed near! Already she is possessed of the graces an intelligent, discerning man appreciates. What she will be when she has reached maturity takes one's breath away!"

"She is but sixteen, Dy!" Darcy remonstrated, alarmed at the intensity he heard in his friend's voice, "and I had your hand that you—"

"That I would not be a danger to her!" Brougham turned back

to him. "You have my hand still, my friend. I do not and would never play with Miss Darcy's heart! I have been at some pains to keep my own feelings at bay, hidden beneath layers of mutual interests and friendship. Upon my honor, Fitz," he protested vigorously in the face of his friend's silence, "I have taken the greatest care that Miss Darcy know me foremost as friend. I am only too aware of her age; give me some credit for delicacy, I beg you!"

"But it will be some years before I would even consider giving her in marriage." Darcy put as much disapproval into his tone as possible. "And the disparity in your ages, Dy!"

"Well do I know it." He laughed grimly. "I would not have believed it myself. The baby sister of my best friend! How absurd! But there is this, Fitz. I'm old enough to know my own mind and know what love is. After this bloody war is over, I know what I shall do with the rest of my life, and it shall not be performing as London's prize idiot, I assure you! You know me, Fitz, despite these last seven years. You know that I would cherish Miss Darcy above my own life, and if I ever did not to your satisfaction, you have my leave to thrash me within an inch of it!"

Darcy stared at his friend in silence. He could not doubt that every word Dy spoke was true and from the heart, but the idea that he loved Georgiana and wished to make her his wife was more than Darcy had ever expected to entertain today or any other. "Dy—"

"Please, let us not speak of this further for now," Brougham interrupted. "She is too young, as you say; and I am entangled in this snarl of intrigue that makes my life not worth a tuppence. Nothing may come of this confession, you know! Any day a notice may appear in the papers. Until this war is done, I can say nothing nor ask anything of you or Miss Darcy. Perhaps, by the time Napoleon is finally dispatched, she will be of age to listen to my proposal. I leave it to you, my friend, to decide in the interim whether you will allow me to make it. Now . . ." He straightened and gestured toward the door. "Shall we go in to supper?"

"Dy, in all honesty, there is something you must know first." Darcy made one last attempt to deflect his friend from his determination to wait for his sister.

"Yes?" Brougham stopped with a look of amusement. "Is there some dark Darcy secret that will deter me?"

"Dark?" Darcy bit his lip. "No, but you must know that she . . ." How was he to put this? There was no delicate way—

A knock sounded on the study door, causing the open expression that Dy had worn during his narrative to be replaced by one of wariness. "Enter," Darcy called and watched with fascination the stages in the transformation of his friend from the sincere lines of the man he had been during their interview to the supercilious ones of his public persona. In the few moments it required for a footman to open the door and Georgiana to enter, the metamorphosis was complete.

"My Lord Brougham!" The pleasure in her eyes was unfeigned. She cast them down only briefly as she did him her curtsy and turned to Darcy. "Have you closeted with His Lordship long enough, Brother, or shall I have supper sent back to the kitchen?"

"Oh, we are quite at an end, Miss Darcy," His Lordship interposed. "We have exhausted between us every topic of conversation. I fear it will fall upon you to keep us civil to each other through supper."

Slipping back into his pose with uncanny ease, Dy proved an excellent dinner guest, entertaining them with anecdotes and absurd homilies interspersed with informative bits concerning the great, the famous, and those who aspired to be so. Darcy could almost believe their earlier meeting had been a dream, so little did the man sitting at table resemble what he had confessed. Still, Darcy watched with a heightened awareness for indications of the strands that might one day bind his sister to his friend. Certainly, Georgiana blossomed under his regard, losing her reticence in Brougham's company even more than when among their relations; but he could detect no feeling for him other than a delighted friendship. On Dy's part, there were no secret glances or soulful sighs. He continued to play the amusing rattle Society thought him, sometimes ridiculous, often ironic; yet his edges were softened in their company with occasional displays of his true intellect and powers of discernment.

Darcy knew that his friend would keep his promises, but when Dy took his final bow in wishing Georgiana a good night and pulled him into a conspiratorial huddle at the door to inform him that his "duties" would require his absence from Town for an unspecified period of time, Darcy was not sorry. "What I most regret is that I shall not be here for the unveiling of Miss Darcy's portrait," Dy said as he shrugged on the coat a footman held for him and reached for his beaver and gloves.

"You shall miss nothing," Darcy replied, continuing at Brougham's upraised brow with "I have concluded that Georgiana has the right of it. Family only, then it shall be packed up for Pemberley."

"Excellent!" Dy beamed at him. "That was well done of you, Fitz! Although I appreciate Miss Darcy's dissatisfaction with her portrait, I hope that one day I may have the privilege of seeing it displayed in proper state in your gallery." He extended his hand, which Darcy immediately clasped in a hard grip.

"Have a care, old man." Darcy choked on the words of farewell, the inestimable value of the man before him filling him with gratitude and fear. "You play a dangerous game, which it is my heartfelt wish you survive and without injury."

"I shall, Fitz," he replied with equal emotion. "You cannot imagine what a relief it has been to come honest with you about it . . . and the other. I shall be Lord knows where during the next several months, but if you should need to contact me, send a note to the sexton at St. Dunstan's. He will make sure I receive it."

St. Dunstan's? Something from the past stirred inside Darcy at the name. Where had he heard of St. Dunstan's before?

Dy took a deep breath. "Good-bye then, my friend," he said

and clapped his hat upon his well-ordered curls. "Watch over Miss Darcy, and think of me. I will require an accounting when next we meet." He laughed, then asked, "What is it that you frown so?"

"St. Dunstan's! Why should I have heard of that parish before? I certainly do not frequent that part of London!"

Brougham grinned provocatively. "Oh, I should be very surprised if you did! Where have you heard of it? I would imagine you ran across it in the references provided you by the excellent Mrs. Annesley." He nodded to the footman to open the door.

"Mrs. Annesley!" Darcy stood rooted to the floor of his hall, staring stupidly at his friend while he scrambled to recall the contents of the woman's letters.

"St. Dunstan's was, before he died, Peter Annesley's parish. Her late husband," Dy offered to the blank surprise that continued to render Darcy immobile. "I beg you will not mention to her that I knew Peter, or apprise her of any notes you send there in search of me. She is not aware of our connection or the circles in which Peter was involved, and he wished it to remain so."

Darcy nodded. "Good Lord, Dy, what next?"

"The end of this damned war in the defeat of Napoleon, I should hope!" he answered grimly. "I must be off!" He sighed, then turned on his friend a smile that spoke warmly of their years of high regard each for the other. "Have a care, Fitz." He turned and in a breath was swallowed whole by the darkness.

CHAPTER 6

Under Transgression Bowed

"The next time you and Brougham decide to have a go at each other, I trust you will send me notice." Sir Hugh Goforth used his queen of clubs to scoop up the trick he had just won. "Heard it was one damned fine show of swordsmanship!"

"Would not have thought that frippery rattle pate knew which end of a sword meant business," Lord Devereaux drawled as he threw his cards into the middle. "Although, I will grant, he is a regular hell-for-leather in the saddle. Ran his horse into the ground at Melton last year, I understand. Had to put a bullet through him."

Squarely caught between a desire to defend his friend and fear of revealing something he ought not, Darcy gathered up the cards and confined himself to shuffling them. It had been more than a week since their confrontation at Genuardi's, but he had only today looked in at Boodle's, where both their absences from the clubrooms had prompted speculation.

One by one, Sir Hugh soldiered the cards Darcy dealt him into the company in his hand while Devereaux and the fourth of their rubber palmed theirs all at once before setting about to order them. Darcy glanced again at his unlikely partner across the table.

Lord Manning met his speculative regard with a mocking lift of a brow. "If you had been at Cambridge instead of Oxford, Devereaux," Manning observed, "you would not labor under such a misconception. Brougham is, or was then, an excellent blade. When he and Darcy were not flinging academic prizes in each other's face, they were drawing edges."

"Ah, inside information!" Sir Hugh closed the fan of his cards. "The betting books are in Darcy's favor at the moment. A pony on Brougham or Darcy, Manning?"

"Oh, on Darcy"—Manning sneered—"but only to annoy him. He hates to be the subject of public interest; do you not, Darcy?"

"Shall we play, gentlemen?" Darcy deflected Manning's question. "Your bid, Devereaux." With His Lordship's bid, the game and the evening proceeded with no further mention of a possible rematch, but with a shift of his shoulders Manning ably communicated that his point had been proved. The appearance of his old antagonist in the club's rooms had surprised Darcy, for although Manning was a member of Boodle's, he was also a member of White's and had demonstrated his preference for the latter with a prolonged absence from the former. Darcy had not seen him to exchange even a word since the horrible business at Norwycke Castle. There was no telling why Manning had suddenly chosen to grace Boodle's with his presence unless it was for the perverse pleasure he took in pinching at Darcy, as he did now. For that, Manning had certainly positioned himself well, offering himself as Darcy's partner when, upon reception of an urgent note, Sandington had to quit the game.

Although he could not enjoy his company, Darcy could not fault the man's play. Manning was as shrewd at cards as he was at provocation, slicing at their opponents' strategy as deftly as he did the reputations of those other club members who chanced to pass by. Both Goforth and Devereaux snorted with amusement at the remarks, leaving Darcy alone in disgust of the Baron's entertainment and wishing himself elsewhere. They ended the evening victors, but Darcy took little pleasure in it or in Manning's curt expression of satisfaction. Nodding his reception of his partner's tight-lipped compliment, Darcy rose from the table, intent upon departing for Erewile House when Manning stepped around to him. "A word?" The tone of his request was almost civil.

"Your servant," Darcy replied evenly, masking his irritation. Manning motioned him over to a small table away from the swell of activity. Taking chairs, they once again faced each other. "What is it, Manning?" Darcy demanded without preamble. "I am for home and have no desire to tarry."

"I wish to speak to you . . . about a personal matter." His Lordship's arrogant voice faltered even as his eyes shifted away from Darcy's. "I know how incongruous that must sound. Imagine me asking something of you! Only the most pressing necessity would, I assure you, bring me to you with this. Damn!" He fell back in his chair, his aspect stormy. Everything tempted Darcy to rise and leave, but something in the picture Manning made stayed him. Sitting back, he waited for the Baron to continue. "It is Bella; you remember my sister?" His Lordship looked back at him.

"I hope that Miss Avery is well." Darcy's brows came together. What could Manning want with him concerning his sister?

"Yes . . . and no! She is not ill in the common sense of the term." His Lordship scowled. "But you know how she is! Ever the colorless little mouse. And that blasted stuttering of hers!" Darcy's frown deepened. Yes, he knew quite well Manning's opinion of his younger sister and his careless mistreatment of her. Returning him what he trusted was a look communicating his disapprobation, Darcy was gratified to see His Lordship had the grace to flush and cease his complaints.

"Here it is, Darcy." He lowered his voice. "I have come to see that Bella has lacked proper guidance. Our parents died before she was eight years old. Her governesses since have been adequate but not inspired. I have never known what to do with her." His voice rose again in irritation. "And, Lord knows, my sister, Lady Sayre, never showed her a particle of interest even before the business last January. I have wasted a Season on her already and am in a fair way to be doing so again this year."

"My sympathies go out to your sister—"

"Yes!" Manning stopped him. "I thought they must. You handled her so well at Norwycke. That is why I have come to you." Darcy stared at him uncomprehendingly. "You are very close to your own sister, I believe."

"I have that honor." He regarded Manning with suspicion.

"I have noticed your unusual esteem for each other; so has Bella."

"When—?"

"Saw you together at the theater, Monday last, Lady Lavinia's recital on Thursday, although you came late and left early, and the opera on Saturday." He ticked them off. "The short of it is this: Bella stands in admiration of you and Miss Darcy." His Lordship's rancor was unmistakable. "And frankly, although you are insufferably correct in all particulars, it is obvious that you do more than suffer the company of your sister. A man of your intelligence . . ." Darcy's brow lifted, feigning just a bit more astonishment than he truly felt at this, the first genuine compliment he had ever received from Manning. "Yes, I admit to all your talents and graces," Manning conceded. "A man of your intelligence and temper would not be so attentive to his much younger sister if she were a hubble-bubble, bird-witted miss on the one hand or a damned nattering bluestocking on the other. Bella would do well to acquire some of your sister's self-possession and intelligence." He paused as a servant came by with a tray. "You there, what is on deck?"

"Brandy, my lord." The man bowed and offered the tray.

"Excellent! Dry work this!" Manning snatched a glass. "Darcy?"

"No, I thank you." He watched as the Baron attempted to soothe the discomfort of the distasteful position in which he found himself.

"Would you—despite our long-standing antagonism—would

you allow an introduction, encourage a friendship between Miss Darcy and Bella?" The proud look, so briefly abandoned, returned, daring Darcy against pity or triumph in whatever his answer might be.

Everything inside Darcy went very still as he made shift to recover from the surprise of Manning's request. How could he answer him? It involved so much: years of what Manning had rightly called an "antagonism," of which he had taken the brunt, the foisting upon Georgiana of a "friend" not of her own choosing, and the increased contact with Manning that this meant for both of them. This was not to mention that Manning's Sayre connections were in serious social and financial disgrace, one of whose members was up to her lovely neck in sedition! Narrowing his eyes on the man across the table, Darcy looked for anything that indicated some feeling in his bosom for his sister's difficulties beyond irritation and the desire to be relieved of responsibility for her. The fact that Manning had come to him for assistance was unaccountably wonderful and spoke in favor of more than a concern for his sister's effect on his purse, but the hard eyes and arrogant demeanor Manning displayed as he waited for his answer mitigated against the possession of softer affections. If Darcy agreed, it appeared that it would make no real difference in Manning's disdain of him, a disdain he had never understood or discovered how he had earned. If there were any justice in the world, he should take this opportunity to—

Though justice be thy plea . . .—as his jaw hardened to deliver his refusal, Georgiana's soft vow to be his Portia, his advocate, recalled itself—*we do pray for mercy.* What more would be his bid for justice in this than revenge for his own offended pride? In his struggles, had it not been Georgiana's mercy and Dy's rougher sort that had pulled him through?

"Well?" Manning barked at him, his lips preparing to curl into a sneer when the refusal came.

"Would Thursday morning be convenient for Miss Avery?"

Darcy inquired. "Perhaps eleven o'clock?" The astonishment on Manning's face was, he found, worth every ounce of his surrender to mercy's better angels.

"You agree? I'll be damned!" Manning sank back against his chair, astonished. "Dashed decent of you, Darcy!" he managed after several speechless moments. "I did not expect . . . Well, that is neither here nor there. Yes, eleven on Thursday; Bella will be ecstatic." He rose and awkwardly extended his hand. "Th-thank you."

"You are welcome." Darcy gripped His Lordship's hand. He had done the right thing; he was sure of it now. But that conviction did not include spending any more time with Manning than was strictly necessary. "Now, I am for home. Can I drop you anywhere, Manning?"

"No, no," His Lordship quickly responded, evidently no more at ease with this new way of relating to him than Darcy was with him. "I shall look in at White's a bit, and then my dancer will be waiting . . ." He let the sentence dangle and shrugged. "Until Thursday."

"Thursday." Darcy nodded, then took his leave of Manning and his club. Sauntering down to the sidewalk, he smiled to see Harry jump from the carriage and move swiftly to open the door and bring down the steps.

"Evenin' Mr. Darcy, sir." The groomsman pulled on his forelock.

"Good evening, Harry," Darcy returned as he mounted the small steps. "Tell James to take us home. I have had enough for one evening."

" 'ope it were a good un, sir."

"Oh, it was an extraordinary one, Harry! Proof of your assertion, I would say."

"Which one 'ud that be, sir?"

"That 'the Quality be a strange lot.' " He quoted Harry's sage observation back to him.

"Humph!" Harry snorted. "Proof o' that ain't in want!" He

made to shut the door and then stopped short and ducked his head, apparently scandalized by his own free speech. "Beggin' yer pardon, Mr. Darcy!"

"Close the door, Harry."

"Yes, sir."

The door clicked shut, but Darcy waited only until Harry was back up on top of the carriage before he gave in to the humorous truth of his groomsman's philosophy. "Strange" surely described Manning's seeking him out tonight and the odd turn their association had taken.

"I cannot tell you what a relief it is to be back in London." Miss Bingley accepted a cup of tea from Georgiana's hand and settled back comfortably in her chair. "The shops and theaters of Scarborough are nothing, never mind what my aunt may claim for them! You may imagine, Georgiana, how I longed to return to civilization."

Darcy watched as his sister responded with a politely sympathetic smile before pouring out the next cup for Bingley. "It was not so bad as that." Bingley looked up at him. "Though I will admit to feeling more at ease here in London than among our relatives and our parents' older acquaintances in Scarborough. I fear we have quite lost touch with them. Another life altogether, it seems." He ended on a pensive note but then rallied. "It has been weeks since we were last here! How was your visit in Kent, Darcy? Warmer than ours in the North, I should imagine."

"Yes . . . warmer." Darcy's voice caught only briefly. Georgiana looked up into his eyes, extending him a supporting smile. He nodded his receipt of it. "But it did not last. Both Fitzwilliam and I were more than glad to return to Town."

"And your portrait, Georgiana." Miss Bingley's voice bridged the lull that threatened to settle upon them. "I am so distressed that we returned too late to see it. Was the Unveiling well attended?" She paused, then shook herself with a throaty laugh. "But of course it was. I should rather ask who attended. Come, you may crow your triumph to us!"

Such an invitation! Darcy looked hard at Bingley's sister, wondering again how she could have so little understanding of Georgiana. Mistaking his observation of her, she cast him a sideways smile that spoke of a conspiracy of indulgence in which he declined to claim his share. "You are mistaken, Miss Bingley; I acceded to my sister's wishes and issued no invitations. The portrait was displayed to family only and is on its way to Pemberley as we speak."

"Really?" Miss Bingley looked between brother and sister in puzzled disbelief.

"It was my wish, Miss Bingley, which my brother was kind enough to grant." Georgiana held out his cup to him with a tender smile. "He is very good to me, is he not?"

Her lips pursed in an uncertain smile, Miss Bingley assented to her proposition.

"What are your plans now that you have returned?" Darcy directed the conversation away from himself. "Society will soon explode into activity, and you will be much in demand."

"I have not altogether decided." Bingley set down his cup. "My desk is already awash with invitations and notices."

Darcy nodded his understanding. "You must take care that you hold the reins, Bingley, and are not driven by Society's whip. Else, my friend, you will end in the ditch."

Bingley grimaced. "I shall keep your advice in mind. It is just making a beginning—"

"Upon which subject I have spoken to Hinchcliffe."

"Hinchcliffe!" his friend exclaimed, a glimmer of hope gilding his features.

"The same." Darcy grinned to see the cautious relief in Bingley's face at the mention of his formidable secretary. "He is of the opinion that his nephew might well start in your service as an undersecretary in charge of your social affairs, if you are agreeable."

"Agreeable! I should say!"

"It is done, then. Shall he report to you tomorrow?"

"Tomorrow— Yes! He may come tonight! I shall send a note round this minute if you will allow."

"By all means!" Darcy gestured to the door, then turned to his sister. "If you will excuse us." Once in his study, he pushed a sheet of paper across his desk and flicked open the inkwell as Bingley availed himself of a chair.

"This could not have come at a better time." Bingley grinned as he took the pen Darcy offered and then bit his lip in all seriousness as he dipped it into the inkwell and set himself to writing. Darcy sat back and watched Bingley scratch away at his note, content with both the utility of the help he was able to offer and its glad acceptance. "There," his friend exclaimed, dotting the *i* of his name with a flourish and pushing the note toward him. "Tell me if it is acceptable. I would not wish to risk Hinchcliffe's opinion with a misspelled note."

The short epistle was soon read, but as Darcy looked back to Bingley with assurance upon his lips, he caught him in what could only be termed a dejection of spirits, his eyes focused on nothing present in the room, the laughter lines about his face gone slack. Even as Darcy watched, Bingley's shoulders slumped and a furrow appeared across his brow. Quickly returning his gaze to the note, Darcy felt his contentment vanish. The prescription he held in his hand for the relief of Bingley's social obligations would do nothing to cure the heartsickness that resided still in his friend's bosom. As he trained his eyes upon the note, a wave of wretchedness engulfed him. What a pitiable pair they made! Bonded now in more than friendship, each had found his soul's match in a Bennet sister; and as a result of Darcy's interference, they both suffered the certainty of living the rest of their days only half alive. Yes, Charles loved Jane Bennet just as surely as Darcy loved Elizabeth. He had eyes to see that now. It was worse in Bingley's case, for Jane Bennet loved him back, if Elizabeth was to be believed; and he believed Elizabeth. How damnably conceited of him to have held himself the arbiter of love! He had wronged Charles, wronged him unforgivably in a high-handed manner and in a matter that Charles's own heart should have sought out, free from his influence or interference. What recompense for such a grievous error could he ever make him? Even this kindness smacked of a patronizing superiority.

"Ahem." He cleared his throat and straightened his waistcoat, giving his friend opportunity to recover himself. When Bingley's head came up, Darcy pushed the note back across the desk. "It will do. Shall it be sent?"

"Yes, by all means," Bingley returned with a quick, faint grin. "I would not wish to accept the wrong invitations." He took up the note and slowly creased it into precise thirds as Darcy looked on, dismayed at his quip. Did Charles truly have so little faith in his own judgment? Had Darcy's attempt to act his mentor convinced him instead that it was safer to put his life in the hands of others he held wiser than himself? If this was so, he had done Bingley a further wrong.

"You need only take young Hinchcliffe's recommendations as suggestions, Charles. The final word is yours in this as in all your dealings. If you should find yourself somewhere you discover you would rather not be, you will know what to do. You have ever landed on your feet in any social occasion in which I have observed you."

"Is that so?" Bingley's face brightened tentatively. "A compliment, Darcy?" His uncertainty cut Darcy to the quick. When had he fallen into the pattern of treating his friend as less than his equal? How had the man borne his condescension?

"No, the truth, Charles." He faced him squarely. "If more of humanity was possessed of your innate good nature, your ability to make those around you comfortable and well disposed toward the world, Society would not be half the gauntlet that it is." He paused to see the effect of his words. The brightness in Bingley's face had

gone a bit flush, but the grin on his lips assured Darcy it was from
pleasure rather than anger or embarrassment. "Lord knows, I
could profit from some of your talent." Darcy sighed both for the
truth of his confession and for his relief that Bingley was coming
back to himself. "Perhaps I should apply to you for lessons!"

"Lessons!" Bingley laughed and rose from his seat. "Shall the
master and student change places?"

"No." Darcy shook his head and stood. "You are graduated,
Bingley! I have encouraged you, wrongly, to lag behind in the
classroom. I would rather we were friends coming to each other's
aid." He extended his hand, which Bingley, though surprised, took
readily. "Equals standing ready to assist each other along the way."

"Of course, Darcy, of course!" Bingley beamed at him.

Darcy nodded and strengthened his grip on Bingley's hand. "I
overstepped the bounds, my friend. What I can rectify, I shall. I
promise you."

A knock at his study door a week later brought Darcy's head up
from his book and that of his hound from close contemplation of
that activity. Trafalgar rose from his station at his master's side and
padded over to the door, his nails clicking against the polished
wood floor between the islands of carpet laid about the room. As
Darcy watched, the dog reared on his haunches against the door
and batted expertly at the knob until the latch disengaged, then
jumped back to nose open the portal. A happy whine from deep
within the animal's chest told Darcy who would soon appear.

"Trafalgar has become quite the gentleman, Fitzwilliam." Georgiana leaned down to stroke the broad, silky brow above liquid
eyes turned to her in hope.

"A highly discriminating one, though." Darcy shook his head at
his sister's fawning supplicant as he rose to greet her. "He will do
the pretty only for those of whom he approves. You, my girl,
merely happen to be one of that select party."

Georgiana laughed and, with one last pat, straightened. "I have come to inform you that Miss Avery has gone, and you may leave the safety of your den for other parts of the house."

Darcy looked askance at her. "Do you mean to imply that I have gone to ground?"

"I cannot help but notice that you have managed to be absent or to find pressing business in here every time Miss Avery calls." She smiled at him as she came to his side. "Even so, she thinks you are the perfect gentleman."

"Georgiana!"

"And that I am the perfect young lady." She sighed. "It is a bit difficult, is it not, to be so worshiped?"

Darcy took her arm and led her to a settee. "Is it very hard to receive her? I know I have imposed upon you abominably."

"No, Brother, not 'abominably.' Miss Avery is a very different sort of friend but not an unwelcome one." She laid her head on his shoulder. "Fitzwilliam, she is so crushed by the weight of her brother's scorn one moment and his dismissal of her existence the next. His opinion of her she takes as the world's. It is no wonder that she is so timid. When I think——" She stopped and pressed her face into his shoulder.

"When you think what, sweetling?" he prompted, brushing her curls lightly.

"When I think how kind you have always been to me, encouraging me . . . Oh, thank you, Fitzwilliam!"

He had turned and was halfway back to his desk when it suddenly occurred to him. He turned back. "Georgiana, are you still of a mind to subscribe to that society?"

"The Society for Returning Young Women to Their Friends in the Country?" He nodded. "Oh, yes, Fitzwilliam! Have I your permission?"

"Allow me to look into it further, and if I am satisfied, you may direct Hinchcliffe to disburse what sums you deem appropriate." His sister, her eyes shining, made to rise, but he held up his hands.

"No, do not thank me. I have been remiss in this as well as in my own charitable concerns. Truly, I have done nothing more than authorize the continued maintenance of our father's charities. Neither have I looked beyond Hinchcliffe's assurances that their boards were respectable and their books balanced." He looked away from the bright warmth and wonder in Georgiana's face, his jaw working as he summoned up the words. "I have held myself aloof from such things. That," he confessed in a low voice, "will no longer do."

Trafalgar looked after Georgiana as she left the room but appeared to decide against an impulse to follow, turning back to his master instead. Darcy returned his solemn regard. "Well, perfect gentlemen are we?" Trafalgar yawned broadly and then snorted, shaking his head before laying it back down upon crossed paws. "Quite so," Darcy agreed and rose.

Walking slowly to the window, he leaned against the frame and looked down onto the square. Miss Avery held him to be the perfect gentleman, did she? A drop of rain tapped against the window and then another. Miss Avery had narrowly escaped a wetting, or conversely, he and his sister had narrowly escaped an entire afternoon harboring her from the weather. He traced the passage of a drop as it flowed down the pane. He must be objective, dispassionate, if he was to sort it all out. It had been nearly a month since Hunsford. He ought to be capable of a dispassionate objectivity by now.

What had been Elizabeth's initial impression of him? From their first encounter at the assembly in Meryton, when he had uttered that graceless dismissal of her, she had set him down as a figure of amusement. He had done no less than to prove her right. Like a pompous fool, he had held himself apart, strutting about the social circles of Hertfordshire with nothing better to do than look down a very ungentlemanlike nose at everyone.

How could it be that he, who had the best of examples before him and the most solemn of intentions, had come to this? Somehow, in the long years of his childhood and youth, he had gone off course, taken on the trappings and attitudes that made him seem now a most unlikable man and a stranger to his own heart.

Trafalgar's whine and hard nudge against his hand brought the room back into focus. "Yes, Monster." He stroked the animal's head. "All is well, at least where you are concerned," he amended.

With a low, rumbling sound, Trafalgar pressed his head against Darcy's knee.

"Yes, I know. The questions remain." He stroked the silky ears again. "But the answer would be more than I wish to contemplate."

With a grimace, he ceased stroking Trafalgar's ears, ignoring the nudge and whimper. It was impossible! Even could he bring himself to petition for it, there was no pretext under which he could seek out Elizabeth, nor were their paths ever likely to cross. Nevertheless, the idea was novel enough to force him to his feet. If it were possible, could she forgive him?

His imagination brought her to him so swiftly he almost started. Admire and love her, he had claimed. How could he possibly do so when he had misread her every action, misconstrued her every word? The extent of his self-deception was astounding! He had presumed himself in possession of her mind and heart when, had he been questioned, he could not have stated with any certainty what she thought or felt upon any subject of importance or what she most desired in life.

Love her? No, he had dallied during these many weeks in his rooms at Pemberley, London, and Kent with an imaginary Elizabeth of his own design, woven from the colored threads of his own desires. In such a state he had gone to her, and she, with no money or prospects of her own, had roundly refused him—refused him, even with so much at stake. The consequences Elizabeth had embraced rather than trust her future to his care loomed more solidly before him than had they heretofore. What kind of woman would do so?

Turning his back to the window, Darcy crossed his arms over his chest, presenting such a picture of concentrated intent that Trafalgar raised his head from his paws, his body tensed in hopeful readiness as his master once more took up the pace of the room. He had come thus far to find an answer, a way through to some resolution of this shocking month of self-revelation, and he was determined to bring all his faculties to bear on the question. What had he to offer as proof of his contrition? Nothing! Certainly nothing that a woman of such principle as she exhibited would be inclined to accept or respect! For a moment he stood there, help-less, before it struck him. The road to becoming a man worthy of the respect of such a woman began in seeing the world and meas-uring himself through other eyes, eyes that were sensitive to his defects and shortcomings.

Could he hold to such a resolve? Any idea of her love as his re-ward must be put aside. Even were they to meet, it must be as in-different acquaintances. But no matter! He would honor this woman who had scorned his station and state to her own hurt and brought him to see himself. He would do it, he swore, by striving hour by hour, unseen and unremarked, toward a conduct of his life that would have gained Elizabeth Bennet's approval.

Darcy made for his desk and, seating himself, reached for his pen and knife. He would need a well-pared instrument for this project. Trafalgar hoisted himself up from his recumbent position next to the settee and padded over to where his master labored. With a sigh followed closely by a grunt, his haunches hit the car-pet, and he turned inquiring eyes upon the figure in the chair. Darcy looked over from his task with a ghost of a smile. "Bored are we?" Trafalgar's regard did not waver. "There is no hope of going out in this rain," he told the dog flatly and, having finished a fine, strong point to his pen, set down the knife. "And even were it a perfect day, I could not oblige you. I have pressing business of a re-formational nature, which you"—he bent a censorious eye upon his hound—"would do well to imitate, Monster." Trafalgar sniffed in answer and sank down once more upon his stomach, propping his muzzle upon his paws. "So say you, but it is long overdue." Darcy turned back to his desk and drew forth a sheet of paper before dipping the pen into the inkwell. His brow furrowed, and for a moment he hesitated. Then, adjusting his grip, he put the point to the sheet and wrote, "A Gentlemanly Manner." He underscored it twice. "Long overdue," he addressed the hound lying beside him, "for both of us."

Several days later, following Darcy's weekly session at Genuardi's, his cousin Richard caught him up for the first time since their return from Kent. They had not parted on the best of terms, Richard having tried to tease Darcy out of his "sulks," as he had named them, and he near taking his cousin's head off his shoulders in return. So Richard had taken himself off, lending himself wholeheartedly to his military duties at the Horse Guards and his social duties to the female portion of Society, leaving Darcy to his own devices until such time as Darcy had regained his humor or Richard was in want of pocket money, whichever came first.

"What ho, Cousin!" Richard's wide grin appeared as Darcy lowered the towel from his face. Genuardi had pushed him hard; it had felt good. It was good to see his cousin again too.

"Richard! Come for some practice? Regain your edge? I'll stand you!" He motioned to the fencing floor.

"Oho, no thank you, Fitz!" He shook his head in mock horror. "I heard about your 'practice' with Brougham and have no desire to be publicly humiliated or worse. Came to see if you might be thirsty after all your exercise. Drop by Boodle's perhaps."

"Excellent!" Darcy said, glad for the opportunity to mend this most important of fences. "Give me a few moments." When he had dressed, they sauntered up St. James's Street and on to the club, Richard letting fall family news and select bits of drollery from military life as they went. Finally, when they were nursing glasses across a table from each other, Richard paused, lifted his, and then lapsed into an uneasy silence.

"Is there something in which I might be of assistance?" Darcy asked quietly when enough time had passed.

"Well, I could always use another win or five at billiards, you know." Richard's lips twisted into a rueful smile. "But that is not why I sought you out."

"Regardless of your reason, I am glad you did." Darcy leaned toward him. "I was insufferable, a veritable bore on our journey back from Kent. I do not know how you swallowed your spleen or resisted the temptation to plant me a facer, for I surely deserved it."

"It might have something to do with the results of that quite physical exchange we had in Rosings Park, which left me with some nasty bruises!" Richard chided him, then changed his tone to a nasal whine. "Besides, I was wearing my best traveling waistcoat and did not want it ruined with blood—yours or my own!"

"And you a colonel in His Majesty's—"

"Never mind that!" His cousin cut him off and, laughing, lifted his glass again, and again brought it down with an air of hesitant sobriety.

"You had better tell me what it is before it chokes you." Darcy eyed his cousin over the rim of his glass.

"It has taken me the greater part of a day and a night to decide whether to tell you at all, old man, so give a fellow some time!" His cousin lifted his glass in salute to him and downed what remained. Setting it down with slow precision, he glanced up at him. "I have seen her. Miss Bennet. Here in London."

Everything went still as Richard's words slowly took on sense and meaning. Elizabeth in London—now? "Where?" he asked hoarsely.

"At the theater last night. She was with a small party, an older gentleman and his wife and a lovely creature whom I take to be her sister. And, of course, Miss Lucas."

"Did you speak to her?" Darcy could not help but ask. He

grasped the smooth solidity of his glass as if it could steady him.

"No, I did not think it wise even if I had been able to reach her, for there was a fearful crowd on the floor. I do not believe she saw me. She looked . . ."

"Yes?" Darcy prompted.

"She looked well, as she always does, even amid the opulence. I believe she watched the audience as much as she did the players."

Darcy almost smiled. Of course she would. Had she not professed herself a student of character?

"I hope I have done the right thing in telling you, Fitz." Richard's concern was genuine. "I could not convince myself that you would not wish to know, yet damned if I wanted to be the one to tell you. Better forewarned, I thought, than chance that you might come upon her unprepared or never know that she is here and . . . and . . ."

"You did the right thing, Cousin, and I thank you for it." Darcy nodded slowly, then took a long pull at his drink. Gracechurch Street. Time . . . he needed time to think.

"Will you . . ." Richard stopped and looked away.

"Will I . . . ?"

"Will you . . . ah, be escorting Georgiana to services Sunday?" His cousin's recovery was admirable, Darcy had to admit that.

"Yes, I will. A new clergyman Brougham desires me to forward for installation will be conducting the service, and—"

" 'Brougham desires!' " Richard's incredulous guffaw attracted stares and uplifted brows from every corner of the club's dining room. "You must be joking! Oh, that is rich, Cousin."

Darcy flushed with annoyance at his slip. Naturally, such a statement would be viewed by the world as ludicrous and in perfect opposition to the persona Dy tried to portray.

"I should almost wish to see such a clergyman as would attract Brougham's attention." Richard continued to laugh.

"Then why not come?" The challenge had sprung from his lips without thought and more for the sake of turning the conversation away from Dy than anything else. "Her Ladyship would be pleased, I have no doubt, to hear from your lips an opinion of this new man, and His Lordship—"

"His Lordship would not believe a word of it, but Pater will defer to Mater on this one. Hmm." Richard sat back and pondered the advantages and disadvantages of his cousin's proposal. That he considered it at all meant that his pockets were already to let, or near to it, for the quarter.

"A game of billiards might be had later."

"Five," Richard shot back.

"So, that is how the land lies?" Darcy's brow rose. "Three."

"Done!" His cousin grinned. "Shall we order another round?"

"We?"

"Oh, only in the broadest sense, Fitz. I have not yet won your money!"

Several days later found them elbow to elbow in the Darcy-Matlock pew on a warm May Sunday. In the intervening time, Darcy had not tried to see Elizabeth, nor had he any business, real or imagined, in the vicinity of Gracechurch Street that might make a chance meeting possible. There would have been no point in it. The last thing Darcy wished to behold was the tight look of politeness, or the hurried excuses to be gone that such a meeting would generate. He would deserve no better in return for that uncharitable letter that he would give almost anything now to have written differently. No, it was better to retain his memories of her in a gentler hue. She would not be in London long. Opening his prayer book, he nudged a corner into Richard's arm and pointed to the scripture for the day as Dy's clergyman began the reading.

The shadows were lengthening, the corners of his study already in darkness, when Witcher knocked and delivered a calling card. "Who is it?" Darcy asked, reaching for the card.

"The Honorable Mr. Beverly Trenholme, sir. I cannot say that I recall the gentleman." The old butler's brow wrinkled in distress. "But he says he is an old friend." *Trenholme!* Darcy thought. *What in the world . . . ?*

"Yes, Witcher, but from university days. I do not believe he has ever called on me here in Town. I spent some time after Christmas with him and his brother, Lord Sayre, in Oxfordshire."

"Oh, begging your pardon, sir. Of course, Oxfordshire!" Witcher shook his head. "Shall I bring him in, sir?"

"Please, Witcher. There's a good man." Darcy rose, straightened his waistcoat, and pulled at his cuffs, the habitual motions helping to clear the tumble of questions Trenholme's sudden appearance had provoked. Dy's warning stood out starkly from among them all, and Darcy wondered whether agreeing to see the man might be more than Brougham would think wise.

The door opened. "Mr. Trenholme, sir."

"Darcy! It is good of you to see me!" Trenholme advanced into the room, one hand extended. In the other was a handle attached to a long, thin leather case.

"Trenholme." Darcy nodded his greeting and took his hand. It felt cold, and he could almost swear that it trembled as they shook. "Please, be seated." Trenholme pulled forward a chair and then, after laying the case gently on the desk, he sat down with a sigh.

"Can you believe that it has been almost four months since last we saw each other?" He sighed again. "Such an awful business. Sayre and I are more than grateful that you have kept mum about my step-mother's suicide and Sayre's financial straits. It only post-poned the inevitable, but one is glad for whatever time the wolves may be kept from the door."

"It is over, then?" Darcy asked evenly.

Trenholme shook his head. "I will not pretend it is not, not with you. Everything movable has been stripped and delivered here for auction at Garraway's. The estate itself goes on the block at the end of the week." A look of murderous hatred shaded Trenholme's face. "It should have been mine! Sayre never cared about anything more than the coin he could wring from it for one more go at the tables. And then that Irish b——!" His voice rose. "Turned our own people against us. You watch her, Darcy! Watch her for the lying little traitor she is! She'll stab you in the back without a thought."

"What do you mean?" Darcy stared hard into Trenholme's eyes while in his mind he tried to piece together names, faces, and conversations from his fractured memories of Sylvanie's soiree. "Traitor? What do you know?"

"What I know is that, between her and Sayre, I no longer have enough money to get drunk on, which is the only state in which I do not wish to send them to—" He stopped. "That is not why I have come. I came to deliver this." He leaned forward and nudged the case toward his host. "You won it fairly, and it should not be sold to pay one farthing toward Sayre's debts."

Darcy opened the case; his breath caught in his throat. The Spanish sword lay there, cradled in velvet. It caught the lamplight immediately he picked it up, blazing in a living fire.

"I may be a coward and a drunk, but I know what is right in a debt of honor. Sayre will damned well pay this one!" Trenholme declared with vehemence.

Darcy hefted it, adjusting his grip on the pommel. It was every bit as perfectly suited to his hand as he remembered.

"Trenholme, I hardly know what to say!" Darcy placed the exquisite weapon back in its velvet swathing.

"There is nothing to say. It has been yours since that night, and you had every right to it all these months. You certainly had enough witnesses to go to the Law if you had wished. Sayre should be grateful that you did not, grateful enough to have sent this to you himself."

"He does not know you brought it to me?" Darcy asked sharply.

"He does now!" Trenholme laughed mirthlessly and rose. "Left him a note!" He nodded his leave. "I'll not take up any more of your time, Darcy, but remember what I said about Sylvanie. Mon-mouth's taken a viper to his bosom, no doubt about that. If there is any deviltry afoot, Sylvanie will be in the thick of it, make no mistake."

"But what will you do?" Darcy's question stopped the Honor-able Beverly Trenholme as he reached for the doorknob. There must be something! Darcy cast about for anything he could offer the man that would answer yet not offend or humiliate him.

"I am for America, I think." Trenholme turned back. A grim smile played upon his face, but even the slight animation that lent never reached his eyes. "I hear English gentlemen are still welcome in Boston, even if tea is not."

"Tea?" Darcy looked askance at him. "I do not believe the cur-rent grievances of the Americans have anything to do with tea, Trenholme."

He shrugged. "I thought they sent a shipload of tea overboard into Boston's harbor."

"Over thirty-five years ago! Tea has been safely shipped to Boston for thirty years and more!" Darcy's jaw worked fiercely to suppress the laugh that threatened insult to his guest. "You need have no fear of going without tea in Boston."

"Oh. Well . . ." Trenholme seemed to have run out of life as well as words. *Passage!* The word pealed in Darcy's ears.

"Wait a moment!" He left Trenholme and went to his desk, drawing out a diary from the top drawer. Flipping through the pages, he came to the section detailing his shipping interests. "If I could arrange your passage to Boston, would you take it?"

"Free passage?" Trenholme's eyes sparked faintly.

"Free passage," Darcy affirmed. "I have controlling interest in a ship bound for Boston, but it leaves tomorrow morning. That is little time . . ."

"I do not require any more time than it would take to gather my things and get to the docks. Do you know what this means, Darcy?" the man cried as his host bent to write out a note to the ship's captain. "Saving the passage money, I shall not arrive in America a pauper."

"Certainly inadvisable." Darcy straightened and handed Trenholme his authorization. "Give this to the captain, and he will take you aboard. It will not be comfortable, not what you are accustomed to . . ."

Trenholme took the note and then Darcy's hand. "You're a good man, Darcy. I shall never forget this." He gulped once and then, turning swiftly, walked out the door, leaving his benefactor to look after him in hope that it was true.

"Why do you continue to check your watch?" Georgiana asked her brother as he pulled the timepiece once more from his waistcoat pocket. The weather continuing so fine the next day, they had decided to take a turn in St. James's Park.

"A friend left for America early this morning. According to the schedule, his ship should reach the open sea within the next quarter of an hour. I suppose I was trying to guess exactly where he might be."

"A good friend?"

"Perhaps. I hope I was a 'good friend' to him whatever the case."

The sound of a horse's hooves pounding the turf at a reckless pace caused Darcy to turn sharply about and then to push his sister behind him and away from the path. The horse and rider continued toward them, checking only at the very last moment.

"Darcy!" the rider gasped, his eyes wild and hard.

"Good God, Dy, what do you think you are doing?" Darcy shouted angrily.

"No time for that! Where is Trenholme? Do you know where he is?"

"On a ship bound for America! Why? What is this?" A cold fear clutched at his vitals.

"When did you see him last? Did he say anything about Lady

Monmouth's whereabouts?" The horse under Brougham danced, putting into motion the desperation in his voice.

"Last night, and no, he did not say where she was. Only that he wished her dead and warned me to watch for her. What is it, Dy? What has happened?"

"The Prime Minister . . . Perceval." Brougham looked beyond him, seeking Georgiana's eyes. Darcy knew the moment Dy found them, for they softened, but in less than a breath he withdrew back into himself and looked again at Darcy. "The Prime Minister was shot dead not fifteen minutes ago in the halls of Parliament."

Darcy barely heard Georgiana's cry for the force of his own shocked "No!"

"It is true." Dy pulled at the reins, his mount's agitation increasing. "We have the assassin, but there are others."

"Sylvanie?" Darcy breathed, "You believe Sylvanie to be involved?"

"The murderer is John Bellingham, Fitz, the man who insulted you, who kept so near Sylvanie at her soiree. Her Ladyship must be found!"

"What can I do?" Darcy caught at the reins and drew Brougham closer. "Anything!"

Dy shook his head. "Nothing directly. I must be off and can give you no assurance of my quick return. Take care of Miss Darcy, Fitz! I know you shall, but do so for my sake as well? It could be quite some time."

"Of course, without question! Take care, and Godspeed, my friend!"

"And you." Dy looked down on him with a wistful smile. "Miss Darcy." He nodded to her and was gone.

Georgiana was in his arms in an instant. "Oh, Fitzwilliam. What has happened? Where is Lord Brougham going?"

"The world has turned upside down," he whispered against her hair, "and Dy has gone to fix it."

CHAPTER 7

An Unperfect Actor

"I assure you, I shall manage perfectly." Darcy looked past his long-faced valet to nod his acknowledgment to the serving man who had appeared at the inn door with the information that his horse was ready at the mounting block. "You are merely hours behind, a day at most."

"Yes, sir," Fletcher answered, a sigh all but audible in his voice. The heat of August had not quite rendered the journey from London unbearable, but the addition of Mr. Hurst's new valet to the servant's carriage had set all of Darcy's people, particularly Fletcher, on edge. "A sneaksby and a mushroom!" Fletcher had pronounced Hurst's man as he attended Darcy their first night out of Town, and his reports worsened at each stop along their way. Darcy was not without sympathy for his valet's complaints, for the company of Miss Bingley also grew increasingly tedious in direct proportion to the hours spent confined with her in the coach. Her brother's conversation offered some respite, as did Georgiana's attempts to interest her in a book or the scenery, but Darcy could only thank Heaven when, upon arriving at the last coaching inn before Derbyshire, he had found waiting for him an urgent note from Sherrill, his steward, requesting his immediate presence at Pemberley. The call of duty could hardly have been sweeter, its siren tone reaching Fletcher's ear as well, but it was impossible that Darcy's valet should accompany him. Nor did he desire any company. These last miles before home he wished to spend alone, with only his thoughts for companions, before he entered into the incessant demands of master and host of his great ancestral estate.

A knock at his door brought Darcy around to see his sister poised at the threshold, a somewhat strained look upon her face. "Sweetling," he sighed as he strode to her, "I am sorry to leave you so!"

"Not so *very* sorry." She sent him a rueful but understanding smile. "I wish we were near enough that I might ride ahead as well."

He bent and bussed her forehead. "When you get to Pemberley—"

"It will be better, I know," she finished. "We will not be in each other's pockets, especially when Aunt and Uncle Matlock arrive with D'Arcy and his new fiancée and family. I hope—" She stopped then and bit her lower lip.

"What, dearest?" He looked down tenderly into her wistful eyes.

"That I shall find a friend among these new relations D'Arcy brings us." She rested her head upon his shoulder. "My own friend."

"As do I." He embraced her and then, gently setting her from him, chucked her under her chin. "I *must* go, but I promise you, we shall look into this business. Perhaps Aunt Matlock may have some suggestions."

Pulling on his gloves and gathering his hat, saddlebag, and crop, Darcy saluted his sister and made for the door, his stride becoming a run down the steps when he heard a door behind him open to the sound of women's voices. Turning the corner at the base of the stairs, he quickly passed through the public rooms and out into the sunlight of what promised to be a warm Der-byshire day.

"Darcy!" Bingley's cry from behind him brought him to a halt. He turned and, smiling at the figure of his friend, waited for him to catch up. The last three months had not only brought Darcy peace from his crushing rejection at Rosings Park but had wrought significant changes in the manner of his friendship with Bingley, but also, Darcy was convinced, in Bingley himself. The man strid-ing purposefully toward him was not the same Bingley of a year or even three months ago. There was more confidence in his carriage and assurance in his lineaments.

"Bingley!" He grinned at the look of reproach his friend freely cast him. "Your pardon for leaving without saying farewell, but I truly must be off if I am to reach Pemberley in good time."

"Say no more." Bingley grasped his hand and, falling into step with him, accompanied Darcy to the mounting block and his waiting horse. "I did not expect it; I just wish I could accompany you." He peered down the road and, with a frown, turned back and addressed him. "Is it wise to go alone?"

"I expect to catch up with the baggage coaches in an hour and will have them release Trafalgar. The two of us should pass rela-tively unnoticed through the backcountry of Derbyshire." Darcy patted the pistol in his saddlebag. "If not, we are not without re-sources should we be ascosted."

"Well then, I shan't detain you except to wish you Godspeed and to promise to deliver Miss Darcy and all my relations upon your doorstep tomorrow." Bingley grinned and shook Darcy's hand once more but solemnly. "Take care, Darcy."

"And you, my friend," Darcy replied and swung up into the saddle. "Until tomorrow!"

The mount beneath him was not Nelson but rather a less un-predictable cousin dutifully sent forward from Pemberley by Darcy's steward. Nevertheless, the animal's bloodlines ran true, and the ground between the inn and the coaches was eaten up in less time than Darcy had thought. Even so, Trafalgar's affronted bark, alternating with a beseeching whine, reached him before he had even sighted the coaches. Upon being released and restored to his master's side, the hound first trembled from nose to tail with undisguised joy, then with equal enthusiasm, rolled in the dust of the road, ran around Darcy's horse in circles, attempted to leap up, and pawed ecstatically at his boot.

"Down, Monster!" Darcy thundered, then winced at the deep scratch that now transected his right boot. Fletcher would not be pleased. The hound sat dutifully, but his twitching tail beat out the quickly passing moments that might have been expected to contain such strenuous obedience. Nodding to Trafalgar's keeper, Darcy urged his horse on, issuing a curt "Come!" to his erstwhile devotee. With an explosion of compliance, Trafalgar raced ahead, circled back, repeated the maneuver, and finally fell into a trot beside him, his happiness so complete that Darcy could only laugh and marvel at how very good it felt to be exactly where he was.

Now that the Monster accompanied him, Darcy slowed his pace to a steady, comfortable one, which he judged would bring them home to Pemberley by late morning. Pemberley! On the one hand, he was impatient to be there, to sluice away the pervasive dust of summer travel and breathe in all the familiar tranquillities of his beloved home. There was even a pleasant anticipation, he found, in setting into motion his solutions to those alarms forwarded by his steward and in meeting the routine seasonal obligations of his lands. On the other hand lay a profound sense that these hours by himself without duty or obligation to distract him, this time to reflect and consider, was essential to his well-being and future. Here, on this road through Derbyshire, before God and any man who might pass him by, he was nothing more than a man alone with his horse and his hound and his conscience.

After the terrible days following the assassination of the Prime Minister, caution had urged Darcy that he ought personally to escort Georgiana out of the city and to the safety of Pemberley.

Rumor at first ran amuck, suggesting that the entire country was on the verge of rebellion. The unknown temper of the countryside militated against chancing their safety on the road; therefore, they had stayed in Grosvenor Square behind closed doors until some reliable report was to be had. When it had become apparent that the Government still stood, London had settled down to going about its business in the usual fashion in shockingly short order. With the certainty that the plot had been centered in the person of John Bellingham, the entire population seemed to throw the incident over its shoulder and pick up the Season where it had left off, and a removal no longer appeared necessary. Lady Monmouth had disappeared, her abandoned lord knowing not where; and although it had been almost three months, they had still no word from Lord Brougham. Darcy suspected that his friend had pursued the Somewhat-Less-Honorable Beverly Trenholme to America. If so, it would be some time before Dy reappeared in London.

In a few weeks Darcy's life was returned to its normal rhythms but not, he had discovered, to his habitual courses. Something had changed in that terrible time since Hunsford, had changed profoundly. He was not the same man he had been. Looking back at that arrogant suitor of last spring, he wondered at himself as he would a stranger. It all seemed so very long ago. What a figure he had cut, striding with such exalted confidence down the steps of Rosings Hall and along the path to the village! From a three-month perspective, he considered that impeccably dressed man as he made his way to Hunsford parsonage, so self-assured, so certain of his reception and answer. For a moment, he felt again the pangs of the humiliation that lay before him. In a very short space, that stranger's world would be turned on its head, changed forever.

He had been the recipient, he now gratefully acknowledged, of a rare and precious gift. In demanding the hand of a woman he neither understood nor was capable of knowing, he had instead received from her the chance to see himself and the opportunity to become a better man. And he had changed. He knew he had. He knew that he was not that man stalking angrily back to his chambers in Rosings Hall. What had happened to him in those intervening months? He was not sure; he could offer no complete explanation, but the man who had opened Rosings's doors, already prepared to write an angry letter, was a stranger, a man who had been walking through his entire life asleep. But now, he had awoken.

Some things, such as his more equitable relationship with Bingley, had changed quickly. Others, Darcy had to admit, had come more slowly. Some had been painful—the honest inventorying of his offenses tallied an alarming list—while others had furnished his life with new purposes and pleasures. The result had been that the world had become a much more interesting place, filled with fellow travelers whose joys and sorrows he no longer disdained to know and whose shortcomings he was far more inclined to overlook. He knew that he would never be one of that hearty sort who immediately attracted the interest and goodwill of all he met, but no longer would he allow himself to stand aloof, even among strangers. *He* would accommodate; *he* would seek to set at ease rather than silently demand to be pleased. It was difficult at times, but a newborn compassion joined with determined practice made surmounting his reserve easier. One day, he hoped, it would be part of his nature.

Nature? He looked about for Trafalgar, who possessed with those reserves of energy that encouraged him to follow his nose, had been largely absent from his company. Loping back at Darcy's whistle, the hound presented a tired mass of burrs and stickers. "It appears that a rest is in order," Darcy remarked to the panting wretch below him. Truly, the animal did look terrible, but it was a result more of his own adventures in the brush than the arduous nature of their pace. Reining in, he drew his leg over and dropped to the ground, then reached for his saddlebag and pulled out the flask of water inside. "Here, Monster." He waved the flask before the hound but then realized that he had nothing into which to pour it. Pulling off his glove, he cupped his hand under the lip and then bent down, slowly pouring the water into his hand while the hound frantically lapped it up. "There, that is enough." He straightened, shaking droplets from his hand. "I am thirsty as well!" he protested to the pathetic whine and took a long draw of what remained. "Ingrate!" he accused Trafalgar, wiping his lips. "You do not hear Seneca complain, and he has had to carry me all these miles!" Hearing his name, the horse nickered and tossed his head, to the supreme disinterest of Trafalgar, whose eyes remained trained upon the flask.

Darcy stretched and then took a deep breath of Derbyshire air, happy to be out of the soot-laden grime of Town, happy to be within an hour of home. He returned the empty flask to his saddlebag, pausing to stroke Seneca's thick mane. The animal stopped in his pull at a clump of grass just long enough to nudge him roughly, whether in affection or to move him away from the clump he now attacked, Darcy was not certain. He laughed, scratching the horse vigorously along his withers as he considered the intense anger, the indignation he had nurtured that first dark week back in London. It seemed the experience of another man. How different Elizabeth's refusal appeared to him now.

A sharp bark recalled him to his errant hound. Trafalgar's luminous brown eyes and twitching tail communicated his impatient anticipation of home. "It will not be long." Darcy bent and ruffled the animal's ears. "We are almost home." The hound was a bit battered from his forays into the brush, but likely better for the experience. Not at all unlike himself, Darcy mused. Yes, he indeed owed Miss Elizabeth Bennet a debt. In her principled refusal of him, she had done him no harm; rather, she had done him incalculable good. What an incredible young woman! The wretched letter had been, in part, a bid for some little of her respect.

He gave Monster a final pat before hoisting himself back atop Seneca. "Only a few more miles and we shall cross into the home wood," he informed the hound. "The lake is just beyond, and I strongly advise that you avail yourself! You do not look or smell like a gentleman in the least, and if you do not take care of it, a stable lad will!"

Refreshed, he gathered the reins and pressed on, the nearness of his own lands increasing the longing in his heart to be home. With new energy, his horse pounded through the home wood. The path, hard and dusty from a dry summer, wound its way up and down the rugged Derbyshire hills before it emptied into the broad valley through which the Ere wound until it reached the dam that formed it into a perfect reflection of Pemberley House. In his anticipation, Darcy had left Trafalgar scrambling far behind and so pulled Seneca to a halt just as they broke through the trees above the valley. The both of them breathing hard, he let the reins go slack and leaned over Seneca's neck to stretch out the muscles in his back while they waited for the third of their party. As he returned upright, his eyes were drawn immediately down the expanse of valley.

How many times had he seen his home from afar, whether from this vantage point or some other? Yet he could no more stop his eyes from traveling over every aspect of the majestic structure than he could prevent himself from rejoicing in the beauty of the gardens or the natural loveliness of the river and wood. Pemberley. Home. This time, however, there resided something new in that part of him which swelled at the sight. He looked down on Pemberley House, questioning every exquisite line until that something found a name. *Gratitude.* Gratitude for what he had been given filled his breast. And for the first time in his life, Darcy felt that he might possibly be worthy to hold the great gift that had been entrusted to him.

A scrabbling sound in the brush behind him alerted Darcy to his companion's arrival, and looking down from Seneca's height, he noted it with a sympathetic laugh. Trafalgar was, if it were possible, in an even more disreputable state, his sides heaving and tongue lolling as he threw himself at the horse's feet. "Do not blame me!" Darcy addressed the weary animal. "Perhaps next time you will not indulge your curiosity quite so often and attend to business." The flash of a canine grin at his tone put the possibility of such a lesson learned firmly outside the realm. "Very well, then, Monster." He laughed. "Shall we see who reaches home first?" At the word *home,* a miracle of sorts occurred, followed by a blur of movement, and the next he knew, Trafalgar was no more than a streak moving down the valley. "Ho!" Darcy yelled to Seneca and, putting heels to his sides, gave the horse his head in pursuit. That they both clattered into the stable yard within feet of each other he charged to the loss of his hat. Forced to stop and retrieve it, he could do no more than recover the ground between them, which was not enough to decently call it a tie. When he dismounted, he almost landed upon his preening competitor, who danced about Seneca's legs. "Yes, you win!" he conceded and, suffering Trafalgar's triumphant bark with good grace, was rewarded with a consoling but wet tribute to his sportsmanship.

"Welcome home, sir!" The head of Pemberley's stables motioned to the lad with him to take Seneca's reins.

"Thank you, Morley. It is good to be home." Darcy nodded and handed over Seneca. "See he is well cooled," he called after them as the lad led him away.

"Hard ride, sir?" Morley watched his young charge as he led the horse to a paddock.

"Not bad. How are things here?" Darcy stripped off his gloves and, taking off the troublesome hat, threw the gloves into its depths and, with a quick smile, handed the lot to another lad who had run up. Morley waved the boy off to the servants' entrance to Pemberley House and then fell into step with his master.

"Vera good, sir. Everythin' is right and tight. All the young uns are comin' fine, sir, comin' fine. Not a weak or sickly one in the lot this year. I think you'll be pleased."

"Excellent! No problems, then?" Darcy looked past his stable master as a team that he did not recognize was led away from the traces of an unknown carriage. "Visitors?" His gaze returned to Morley.

"Day trippers, sir, come to view the house an' grounds. We just got notice from the house that they intend to walk the gardens when they're done and maybe the park and we were to unhitch the horses."

Darcy grimaced. "Visitors! Well, I shall take the long way around then. I meant to send Trafalgar into the lake anyway. The beast is in sad want of a bath." He looked about, but the hound was nowhere to be seen. "Now where did he go!" He sounded a sharp whistle and then shouted, "Trafalgar! Monster!" A bark from the direction of the lake answered him back.

"Sounds like he's afore you, Mr. Darcy." Morley laughed.

"He usually is! Good day to you, Morley." Morley's "An' to you, sir," followed him as he strode purposefully after the hound, as much to stretch out the cramped muscles in his legs as to make sure the animal became intimately acquainted with the benefits of Pemberley's lake. As he walked, Darcy breathed in the flower-freshened breezes wafting from the gardens and smiled to himself. He had made good time; it was still early in the afternoon, and he was home. He looked toward the house. No sign of the visitors whose intrusions were part and parcel of the obligations of a great house. Good! Hurrying on to the lake, he found the hound nervously pacing its edge, looking over his shoulder in anxiety for Darcy's appearance.

"Here I am, Monster, but you need not have waited. Get on with it!" he urged him. Trafalgar sat down and whined. "Swim!" Darcy commanded. The hound looked at him, dumbfounded. "Swim!" He motioned toward the water, but the animal seemed unable to comprehend his meaning. "Humph!" Darcy looked narrowly down into his dog's face, studying whether he was truly confused or merely being recalcitrant. Too canny for him, Trafalgar avoided his gaze, looking away across the lake and up to the gardens. "So that is the way of it." Darcy searched about him and, breaking a dry branch in two across his knee, he returned to the lake's edge to find he was now in possession of the hound's undivided attention. They regarded each other in silence, each watching for any movement, any drop in the other's resolve. Suddenly, with a swift jerk of his arm, Darcy threw the branch far into the lake. "Fetch!" Without the slightest hesitation, the hound sprang into the water and paddled determinedly after the prize.

Darcy skirted the edge of the lake, laughing and shouting encouragement to the hound as he swam, and met him on the other side, taking care to arrive only after Trafalgar had emerged and shaken off the worst of the water that clung to his coat. "Good man!" Darcy accepted the branch from the dog's jaws. "Now, up to the house with you!" With a last, soulful glance at his prize, the animal loped off toward one of the gardens, leaving Darcy to follow. He tossed the branch away and turned his face toward his home. Home! The pleasant, grateful elation of earlier returned, warming his heart. Rejoining the road from the stable, he determined to make his way through the lower garden and thus avoid the hall, for he was in no proper state to greet strangers after this morning's ride, and although the elation remained, he was not long on his way before he began to feel the morning's exertions. He tugged at his cravat until it hung in loose, sweat-stained loops about his neck. His coat he had already unbuttoned, nor did he have the will to rebutton it. He was both hatless and gloveless, having sent these items ahead with a stable boy, and he could feel the dust and grit of the road being rubbed against his skin by the weight of his clothing. His face . . . He paused to rub at his eyes and chin. No, in no state at all!

Dropping his hand, Darcy turned into a parting in the tall hedge that marked the boundary of the lower garden's lawn only to be brought up short. The visitors! He hesitated at the sight of the three strangers whose backs were, fortunately, turned to him as they inspected the exterior of his home under the care of Old Simon. He had mistaken the time, Darcy groaned to himself, and they were already arrived in the gardens. Perhaps he could retreat quietly the way he had come. As he took a step backward, one of the ladies turned, her eyes coming to rest full upon him. The light in them struck him like a bolt. *Elizabeth! My God, Elizabeth?* Every nerve in his body came alive, yet he seemed unable to command them to any purposeful action. Elizabeth—here! The truth of it raced through him, yet his mind reeled into denial. How could it be? But it must be; for there she stood not twenty yards away, her lovely eyes wide in surprise and then turned from him as a blush suffused her cheeks. An answering heat flushed his face as he searched for a sign, an indication of how he should approach her. None came, and she remained a picture of beautiful confusion. That he must relieve her anxiety was his only thought; he must be the one to make a beginning. Willing his limbs forward, he went to her.

"Miss Elizabeth Bennet." He offered her a slow, honoring bow. He could barely hear her answering acknowledgment and found, upon rising, that her blush had deepened further and that her eyes looked almost everywhere but at him. "Please allow me to welcome you to Pemberley, Miss Elizabeth." Her "thank you" was soft as a breath and no more substantial. She was clearly uncomfortable. Somehow he must set her at ease. "I was not aware that you planned to visit Derbyshire," Darcy ventured. She made no reply. "Have you and your companions been long on the road?"

"We left Longbourn a little more than two weeks ago, sir." Her answer to this was stronger-voiced but still quavered in the summer air.

"Ah . . . and your family is well? Or was well?" he amended. "Your sisters? Have you received any communication?" He grimaced inwardly at his jumbled, awkward sentences.

"Yes and no, Mr. Darcy." She bit her lower lip. "Yes, they were well when I left, but no, I have not received any communication as yet."

"Oh, I see . . . Your trip, it has been pleasant?" he persisted.

"The weather, it seems, has been in your favor. Have you found it so?" She smiled slightly at that and agreed that the weather had, indeed, been fine. "Yes, so I have found," he affirmed, ''although I have been on the road only three days. You have been traveling how long?"

"Two weeks, sir."

"Yes, you did say that. Two weeks. Do you stay in Derbyshire long? Where are you staying?" Good Lord, that was blunt of him!

"The inn, the Green Man, in Lambton, sir."

"Ah, yes, the Green Man. Garston, he is the proprietor, keeps a fine inn. But watch for all his grandchildren," he responded, "especially when he discovers you have been a guest at Pemberley. There will be no end to their courtesies. Did you say how long you would remain in the vicinity?"

"No, I did not." She glanced away nervously in the direction of the others. "I remain at my companions' pleasure. It has not been decided as yet when we shall leave."

"I see." He paused. What else to say? "And your parents, they are well?"

She did smile fully at that and even looked him directly in the face. A breeze played with the curls about her temple, and the color or style of her bonnet, he knew not which, did lovely things to her eyes and enhanced the radiance of her face. Good Lord, it was a wonderful sight! "To the best of my knowledge, Mr. Darcy," came her reply. He smiled back. She looked away. Was it distress that wrinkled her brow? Had he said something wrong? Perhaps it was himself, his present unkempt appearance. Did she doubt her welcome? She must never think that! If he said nothing more, he must assure her at least of that.

"You are very welcome to Pemberley, Miss Elizabeth, you and your companions." He bowed. "Please, take all the time you desire to walk the park and grounds. Simon knows all the best views and the most pleasant walks. You are in excellent hands with him. If you will excuse me, I have just arrived and must attend to some business." He bowed again, receiving this time her soft leave of his departure.

Moving past her, he continued on, the exultation in his heart at her presence at his home vying with embarrassment with his miserable performance and, he looked down in dismay, his disheveled appearance. What must she think of him? With a groan, he hurried on. If only Fletcher *had* accompanied him! Under his valet's care, he could have been presentable in a quarter hour. It could not be helped. He ran up the steps and into the hall, surprising Mrs. Reynolds as she was locking up one of the public rooms.

"Mr. Darcy, sir!"

"Mrs. Reynolds! Yes, I arrived not long ago." He flashed her the smile that had served him well with her for twenty-four years. "How long would it take for hot water to be sent up?"

"Fifteen minutes, sir, unless you desire a bath." She looked at him curiously.

"No, that will not be necessary. Make it warm and in ten minutes and send up one of the footmen to help me dress, if you please!" he said as he made for the staircase. He stopped halfway to the top and looked back down the hall. "Oh, and Mrs. Reynolds, Trafalgar is with me or, rather, somewhere. Perhaps a boy should be sent to the garden?"

"Yes, sir. We shall attend to Master Trafalgar." Mrs. Reynolds looked up wonderingly at him.

"Excellent! Ten minutes, Mrs. Reynolds!" He continued up the stairs and all but ran to his dressing room. He shed the dusty clothes of his morning while at the same time searching through the neatly hung and ordered garments. Good Heavens, what should he wear? Nothing too imposing. Would hunting attire be too casual? Would she regard it an insult? His gaze ranged over the choices before him. "Fletcher!" he groaned aloud. "What in blazes should I—" A knock at the door interrupted his plea. "Enter!"

"Mr. Darcy, sir! Is there aught amiss?" Mr. Reynolds poked his head in first and then, seeing his master's distraction, entered.

"You required a footman, sir. Is Mr. Fletcher not with you or shortly to arrive?"

"No, Sherrill's note brought me ahead on horseback, but it is very urgent now that I attend to my guests."

"Guests, sir?" Reynolds was confused. "None of your guests have— Oh, the visitors! But they are out in the park, sir; you need not trouble yourself." Another knock sounded.

"The water!" Darcy jumped to the door, much to Reynolds's surprise. "Come in; pour some in the basin and set the rest over there," he directed the brawny youth. "Very good; that will be all." He turned his attention back to his astonished butler. "It is of incalculable importance that I trouble myself for these particular visitors. If I can prevail upon them to return to the house, they should be treated with the utmost courtesy." A sudden anxiety seized him. "They were well cared for earlier, I trust?"

"Yes, sir. Mrs. Reynolds conducted them personally. The young lady claimed some little acquaintance," he offered.

"Yes, that is true . . ." Darcy turned back to his wardrobe and stared at its contents.

"May I help you, sir?" Reynolds briskly stepped forward. "I believe I may be of equal or better service than a footman."

Surprised at such condescension, Darcy turned to his butler, a man he had known most of his life, to behold one still possessed of all the dignity of his office but with an understanding twinkle in his eye. "Yes, you may." He nodded toward the wardrobe. "The doeskin breeches, I think, the tan waistcoat and dark brown coat. A plain neckcloth, mind you, and shirt. The brown-topped boots . . . and a clean set of all else."

"Very good, sir. All shall be ready." The old man straightened his shoulders before this new duty.

"Thank you, Reynolds." Darcy's lips twitched against an incipient grin. "I will not be long."

Despite his impatient speed and Reynolds's surprising alacrity with his clothes, it was almost a half hour before Darcy clattered down the courtyard's steps and onto the drive. Where Elizabeth was now in the vast expanse of the park had occupied his thoughts as he had finished dressing. Old Simon would keep them to the usual paths shown to visitors, but where exactly might they be? He scanned the perimeter of the wood that girdled the near park. Knowing her stamina, they might be anywhere, but he doubted the endurance of her older companions. He narrowed his search. There! A flash of color among the trees that overhung the path meandering by the river gave him his course. He set off, judging that even at such a pace he had a quarter hour in which to prepare to meet her.

They had made a beginning, but he was in no position to say how good a one. It was very possible he was striding toward a woman who would rather he were at the Antipodes than coming to escort her to his home. He called up the emotions that had crossed her countenance as they had spoken. Confusion, embarrassment, both had cast their shades over her loveliness, but there had been no trace of aversion or the cool politeness he had feared in an imagined encounter. Nor welcome either, he reminded himself. Well, there was no help for it! He could not stay away from her, not here on his own lands, where he had the best chance of showing her, expressing to her, his gratitude for what she had done for him. A fullness of heart came hard on the heels of that thought, and the incredible good fortune of her visiting Pemberley seized him again. He strode on until, rounding a curve in the walk, he came upon them.

This time she was able to greet his arrival with her usual self-possession. He had hardly risen from his bow when he heard the words "charming" and "delightful" applied to all she had surveyed. Schooling his features to display a more moderate pleasure at her words than he would have liked, he thanked her. "Charming" and "delightful" were commonly ascribed to Pemberley by visitors, but never before had the accolades held such significance. Elizabeth found his home charming and delightful. Better and better. His elation was short-lived, however; for no sooner had he thanked her than she colored and fell silent. At a loss for the change in her demeanor, he hesitated. He must engage her again, restore her ease in speaking to him. What? Her companions! How could he have ignored them for so long! They must think him . . .

"Miss Elizabeth, would you do me the honor of introducing me to your friends?" The look she returned him to this request was a curious mixture of surprise and amusement. Whatever it meant, he promised himself as he followed her to where her friends awaited, he *would* meet it with credit.

"Aunt Gardiner, Uncle Gardiner, may I present Mr. Darcy? Mr. Darcy, my uncle and aunt, Mr. Edward Gardiner and Mrs. Edward Gardiner."

Relations! He looked at them in surprise. He should have guessed, but the placid gentleman and lady before him were as unlike the family members with whom he was familiar as he could imagine. "Your servant, sir." He bowed.

"And yours, sir," Mr. Gardiner replied. "We have been thoroughly enjoying your house and lands, Mr. Darcy, and must tell you at once what wonderful attention your servants have bestowed upon us. We have been made more welcome at Pemberley than at any other great house we have visited on our holiday."

"I am glad to hear it, sir!" Darcy smiled at the genuine pleasure in the man's voice. "We are pleased to have earned such a good report." He turned to the lady. "Ma'am, I hope that the park has not been too fatiguing for you. It is quite a distance around."

Mrs. Gardiner smiled brightly up at him. "I confess, sir, I am tired but have rarely been so pleasantly rewarded for the effort. Pemberley is lovelier than words can tell."

"Thank you, ma'am." He bowed. "If I may, please allow me to conduct you back in Simon's place. I think I may know almost as much as he about the way." To this they readily assented, and dismissing the grateful gardener back to his pruning, Darcy took up a place next to Elizabeth's uncle as they set out. It was but a few minutes before he discovered Mr. Gardiner to be not only a man of particular intelligence and taste but a fellow fisherman as well. Delighted to have hit upon something they held so closely in common, he invited his guest to fish the river whenever he desired and offered him tackle and advice on the best spots for sport.

In the midst of the men's fishing stories, the ladies before them descended to the river in exclamation over some water plant of unusual parts. Mr. Gardiner, in fine humor, recommended they stay on the path until the feminine raptures were done and the ladies returned. Although he would have liked to have had a part in Elizabeth's short expedition, Darcy remained with her uncle, watching the proceedings closely lest any accident befall them.

"My dear," Mrs. Gardiner addressed her husband upon returning to the path. "Your arm, I beg of you. I fear I am more fatigued than I had believed."

"Of course, my love." Mr. Gardiner stepped forward smartly. Darcy's hopes expanded. As the Gardiners fell behind them, he moved forward to Elizabeth; but she greeted this new arrangement with silence, the brim of her bonnet serving as a barrier to him. Committed to his course, he prepared to begin again with her.

"Mr. Darcy." Elizabeth's voice issued from behind her bonnet brim. "It seems that your arrival today was very unexpected, for your housekeeper informed us that you would certainly not be here till tomorrow; and indeed, before we left Bakewell we understood that you were not immediately expected in the country. Otherwise, we would never have dreamt of invading your privacy."

"Indeed, that had been my plan," he acknowledged, "but I received yesterday a note from my steward that required my presence sooner rather than later, and I came forward a few hours before the rest of the party with whom I am traveling. They will join me early tomorrow." He paused, wondering how she would receive the information, then continued. "Among them are some who will claim an acquaintance with you—Mr. Bingley and his sisters." Only the slightest of bows indicated that she had heard him. Darcy looked away, his lips pressed together in dismay. The conversation was circling in upon itself, and he had no notion of how to elicit something more from her. In fact, his mention of the Bingleys may have prompted her to decamp from the area as quickly as possible. But she could not go! Not before he had shown her that he was, indeed, a different man than that one who had accosted her in Hunsford's parlor. Not before Georgiana had had an opportunity to meet her whom she had so wished to know since his mention of her last autumn. He laid hold of that thought.

"There is also one other person in the party who more particularly wishes to be known to you." He took a deep breath. "Will you allow me, or do I ask too much, to introduce my sister to your acquaintance during your stay at Lambton?" What followed as he bent to hear was a jumble of expressions, the sum of which tended to her willingness and pleasure in fulfilling Miss Darcy's wish of acquaintance and that, yes, she would be happy to receive Miss Darcy the day after she arrived home. When she had finished, silence again descended upon them, but it seemed to Darcy it was of a different sort than had plagued them before. She was pleased; he could tell it, and he was content.

They were soon quite in advance of her relations, nearly to the house. As they approached, they slowed, and looking down at her, he asked, "Miss Elizabeth, will you walk into the house?" He was rewarded with a brief upward flash of her eyes. "You must be in want of rest or refreshment, and within you might await your aunt and uncle in some comfort."

"No, I thank you, Mr. Darcy," she replied, "but I am not at all tired." There followed more silence. He observed her anxiously, wondering how he should go on. Then, suddenly, Elizabeth began to speak of the other great houses she had seen during her holiday, and they were able to share observations and opinions on estates and gardens in the neighborhood until Mr. and Mrs. Gardiner arrived. His invitation to walk in was repeated, but to no avail. They were much obliged but it had been a very long day and they must return to the inn. A lad was sent to the stable yard, and in short order, the carriage was brought forward.

"Mrs. Gardiner." Darcy handed her up into the carriage with care. "Miss Elizabeth Bennet." He turned to her and performed the same office, not caring that her relations might notice the softness in his voice or the lingering of his hand upon hers. He stepped back from the carriage but stayed to watch them long after it was needful, and even then, he walked slowly back to his door. He had made a beginning, and she had consented to receive him in two days' time. It was enough.

Darcy's gaze searched the confines of his book room in growing exasperation. Was there nothing that could distract him long enough to allow his mind and body to settle into more rational courses? How was he to meet the mundane and obligatory when every part of him was so very alive to the events of the afternoon? After leaving the pleasurable sight of Elizabeth's curious, backward gaze at him from the carriage, he had retired to his book room and study with the intent of preparing for the interview with his steward that had called him forward. But when the study door was safely shut against any chance observance by his staff, he found himself utterly unable to do so. For a quarter hour now he had paced the room, incapable of any thoughts save those that centered upon the surprise and delight of discovering Elizabeth at Pemberley. The words they had exchanged, the time spent so closely in her company crowded his brain and heart. Jostling them for room was the anticipation of their next meeting, an appointment that sent distracting sensations flashing along every nerve. It was not until Witcher's knock and the announcement of Sherrill that respite from the sweet agony of his reflections was forced upon Darcy and any other subject could be entertained.

His steward's concerns required he return to the saddle and accompany him out to deal with several difficult cases among his tenants and examine an unexpected obstacle to the draining of a field bordering the Ere. Several hours later found them still pondering balance sheets and hay production estimates spread out upon his book room desk. Finally, nodding his leave to go with a reassuring smile, Darcy dismissed his much-relieved steward to his dinner and the task of putting his directives into motion. The difficulties that had occasioned his early return he had met with some rather innovative solutions that had not easily won Sherrill's confidence. In the end, Darcy had prevailed, not an uncommon scene within these walls over the generations of Darcys who had ruled here. But as he looked about him from the perspective of his desk, the events of earlier that day returned to possess Darcy, and this, his haven and seat, strangely became too small to contain all that now strove in his breast. Rising, he took a deep breath. He must steady himself, somehow integrate that hard-won sense of himself into this opportunity Providence had bestowed. In short order he found himself pushing open the doors to the conservatory, the Eden of his parents' creation.

The fragrance of fertile earth and summer blossoms enveloped him as he stood just inside, the doors behind him swinging shut of their own accord. In the gathering dusk he could still distinguish his mother's favorite chair among the vining exotica and, near to it, the lounge upon which his father had spent his last painful days surrounded by the living tribute to his wife's artistry and their deep affection, each for the other. He looked up between the branches and vines into the darkening sky, where a clutch of stars was already visible, and inhaled the encompassing peace. Elizabeth was near. He imagined her at table with her uncle and aunt, smiling yet pensive behind those lovely, bright eyes as she reviewed their encounter in the privacy of her heart. With what anticipation did she regard their forthcoming meeting? Had she been as pleased with the conclusion as he had at first thought? It would be more than he deserved. Or had she been merely polite, caught as she had been on his lands?

He sighed and set out slowly for the far end of the conservatory. And Georgiana! He smiled at the thought. She would be overjoyed with his news! How keenly she had regretted never having had the opportunity to make Elizabeth's acquaintance. She, who so longed for a friend of the heart, could never find another of such perfect sanguinity. He would watch them closely. If they delighted in each other, as he hoped, what better friend or confidante could he desire for his sister?

He had reached the end and stopped, peering out into the darkness of the gardens beyond Eden for a moment before turning about. Above him, through the glass, he could see the pale walls and brightly lit windows of Pemberley shimmering in the night. Elizabeth was near, as were Georgiana, the memories of his parents, what he had been born to, and what he had lately learned that truly meant. Here, in this place, they together filled his soul, propelling it upward in renewed gratitude and a sense of peace. He started back through the conservatory, a smile upon his face. Yes, Georgiana would be overjoyed. So much so that, perhaps, she might not wish to wait an entire day to begin her new acquaintance. He devoutly hoped that would be so!

"Mr. Darcy, sir, the carriage has been sighted." Darcy looked up from his book and thanked the footman before inserting his mark and putting it aside. He had read little and understood even less, the volume being more a prop in the masking of his expectations for the day than a true endeavor. Pulling at his cuffs and waistcoat, he strode to the door and out into the hall. The wide main door was open to what summer breeze might chance by as well as to the broad sweep of the carriageway, where he did, indeed, spy his own coach bowling smartly down the lane followed closely by Bingley's equipage. The vehicles raised such dust that a breeze carried a shower of it toward the door and desposited a layer upon his coat as he stepped outside to meet them. Flicking away the undesirable patina so as not to mar Fletcher's brushing of that morning, he composed himself to greet his sister and friends.

Lads from the stables quickly stepped up to the leaders while an army of footmen opened doors, pulled down steps, and retrieved the guests' cloaks, cases, and portmanteaus. As Fletcher had predicted upon his arrival in the servants' coach earlier that morning, Bingley's brother-in-law was the first out, his face red and perspiring from a cravat tied entirely too high and a corset laced much too tightly for travel. Darcy bit his lip at the picture Hurst presented while the scathing adjectives with which Fletcher had rightly decried the talents of Hurst's new valet repeated themselves in his mind. But Hurst was not his immediate concern, nor were any of the Bingley entourage. Rather, his desire was for his sister and the happiness he hoped soon to be able to bestow upon her.

"Bingley! Welcome!" He clasped his friend's hand.

"Darcy!" Charles breathed out an exasperated sigh as he grasped his hand in return. "Thank God, we have arrived! You would not believe what was necessary to transport my family a mere three hours' drive." He looked daggers at his brother-in-law's back. "And the only ally you supposed is the worst of the lot!"

"You have my sympathy." Darcy clapped him on the shoulder. "And a glass of restorative awaits you in your rooms."

"Marvelous!" Bingley grinned and headed up the front stairs.

Darcy turned then to Hurst. "Please walk in and allow Reynolds to attend to you, sir. You do not look well. Ladies." He turned to Miss Bingley and her sister and bowed.

"Mr. Darcy." Miss Bingley extended her hand. "To be at last at Pemberley! It seemed we would be forever upon the road this morning."

He briefly touched the fingers offered to him. "You are welcome. I trust your journey—"

"Tedious beyond belief!" Miss Bingley cast her eyes to Heaven. "But who would not suffer more and gladly if Pemberley be their destination!" She cast him a soulful glance. "Such perfection! Why, it is recompense enough merely to breathe the air. You are, sir, justly within your rights to be proud to command such a noble estate."

"Proud, Miss Bingley?" His brow rose. "I hope not!" He smiled then into her startled countenance and indicated the door. "Please allow Mrs. Reynolds to show you to your rooms. You must be wishing to rest after such tedium as you have endured."

Darcy's eyes strayed past her, his smile lengthening into a broad grin when at last Georgiana appeared at the coach door. Quickly, he strode to her and handed her down himself. "Sweetling!" He kissed her brow and, tucking one of her gloved hands under his arm, bent and whispered, "I have been at my wit's end awaiting your arrival. The most wonderful thing has happened!"

"What can it be!" She laughed up at him. "It must be wonderful indeed for such a smile as you wear!"

"It is," he whispered. "Go, refresh yourself, and come to my book room directly. Try to come unobserved." He lifted his chin toward Miss Bingley and Mrs. Hurst and, urging her onward, added, "Hurry!" With an excited giggle, Georgiana obeyed, falling quickly into Mrs. Reynolds's welcoming arms within the door before hurrying to the stairs. Satisfied with her reaction, Darcy followed behind but waited until all his guests were abovestairs to send word to the stables and then turn in through his study door. He was not forced to wait long. Before fifteen minutes had elapsed, Georgiana was seated on the divan, her face wreathed in such expectant smiles he could do nothing but smile back at her.

"Yes?" She looked to him inquiringly, but her pert expression and the expectation of the joy his news would bring made it impossible to begin. Instead, he threw back his head and laughed. "Fitzwilliam!" Georgiana tugged at his hand much as she had when a child. "Tell me!"

He dropped onto the divan beside her and with great effort schooled his features and asked with the utmost solemnity, "How should you like to meet Miss Elizabeth Bennet?"

His sister's eyes widened, incredulity writ large in them. "Miss Elizabeth Bennet? Fitzwilliam, you tease me!"

"No, I swear!" He laughed again. "She is here . . . in Lambton, rather . . . the Green Man!"

"But how . . . ?"

"She travels with her aunt and uncle on a tour of Derbyshire." He settled in beside his sister, happy at last to tell all his news. "Her aunt is from Lambton, and Mrs. Gardiner must have it that they visit the scenes of her girlhood. Pemberley's reputation enticed them, and our reported absence convinced Miss Bennet to chance a tour. I found them in the gardens yesterday on my way from the stables."

"How she must have felt upon seeing you!" Georgiana murmured sympathetically. "And you! Oh, Brother!"

"I was stunned to be sure." He squeezed one of her hands. "I hardly know what I said, but later . . ."

"Yes, later?" she prompted.

He smiled hesitantly. "I believe I did better." He took a deep breath. "I asked her permission to introduce you."

"Fitzwilliam, truly?" Georgiana almost wrung his hand.

"Yes, dearest, truly"—he laughed again—"and she has given her consent."

"When? When shall we meet?" Georgiana was every bit as excited as he could have wished.

"I hoped"—he looked askance at her—"you might be agreeable to setting out for Lambton immediately."

"Now?" Georgiana's countenance fell. "Oh!"

"I know you have just arrived," he rushed to explain, "but there is so little time to accomplish an introduction with some assurance of . . . of privacy." A knowing expression crossed his sister's face. "I see you understand me. Come, will you oblige me and Miss Elizabeth Bennet? The curricle is on its way." He could see her hesitation, the return of shyness to her eyes at the prospect of this meeting taking place so precipitously. He took both her hands in his and kissed each one. "Georgiana? You will adore her; I know it! I could wish for you no better friend."

"Of course, Fitzwilliam." She freed a hand and placed it upon his heart. "Let me get my bonnet."

"Send for it," he whispered. "We must be off without discovery." Still in possession of one of her hands, he rose and pulled her to her feet, and giggling with pleasure, Georgiana trailed behind him. In haste he led her to the door, and laying hold of the knob, he flung it open, only to be brought up short by a much-startled Charles on the other side.

"Here, what is this?" Bingley jumped back and stared at the two of them framed in the doorway. "Darcy?"

"Bingley!" Darcy paused. What to do? "My sister and I have an urgent appointment to keep in Lambton," he added as they all turned to observe the curricle being drawn to a halt before the door.

"In Lambton?" Bingley's brow rose. "We just drove through Lambton."

"Yes, well." Darcy cast about him for something to satisfy Bingley's curiosity.

"We go to meet someone," Georgiana supplied. "Someone visiting."

Bingley turned back to Darcy. "Really? Must be someone dashed important to hie Miss Darcy back out upon the road immediately we arrive!"

Darcy held his silence, hoping Bingley would not persist, but he could sense Georgiana's discomfort under his friend's interrogation. There looked to be nothing for it but to bring Bingley along. "It is Miss Elizabeth Bennet," he spoke lowly, taking Bingley by the arm and propelling him toward the door. "Shh! Do not repeat it!"

"But, Darcy!" Bingley protested in a sharp whisper as he was pushed outside. "Miss Elizabeth?"

Darcy helped his sister into the conveyance and handed up her bonnet, which had just arrived. "No, only Miss Elizabeth and her aunt and uncle from London. I understand that Miss Bennet is well," he offered at Bingley's crestfallen expression, "but that is all I can tell you."

"I should very much have liked to have seen Miss Elizabeth, regardless," Bingley said.

"And you will, soon after," Darcy assured him. "I wished to introduce Georgiana to Miss Elizabeth in a less public situation than would be the case at Pemberley among my guests." He looked meaningfully at his friend.

"Oh, without Caroline and Louisa about, you mean." Bingley stood back smiling. "Say no more, old man. I understand completely." He looked at Georgiana. "I will stay out of sight until your introduction is made. Then, I beg you will ask Miss Elizabeth if I may come up. Darcy?" He turned to him. Darcy nodded his assent. "Right, then! I shall be close behind you." He beamed at them both. "Capital!"

The five miles to Lambton was accomplished in a silence dictated differently for each of the curricle's occupants. Georgiana contemplated her hands in her lap and the scenery as, her brother suspected, she prayed and prepared for this unexpected interview, on which she could not help but know he placed great importance. For himself, the rapid progression of events had carried him through the morning, but as he drove toward Lambton and Elizabeth grew ever closer, an uneasiness took up residence in his chest. His earlier question of her pleasure in the introduction returned, accompanied by the disquieting realization that she could not know they were even now coming. He doubted she would thank him for what could only appear as another example of insufferably high-handed behavior. Had he overstepped himself yet again, read too much into her conversation, her eyes? He felt certain that she would be kind to Georgiana. She might even welcome Bingley. But would she turn cool and distant under his regard?

As was usual, the news of the approach of a vehicle from Pemberley was known in Lambton before they arrived. Darcy almost swore that both Matling of the Black's Head and Garston of the Green Man paid some village urchin to keep watch, for they were out in front of their respective establishments, each determined to tally one more stroke against the other in their personal contest for the notice of the district's greatest house. Therefore, it was with great triumph on the part of one and high dudgeon on the part of the other when it was realized the curricle was actually stopping in the village and coming to rest before the Green Man. In a rush and tumble, Garston's innumerable grandchildren formed a guard of honor from the curricle's steps to the inn's door, where Garston himself awaited them, nigh bursting with pride for his house.

"I shall knock about in the taproom." Bingley waved them on as Darcy and Georgiana prepared to follow the innkeeper up the stairs. "But do not, on your life, forget me, Darcy!"

Putting a hand under Georgiana's elbow, Darcy made to assist her up the inn's narrow stairs when he sensed her holding back. He stopped and peered down at her. "Georgiana?"

"I'm sorry to be such a goose, Fitzwilliam, but I so want her to like me!" She cast an almost desperate look up at him.

"She will! She *will* like you; have no fear," he assured her firmly. "She will like you more than ever she liked me," he added with a wry smile, "I promise you!" Georgiana shook her head at him, but a smile played upon her lips at his comment, and it was she who took the first step forward. Seconds later, Darcy heard a knock sound on a door above them, and the innkeeper's announcement of visitors echoed down the short hall to meet them. Although his sister seemed to have accepted his assurances, the apprehension he was feeling increased with each step toward Elizabeth's door. The door opened.

"Mr. Darcy and Miss Darcy," Garston intoned, stepping back to usher his exalted visitors into the presence of guests who now assumed an unprecedented degree of importance in his estimation.

He heard Georgiana's intake of a quick, deep breath, and then . . . there was Elizabeth. He swallowed nervously as he stood outside the door, unable to pull his eyes away from her face. Her smile, though tentative, was tempered by the lively interest in her eyes as Mr. Gardiner greeted them.

"Mr. Darcy, you are most welcome, sir." Elizabeth's uncle bowed as his wife and niece did their curtsies. The man's calm demeanor and generous tone brought Darcy to a sense of his limbs. He and Georgiana stepped into the room.

"Mr. Gardiner, Ladies." Ingrained habits swept him into his own bow. "Please allow me to apologize for our intrusion, sir. We have come unannounced and a day before expected."

"Tut, tut, sir." Mr. Gardiner would not have it. "Did we not arrive on your own doorstep unanticipated? Please, allow us to welcome you and your companion."

Although the circumstances could in nowise have been deemed similar, Darcy inclined his head and, after glancing at Elizabeth, responded with a grateful smile. "You are very kind, sir. Mr. Gardiner, Mrs. Gardiner, Miss Elizabeth Bennet, please allow me the pleasure of presenting to you my sister, Miss Georgiana Darcy." He stepped a little behind Georgiana as she made her curtsy, the better both to put her forward and to observe what might happen. Mr. and Mrs. Gardiner exhibited all that might be expected in the nicety of their response, but it was Elizabeth whose actions were his primary concern. Her aspect seemed a mixture of hesitancy and curiosity as she waited for her relatives to accept the introduction. Then, finally, she stepped forward.

Darcy was conscious of his heart booming in his chest even as he placed an iron hold on his breath and watched the two he held most dear in the world meet for the first time. Georgiana curtsied, her smile shy but her countenance open to Elizabeth's scrutiny. "Miss Elizabeth Bennet."

"Miss Darcy, I am so pleased to meet you." Elizabeth returned her courtesy with a warmth in her smile and voice that spoke quiet assurances to Darcy's heart. Georgiana's smile deepened; he let go his breath.

"And I you, Miss Bennet. You are so kind to overlook our haste in seeking you out."

"Please think on it no more, Miss Darcy," Elizabeth averred. "Truly, we are delighted. But you must have only recently arrived." Georgiana's eyes strayed to her brother's at Elizabeth's comment; then Elizabeth's did also.

"The journey was not a long one." Georgiana reclaimed Elizabeth's attention.

"Oh?" Elizabeth's eyebrow arched provocatively. "But then I have been told that fifty miles is 'an easy distance.' Perhaps you are of your brother's persuasion in this?" Darcy smiled on hearing her quote his words. Oh, how he had missed her repartee!

"Fifty miles! In my brother's care it is easy, indeed!" Georgiana replied seriously, "but I would not regard it generally so!"

"Miss Elizabeth teases you a little," Darcy put in. "She is quoting to you some nonsense I taxed her with several months ago. Yet, Mr. Gardiner, sir." He looked to Elizabeth's uncle. "A well-sprung carriage and good road might make fifty miles little more than a trifle, would you agree?"

"A mere nothing, sir," Mr. Gardiner concurred but cast his niece a droll look, at which all of them laughed.

"Then we are of the same mind in this as well as fishing, in which sport I hope you will indulge tomorrow as there are now several gentlemen at Pemberley who share our passion. A party will surely be made up in the morning." Darcy's invitation was readily accepted and with such grace as encouraged him to like the man even more and anticipate some real enjoyment in the proposed expedition. Bingley and Hurst fished, but in Mr. Gardiner he sensed a true angler. The thought of Bingley reminded him then of his promise, and excusing himself, he stepped over to the door and instructed the servant outside to collect the young man in the taproom and bring him up.

Turning back, he was gratified to see Elizabeth and Georgiana in earnest conversation. Elizabeth had taken the lead, but her gracious drawing out of his sister sprang from more than correct manners. He knew her quite well enough to be sure that the lively interest in her countenance and the soft encouragement in her eyes were unfeigned. They had hit upon the subject of music, it seemed, and Georgiana was fairly blossoming under Elizabeth's regard as each of them expressed admiration for the reputed talents of the other. Then Georgiana laughed, at what he could not hear, but one thing was confirmed to him as he watched them drawing together. He had not appreciated Elizabeth, loved Elizabeth, rightly before. What was arising in his breast now was nothing like those previous petulant desires. Rather, it was a fullness of joy that wished to be of service to her in any capacity she might choose, to provide for her that place where her talents and graces might come to complete fruition. *Command me,* his heart whispered, *try me!*

Bingley's knock at the door recalled him to his manners, and upon his friend's entrance, he made Bingley's introduction to the Gardiners as well. There followed an enjoyable half hour for the entire party with such abundance of easy conversation that Darcy was confident that an invitation to dine at Pemberley would be welcomed on the Gardiners' part. He glanced again to Elizabeth. Although they had spoken little, she had not completely avoided his gaze. He sensed an awkwardness, or was it nervousness, in her demeanor toward him. She made no obvious bid for his attention, centering all her effort on Georgiana; yet her eyes strayed to him with something unreadable in their expression. No, the clues she had scattered this morning were not enough for him to discover her mind on this reacquaintance. If he were to do so before the precious few days she was to stay in Lambton ended, he must make more opportunities.

"Georgiana." He gently drew his sister away from the others. "Shall we invite them to dine?"

"Oh, yes, Fitzwilliam!" She leaned closer. "Miss Elizabeth Bennet is wonderful! I long to hear her play and sing, and . . . and she is so very kind!"

He smiled down into her joyful face. "Then do the honors, my dear! Invite them!"

"I?" Georgiana shrank a little.

"You are the lady of Pemberley, and they do not appear such frightful people that they would spurn your invitation," he teased. "For the day after tomorrow." His hand closed on her shoulder in assurance. "Go!" he whispered.

With a tremulous breath, Georgiana turned. "Mr. Gardiner, Mrs. Gardiner, Miss Elizabeth Bennet." She waited, trembling a little as they all turned to hear her. "My brother and I would be most honored if you would dine with us at Pemberley. Would the day after next be acceptable?" Darcy looked past her to Elizabeth to gauge her reaction, but as she apprehended the intent of Georgiana's words, she looked away; even her aunt could not see her expression. Did he then have his answer? He glanced back at Mrs. Gardiner, who oddly enough, was allowing a smile to play upon her face. Did she know something? Did she have Elizabeth's confidence? He watched as she caught the eye of her husband, and for a moment something passed between them.

"Miss Darcy, Mr. Darcy." Mrs. Gardiner came forward and curtsied. "We would be most happy to accept your invitation to dine at Pemberley."

At his snap of the reins, the curricle lurched forward. Darcy's first task was to navigate down the narrow village street toward the bridge over the Ere, but when the horse had established a comfortable gait and the high wheels no longer bumped against cobble or rut, he was able to turn over in his mind the events of the last hour. The journey down the inn's stairs, he mused, had been taken with much lighter hearts than the journey up had been. He had felt Georgiana's pleasure and happy ease as he took her arm down the steps and out into the afternoon sun, and if that were not enough, the smile on her face would have told the story. As for his own features, he had found himself hard-pressed to keep an even mien for the smile that still tugged at the corners of his lips. Pointing the horse for the bridge out of Lambton, he was more than pleased to feel his sister tuck a hand snugly inside his arm and the tickle of her sigh against his cheek.

"Oh, Fitzwilliam, I do so like her! Do you think . . ." She paused. "Do you think she likes me? She was so kind, so amiable; she seemed to know exactly what to say. And she listened to me even though I hardly knew what to say. But, then we talked about music and family and you . . . a little." Darcy's ears pricked up at the last, but he allowed it to pass. "It was easier then."

"Then you look forward to their coming to dine," he asked, "and do not regret the invitation?"

"Yes, oh, yes! Mrs. Gardiner is all that is amicable, and Mr. Gardiner seems a jolly, indulgent sort of gentleman whom no one but a complete goose would fear for long!"

Darcy chuckled at the scorn for her earlier fears in her voice. "Yes, only a *complete* goose, I grant you!" The horse's gait slowed as it prepared to pull the curricle over the high arch of the bridge. The rush of the merry waters and the clatter of hooves against cobblestone drowned out Georgiana's response. When they were crossed, he looked over to her. "You realize that Miss Elizabeth Bennet and Mrs. Gardiner will likely return the call tomorrow. Will you be easy? Shall I return early from fishing?" He presented his offer with what he hoped was light disinterest, but in truth he struggled with competing desires. On the one hand, he should absent himself from the salon if he truly wished to remove every obstacle to the growth of a friendship between Georgiana and Elizabeth; on the other, he could hardly think how he could know Elizabeth was at Pemberley and stay away from her.

"Miss Bingley and Mrs. Hurst will be there. Will they not be happy to see Miss Elizabeth as well?"

"I would not depend on the joy of either of those ladies to carry the morning," he replied, "but Mrs. Annesley will know how to make your guests feel at ease."

"Of course, Mrs. Annesley." Georgiana nodded and then looked askance at him. "Still, it would be good if you came . . . just to be sure. Near the end of their visit, perhaps?"

He briefly looked down on her and then away. Was this a bit of feminine subterfuge or a resurfacing of her shyness? Whichever, it was an open door that he was glad to step through. Taking both reins in one hand, he reached down to squeeze the gloved fingers curled about his arm. "I shall make an appearance then, near the end."

Mr. Gardiner's grasp of the art and nuances of angling was a pleasure to behold, but it was his easy, companionable silence that particularly recommended him to Darcy's growing circle of those he respected. That Bingley or Hurst would ever achieve the status of true angler was doubtful; Bingley's laughter and Hurst's roars gave neither him nor the trout in the river any peace to be about their business. It was not long, therefore, before he and Mr. Gardiner found themselves side by side away from and above the spots along the Ere that the other two gentlemen had staked out. Glancing over at the older man, Darcy was reminded of the last angling trip to Scotland that he and his father had taken the summer before he entered Cambridge. Although he had not then been his sire's equal in the sport, he had been treated as such, and the quiet companionship and good humor of that expedition were not unlike what he felt at this very moment. If it were not for the distracting awareness that even at this moment Elizabeth was in Pemberley's salon and a raging curiosity about the events taking place there, he could have put it down as a satisfying expenditure of a morning.

"Mr. Darcy, allow me to thank you again for this invitation,"

Mr. Gardiner offered, his voice low. "I hesitate to say how long it has been since I have had this pleasure and did not think that, as escort to two ladies, such an opportunity would come my way. Quite providential!"

"It is my pleasure, sir," Darcy responded and was gratified to discover that he truly meant it. "I hope that you will not pass Pemberley by on any future holidays in Derbyshire. If I am not in residence, Sherrill, my steward, will be happy to see to you."

"You are very kind, sir." Ten minutes of silence ensued before the older man coughed and cleared his throat. "Ah, Mr. Darcy, I beg you will not think you need attend me. I am quite content to spend the next hour communing with Providence and the trout on my own should you have obligations elsewhere." The guileless eyes rested on him briefly. "You must not let me detain you."

Had he been so obvious? Looking narrowly down at the man, Darcy could detect no sly or conspiratorial humor, only a quietly blissful gladness to be just where he was. Another open door? He pulled in his line and set the tackle down next to the box they shared. "There is something that I promised Miss Darcy that I should see to before her guests leave," he explained. The excuse sounded weak and insubstantial to his ears, but Mr. Gardiner nodded sagely, as if his explanation bore all the marks of reason. "If you will excuse me, I will attend to it directly." Leave was promptly given, and with a deep breath, Darcy turned for home, his pace increasing the closer he drew to the house. Forcing himself to walk up stairs he wished to take in bounds, he paused only long enough to straighten his waistcoat and coat before nodding to the footman to open the salon door.

As soon as he stepped inside the room, all conversation ceased, and Darcy found himself under the curious regard of every feminine eye in the room. "Ladies." He made his bow after sweeping them all with a polite smile. "I hope you will excuse my intrusion." Although all his being was alive to Elizabeth's presence, he knew at once that Georgiana was under some strain. The source he could easily guess, for Miss Bingley's countenance was wreathed in one of the most false smiles he had ever had the misfortune to receive. But Caroline Bingley was not his concern on this excellent day, and he passed by her quickly to take Georgiana's hand in his. "Come, my dear," he whispered, moving her from Mrs. Annesley's side to sit next to Elizabeth on one of the divans. "Miss Elizabeth, has my sister told you of the last concert we attended before leaving London?" He took up a station on the other side of Georgiana and dared to look down into Elizabeth's smiling face. She wore a simple but becoming gown of pale yellow muslin sprinkled with delicate flowers that enhanced everything about her. He particularly noted the curls at her nape, which brushed her shoulders and played enticingly with the lace at her throat. It was all he could do not to reach out and entwine his fingers in them.

"No, she has not, sir!" Elizabeth turned her beautiful, laughing eyes upon Georgiana. Good Lord, she positively glowed! "Please, Miss Darcy, you must tell me. Whom did you see, and what did you hear?"

Georgiana colored a little but responded readily enough, and Darcy could have asked for no better than the gentle questions and sincere exclamations that Elizabeth contributed to their conversation. He could sense his sister's tension slipping away as, with either Elizabeth's help or his, their conversation flowed from one topic to another in a seemingly natural manner. As for Elizabeth, she gave every indication of developing a warm regard for Georgiana, which made his heart rejoice. It was not long before he had the further satisfaction of assuming the part of observer only, withdrawing from participation as the exchanges between the two became more animated, until all he needed to contribute was the broad smile that would not be contained.

"Pray, Miss Eliza." Miss Bingley's voice carried imperiously across the drawing room, bringing all other discourse to a halt. "Are not the —shire Militia removed from Meryton? They must be a great loss to *your* family."

Darcy stiffened as the room fell into shocked silence. What devil had seized control of that woman's tongue that she would attempt to introduce Wickham into his drawing room? What could be her purpose? Surely Caroline Bingley could not know of Wickham's attempts against Georgiana! No, that was impossible! He glanced at Elizabeth, who had gone very still at the mention of her name. Yes, it was Elizabeth whom Miss Bingley wished to defame in this exceedingly ill-bred attack. His blood raged at the thought, but even so, it was his sister for whom he feared. As he looked down into Georgiana's pale face and large eyes, he saw that the damage had been done, for at his glance she quickly lowered her head and looked away, all her former animation having fled. His color heightening in helpless anger, his eyes sought Elizabeth's. *It remains with you,* he tried to tell her through the agency of his earnest regard. Miss Bingley must not delve further.

The glint of steel that had preceded so many of their own verbal fencing matches flashed past him, and Elizabeth's chin, accompanied by the most enigmatic of smiles, rose. "Yes, it is true; they have removed to Brighton, Miss Bingley," she replied airily, "a necessary event for the Militia and a most happy event for those who are now relieved of the necessity of entertaining them."

Darcy did not trust himself to turn back to note Miss Bingley's reaction lest she see the grateful relief that flowed through his frame and across his face. Instead, he gave himself over to the pleasure of observing the satisfaction her parry had induced in Elizabeth's eyes and the puzzle of how he was to thank her. Before he could come to any conclusion, she leaned toward Georgiana and lightly brushed her hand. He caught his breath, the wonder of her concern for his sister holding him, warming him as she turned her face up to meet his. No words, of thanks or gratitude, were needed, her eyes told him. She already knew his heart on this matter, and his trust of her was not misplaced.

His heart swelling, Darcy took a seat opposite them and engaged her directly, carefully choosing his subject for both his ladies' sakes. "I must say, Miss Bennet, your uncle is a true disciple of Mr. Walton, possessed of an excellent disposition for the sport. I left him in high spirits happily pursuing my trout."

"Indeed?" Elizabeth smiled back at him, her light scent of lavender entrapping his senses. "He has often mentioned how his concerns have kept him from indulging in what was once, before his marriage, a passion of considerable proportion. I am glad he has had the opportunity to enjoy it, especially as he has so good-naturedly put himself at the disposal of two demanding women for his entire holiday. I thank you for his invitation."

"It was my pleasure," he managed to reply, then tore his gaze away to glance at Georgiana. She remained silent, as yet unequal to even this inconsequential an exchange. His pause seemed to have decided Elizabeth, and she rose.

"I fear we must be going, sir."

He rose immediately as well, reasons and schemes to detain her coming quickly to the fore; but there was that presence about her that stayed him, and he held his peace. Mrs. Gardiner came then to stand beside her niece and offered her thanks for their welcome and for her husband's invitation. Darcy bowed his acknowledgment. "Your husband's skill has not diminished, madam. It was a privilege to observe him. If you and Miss Elizabeth Bennet must go," he continued, "please, permit me to see you to your carriage." Of course, they could not refuse, and with smiles of thanks they allowed him to usher them to the door after taking leave of his sister and the other ladies.

Standing in his hall, Darcy looked down upon Elizabeth, her glorious crown of hair coming only just to his shoulder, and was beset by so many emotions that he could barely sort them out, save for one. He loved her. It was as simple and as complicated as that. The simplicity lay in the nature of his love, for it was centered upon Elizabeth rather than himself or his desires and arose from the deepest wish to be the one whose privilege it was to do her good all her days. The complication lay within him. He could not make her love him or arrange for it as he did all his other concerns. He could only show her who he had become and was becoming . . . and hope.

Little of import could be said while they waited the few minutes required for their carriage to pull up to the entrance, but he could not let even so small an opportunity pass him by. "Miss Darcy and I look forward with pleasure to your visit tomorrow."

"As do we, sir," Mrs. Gardiner replied.

It appeared that Elizabeth would remain silent, allowing her aunt to offer all the civilities, but then she lifted her face and met his hopeful gaze with a sincerity that took his breath away. "Indeed, sir. Please, say as much to Miss Darcy, also?"

"I shall," he promised, hope taking a small foothold in his heart. He waited until the carriage settled before handing Mrs. Gardiner up, then turned to Elizabeth. This time he was not made to wait for her hand. She gave it to him willingly. As his hand closed around her gloved fingers, delight coursed through him; and as she depended on his arm to assist her up, deep feelings of protectiveness followed it.

"Until tomorrow." His voice was hoarse with all that possessed him, but Elizabeth heard him. Her answering smile was soft, its sweet contours remaining with him as the carriage bore her away. He watched after her until the trees of the park swallowed up the carriage. Even then, he was reluctant to rejoin the ladies in the salon, but he had to return to Georgiana to see how she fared. He stepped into the room just as Mrs. Hurst was agreeing with her sister upon some matter, a not unusual occurrence in their filial relationship, only to be addressed by Miss Bingley upon the same subject.

"How very ill Eliza Bennet looks this morning, Mr. Darcy. I never in my life saw anyone so much altered as she is since the winter!" She sniffed her incredulity. "She is grown so brown and coarse! Louisa and I were agreeing that we should not have known her again."

A thorough disgust with Caroline Bingley gripped him. Not only her words but her very tone and manner were offensive to him. "Haughty as a duchess and heartless as a jade," he had once named her. She had not improved a wit since but was, in fact, hardening into a caricature of both. "I perceived no alteration in her," he replied coolly, "save in her being rather tanned. That is no miraculous consequence, as she has traveled some distance and in summer."

Miss Bingley was not to be prevented her declamation but continued on despite the note of caution a wiser woman would have recognized in his voice. "For my own part, I must confess that I never could see any beauty in her. Her face is too thin; her complexion has no brilliancy; and her features are not at all handsome." Darcy ground his teeth, his jaw hardening; but her list was not yet complete. "Her nose wants character; there is nothing marked in its lines. Her teeth are tolerable, but not out of the common way; and as for her eyes, which have sometimes been called so fine"—she glanced at him but, to his disbelief, continued on— "I never could perceive anything extraordinary in them. They have a sharp, shrewish look, which I do not like at all; and in her air altogether, there is a self-sufficiency without fashion, which is intolerable." The last she had said to his back as he turned sharply away and sat down next to Georgiana. His sister looked at him with amazement at what she heard and what he was tolerating. She laid a hand upon his.

"I remember, when we first knew her in Hertfordshire, how amazed we all were to find that she was a reputed beauty." Darcy's jaw flexed. She had reached the limit of what he was prepared to countenance. Only care for Elizabeth's name prevented him from confirming Miss Bingley's suspicions with a demand she vacate his home at once. "And I particularly recollect your saying one night, after they had been dining at Netherfield, '*She* a beauty! I should as soon call her mother a wit.' But afterwards she seemed to improve on you, and I believe you thought her rather pretty at one time."

At this last pronouncement he could contain himself no longer but rose with a bound and turned upon her an eye that had made grown men step backward. "Yes," he replied icily, "but *that* was only when I first knew her; for it is many months since I have considered her as one of the handsomest women of my acquaintance." The shock on Miss Bingley's face gave him no pleasure, but neither did her company or her conceits. He could no longer bear any of them. With the briefest of bows, he left the room, his disgust taking him straight out the door and toward the river. With any luck, Mr. Gardiner and his own tackle would still be there . . . and Hurst and Bingley would not. At this particular moment the silent counsel of creation and the serene example of Elizabeth's relative would best quiet his angered spirit. Suitably obliging trout, he mused, would not be amiss, either!

Not only had Mr. Gardiner remained for the rest of the afternoon but the trout had been most cooperative as well, exhibiting sufficient cunning to offer a challenge yet being sensible enough to yield themselves to the inevitable at the appropriate moment in the game. Only a punishing gallop atop Nelson over rough ground could possibly have diverted Darcy better from the wonderful fact that Elizabeth's company and companionship had that day been his. To see her at Pemberley, in his home and in those rooms in which he had long imagined her, was more than he ever had had reason to hope for after Hunsford. It was a thing to be dwelt upon, which he did, alternating between such pleasure and doubt that Georgiana had been forced to clear her throat several times through dinner in order to recall him to his surroundings and guests.

"As I was saying," Bingley began again after one such lapse, "the attraction of angling continues to elude me, Darcy."

"As did the trout, damn them," Hurst interrupted.

"Well, you *would* roar and stamp about. Frightened them so they were only too happy to have Darcy or Gardiner catch 'em." Bingley turned back to his friend. "As much as I should like to accommodate Mr. Gardiner, I hope our next visit to your river will be no more demanding than a picnic."

"A picnic!" broke in Mrs. Hurst. "Oh, Caroline!" She leaned toward her sister. "Would not a picnic be just the thing?"

Miss Bingley lifted a quelling eyebrow in response. "Perhaps," she said slowly and then bid for Darcy's attention. "If that is agreeable, sir, allow me, I beg you, to spare Miss Darcy the arranging of it?"

He inclined his head in permission but offered her not even the encouragement of a smile. He had suffered Caroline Bingley for Charles's sake, but her jealousy and ill-bred disparagement of Elizabeth had now rendered her presence utterly distasteful to him. Let her be kept busy with ordering his servants about if that would amuse her. The experience would be short-lived, and his people would survive it with reasonably good humor once he had given Reynolds the word.

"Tomorrow, then." She pounced upon his acquiescence. "We shall breakfast at the river alfresco! What will be the number? We expect no one in the morning, I trust?"

"No, no one, Miss Bingley," he affirmed, his irritation rising with both the woman and her transparent implication.

"Miss Elizabeth Bennet, her aunt and uncle will be with us tomorrow evening," Georgiana reminded her gently. "I do hope we may prevail upon her to play and sing for us. You have heard her before, have you not, Miss Bingley?"

"Yes," Miss Bingley responded in a clipped tone, but when Georgiana drew away from her, a slight frown creasing her young brow, she stumbled on. "Yes, I have; we all did . . . at . . . oh, that man's. What was his name?"

"Sir William Lucas, a most congenial gentleman." Bingley reproved her with a frown deeper than Georgiana's. "As I remember, she played and sang beautifully, and was universally importuned for another. It will be an uncommon pleasure, Miss Darcy, if you are able to persuade her to perform. Do so, I beg you."

Darcy did smile at that. Bingley's confidence and willingness to assert himself had increased steadily since that day in Darcy's London study. His friend certainly moved with more assuredness among his contemporaries, but it was in his own family that Darcy particularly appreciated Charles's new self-confidence. If he could school his sister in some discretion, she might continue to be received in his house after this visit. The issue that occupied him to the exclusion of his present guests, though, was not Miss Bingley's future visits to Pemberley but, rather, whether such might be hoped for by Elizabeth Bennet.

Had she been pleased with his home? She had affirmed so upon their first encounter, but had her opinion been no more than that of any visitor on holiday? Now that she had been a guest, what did she think? He closed his eyes and shook his head slightly, annoyed with himself. Yes, he wished her to think well of Pemberley, but what truly lay at the bottom of his speculation was whether she as yet thought well of Pemberley's master. His anxiety to know if he had progressed in her estimation was consuming every thought that was not strictly needed to maintain an appearance of attention to his guests. They swung from hope to doubt and back again with alarming swiftness. Her quick-witted response to Miss Bingley's implication joined with her silent collusion in Georgiana's protection were encouraging, as was her willing acceptance of his assistance into the carriage and her soft smile of farewell. Could he credit these incidents with any substance, or were they merely general politeness?

"Ahem." Startled, Darcy looked over at his sister as Georgiana cleared her throat yet again. Her lips pursed in a bow of rueful amusement.

"Brother." She prodded him with a gesture to the door. "Shall you and the other gentlemen want your brandy now?"

The mystery of Elizabeth's regard for him plagued Darcy for the remainder of the evening and followed him to his chambers after wishing Bingley and Hurst *bonne chance* over the billiard table. Tomorrow evening she would be here . . . possibly for the last time. The thought chilled him as he reached for the bell pull. Her aunt and uncle might have been done with Lambton and, desirous of continuing on in their holiday plans, might whisk her off the following day to the next great estate or praised natural view. A great, painful *No!* arose in his chest. She must not! She must not disappear, perhaps forever this time, before he could make some substantial determination of where he stood in her esteem! But how? How was it to be done? He turned slowly toward his dressing room.

"Mr. Darcy, sir." Darcy started in surprise at Fletcher's voice.

"Good Heavens, man! I only just summoned you!" Darcy said sharply. Then, realizing his valet must already have been there, he added, "Make a bit of noise if you are about, will you?"

"Yes, sir." The man bowed and approached him. "May I assist you, sir?" Nodding, Darcy unbuttoned his coat as he turned his back. Fletcher's sure fingers carefully stripped him of the garment. "Your fobs and watch, sir."

"What?" Darcy demanded and then looked down at his waistcoat. "Oh, yes, of course." He pulled the items from their pockets and laid them on the table. What he needed was time, more time, and time that would not be interrupted or curtailed by others. Time, he mused, staring down at his watch while Fletcher removed his waistcoat, a commodity that, regrettably, was not in his power to command or create.

"Is there aught amiss with your pocket watch, sir?" Fletcher scooped up the mechanism and peered at its face before pulling out his own and comparing the time.

"No, Fletcher. I was woolgathering, musing over the inflexible independence of Time." He let out a short sigh and began unbuttoning his shirt while the valet worked at the knot of his cravat.

" 'Inflexible independence,' sir?" Fletcher pulled at the neckcloth and then tossed it onto a chair.

"Yes." Darcy bent and removed his shoes. "Men invariably need more or less of it but cannot command it to be still or bid it go faster. Time proceeds as it will and will not be bridged or created."

"Indeed?" Fletcher responded. "Is man then merely 'Time's fool'?"

"You misquote the Bard, Fletcher," Darcy snorted. "I believe he said 'Love's not Time's fool.' "

Fletcher smiled. "Forgive me, sir, as I trust the Bard would also. But as the only love that is subject to Time is man's, it is all one. As for its 'inflexible independence,' that is a matter of perspective; is it not, sir?"

"What can you mean? Sixty minutes always equals one hour!"

"Yes, sir. But an hour with the toothache is an eternity; whereas an hour with one's beloved is as a moment gone." Fletcher's voice dropped. Then he shook himself and continued firmly. "No, I believe Time is perfectly flexible if we have the wit or nerve to mold it to our use."

Wit or nerve. Fletcher's prerequisites for the command of Time repeated themselves in his mind as Darcy lay unsleeping in his bed. The clock on the mantel chimed out the hour. One o'clock. Time, more time, was what he needed in order to determine Elizabeth's mind, but he could count on no more time than what tomorrow afforded. Tomorrow, dawn to evening, was all that he could foresee; therefore, it was tomorrow that he must bend and mold. *If you have the wit or nerve to do so,* he reminded himself grimly. His mind ranged over the next day's schedule. Accomplishing anything to his purpose at dinner was summarily dismissed. Too many interested parties about for the privacy he desired! Further, waiting until then left him even less time to bend. Morning and afternoon, then, were all that remained to him.

It came to him all in a moment: the picnic Caroline Bingley had been so eager to marshal! All of his guests would be gathered at the river for her alfresco, at which time he could send a servant with his regrets that he had been called away and to proceed without him. Ah, yes, there was the wit; what about the nerve? He would call on Elizabeth and the Gardiners. Nothing unusual in that! He would ask for permission to escort her, or all of them if need be, on a stroll of the village path which followed the Ere. Then, when opportunity arose, he would thank Elizabeth privately for her kindness to Georgiana. Her response and subsequent conversation would, he hoped, reveal something of her estimation of him that might be built upon at dinner that evening.

Darcy heaved a sigh as the mantle clock chimed out the quarter hour. It was not an elegant plan. Rather, it was fraught with countless opportunities to go wrong. But it was all he had, and he meant to use it.

"No, Fletcher." Darcy looked over the clothing his valet held out for approval. "Riding clothes, if you please, ones fit for a call." He finished drying off his freshly shaved chin and cheeks and ran a hand through his damp hair.

"Riding clothes, sir? I was not informed, sir!" Fletcher frowned mightily at such an oversight. "Shall I send notice to the others?"

"No, only I shall be out. The others are still to attend Miss Bingley's alfresco." He paused to see what effect the announcement produced in his valet. Fletcher, however, appeared more concerned with the new demand placed upon his art than with its cause.

Grateful for Fletcher's lack of interest, Darcy channeled away the man's thoughts with a question suited to his other talents. "How is that progressing . . . the picnic?"

Fletcher rolled his eyes. "The staff has been harried through four refinements of the menu and three changes of location since last evening, sir; but they press on with good humor," he said, disappearing into the closet in search of the required clothing.

"Good humor?" Darcy called after him.

Fletcher emerged, a complete ensemble and several alternates in hand. "They have eyes, sir, and ears, and know you have all our best interests in hand." Darcy cocked a brow at him. Clearing his throat, Fletcher continued. "Forgive me, sir, but we . . . ah, the staff, sir, can bear with whatever the lady may demand during the *short* time she will be here."

"I see." Darcy strode to the window and leaned against the frame. What faith they all had in him! What hopes were invested in his every decision! He sighed and bowed his head. The happy future that his people wished him and themselves was not so easily accomplished, for they were not privy to the irony that ruled their hopes. Yes, Elizabeth's place in *his* heart was sure, but that place meant little to the woman who had last spring, without a moment's hesitation, refused the offer of his hand and the prestige of Pemberley. He could make that same proposal to Caroline Bingley or nearly any other woman in England and be assured of success. Yet here he was, setting out to pursue the one exception . . . perhaps for that very reason. He knew her worth. If Elizabeth's opinion of him had softened, if she turned toward him in any way, he would not let her disappear from his life. He would pursue her, court her as she so richly deserved, and God willing, win her respect and her heart.

Turning back to his valet, he examined the attire held out for his inspection. Doeskin breeches, of course, and boots polished to the highest gloss were at the ready. "The silver-gray waistcoat, I think, and that coat." Fletcher's brow went up in question. "The green one, yes." He nodded as the valet held it out. "Now, hand me the breeches . . . hurry, man!"

The interior of the Green Man was dark and still cool when Darcy took off his beaver and bent to enter the inn's door. For the first time in his adult life he had escaped the elaborate attentions of its proprietor and been greeted only by a servant, to whom he conveyed his desire to be conducted to the rooms occupied by the Gardiner party.

"The Gardiners, sir?" Forced to disoblige the village's most esteemed patron, the young man looked panic-stricken. "The Gardiners 'ave gone out awalkin', sir." Disappointment that Elizabeth was not immediately available put a check upon his eagerness, but Lambton was not large. He should be able to find them; it was the loss of time he rued.

"Which direction—" he began to ask, but the nervous boy interrupted him.

"The young lady is still above, sir. Would you be awantin' to be taken up for jus' her?"

He could not stop the laugh that welled up inside him at the lad's apologetic tone. Did he want to be taken up just for Elizabeth? His heart expanded. This was perfect, much more to his purpose than he could have hoped or planned for.

"Yes, if you please." He grinned down at the boy and gestured that he should take the lead up the inn's stairs.

The upper hall was quiet, the public room below not yet belabored with patrons and the inn's other guests out about their business. The tread of their boots upon the wooden floor rang loud in Darcy's ears but did not mask the sound of a chair being scraped across the floor behind the Gardiners' door. Elizabeth! His heart turned over as he came to a halt behind the servant and waited. The sound of light footsteps reached him. His breath caught in his chest. The serving boy reached for the latch and, stepping back, pulled the door open.

Elizabeth's pale face appeared suddenly, looking up at him with such wild pain and desperation that he started back, speechless at beholding such stark need in her every line.

"I beg your pardon, but I must leave you," she gasped out. "I must find Mr. Gardiner this moment, on business that cannot be delayed; I have not an instant to lose."

"Good God! What is the matter?" Darcy demanded, the misery in her face eliciting both alarm and every tender feeling he possessed. Find the Gardiners? Impossible for her in this state! "I will not detain you a minute; but let me, or let the servant, go after Mr. and Mrs. Gardiner." He seized command of the situation as well as he might, ignorant as he was of the particulars. "You are not well enough; you cannot go yourself." Darcy expected that she would gainsay him and prepared to insist that she not attempt the mission. She did not. Instead, she hesitated and, to his concern, trembled visibly before nodding and, after calling back the servant to entrust him with the task of recalling her aunt and uncle, sank heavily into a chair.

What should he do? Darcy looked down into her pain-filled countenance, the droop of her fine shoulders, and knew that he could not leave her. His hand reached out, every impulse urging him to gather her into his arms and vow to make all things right again, but he was forced to let it drop to his side. He had no right. "Let me call your maid," he said to her gently instead. At the shake of her head, he pursued a different tack, but in the same tone. "Is there nothing you could take to give you present relief? A glass of wine; shall I get you one?" Again, she shook her head. Darcy's feeling of helplessness increased. Perhaps she was too distressed to realize her condition? "You are very ill," he told her softly.

"No, I thank you." Elizabeth's back straightened a little. "There is nothing the matter with me. I am quite well, I am only distressed by some dreadful news which I have just received from

Longbourn." Tears that had been stayed by her anxiety now burst forth, rendering her incapable of speech, and left Darcy no further enlightened save that the cause was news from her home. A death in her family seemed the likeliest answer. Had there been some terrible accident? His heart went out to her, desperate to be of some use, some comfort in her throes of sorrow and pain. Again, the desire to hold her, lend her his strength seized him. Good God, how much longer could he stand to see her thus and maintain his place! He lay hold of the back of the chair opposite hers and gripped it so tightly his fingers ached.

"Miss Elizabeth, please . . . allow me to be of service to you in some manner," he importuned, but her tears continued and there was nothing more he could say or do but wait.

"I have just had a letter from Jane, with such dreadful news." She finally looked at him, although her words were halting. He leaned toward her, intent on her every syllable. "It cannot be concealed from anyone." She gasped for breath and then continued. "My younger sister has left all her friends—has eloped; has thrown herself into the power of—of Mr. Wickham."

His shock could not have been more complete. Wickham! The Devil take him! But how had this happened?

"They are gone off together from Brighton," Elizabeth continued disjointedly. "*You* know him too well to doubt the rest. She has no money, no connections, nothing that can tempt him to—" She gasped again. "She is lost forever."

Darcy's mind reeled at her account and its implications, rendering him both enraged and speechless. Had the man no conscience at all? At least with Georgiana there had been the motive of revenge and gain, but what had been his purpose with Lydia Bennet? Elizabeth was entirely correct; she had nothing to tempt him to marriage. Her attractions were youth, heedlessness, and the promise of sensuality. When Wickham had had his use of them, he would abandon her without a thought.

"When I consider that *I* might have prevented it. *I* who knew what he was." Elizabeth bitterly berated herself. "Had I but explained some part of it only—some part of what I learnt, to my own family! Had his character been known, this could not have happened. But it is all, all too late now." She buried her face again in her hands.

Darcy looked down helplessly upon her bowed shoulders. What could he say or do to mitigate the disaster in this turn of events? Little, so very little! "I am grieved, indeed, grieved—shocked," he whispered. "But is it certain, absolutely certain?"

"Oh yes!" she answered with a wretched laugh. "They left Brighton together on Sunday night, and were traced almost to London, but not beyond; they are certainly not gone to Scotland."

Here was something—time and a location! Darcy's mind began to function more rationally. When and where! "And what has been done, what has been attempted, to recover her?"

"My father is gone to London." Elizabeth gestured in a hopeless manner. "And Jane has written to beg my uncle's immediate assistance; and we shall be off, I hope, in half an hour. But nothing can be done; I know very well that nothing can be done." She sighed bitterly. "How is such a man to be worked on? How are they even to be discovered? I have not the smallest hope. It is every way horrible."

That might very well be true, Darcy thought to himself, *or not!*

"When *my* eyes were open to his real character. Oh! had I known what I ought, what I dared to do!" Elizabeth wrung at her handkerchief, anger displacing her grief. "But I knew not—I was afraid of doing too much. Wretched, wretched mistake!"

Elizabeth's misery pulled at his heart. The sight of her there, weeping, blaming herself for the rash behavior of a sister who had been allowed to run wild and the perfidious treachery of a practiced seducer would have tempted Darcy to fresh anger if his own fault in the affair had not then struck him with punishing force. Her mistake? No, it was his . . . it was his pride, his care for nothing beyond his family circle that had allowed a blackguard freedom to prey upon young women. And now the wolf had fallen upon another family, the family of the woman he loved so well and to whom he owed so much. The blow threatened to send him back into the emotional tangle that he had felt at the first glimpse of her face and revelation of her news. But no! If he allowed that, he would be of absolutely no use to her. Turning away, he began to walk up and down the room, latching on to every fact Elizabeth had conveyed as a puzzle piece. Where would Wickham have gone to ground in London and who might know? Possible avenues of inquiry recommended themselves. If only Dy were back in Town! Whether Dy was available or no, Wickham's trail must be picked up with the utmost speed before he tired of Lydia Bennet and disappeared to some other corner of the kingdom.

Darcy turned, then, and observed Elizabeth. She had covered her face with her handkerchief, lost to all but the terrible facts of her family's disgrace. He had every reason to stay with her in her distress, but no right. He ought to excuse himself, but how was he to do it? He hesitated, then plunged into an awkward apology. "I am afraid you have been long desiring my absence, nor have I anything to plead in excuse of my stay, but real, though unavailing, concern." Slowly, she straightened and listened with tear-brightened eyes. Please God, he hoped she believed him! "Would to Heaven that anything could be either said or done on my part, that might offer consolation to such distress! But I will not torment you with vain wishes, which may seem purposely to ask for your thanks." He could see that she was regaining countenance. Her chin lifted ever so slightly at his words. "This unfortunate affair will, I fear, prevent my sister's having the pleasure of seeing you at Pemberley today."

"Oh yes." She wiped her eyes and sniffed. "Be . . . be so kind as to apologize for us to Miss Darcy. Say that urgent business calls us home immediately. Conceal the unhappy truth as long as it is possible," she pled. "I know it cannot be long."

"You have my word," he promised her, looking down into eyes

that now seemed to withdraw from him. "I am sorry, truly sorry that such distress has come upon you and your family." He paused, wishing there were some better comfort he might give, but none was vouchsafed him. "And there may yet be hope for a happier conclusion than you presently have reason to expect." She looked at him dubiously but inclined her head. There was no more he could do. He answered with a bow. "Please, convey my compliments to your relations and that I hope you may all return to Pemberley at some happier time," he offered, and with a last searching look to impress upon her the sincerity of his words, he stepped into the hall and quietly shut the door.

CHAPTER 8

What Silent Love Hath Writ

*T*he ride back to Pemberley might have taken a quarter hour or much longer; Darcy could not say. All that he remembered was mounting Seneca at the block outside the inn, and now here he was being jarred into awareness of his surroundings by the clatter of his horse's hooves upon the cobblestones of his own stable yard. When he took out his pocket watch as a stable lad led his mount away, his eyes opened wide at the story the hands told. An hour! He looked after his horse, his tail swishing slowly as he was led to the grooming post. Truly, Darcy had only Seneca to thank for his eventual arrival home, for the time and scenery that had passed between those two events were completely lost to him. An hour. With any luck the others would still be working their way through Caroline Bingley's alfresco and leave him to continue uninterrupted the wrestling within his chest that had begun at the first sight of Elizabeth's stricken face.

What should he do? The question had consumed him during the entire course of his return. What he *could* do, he had quickly determined. His resources, his connections, his personal knowledge of Wickham's tastes and habits urged upon him the conviction that it was he who was best placed to find the missing couple or direct others in the recovery of Lydia Bennet. But what he could do was not the decisive factor in what he should do. Here was the sticking point, for to this juncture his success at choosing *shoulds* had been worse than lamentable. Indeed, his missteps in this area were the origins of the crisis at hand. With a shudder, the guilt of it struck him anew.

More to the point, in a family matter as delicate as this, the hand of a virtual stranger would be most unwelcome. Well did he know the lengths to which a family might go to protect itself. It had to be the object of Elizabeth's family to involve as few as possible before the final disposition of their daughter was accomplished, whether in honorable marriage, distant seclusion, or eternal disgrace. Further, the Bennet family certainly had no sort of claim upon him that might prompt them to enlist his aid or justify his offering of it. Presumptuous ... interfering ... unwelcome! Darcy stripped off his gloves and slapped them against his thigh in high irritation with the frustrating but accurate descriptions of any assistance he might offer or action he might take. It seemed that the only acceptable action was complying with Elizabeth's plea that he say nothing.

Entering his study, he quickly closed the door and threw himself into his chair. A deep frown sharply slanted his brows as he mentally reviewed the situation. *Say nothing!* Of course, he would comply with her plea when it came to society in general; but his entire being strained against the inaction that propriety demanded. It was all so absurd! He knew how to begin, where to go, whom to enlist. He had the resources to buy any information he might need in pursuit of an acceptable conclusion to this disaster, and he was, without doubt, sufficiently motivated to accomplish it all as well! The memory of Elizabeth's inconsolable weeping swept through him once more with painful clarity. Oh, he would never forget the encounter! Even now, her helplessness and misery grieved him so acutely that his entire fortune seemed a small price to relieve her suffering.

"Wickham!" Darcy ground out as he pounded his fist on the

desk and bounded from his seat. Running a hand through his hair, he strode about the room. What would be the outcome if he did not involve himself? Ghastly! It was highly unlikely that a man of Mr. Bennet's limited resources and country temper would alone succeed in finding his daughter in the stews of London. The pursuit could bankrupt him and take months or longer. Even were he successful, the girl's reputation and, therefore, her family's would be torn to shreds. Certainly, no one in Hertfordshire would ever forget the scandal, and the disgrace would cling to the remaining sisters, following them anywhere in England they might go. Scandal! He shook his head. The power and fear that word could evoke! Yet its effects fell so very unevenly across Society. What caused gasps and titters when committed by one—Lady Caroline Lamb's highly public indiscretions flashed through his mind—was the ruination of whole families in others.

Darcy checked his stride and paused at a window to look out on the neat, orderly gardens of Pemberley. The horror of scandal had kept him silent before. Oh, he had saved Georgiana and jealously guarded the Darcy name, but with that he had been content. He knew Wickham, had known what sort of man he had become, known that if he could so use Georgiana, he could have no compunction about seducing others. Who knew what other young women Wickham had deceived, debauched? But Darcy had been satisfied with fencing his own pasture and had spared no thought for the defense of his neighbor's. Here was the result! Elizabeth's family was only the most recent to suffer, but that it was the family of the woman he loved and to whom he owed so much cast his neglect into even darker hues. Darcy took a deep breath. It was certain that the only possible path to resolving the matter for the Bennets was a marriage. A less satisfactory solution would be a respectable but distant retirement for the girl and prison or a foreign military post for Wickham. Either solution would require financial and social resources far beyond those available to Elizabeth's father or uncle.

And then, Darcy's breath caught, there was Elizabeth! His mind, his heart flooded with waves of longing that threatened to drown his every rational faculty. The chances for Elizabeth to contract an advantageous marriage had always been slim. Now her prospects were all but nonexistent. The thought of her as another man's wife had never been anything other than difficult for him to contemplate, but now the prospect of any sort of happiness attending her future was deeply in question. Darcy closed his eyes against the yearnings of the past that would enfold her into his protective care. He must think clearly!

Both she and her sisters—he pulled himself back to the question at hand—both Elizabeth and her sisters would be forced to marry below their station if they married at all, and if respectable men could be found who would overlook the taint upon the family. Unbidden, a picture arose of Elizabeth as the wife of some poor farmer or clerk, toiling daily through a mean existence that drained every ounce of her vivacity. Darcy's teeth clenched as he leaned his forehead against the cool glass of the window. Groaning, he tried to push the vision away, but it would not quit the center stage of his imagination as he saw her, a shadow of the woman she could have been. It nearly drove him mad! It also decided him. He turned back to the room, his gaze taking it in as if it were all of Pemberley laid before him. No, he would not stand aside from her need! If his fortune could purchase an acceptable solution and give her a chance for happiness, perhaps his prestige carefully applied to the right man—Elizabeth's uncle came immediately to mind—could override objection to his involvement.

With new energy, Darcy returned to his desk and pulled open his calendar. Running a finger down his schedule, he noted his appointments and then pulled out paper and ink. His steward would be scratching his head at what he would read, but that could not be helped. Sherrill was a good man and would rise to the challenge of the responsibilities Darcy was about to give him. What mattered now was speed. He must be in London as soon as possible, even if it meant little rest or traveling on Sunday. In a hand that reflected his haste, Darcy put his signature to a second letter, this one to be sent ahead of him to the city, and blew lightly upon the wet ink while his mind raced to all that he must accomplish before he could leave. Then, folding it, he made for the door and handed both letters to the first footman he encountered with instructions for their direction. The sound of voices in the main hall alerted him to the return of his guests from their breakfast picnic. He could ill afford the time for engaging in social niceties or foiling Caroline Bingley's little plots and stratagems. Turning to the stairs, he took them two at a time and, when he had reached his chambers, pulled insistently upon the bell.

"Fletcher!" Darcy was upon his valet before the man had a chance to catch his breath from his unexpected summons up two steep flights. "We are leaving for London tomorrow. You must pack only what is necessary, for I will not be entertaining or going about Town in the usual manner."

"London, sir?" Fletcher wheezed in surprise. "Tomorrow? Good Heavens, sir!"

"Pray that it is so, and that Heaven will be good." Darcy paused, the look of bewilderment on Fletcher's face setting him to wonder whether taking his valet into his confidence might be the wiser course. "We go to the rescue of a young woman, Fletcher," he finally added, a ghost of a smile creasing his face, "an activity with which you and your finacée have some experience, if I recall."

"Y-yes, sir," his valet agreed uncertainly. "When do you wish to depart?"

"Six, absolutely no later. That will be all— No, wait!" Darcy caught the man before he could bow. "Tell no one until later tonight; then you may let it be known among the servants. I will inform Mr. Reynolds, but my guests are not to know until I tell them."

"Yes, sir." Fletcher bowed.

"And send a servant to find Miss Georgiana. I wish to speak with her at once."

"Immediately, Mr. Darcy!" Fletcher quickly bowed again and disappeared behind the servants' door. For a moment, Darcy stared at the closed door, his valet's steps receding into silence. A deep sense of wholeness spread through his soul, accentuating as it did so the sweet freedom of a clear conscience granted by having come to a decision that he could act upon.

"Fitzwilliam?" Georgiana appeared in the doorway in response to his call of "Enter!" Darcy looked up from his portmanteau just in time to catch the smile upon her face fade into puzzlement. "What are you doing? Packing?" She looked at him in astonishment.

"Yes, dearest, I leave tomorrow at first light." He dropped what was in his hands and went to her.

"But, our guests . . ." She looked up at him as he took her hands in his. "And Miss Elizabeth?"

Darcy looked down into her eyes and marveled at the calm self-possession he found there. *The quality of mercy . . .* Yes, that was what he saw there, the effects of mercy and the wisdom its bestowal had brought to her. The urge to tell her his plans was strong. Georgiana, of all people, would understand what he was about to do.

"It is on behalf of Miss Elizabeth that I must leave you here to entertain our guests, sweetling, and travel to London for I know not how long."

"London! For Miss Elizabeth?" He could see her curiosity warring with an awakened concern and a proper reserve.

"Yes. Elizabeth . . . Miss Elizabeth received some distressing news by post just moments before I was introduced. She was so distraught that she confided its contents to me in a most unguarded fashion." He paused. "It is a matter, oddly enough, that touches on our family and for which I hold my own actions to be a highly significant factor." He looked deeply into his sister's eyes. "I promised Elizabeth my silence, but it involves Wickham, my dear." Georgiana gasped, and for a moment, the old look of pain and shame crossed her delicate features, but these emotions were rapidly replaced by intensity.

"Wickham and Miss Elizabeth? You must tell me, Fitzwilliam!" she demanded, her grip on his hands tightening, her regard of him steady.

"Wickham has . . . has compromised Miss Elizabeth's youngest sister—"

"No!" Georgiana breathed it out in a strangled whisper.

"I fear it is so." He looked at her apprehensively, but she nodded and motioned that he continue. "He has taken her to London and effectively disappeared. The post pled for Miss Elizabeth to return home to Hertfordshire and for her uncle to assist her father in his search. I expect they are already gone, Georgiana." He sighed. "I cannot think but that if I had exposed Wickham for the danger he was, this could not have happened. Perhaps I am wrong, but at the moment I can only accuse myself of behaving with no thought for the protection of anyone beyond our own family."

"And so you go to London to assist in the search?" Georgiana finished for him. "They will not want it."

"No, they will not; therefore, I will make them no offer but will employ my own means in secret. Which brings me to this next." He caught her eye. "You must tell no one and carry on here yourself. Can you do that?" He cocked his head at her. He was asking much of his young sister, but as he put his hands on her slim shoulders, he felt them straighten to the task.

"Yes, I can; it is the least I can do." She looked him full in the face. "It was for me that you kept silent, Fitzwilliam. We must put that right; we must help Miss Elizabeth."

Darcy smiled at her "we" and put a palm to her cheek. "You have become such a lady that I dare not call you 'my girl' any longer. Lord Brougham warned me it was so and, as in so much, he was right." He kissed her forehead. "Now, I must finish my packing. I will announce my departure at dinner tonight, not before; and you must plan your own strategy, Miss Darcy!"

The profound consternation of his guests when informed that Darcy was leaving them to their own devices might have gratified the conceit of a lesser man, but after briefly acknowledging their disappointment, he refused to entertain long faces or petulant looks. Instead, he plunged into the next matter, that of insisting that his guests treat Pemberley as their own while he was gone from them, ending with the small caveat that any large entertainments should be discussed first with his sister.

"Dash it all!" Bingley exclaimed at the news of the unnamed emergency. "What deuced bad luck! And everything has been so agreeable . . . more than agreeable," he murmured. "When will you return, Darcy?"

"I cannot say. It is completely in the hands of Providence." Darcy's mouth assumed grim lines. "But I believe it will be a matter of weeks rather than days."

"Then p'rhaps we should think of pushing on to Scarborough." A new chorus of disappointment from his sisters greeted Bingley's words, but he pointedly ignored them. "Unless"—he peered into Darcy's face—"unless there is any way in which I might help you." Bingley's earnest offer was gratifying to behold, for not long ago he would not have dared even to think he could stand as his friend's support.

"No, I thank you." Darcy steadily returned his regard. "If the matter were such that you could help, I would pounce upon your offer; but as it is . . ." He let the sentence dangle.

Bingley nodded. "Well then, we shall keep Miss Darcy company." He winked at his friend. "And plunder your trout stream in the meantime. I know of nothing else so likely to hasten your business in Town."

"Indeed." Darcy smiled back. "But having observed your skill with rod and reel, I have not the least concern for the health and safety of my trout."

Upon bidding his guests adieu and retiring to the sanctuary of his bedchamber, Darcy found his valet awaiting him in his dressing room with all at the ready. A single trunk, closed but as yet unbound, stood discreetly to one side awaiting his inspection while a solemn-eyed Fletcher, caught in the midst of evening preparations that would end only after Darcy ordered him to bed, bowed.

"Good evening, Fletcher." He looked down at the trunk. "Packed to satisfaction?"

"Yes, sir. I believe so, sir." His man moved toward the article in question. "Do you wish to—"

"No, I have every confidence that it is complete for our purposes. Send it down with my bag, if you please." Fletcher bowed, reached for the bell rope, gave it a stout pull, and then bent to the task of strapping and locking the trunk.

When he finished, he turned back to his master, the solemnity of his manner unchanged. "If I may, sir?" Darcy nodded his assent to the curiosity he knew Fletcher had manfully controlled throughout the evening before turning him his back to begin disrobing. "May I know more about our mission?" He eased the coat from Darcy's shoulders and placed it on a chair. "A lady in distress, I am to understand?"

"Yes, but wait!" A knock had sounded at the servants' door, causing both men to tense. "Enter!" Darcy called out. "There." He motioned the entering footman toward the trunk. "Take it below for tomorrow morning, if you please; and remind Morley that the coach is to be ready by first light. Thank you."

"Yes, sir." The footman hoisted the trunk to his shoulder and headed back down the servants' stairs. Darcy waited until the sound of his footsteps had receded to silence before turning back to his valet.

"Yes." He unbuttoned his waistcoat. "That is correct—or almost correct." Fletcher's eyebrow went up. "The lady may not yet realize that she is in distress, but she most certainly is. Of that there is no question!" Darcy leaned toward his man as he handed him his waistcoat. "Your discretion is of the utmost importance in this matter, you must realize, the utmost importance!"

"Yes, sir!" Fletcher's eyes lit up even as Darcy fixed upon him an intense look.

"It involves the Bennet family."

Fletcher's excitement turned to horror. "No, sir . . . not Miss Eliz——"

"No! Rest easy on that score." Darcy began untying his cravat. "But it is one of her sisters, the youngest. She has run off in what she expects to be an elopement but what I am most certain is not. I know the character of the man," he explained grimly. "It is George Wickham."

"Wickham? One of Colonel Forster's lieutenants?" Fletcher questioned. "'A Plumper and too ripe by half' was the word among the servants in Hertfordshire, sir. But I understood that the Colonel's regiment was in Brighton."

"You understand correctly, but the Colonel's wife must have Miss Lydia Bennet as companion. So off she went to Brighton as well, without her parents or other relative as chaperone."

"A bad business, sir." The valet shook his head.

"As is now seen," Darcy agreed, handing him the cravat. "I came upon Miss Elizabeth Bennet only moments after she received this news from home. She was understandably distraught and confided to me more than she might have otherwise, I am sure. You know what this means, Fletcher."

"Yes, sir. 'Disgrace with fortune and men's eyes,' censure for all concerned unless the young people can be found and made to marry." The valet's features sank into lines as grim as those of his master, reminding Darcy that the widening effect of Wickham's perfidy encompassed Fletcher's nuptial hopes as well. Until Elizabeth was wed, Fletcher's Annie would not entertain thoughts of leaving her mistress for her own matrimonial desires.

"There you have it." Darcy nodded and passed his shirt to the valet. "It must be accomplished, or the parties must be bought off and sent into a sort of semiexile. I can conceive of no other acceptable solution that will provide the family—the young ladies—protection from the 'outcast state' of your sonnet. As it is, even should we succeed, the seemliness of the affair will be as thin as a veil." He paused before his mirror, ready to avail himself of the hot water from the washstand in front of it. "So thin, so very thin, Elizabeth!" he whispered before bringing the water to his face. He then turned back to Fletcher. "But perhaps that is all that will be needed. Society has certainly entertained greater scandals with less concern. Let us hope that this may be one of them."

"I devoutly pray it be so, sir." Fletcher's chin hardened as he held up Darcy's dressing gown and pushed it over his shoulders. "And how shall I assist you, sir? I am even more at your command."

"I have no conception as yet, save for the conviction that I shall stand in need of your powers of observation and your uncanny ability to come upon information when needed, which you displayed so well at Norwycke Castle last winter." A slight smile creased Fletcher's face. "Not to mention that I expect to be keeping very irregular hours, which must not be allowed to alarm the rest of the staff. It will be a dicey bit of work, Fletcher."

"Yes, sir." The valet gathered up Darcy's discarded clothes. "But allow me to observe that the lieutenant, as despicable as he is, is in nowise the same class of fiend as was Lady Sayre or her daughter. I would not lay any odds in favor of him eluding you, sir."

"Let us hope that will prove true. Now, get some rest." Darcy waved him off. "We leave at six; I shall expect you at five-thirty."

Fletcher bowed at the servants' door. "I have no doubt of your success, sir," he replied as he rose and, for a rare moment, looked Darcy full in the face. "No doubt at all. Good night, sir." Inclining his head once more, he closed the door.

Two evenings later found Darcy encamped at Erewile House with only a skeleton staff to do the small amount of cooking and cleaning that were required in the extraordinary circumstance in which he had chosen to put himself. As an added precaution, he had directed that whoever answered the door admit only those on a select list, claiming that the family was not home to any others. Mr. Witcher's bushy white eyebrows went up for a moment at such instructions, but trust and affection for his young master carried all questions before them, and the old butler merely nodded his head at the strange orders.

The first thing was to locate Wickham in the interminable warrens of London. When Darcy had given his final instructions to the staff and sent Fletcher on an errand, he sat back wearily at his desk, stretching his limbs and rubbing at his eyes. There were any number of mean districts in Town that might harbor a couple bent upon anonymity, and he was familiar with none of them. Even if he should go and make a search, he would immediately be noted as an outsider and mouths would close. A bribe would, undoubtedly, serve as an adequate wedge, but word of his presence would have gotten out, and the birds would have flown before he located the nest.

There were only two avenues into the underworld of London, he had determined, that held any promise—Dy's contact at St. Dunstan's church and the network developed by the Society for Returning Young Women to Their Friends in the Country, to which Georgiana had introduced him. First, a note to the head of the Society must be sent off at once. Then, since he had had no word from Dy since the day of the assassination, he would need to meet personally with the sexton at St. Dunstan's and, if at all possible, tonight. Pulling a sheet toward him, Darcy flipped open the inkwell and drew out a pen.

"Dear Sir," he wrote. "I have come upon an instance of the deception of a young woman from a respectable family and ask for the Society's assistance."

An hour later the common cab Darcy had hired to carry him and Fletcher pulled to a stop at the back of a darkened church. St. Dunstan's was not a large building, but it was the most solid-appearing structure in a neighborhood that looked to be held together only by the grime and misery long resident there. The heat of summer had accentuated the smells that wound through the fetid streets and alleys, which even as late as it was, still undulated with the wary comings and goings of their wretched inhabitants.

Climbing down, Darcy flipped the driver a coin, which the man snatched handily out of the air and immediately bit. "Remember." Darcy put a hand on the reins. "Back in a half hour and safely to my lodgings and twice that shall be yours."

"Aye, gov; me an' ol' Bill be right 'ere, awaitin'." The cabbie nodded. Darcy released the reins as the cabbie flicked them. "Gee-up now, Bill." The cab moved on into the night. Watching it pull away, Darcy took a firmer grip on his walking stick, the heaviest he owned. Unfortunately, it was also the most ornate and contrasted mightily with the plainest of attire in which Fletcher could be convinced to dress him.

"I see a light, sir." The valet pointed up to a small corner window on the second floor. "It must be the sexton's quarters."

"Good—now to find the door." Both men stepped forward, only to be immediately accosted out of the darkness by a beggar pleading for enough coin for a bit to eat. Before her plea was finished, two others joined them, little more than children. She turned on them, kicking them away. In moments the street was thick with urchins and derelicts, some interested only in the brawl while others were attentive to the strangers who were its cause. "On your life, show no fear," Darcy hissed to Fletcher, "and follow my lead." Slowly he backed up to and along the church's wall, being careful to display the fact of the walking stick as he did so.

"I've found the door, sir," Fletcher gasped. "It is locked!"

"Knock, man!" Darcy brandished the solid brass knob at the crowd that was now hooting and calling out insults as well as demands. It was most likely the noise of the crowd rather than Fletcher's knocking that attracted the sexton's attention, for the door opened suddenly behind them, and heavy hands on both their shoulders drew them in and behind a man of stunning proportions. Cries of disappointment rose from the mob.

"Do no behef so," the giant called out in heavily accented English. "Trit straungers lack dis? No! Go home; pray Fadder forgif. Go!" With that advice or command, Darcy knew not which, the man closed the door, turned to them, and held his candle to their faces. "Who?" was all that composed his simple question.

"Darcy. I am a friend of Lord Brougham."

"Lordt Brougham?" The giant was clearly at a loss.

"Lord Dyfed Brougham," Darcy tried again.

"Oh, Mr. Dyfedt!" Relief shone on the man's face. "Yes, I know Mr. Dyfedt, but I not know Lordt Brougham. Brudder, maybe?"

Darcy smiled. "Perhaps." Of course Dy would not be known by his real name here! What was he thinking? "Mr. Dyfed told me to find you if I needed his help. Can you contact him for me?"

The sexton drew back. "Name again, please."

"Darcy . . . and this is my man, Fletcher. Mr. Dyfed knows us both," he said and pulled out the slip of paper Dy had given him. "Here is his pledge."

The sexton took the paper and held it up to the candle. Nodding, he returned it to Darcy. "Yes, Mr. Dyfed."

"Can you get a note to him?"

The giant shook his head. "Ach, no. Ist business?"

Darcy shook his head wearily. "No, a young woman in danger. He knows people here who might be able to help me find her and restore her to her family."

"Yong voman? Hmm." The man's brow furrowed. "Not business?"

"No, not business; a personal matter in which I know he would wish to lend assistance." Darcy sighed.

"Then perhaps I can help you," came the reply in perfect English. Both Darcy and Fletcher stared at the smiling giant. "But first let me offer you gentlemen some refreshment. You have had a hard night of it, I think."

Drawing back, Darcy stared up into the amused eyes of their rescuer and tightened his grip once more upon the brass-crowned walking stick he had brandished at the unruly lot outside the door. The giant's rumbling laughter in response filled, then echoed off the circular stone walls of the stairwell. "Please, sir, come up. If Mr. Dyfed sent you to me, you can have nothing to fear at my hands. Please . . ." He indicated the steps. Still uncertain as to the wisdom of accepting, Darcy cast a glance at Fletcher, but his manservant was otherwise engaged.

"Tyke? Tyke Tanner?" Fletcher stepped toward the giant, whose regard now swung to him in surprise.

"Who . . . ?" he began, then stopped, his eyes nearly starting out of his head. "Lem? Lemuel Fletcher? I'll be!" Reaching out a great paw of a hand, he clapped Darcy's valet a hearty slap upon his back. "Ten years, has it been? Unbelievable!" That observation summed up Darcy's sentiment as well. How in the world did his valet know this man? "And your parents! How are Mr. Farley and Mistress Margaret? Still atread the boards, I'll be bound!" *Treading the boards?* Darcy turned to his man, his brow cocked, awaiting Fletcher's answer with more than a little interest.

"Ah, no." Fletcher glanced at his employer nervously. "They have retired to Nottingham." He cleared his throat. "But how did you come to be here and sexton of a church? Not your sort of role, Tyke."

Tanner's gaze flicked back to Darcy, and he hesitated. "Perhaps your gentleman would welcome that refreshment and a seat to enjoy it in, Lem. Sir." He tugged at his forelock in Darcy's direction. "I am completely at your service."

Darcy nodded, not at all satisfied with his understanding of what had just passed, but his cause for being in this unlikely situation was too pressing to puzzle it out now. "Lead on." Tanner ducked his head in polite response and started climbing the winding stone stairway. A partially open door lay at the second landing, and at this he stopped and waited for them to precede him into the room. Darcy looked back at Fletcher, one brow quirked in question. The valet's assuring smile was not entirely gainsaid by the wariness in his eyes, but it was a consideration. There was nothing for it but to trust to Dy's instructions and the contacts those instructions offered to him. Really, given what he now knew about his friend, the odd nature of his contacts should not have been surprising. He looked up into their guide's eyes again and wished to Heaven that this one were not so odd and so blasted large at the same time!

Gathering his resolve, Darcy stepped past the giant and into the room, Fletcher treading behind him, and then their host. Tanner paused to close the door and took the further precaution to lock it and hang the key on a hook to the side. Turning, he smiled at them and hurried over to the fire to swing a kettle above the embers, then began a search for the apparently rare clean cup. In an instant the man's large frame became comic rather than threatening as he hurried awkwardly about his hosting duties in the confines of the low-pitched room that served as kitchen, sitting room, and bedchamber, all the while apologizing for its cluttered, unkempt appearance.

"Please, sir, have a seat." He dusted off an ancient chair. "The water'll be hot in no time. Lem, can you lend me a hand?" Fletcher looked down at Darcy. He nodded, and Fletcher followed Tanner to a table that served all its owner's needs for a flat horizontal surface. Evidently, they had interrupted their host's meal, for a plate with an enormous haunch of meat lay at one end while a mound of papers, pens, and an inkwell graced the other. True to Tanner's word, a cup of hot tea appeared at Darcy's elbow in record time. After handing Fletcher another, the great man stepped before Darcy and tugged again at his forelock. "Sir? How can I help you?"

"Tanner." Darcy looked up into the curious eyes of Dy's contact. "Mr. Dyfed gave me to know that any time I needed to find him, I was to come here, but he is not to be found, you say."

"No, sir, and I cannot say when he will be found. More I cannot say, sir." Tanner's jaw flexed firm. There would be no more information in that quarter. "But perhaps I myself or some others of Mr. Dyfed's friends may be of service?" Tanner's eyes did not flinch from Darcy's studied scrutiny, nor did he seem uncomfortable in his humble stance before him. Darcy considered his options. They seemed to come down to the fact that Dy trusted this man. Could he claim any more delicate a need for secrecy than Dy?

"It is a personal matter requiring the utmost confidentiality and discretion," Darcy began slowly. "A young woman's reputation, rather her entire family's reputation, is dependent on her swift location and rescue from a man of base character. All my information indicates that she and the man came to London a week ago and have disappeared into the meaner parts of the city."

"A kidnapping, sir?" Tanner's beefy face hardened.

"No." Darcy shook his head. "The young lady went willingly, and it may yet be that she remains enamored and desires no rescue. But she must be found and brought to her senses and out of the power of this man." Darcy took a deep breath and fixed his eyes on their host. "I desire only help in locating her. I will endeavor to do the rest. Can you help me?"

Tanner's eyes flicked to Fletcher's for the briefest moment and then returned to Darcy. "Yes, sir, I can help you; and I will." An angry whistle escaped him. "A common enough story; though it still makes my blood boil, begging your pardon, sir."

Darcy negated the apology with an upraised hand. "The man's name is Wickham, George Wickham, and the lady's is Lydia. I will not say her family's name. Lydia should suffice. She is a small, young woman, only sixteen years old, of good but not noble family. Wickham holds the rank of lieutenant and is absent without leave from the ——th Militia stationed at Brighton. He has little money and few friends. He is about my height, dark hair, thin. He has a weakness for gambling." Darcy pulled a small package from his coat pocket. "You will find a tolerable likeness of him in this." He handed it to Tanner.

"Oh, this will be of great help!" the giant exclaimed as he unwrapped the parcel and held the miniature up to a candle. "How shall I contact you, sir? You must know, you should not come here again."

Darcy nodded. "Leave messages with my groomsman, Harry, at the mews for Erewile House, Grosvenor Square. Harry has no notion of this affair but will faithfully deliver whatever is given him."

"It shall be done, sir. Whether there is news or no, I will send to you morning, afternoon, and evening of what has been done and discovered."

"Excellent!" Darcy stood up. "I could ask no more!" He looked around the room again, curious about this man who probably knew more about the real Dy Brougham than he did. His gaze came to rest on the piles of papers on the table, unusual to be sure. "That is a prodigious amount of paperwork. I had no idea a sexton . . ." He paused, his curiosity overcoming his caution. "If that is what you truly are."

Tanner's smile was guarded. "Oh, I am the sexton, sir, when there is time. But people don't bother the sexton in a place like this, especially one who speaks little English."

"How *did* you come to be here, Tyke?" Fletcher joined them. "My father wrote when you left eight years ago, and he had not heard from you since."

Tanner sighed. "Lem, it was the worst decision I ever made, and yet the best, given the way it ended. I left your father's company and followed this troupe down here to London, believing the leader's big talk of fame and fortune. We never got into even one respectable theater. Soon it was steal or starve; and when I said I would rather starve, they let me. Then, it was sick with the pneumonia. No place to go; sick as a dog and weak as a kitten." Tanner's eyes misted. "The minister here found me on the street and took me in. Nursed us with his own hands, he did, and was rewarded with a fatal case of it himself." Tanner wiped at his eyes and sniffed. "Pardon me, sir," he said to Darcy, "Peter Annesley . . ." At the name, Fletcher started; but at Darcy's look, he remained silent. "Peter Annesley was a prince among men. He introduced me to Mr. Dyfed, and between them . . . Well, a lot has changed for me. Mr. Darcy . . ." Tanner turned back to him. "Will you stay here while I find you a cab? The street is likely clear, as much as any street in this part of London is clear; but you saw how quickly a man of your appearance can attract attention."

"I required the cab we arrived in to return for us. It should be along soon," Darcy stated with more conviction than he felt.

Tanner looked at him dubiously. "Well, that may be, sir; but I'll have a step round and make sure before you venture out. If you please, sir," he added as a sop to what they both knew was Darcy's privilege to do as he desired.

Darcy nodded. "If you will, but we shall accompany you as far as the door. Fletcher," he called over his shoulder.

"Here, sir." Fletcher put down his cup of tea directly, smoothed out the creases in his coat, and presented himself to his master. Tanner unlocked the heavy portal, swinging it wide on well-oiled hinges, and they walked down to the entrance door in silence.

"If you would wait here a moment, sir." Tanner's request rumbled down more like a command. He was out and closing the street door behind him before Darcy could make any reply. Snorting at the giant's high-handedness, he turned to Fletcher, whose eyes shifted away immediately he caught them. Ah, yes . . . Fletcher. Darcy warmed to this new mystery and turned his full attention upon his manservant.

"Fletcher, you will oblige me by explaining exactly how you know this man." He crossed his arms and settled back on one heel, his brows raised. "I am *all* anticipation, I assure you."

"Ah . . . well, sir," the valet began but then stopped. "You see, Mr. Darcy . . ."

"No, I do not; that is why you are going to tell me . . . in plain, truthful English! I received the distinct impression that Tanner was part of an acting troupe both before *and* after he left your family." Darcy fixed his valet with a piercing regard.

With a great sigh, Fletcher nodded his head even as his shoulders slumped. "Yes, sir. It's the truth, sir. My parents are—rather, they were—actors."

"Shakespearean actors, I assume." Darcy waited for the assent he knew would be forthcoming. How much this explained! No wonder Fletcher quoted the Bard like a son; he had been raised on him!

"Yes, Mr. Darcy, although they were never what one might call 'famous.' The troupe played only small to middle-sized towns, never London, nor even York or Birmingham. But they did know Shakespeare, sir, all the comedies and a number of the histories. They are retired now." Fletcher put an emphasis on the "now." "They were respectable in their own way, sir. Never cheated a customer nor stole." He drew himself up painfully stiff. "But I quite understand if my services are no longer required."

"Do not speak such rubbish, Fletcher." Darcy snorted. "I am sure your background can have no influence upon your present position. It might explain your flamboyant attitude with respect to neckcloths and your ability to quote the Bard so handily, but it is no reason for me to discharge you. And," he ended, "I have no doubt that your parents are exceptional people."

"Thank you, Mr. Darcy." Fletcher's shoulders relaxed.

The doorknob turned, and Tanner slipped his impressive frame around the door and back in. "Your cab is waiting, sir. You need to leave straightway, before it attracts attention."

"Thank you, Tanner." Darcy offered his hand to the surprised giant, who took it wonderingly into his. "You have my confidence in this. Any expenses you incur shall, of course, be covered; so do not fear to spend what is needed to acquire what I want."

"Yes, sir, and you are welcome. Now, you must go! You will hear from me soon." Tanner drew open the door and bustled them out into the night and up into the cab. "Grosvenor Square, and look sharp, Jory," he rumbled at the cabbie. "He be Mr. Dyfed's friend. No tricks!"

Monday morning saw Darcy in Lord ———'s study, where he laid out the matter of Lydia Bennet to the president of the Society for Returning Young Women to Their Friends in the Country. His Lordship listened carefully, taking notes as Darcy labored to give him all the particulars he could without putting the identity of Elizabeth's sister in jeopardy.

"A difficult case, indeed." His Lordship sighed as he put down his pen. "Unfortunately, it is not a unique one. On the contrary, it is quite common. Young country miss meets dashing officer smacking of the world and excitement, and there is no stopping the mischief that results. You realize"—he looked at Darcy earnestly—"that she may not yet wish to leave her officer. Depending on how flush he is, it may be quite some time before disillusionment sets in or until he tires of her."

"Yes, My Lord, I realize that."

"I fear that if the young lady is as heedless as you indicate, Darcy, there are only two realities that may move her. The better is that the officer has or will shortly run out of money. The other, far less desirable"—he dropped his eyes momentarily before fixing them upon Darcy again—"is that he has been cruel to her."

Darcy nodded grimly. "I am prepared for both eventualities, but thank you for your warning."

"Then I shall advance this information to our people." His

Lordship rose and extended his hand. "You will hear from me directly any news arrives. They needs be buried very deep in London to escape the Society's notice, sir, very deep. They shall be found."

Pushing away the remainder of a light repast, Darcy rose from his desk, scattering the scraps of notes from Tanner that lay among the dishes and the first draft of a note he'd sent off to his cousin Richard. Wearily, he pulled his pocket watch from its resting place and held it up to the study's clock. Three-twenty. His morning interview with the head of the Society seemed an age ago, but the times of clock and pocket watch marched together perfectly, each click of the hands marking off another moment of his lack of progress in relieving the disgrace Elizabeth endured. The scene at the inn at Lambton, her shame and desperation, and the tears that had traced down her cheeks were ever before him, spurring him on. Yet time perversely dragged its feet even as his feelings of urgency mounted.

A knock sounded at the door. "Enter!" Darcy called out. Another note from Tanner lay on the servier Witcher placed upon his desk.

"From Harry the Groomsman, sir." The butler sighed. "Yet again. What could be so important that he must be sending notes all morning . . ." His query faded away at his master's expectant face.

"Thank you." Darcy snatched up the scrap of foolscap. What he read caused him to call after his retreating butler. "Witcher, hold there."

"Yes, sir?"

"I will be going out and have no notion of when I may return. Please tell your good wife to lay by something in the larder for later tonight. I shall find it when I return."

"I shall tell her, sir." Witcher's bushy white eyebrows twitched ominously. "But she will not like it, sir, especially with the way you have been keeping to yourself and holding odd hours."

Darcy laughed for the first time in days. "Tell her she may spoil me with her cooking soon!" He waved the note at his butler. "This may lead to what I have come to London to discover." He tucked it into his waistcoat pocket. "Send a boy for a hack, Witcher. I must leave at once."

A half hour later, the hackney driver opened the door of his cab with a flourish at the sight of Darcy's somber elegance. "Where will it be, sir?"

"Edward Street," he called over his shoulder as he mounted the carriage's step. "Yes," he affirmed when the driver's widened eyes darted up at him, "Edward Street and as quickly as can be."

Tyke Tanner's note had been brevity itself. "Mrs. Younge. 815 Edward Street." Darcy stretched out his legs as much as the hackney carriage would allow. He had supplied Tanner with the name of Georgiana's former companion even though he could not guess whether the lady and Wickham had remained on good terms since their connivance against him at Ramsgate. For her complicity, she had been turned off without a character reference. She might well hold a grudge against him for the loss of a highly remunerative situation. But if thieves were thick, as the saying went, perhaps she would have rumor of Wickham or even have seen him.

Darcy settled back into the cushions of the hired carriage and noted their progress through Mayfair, then the government districts, and into the east side of London. He gripped his brass-knobbed walking stick. Edward Street was unknown to him, but he guessed it would not be in the best part of Town. Therefore, when the hack came to a stop in an upper-working-class neighborhood, he was somewhat relieved that the walking stick he carried would find no more employment than as the article of distinction for which it was intended.

"Edward Street, sir," the cabbie called down. "Any particular address?"

"No, let me out here," he directed. "I wish to walk." The cabbie clambered down and opened his door. Darcy gave him the fare and two shillings more. "Walk your horses around the block until I am ready, and your time will not be wasted."

"Your obedient." The cabbie tugged at his forelock. "Me and my lady 'ere will jus' take the air, so to speak, sir."

Darcy nodded and, tucking his walking stick under his arm, began a saunter up the street. It looked a respectable neighborhood. If Wickham and Lydia Bennet had taken refuge here, he would at least give Wickham credit for seeing her protected from the rougher elements of Town. Not every building retained its number, but 815 Edward Street was easily discerned, its number artfully painted on the door below the sunset window at the top. Steeling himself for the confrontation, Darcy mounted the stairs of what appeared to be a rooming house and rapped his stick upon the door. It opened at the hand of a young maidservant.

"I'm sorry, sir, but there ain't any rooms. Try the inn down the street an' over one." She motioned after his retreating cab. "Jus' follow the cab there, sir, an' you'll see it."

"Thank you," Darcy responded to her bid at helpfulness, "but I have come to see Mrs. Younge. I was given to understand that she lives here."

"The mistress?" She looked at him, taking in the quality of his coat and his complacent air. "No one told me that the mistress was expectin' a gentleman." She warily looked down at the calling card he extended. He gently placed a shilling atop it. Quicker than a Covent Garden pickpocket, she snatched the shilling, secreting it down the neckline of her dress, and took his card. "If you would follow me, sir?" She turned from her guard of the door and let him in.

Instead of asking him to wait while she went up to inform Mrs. Younge of her guest, the girl continued down the hall to a room at the back and knocked on the door. "Mr. Darcy to see you, ma'am." She ducked her head to the room's occupant and quickly stepped back to admit him just as a faint, strangled cry issued from the interior.

"No— Oh! You stupid girl! Close the door!" Darcy stepped into the open doorway as his former employee rose from her desk in agitation. With a countenance the color of blancmange, she stared at him as if at a ghost. "M-Mr. Darcy!"

"Mrs. Younge." He offered her a small, ironic bow as she sank into a curtsy.

"I hope . . . you are well, sir." She examined him covertly, visibly struggling to regain some composure.

"I am well, Mrs. Younge, as is my sister. Miss Darcy is very well, indeed." He looked at her steadily, willing her to meet his eyes. "But I did not interrupt your afternoon to exchange civilities."

"I cannot imagine . . ."

"Can you not, ma'am? Think on it, I beg you." She turned quickly from him, unwilling or unable to meet his gaze. "What possible connection might still exist between us that would bring me to your establishment today?"

Slowly, she turned back to him, a look of caution mixed with cunning on her face. "Wickham." She almost smiled but caught herself. "Miss Darcy—?"

"Is very well, as I said, and in nowise connected to my business here with you."

"I see." The lady sank into her chair behind the desk. "And just what is your business with Wickham, Mr. Darcy?"

"Then you have seen him?" Darcy jumped upon her words.

A tick at the corner of Mrs. Younge's eye revealed her annoyance at her misstep. "Perhaps." She rearranged the papers lying on the desk before her, then looked up at him. "What do you want with him, sir? Do you seek him as friend or foe?"

"That will depend entirely on Wickham, ma'am. If he can quickly be made to see where his best interest lies, he may in the end be glad to have been found."

"Indeed?" Speculation had now clearly joined with cunning. "How glad?"

"That is a matter between Wickham and me." He leaned over

her, fixing her with inflexible purpose. "Tell me, madam," he demanded, "do you know where Wickham is? Is he here?"

Her lips pursed as she boldly returned his stare. "I cannot help you."

"Cannot or will not?" he replied quietly, then looked about her small office. "I imagine that, as a woman of business, you expend yourself in only those endeavors that will result in some form of profit."

A half smile appeared as she inclined her head in admission. "When I was dismissed from your employ, I lost a very good situation. I was fortunate to keep body and soul together. I learned an age ago that I must look after my own interests in whatever form they may come to me."

His mind leapt to her dealings with Georgiana. The carelessness of her words awakened a surge of anger, but now was not the time. They must both measure every word. "That was made quite clear last summer in Ramsgate, madam!" he returned in the same quiet tone. "No one's future may be permitted to stand in the way of your interests."

Mrs. Younge dared to shrug her shoulders at him. "It is the way of the world, Mr. Darcy, certainly of your world no less than mine."

"No, not all the world, Mrs. Younge." He straightened and stepped back. "I will make it worth the while of anyone who can give me Wickham's direction." He made to leave but turned back at the door. "You must know, madam, you are not my only resource. Others, who have no personal interest save in the doing of good, are also looking for him. I would not wait long, were I you, to decide to place your trust with me. They may find him first, and that, I believe, would *not* be in your interest. You know where to send word." He bowed. "Good day, madam."

Walking briskly down the hall, he nodded to the maidservant and let himself out. The hackney was just making the turn to come up the street again when he stepped to the curb and lifted his walking stick in salute. The driver pulled his horse to a halt before him. With one foot on the step, Darcy noticed a movement out of the corner of his eye, and looking over his shoulder, he spied a boy of no more than eight fade slowly into the alley between 815 Edward Street and its neighbor.

"Wait a moment," he commanded the cabbie and strode over to the dark passageway.

"Don't ya be worryin', govn'r," a young voice greeted him from the depths of the alley. Darcy stopped and squinted into the duskiness, barely able to see the face of his quarry as the boy peeped at him from around some barrels and boxes. "Jus' you go home," the voice continued. "I'll be awatchin' the old mort 'n' send word ta yer groom if she bolts." The boy's head bobbed. "Mr. Tanner's compliments, sir."

"And mine to him," Darcy replied and turned back to the waiting hack.

"Fitz! What the Devil is this about?" Richard strode into Darcy's study before Witcher had a chance to announce him. "No knocker on the door, warnings to keep mum that you are in Town, and a dashed imperious command to make my appearance!"

"Was it imperious? I beg your pardon, Cousin." Richard's brow hitched up in wonder at Darcy's apology, but he said nothing. "Lay it down to the urgency of the matter in which I need your help," Darcy went on.

"My help?" Wonder changed to astonishment as Richard fell into a chair. "Say on!"

"I need your help, or rather the help of your connections, in finding Wickham."

"Wickham! By God, it's not Georgiana . . . !" He started back up out of the chair.

"No . . . no, something else entirely but about which I may not speak. He is absent without leave from his regiment, and I have every reason to believe him to be here in London. Where might such a man go to hide from the military authorities? Are there places, people, to whom he might go?"

"Possibly . . . probably! I know where to begin inquiries at any rate." The Colonel looked at his cousin in curious concern. "You cannot tell me anything? Since it is Wickham, I have no doubt as to its perfidy, the poxy little weasel. You could hardly shock me."

Darcy grimaced in agreement but shook his head. "No, I am sorry, but I can say no more. It involves others who may not be named." He sat down in the chair opposite his cousin. "I do not want you to do more than find out where he is; I shall do the rest. Do you understand?"

"Yes . . . and no." Richard drew out the words slowly. "But I shall do as you ask." He paused, looking at his cousin from under peaked brows. "Do you realize how fagged you look? When did you arrive in Town?"

"Yesterday evening."

"Late?"

"Late . . . and before you ask, I left Pemberley that morning."

"Good God, Fitz! This must be of the utmost importance then."

"It is." Darcy sighed, absently rubbing his fingers back and forth over the arms of his chair. "I must find him as soon as is possible." He looked into Richard's frowning countenance. He wished nothing less than his cousin's immediate attention to his task, but common civility and the lateness of the hour demanded a nod to the requirements of hospitality. "But I find that I am quite at leisure for the rest of the evening. Have you eaten?"

"Not if Mrs. Witcher's is the hand!" Richard grinned.

"Billiards after?"

"A rack. I must oversee a new set of blockheaded young officers tonight. Officers? Children!" He snorted. "But I shall begin my inquiries immediately tomorrow and send round should I discover anything."

"Thank you, Richard." Darcy rose and took his cousin's hand in a tight grip.

"You are welcome, I am sure." Richard grinned at him. "But I would rather Mrs. Witcher's plum duff than your thanks. Will supper be ready soon?"

With a certain grim sense of satisfaction, Darcy looked down at the card which had arrived that morning in the middle of his breakfast. It was from Mrs. Younge, of course. The name of her boardinghouse imprinted on the front, it was graced with a simple, straightforward note upon the back: "11 o'clock. £300." Yes, he frowned as he tucked the card into his waistcoat pocket, the woman knew her own interests, and they had not included being unduly coy about the betrayal of a former conspirator. It had taken three days to arrive at the extravagant figure of three hundred pounds, but one had to begin somewhere, and time was precious to both of them. The longer Elizabeth's sister was without the countenance of a relative during her sojourn in London, the harder it would be to retrieve her character, if indeed, that could still be done.

It took only minutes to conclude the business before Darcy was once again in a hired hack, a second card in his hand with the direction of an entirely different part of Town written on its back. As Darcy read it to him, the driver's face expressed more than a little surprise, but with a shrug, the jarvey shut the carriage door, climbed up into his perch, and slapped the reins. Settling back into the greasy cushions as the hack jerked into motion, Darcy contemplated the task before him. As he had planned during the hours between Pemberley and London, he would apply to Elizabeth's sister at the outset. Her response would decide his course. If Lydia Bennet proved to be intractable, as Lord ———— of the Society had suggested, then the success of his mission would rest entirely upon his dealings with Wickham. Darcy knew that the latter was the more likely scenario. Wickham would have to be bought, and bought well, in order to agree to the sorts of conditions that would serve to retrieve the characters of the many he had brought into disrepute. But it was not the amount of coin which would be required that was Darcy's concern. No—his jaw clenched tightly—it was that it was Wickham.

The hack slowly wound its way through meaner and meaner streets until the driver stopped and, knocking on the door, announced that he could take him no farther. Gripping his brass-knobbed walking stick with a firm hand, Darcy descended from the conveyance, purchased the driver's time and promise to await his return, and set off in the man's vaguely offered direction to his destination. Within moments of entering a veritable warren of streets lined with dank, wretched buildings, he was thoroughly confounded and forced to ask for directions. Yes, the fine gentleman was in the right neighborhood, just one street over from his desired address, as it were, and yes—a hand reached out—a few shillings would be appreciated. Darcy dug into his pocket and dropped the coins into the girl's dirty palm. *Good God,* he thought, as he continued on, *in what sort of place has Wickham taken refuge?* The prospect of Elizabeth's sister in such surroundings made his skin crawl. Elizabeth would be horrified! He could only hope that Lydia Bennet shared at least that much of her sister's good sense. She might then be quite eager for rescue.

The rooming inn that answered to the address on his card stood a cut above its neighbors, but that was not saying a great deal. Darcy's gaze encompassed the unsuccessful attempt at the whitewashing of the walls and the yard within. Both spoke of better days gone long before the hostelry had fallen into the bad company of the encroaching neighborhood. He looked down at the card again. This was surely the place. Darcy breathed deeply, his chest filling with the rancid air of this sad place. The time had inevitably come. His chest grew tight. No, no . . . he must rule those old emotions! He forced himself to let the pent-up tension release. The degree of happiness to which Elizabeth was entitled, that which he passionately wished for her, depended upon how he conducted this interview.

Taking a step into the yard, he looked into the small, cramped windows of the upper floor that surrounded it. A flash of movement at one caught his eye, and he looked into the smoky glass to see a delicate-shaped face peering down at him. His heart stopped. It was Lydia Bennet, but her resemblance to Elizabeth was just enough to give him a start. Lydia's face disappeared. He must act quickly. Darcy leapt for the hostelry's door. Ducking his head as he entered, he quickly crossed the tavern floor and ran up the narrow steps to the rooming hall.

"Wickham." He called the name down the hall in a voice that held every expectation of an answer. Silence reigned for several moments; then, suddenly, a door opened with a flourish and Wickham stood there, his neckcloth loose and soiled but his head high. "Darcy," he acknowledged him, a smirk upon his lips as he shrugged his waistcoat closed.

Darcy advanced upon him. "I have come about Miss Lydia Bennet." Stopping directly in front of Wickham, he looked him squarely in the eye. "I know she is within."

A hint of wariness flitted across Wickham's face and as quickly disappeared. "She is why you are here?" His tone was disbelieving. Straightening, he threw back his shoulders in an attempt to block Darcy's view of the room behind him. "What can you possibly want with her?"

"At present, my business is with you, but I also desire to speak with her and her alone. I trust you have no objection." Darcy regarded him evenly, conveying as little as possible in his face or voice.

"Of course, I have no objection . . . if it is business," Wickham replied. He stepped aside and called over his shoulder, "Lydia! You have a visitor," then turned back to Darcy with a speculative gleam.

A pair of wide eyes in a flushed countenance appeared next to Wickham's shoulder. "Mr. Darcy . . . to see me?" The girl looked up at him doubtfully.

Darcy bowed to her. "Miss Lydia Bennet, may I speak with you in a few moments?" he asked, then added with a glance at her companion, "privately." At her mute nod, he bowed and turned to Wickham. "Shall we go below?"

Wickham shrugged his shoulders as he buttoned his waistcoat. "If you wish." With a fleeting salute upon Lydia's cheek, he turned and without a backward glance sauntered down the hall, leaving Darcy to follow.

Ducking his head to enter the taproom, Wickham then straightened, flung his hand toward a shadowed table next to the far wall, and looked back at Darcy with a raised brow. Nodding curtly, Darcy strode to the table while Wickham informed the innkeeper that they required the house's best.

"An' who's to pay fer it is what I wants to know," the man growled. "Haven't seen a bit o' the brass—"

"My companion will pay, never fear." Wickham interrupted his speech. "Two of your best, now, and keep the glasses full." He turned back to Darcy with a brief smirk. "Keeping Lydia is not cheap, and I know you will not mind the expense." He sat at the table and lapsed into silence while the innkeeper brought their brimming glasses and set them down with an indecorous slam.

"I'll see the brass first," he demanded. Meeting the man's pugnacious look with equanimity, Darcy fished inside his waistcoat pocket and laid some coins out on the table. "All right, then." The innkeeper's big hand swept up the coins. Hefting them in his palm, he peered at them for a moment before nodding his satisfaction and leaving the two men to themselves.

Darcy turned back to Wickham in time to catch him warily studying him. Immediately, Wickham looked down to the drink before him and grasped the glass for a long first draw. Darcy did likewise but kept his quarry squarely in his sight. Both glasses were put down on the table, almost in unison. "George," Darcy addressed him with the name of his boyhood.

Wickham's gaze flew up to his at the sound. He then wiped at his mouth and sat back. "Darcy," he responded, a note of tightness in his voice, "perhaps you will now be so good as to tell me why you are here. You must have gone to some lengths to find me. Is it Colonel Forster that you represent? I should think he would believe himself well rid of as unhandy an officer as I."

"You truly cannot guess my reason?" Darcy regarded him with a mixture of astonishment and disgust that he labored to disguise. "It is, of course, the young woman above! What can you have been thinking to play so carelessly with such a young girl and a gentleman's daughter as well?"

"I am not to blame!" Wickham bristled indignantly. "Not entirely, at any rate. She would come with me, the silly chit!"

"Why did you leave your regiment, then, if not for the purpose of taking advantage of her?"

"You know very well why!" Wickham grimaced darkly. "I found myself to be quite impossibly in debt. My honor was vigorously called into question by some sniveling brats with quarterly allowances that would set me up for a year. It followed soon after that satisfaction was demanded forthwith. Naturally, I was obliged to leave!"

Darcy's lips pressed together, stifling a heavy sigh. It was ever thus with George Wickham. "And now what, George? What are your plans?"

"I have not the slightest idea, as yet!" Wickham paused to swallow the last of his glass, then pounded the flat of his hand upon the table to catch the attention of the slatternly woman behind the bar. "Another round, there's a dear." But instead of the mistress, a scrawny boy appeared with the pitcher from behind the smoke-darkened bar and carefully filled the glasses with the frothy brew.

"All right an' tight, govn'r?" he asked with a slow wink only Darcy could see.

"Yes, that will do." Darcy recognized the urchin Tyke Tanner had designated to shadow him. Good, he thought, *Wickham will not be able simply to disappear.* The boy pulled on his forelock and retreated to the other side of the taproom.

"I shall resign, of course, but where I shall go or what I shall live on, I cannot say." Wickham pulled a weary face and sipped at the new foam atop his glass.

"And the young person upstairs?" Darcy persisted. "Why have you not yet married her? Although her father may not be imagined rich, he would be able to do something for you!"

"Marry Lydia? Good God!" Wickham looked at him in mock horror.

"You must have some feelings for her, to have engaged her affections so far as to convince her to fly with you."

"No convincing was necessary, let me assure you." He took a gulp of his ale. "She was quite happy to go adventuring."

"Adventuring! Wickham, she is a gentleman's daughter! She can no more return to her life after this without marriage than—"

"I promised nothing but some fun and a chance to spite those who did not appreciate her lively spirits." Wickham leaned over the table, his hand tightly gripping his ale. "Any ill consequences may be squarely laid to her folly alone." At Darcy's silence, he sat back and took another gulp. "It was never my design to marry the chit!" he growled. "Her family is scarcely wealthy enough to suit my requirements. Believe me, Darcy." He raised his glass to him. "I have finally come to see my limitations. My only recourse is to marry very, very well, and that will not likely happen in this part of the country with my debts shadowing me like a hangman. No, I shall have to go elsewhere. Scotland, perhaps, or I understand that there are some exceedingly rich Americans who think an English son-in-law is just the thing to add to the respectability of their names."

"You realize we are at war with them."

Wickham shrugged his shoulders. "South America, then, or a rich planter's daughter in the Indies. It is all the same."

"I see." Darcy eyed him steadily and prepared to set out his bait. "What if there were a more immediate source of relief for your present situation? Not as great as a planter's heiress, by any means, but a comfortable solution."

The familiar gleam of avarice sprang into Wickham's eyes. "I might be persuaded, if the solution is suitably 'comfortable,' as you say." He paused, regarding Darcy shrewdly, then asked, "But come now, Darcy, what is your interest in this? How is it that you have become involved?"

There it was, the question he knew would come. Darcy slowly leaned forward, his eyes holding Wickham's. "Interest? My interest is simply this: that you cease to be a menace to innocent young women. I kept silent concerning your seduction of Georgiana and in so doing have allowed you to prey upon others. If I had spoken, the girl upstairs—and possibly others—would have been kept safe from your careless use of them. But I did not speak, and your indifference to the consequences of your appetites has brought the respectability of an entire family of my personal acquaintance into disrepute. What my silence has effected, I will all do that is in my power to put right."

"What do you propose?" Wickham had not flinched at the recital of his behavior but shifted forward to the edge of his chair in anticipation. Darcy sat back and held his peace, allowing Wickham to shoulder the weight of beginning the negotiating. "I suppose that a wedding would be expected," Wickham advanced cautiously.

Darcy rose. He had Wickham's attention, and that was all he wished to secure at this juncture. Let him flail about in uncertainty for the present. "I wish to speak to Miss Lydia now, if you please."

"May I come in?" Darcy inquired gently as Lydia Bennet pulled her eyes away from Wickham's retreating figure and turned them up to him in confusion. She was so very young. How had this been allowed to happen? *Neglect,* his conscience answered, *a neglect not so very different from yours.* "I assure you most solemnly," he continued, "I mean you no harm, but I should not wish any neighbors you may have to overhear our conversation."

"If you must," she replied and motioned for him to enter the tiny room. Inside was only the meanest of bedsteads, a rickety table and lamp, and an equally unstable chair. Clothes, bottles, and dishes lay about the place, all in a state of profound disarray. As he turned his regard back down to her, her tense attitude recalled to him Georgiana's protest that his presence was intimidating even to those who loved him. In such cramped surroundings, his height could not help but seem threatening to a very young woman in her circumstances. He carefully lowered his weight onto the chair, composed his face in what he hoped were beneficent lines, and examined his charge.

It was quite obvious that Wickham had done little to see to her comfort. The gown she wore was rumpled and stained, her hair was a tangle. It appeared that she had come with little more than could be packed in a valise. They were, very likely, all but destitute. His hopes for the interview rose. "Miss Lydia, please be at ease. I have not come to offer you an insult," he assured her. "I come as . . . as a disinterested acquaintance to ask you to consider the position into which you have been led and to provide a way to return to the anxious bosom of your family with as much honor as may be."

If it were possible, Lydia's eyes opened even wider. "What?" she replied, every evidence of astonishment upon her face. "Are you joking?"

"I assure you, I am not," he answered, surprised by her response but maintaining his composure.

"I am to be married," she informed him smugly. "I shall be Mrs. George Wickham and quite honorably so, if you please."

"Has a date been set, then?" he asked, his regard steady.

"N-no," Lydia admitted, turning away from him. "We must

wait until some horrible people who are jealous of George can be repaid some trifling sums." Her words were merely a recital of an excuse she'd had from Wickham. Poor girl, she believed the wretch. "Really, it is most unfair!" She rounded on him suddenly. "Why must people be so cruel to my poor Wickham?" She looked at him, her eyes accusing. "And you are among them. George has told me!"

"My relationship with Wickham is a long and difficult one, Miss Lydia.' " He shifted his position, the chair threatening to take him to the floor. "My presence here has nothing to do with that, nor any tale of hardship with which Wickham has entertained you." At his words, Lydia's chin tilted up in a manner so like Elizabeth's that his heart nearly seized. He persisted. "Please, hear me. Your family are beside themselves with worry for your safety. Since Wickham cannot, as you admit, offer you marriage at this time, why not return to your family until he can come to claim you with all honor?"

"It will not be so very long"—she bristled—"and I do not wish to leave." Her pose as a soon-to-be-married woman dissolved into girlish intransigence under his piercing regard. "Oh," she cried, stamping her foot, "why should you be here and say these things to me?" An unhappy thought must then have occurred to her, for she stiffened, her face turning cautious. "Is my father waiting below?"

Darcy allowed a few moments of silence to separate her outburst from his answer. She must understand clearly what little he could tell her. "No, your father is not here. I am here by no one's urging or plea."

"Oh." She breathed out again and shook herself slightly. "Well, then." In a moment, she clapped her hand to her mouth, then giggled and hugged herself. "I've done it, haven't I! Oh, they shall all be green with envy of me, every one! And how I shall laugh!"

"Laugh at the distress of your family and all those who wish them well? For that is what it is, Miss Lydia. They suffer no envy, but fear for you and reproach for themselves." He searched her face, hoping for some twinge of conscience, but his words had not, evidently, found a home with her.

"It all will not matter a jot when I go home a married woman," she informed him airily and turned away to the window.

"You think not? It would be very strange if that were so, and I assure you that your sisters Miss Bennet and Miss Elizabeth do not regard the matter in such a light." His statement appeared to give her pause, for she turned back to him. "You would not wish to live under the disapprobation of two of your closest relations whose chances for an advantageous future would be considerably lessened by such actions on your part."

Lydia's lips formed into a pout as her eyes slid away from him. "My sisters! My sisters will do very well, or would if they . . ." Her voice trailed off and her eyes shifted back to him, now bright with suspicious curiosity. "How do you know of my sisters' regard or, for that matter, about any of this? Lizzy doesn't even like you; no one does that I ever heard, except for Mr. Bingley."

The dart, so inelegantly flung, still possessed a sting. Darcy rose from his seat in irritation with both himself and his antagonist and strode to her. The child was entirely self-absorbed, dangerously careless, and hopelessly naïve. How was he to make her see the truth of her position? He looked out the small, grime-laced window for a moment and then turned back to her. "You must know that your sister was to travel with your Aunt and Uncle Gardiner during the summer."

"Yes, a boring trip north." She sniffed in disdain. "No parties or balls or picnics. Only Aunt and Uncle Gardiner prosing on and on."

"On their travels," he continued, "they stopped to view my estate in Derbyshire. It was there that your sister received word that you had entrusted your future to Wickham. In great distress at this news, your sister confided in me. She and her party left immediately for Longbourn, your uncle to join your father in searching for you." He paused. Here was the difficult part. "My long association with Wickham put me in a better position to find you both; therefore, I resolved to do so and without their knowledge should I raise their hopes but meet with no success."

"I still cannot imagine why you should care to trouble yourself," she replied tartly. "We will be married—in time. My friends will be happy for me. There is nothing so terrible about that, that you should come here and say I should leave George."

"Can you not imagine the precarious position in which this puts the respectability of your family? They will, if they have not already, become a byword in the neighborhood."

"Oh, the neighbors!" Lydia stamped her foot. "Old, catty busybodies with no use for fun! Who cares about them? I do not!"

"But your sisters—"

"I shall see to getting them husbands, shan't I? For I shall be married and before them all!"

Darcy held his silence when she had finished. Lydia Bennet was not to be reasoned with or shamed into leaving her illicit lover. She seemed to have no understanding of the consequences of her actions for herself or her family, nor had she any concern to discover what her behavior would cost them. He looked down at the hat and gloves in his hands in order to conceal the unsettling nature of his thoughts. Unlike Lydia Bennet, his sister had known what she was doing and repented of it, if only at the last. This child—he glanced up at the bedraggled and defiant girl before him—flesh and blood of the woman he loved, had no such advantage. How was he to convince her to give up her dangerous toy? He had only one resource left and, fortunately, permission to use it. Still, he would employ it discreetly.

"Miss Lydia, would it influence you in any way if you knew you were not the first young woman George Wickham has convinced to fly with him?"

"What do you mean?"

"I mean that I have personal knowledge of another who was deceived by Wickham's blandishments and promises into consenting to elope with him. It was clear that his reasons for courting her without the knowledge or consent of her relations were dictated not by passion but by economics. She was an heiress, and Wickham was in need of money."

Lydia's eyes flew open. "What has Miss King to do with anything? George never . . . Oh!" She stamped her foot at him yet again and took a hasty step toward him. "I may not be an heiress, but I know George loves me!"

"Miss Lydia." Darcy leaned forward earnestly. "Wickham is ever in need of money. He has no profession. He has tried to live by his wits and by chance, and has failed at them both. He must marry for money; he has no choice." Compassion welled up in him as he looked down into her set, young face. "You are right; you are not an heiress," he agreed gently, "and whether he truly loves you or not, for that reason, you must believe me, he will not marry you."

A flicker of doubt crossed her countenance. Brightness welled at the corners of her eyes. Was it enough? Too quickly, the doubt faded. She hastily wiped at her eyes, and her chin took on an immovable cast that bore an alarming resemblance to her mother's. "George will marry me, and that is the end of it! Now, I think you should leave!"

Heaving a sigh, Darcy bowed his acquiescence and turned to go. "Miss Lydia." He looked back at her from the doorway. "May I leave you my card should you change your mind?" She shrugged her shoulders, which he took for permission, and laying it on the table, he bowed again and walked from the room. It had been as he had feared. The girl would not be dissuaded. He must deal with Wickham.

CHAPTER 9

The Marriage of True Minds

*U*pon closing the door on his unsuccessful interview with Lydia Bennet, Darcy walked slowly down the hall and stairs to the inn's public rooms and Wickham, considering his next moves. The rogue would believe he held the upper hand, and indeed, he did in immediate particulars. The facts of Darcy's presence and Lydia's obstinacy proclaimed it. But it was a tenuous ascendancy, and it remained to Darcy to impress upon Wickham every uncertainty and danger inherent in his position as acutely as possible while still keeping his birds in hand. For if they flew, all might well be lost.

Wickham turned from the window as Darcy entered the public room, his perpetual smirk widening as he broadly noted that Darcy came down alone. He sauntered over to the table that they had occupied previously, setting down a half-empty glass before sitting. "Amazingly loyal little thing, is she not? I have not quite decided whether that is an advantageous or an unfortunate trait in a woman, but there it is. What shall you do about it?"

"Indeed," Darcy replied, taking the opposite chair. "What would you suggest?"

Wickham laughed as if he had made a joke, but his levity trailed and sobered under Darcy's continued solemn regard. "Well," he offered, "you might carry her off bodily, you or someone hired, kicking and screaming her little head off. I, nor anyone here, would stand in your way for . . ." He looked at him speculatively. "Ten thousand pounds."

"Ten thousand pounds," Darcy repeated without emotion. "But there is the problem of her reputation, and that of her family. Ten thousand pounds in *your* pocket will not restore *them* to respectability. No, your previous assumption of a nuptial is the direction you should pursue." He sat back.

Wickham's mouth turned down in a brief grimace, but his eyes said that he was keen to continue. "All right, ten thousand pounds." He slapped the table as if he were at a horse auction. "And I marry her!"

Darcy affected a look of mild surprise. "And by this magnanimous offer, am I to assume you to believe that, first of all, I am a fool, and second, your name alone attached to hers will confer adequate compensation for your actions and effect the restoration of the entire family's name?"

"What do you—"

"What do I believe? Quite simply, that once any appreciable amount of money is in your possession, you will leave her a grass widow to deal with your creditors, and I shall have financed a considerable amount of gross self-indulgence and future debauchery. Or was a reformation of character an addendum you neglected to mention?"

Wickham cast him a look of cold hatred. "Always the tight-arsed prig afraid to dirty his clothes! Character!" he spat out. "Only the rich can afford character, but most of them seem to dispense with it soon enough. They just have the money or the power to buy their way out of trouble before the whispers get too loud, but poor men . . . poor men are judged without mercy—"

"Yes," Darcy interrupted him, "there *is* the matter of your debts. Do you have any idea how much they are?" Wickham shrugged his disinterest. Darcy pressed the issue. "Let us only consider, then, those since your arrival in Meryton. What is their amount?"

Wickham shrugged again. "I have no notion, except . . ." He looked away a moment before continuing. "Except for what in honor I owe to fellow officers." As if suddenly enlightened, he straightened and pounded the table between them. "They are the cause for this whole damned mess! If those 'fine young gentlemen' had not been so bloody-minded, so damned precise about things, and ready to cry to Mamá, I would not be here!"

"I shall pay your debts."

"What?" Wickham looked at him sharply. "All of them?"

"All of those you have incurred since setting foot in Meryton."

"You must be joking! All of them? Not knowing their sum?" he asked, incredulous.

"I shall pay your debts, whether from tradesman or officer," Darcy repeated. He had not moved since sitting back against his chair nor, oddly enough, had he felt the anger or disgust that heretofore had arisen with little more than the thought of George Wickham. He had an objective, and would hone to it, but something had changed, and he was able to deal with Wickham calmly.

Wickham's incredulity turned swiftly to suspicion. "But that would mean *you* would hold them all. At any time, you could call them in."

"Yes, that would be true." Darcy inclined his head in agreement. "You would be dependent upon"—he paused, searching for the word, and was bemused to find it from his sister's lips— "mercy, which would be excessively large and silent, I assure you, so long as you comport yourself like a gentleman in every sense of the word and treat your wife with honor." Agitated by the prospect, Wickham rose from his chair and strode to the window. "I do not require that you *believe* in honor—you may continue to despise it all you wish—only *act* in such a way that others believe you do." Darcy spoke to his back. Wickham turned to face him, his expression unreadable. "But should it come to me that you are mistreating your wife or contracting unwarranted debt . . ." He let the sentence dangle.

"Bought and shackled!" Wickham's face contorted in anger. "Where is the profit for me in this charming little picture? I could simply walk away from you, the girl, and the whole damned thing this minute, you know."

"You could try, but there are so many interested in your whereabouts: tradesmen, angry fathers, your former fellow officers, not to mention your commander. I found you within days of learning of your flight from Brighton. They will as well."

Wickham blanched, swallowed hard, and then reddened. "You wouldn't . . . ," he ground out from between clenched jaws, his eyes hunted and wild.

"I sincerely hope that it will not come to that," Darcy replied, a sense of calm flowing deep and wide through his body. The veracity of his words took him by surprise no less than they did his adversary. He should have been feeling every sort of exultation in his impending triumph over the one who had bedevilled his life and threatened his family. At least, he should have felt the excitement of closing upon the quarry, but strangely, he did not. Was it pity? Did he pity Wickham? No . . . it was not that, not precisely.

Wickham relaxed from his rigid stance and resumed his seat across the table. "If I agreed to all of this, how shall I go on and with a wife to support? Satisfying the damned bloodsuckers is all well and good, but what shall I live on?" Darcy's lack of an immediate reply appeared to worry him, for Wickham's foot began tapping nervously against the inn floor. "I have no profession." He looked down at his hands and then up at Darcy. "Kympton! Give me the living at Kympton!" Darcy began to shake his head. "It is what your father desired for me! It is perfect!"

"No! Absolutely not!" Darcy's voice cut sharply through Wickham's demands. "There is another possibility, but I desired to

reach an understanding with you before pursuing it further." He
rose from the chair. "Do we have an understanding? You will not
attempt to flee this inn and will meet with me tomorrow to discuss
your situation further, and I will not inform on you or retract any
promise I have made to you thus far."

Wickham considered for a moment and then, sighing,
stretched out his hand. "Agreed." Darcy stared at the outstretched
hand, a tightness springing up within his breast. "Ah, well . . ."
Wickham began to withdraw it.

"No, here!" Darcy smothered the imp that would tease him
back into black resentment and took Wickham's hand briefly into
his grip. "Agreed. I will call upon you tomorrow afternoon." He
spoke hurriedly. "Make my good-byes known to Miss Lydia Bennet." Then retrieving his hat and walking stick, he left Wickham
standing alone in the public room to think as he wished about
what had just passed between them.

Reaching the hired cab, Darcy called up an address to the
driver and climbed inside. As the cab threaded through the streets,
Darcy threw his hat and gloves beside him on the worn, cracked
leather seat and rubbed first at his eyes, then briskly over his entire
face. Sitting back into the squabs, he stretched out his legs and
evaluated his position. He had found them! The sad meanness of
the place in which he had found them was enough to depress the
most optimistic of men, and Wickham was not one of that happy
tribe. Rather, Darcy was certain, he was chafing miserably at the
necessity of being cut off from the life he craved and was desperately eager for a way back into enough respectability to reach for it
again. Were the terms he had proposed enough to tempt Wickham? It appeared so; at least for the moment. After the moment
had passed, it was likely that only holding Wickham's debts over
his head would keep him between the traces.

Darcy closed his eyes, a great sigh escaping him. As onerous as
were the terms to Wickham, the fact of the matter was that the
man's acceptance of his offer to purchase his debts and the meas-

ures required insuring its terms would tie him to Wickham for the rest of his life. Darcy had known this from the outset, and the distaste it evoked had roused his latent antipathy despite all efforts to cultivate an attitude suitable to the delicacy of his task. But then, in the face of it all—Lydia Bennet's childish defiance and selfishness, Wickham's bravado, devoid of conscience—compassion had unexpectedly welled up within him, and what anger and pride could not contrive, the fall of mercy's gentle rain had brought to pass. They had an agreement. It was a beginning that held some hope.

Hope! Darcy's attention shifted to that sweet presence in his heart for whom hope would impart so much—Elizabeth. If only he could relieve her mind with the assurance that her sister was found and that plans were in motion to secure her return. What she must be enduring as she waited for news day after silent day! "Soon," he promised her, his voice soft in the shadows of the cab. "Soon."

The cab slowed to a stop in front of the officers' billet of His Majesty's Royal Horse Guards, and as the cabbie dropped down to open the door, Darcy withdrew a card from the case in his waistcoat pocket. Handing it to the man, he instructed him to take it to the officer on duty and request the whereabouts of Colonel Fitzwilliam. In less than five minutes, he knew exactly where his cousin was.

"Good God, Fitz, what are you doing here and in that!" Darcy laughed at the disapproval on Richard's face as his cousin opened the cab's door and set out the steps himself. How good it was to laugh again! "Here, get your hat, for pity's sake, and make sure you dust it off!"

"Do not offend my driver, if you please!" Darcy warned him with a wink. "He is an uncommon brave one and stands by his word." He turned to the man and pressed thrice his fare in his hand as he looked him squarely in the eye. "I am very grateful to him."

"T'anks, gov'ner . . . ah, sir." The man flushed and, ducking his head while he backed away, clambered up into his seat and drove off.

Darcy turned to see his cousin staring at him in utter disbelief. Clapping him on the shoulder, he said, "Come, I have found Wickham and need your help. Where can we talk?"

A few minutes later, they stood in the doorway of a public house favored by a large number of His Majesty's officers, most of whom looked curiously at Darcy after stepping aside and nodding to his companion. "Not many civilians brave enough to part the 'Red Sea,'" Richard explained as he ushered his cousin to a snug table in the corner. "They are wondering who you are. Now, tell me how the Devil you found the scabby miscreant before I did!"

Darcy shook his head. "Another time, perhaps. I need your help in something else in which you are particularly knowledgeable." Richard grinned slyly at him. "What? No! I refer, my dear Cuz, to your military knowledge."

Richard sat back complacently. "Say on! What do you wish to know?"

"What does a lieutenancy cost?"

"A lieutenancy? It would depend upon the unit and where it is stationed. Anywhere between five hundred and nine hundred pounds." His brow wrinkled. "Why do you— Hold there!" The colonel came forward in his chair and pinned Darcy with a look of horror. "You do not mean it for Wickham!"

"In one crack!" Darcy's lips turned up in amusement at his cousin's expression. "I will never understand why D'Arcy calls you a slow-top!"

"Because he is an idiot! But that is not to the point." Richard's eyes narrowed, and he tapped a finger on the table between them. "You mean to purchase *Wickham* a lieutenancy. Wickham—the blackguard who almost ruined—" He stopped and bit his lip, then continued. "Who has thrown every good you have done him in your teeth, who owes money to every tradesman and an apology to every young woman's father between here and Derbyshire." Richard's face grew more flushed with each charge. "What has he done that he should abandon his militia regiment and you reward him with a career in the army? Lieutenant!" He snorted. "Let him start at the bottom and learn discipline and respect if he is wild for the army!"

"I cannot tell you; it is not mine to reveal the particulars," Darcy reminded his cousin, who sat back in frustration, shaking his head. He relented. "You must know that I do not do this with Wickham's welfare as my object. He has . . ." Darcy paused and frowned. "Damn if he has not compromised another young woman, but this time, she is from a respectable but modestly situated family with whom I have some acquaintance. There is nothing for it but that they must marry, and you know as well as I that George is in no position to support a wife. It is for the young woman and her family that I do this." He traced one of the dark rings on the table left by innumerable pints. "Perhaps, if I had been less proud, I might have had some success in making Wickham's character understood before ever he endangered one of their daughters."

Richard eyed his cousin steadily as he stroked his chin, examining him, Darcy knew, for any weakness on which he could work. "All right, all right!" He finally surrendered, throwing up his hands. "You are set upon this—of which there is much more than meets the eye—and there will be no moving you! What do you want me to do?"

"Find a commission stationed here in England but in an obscure unit, preferably a place that offers few inducements to mischief."

Richard's eyebrows rose. "Bury him, you mean!" He snorted. "Well, your idea sounds better now than it did at first, I must say. Officers wishing to sell out of a stagnant unit in the middle of nowhere should not be difficult to locate. Perhaps I will be lucky and find one with a martinet commander who devoutly believes that tormenting his staff is how to make men of them." He laughed wickedly. "I shall send round a list to Erewile House."

"I need it sooner rather than later." Darcy rose, as did his cousin.

"Yes, sir!" Richard saluted him smartly, then leaned forward to whisper, "But if word should get out that I had *any* hand in foisting that wretch on the army, I shall have no mercy on you, Cuz."

Later that evening a packet carrying Richard's scrawl was laid upon Darcy's desk. "The communication from Colonel Fitzwilliam, sir," Witcher announced quietly at the door, then crossed the room at Darcy's nod.

"Thank you, Witcher. That will be all." He reached for the packet and began to break the seal.

Rather than leave, his butler looked pointedly at the tray at his master's elbow. "Nothing to your liking, sir?"

"No, it is very well." Darcy looked at the artfully arranged repast with dismay. "In the midst of all this"—he indicated his littered desk—"I forgot it was there."

"Shall I remove it, sir?" From Witcher's tone and his own long experience, Darcy knew that sending the food back without touching it would cause undue concern belowstairs.

"No, no, leave it here. Now that this has come," he answered, waving the packet, "I shall feel more at leisure. Thank your good wife, Witcher."

"Yes, sir." The man sighed with relief. "Just so, sir."

The seal broken, Darcy laid out the pages on his desk and reached for one of his housekeeper's lemon biscuits. A half hour later, he drew forward paper and pen and began his purchase of a commission for George Wickham, Esquire, in the regiment from among those in Colonel Fitzwilliam's list that lay the farthest distance from Hertfordshire and Polite Society.

The next morning, following his cousin's instructions, Darcy presented his application to the proper authorities and within an hour was in possession of assurances that, when all the military wheels had ground, his request for a commission in the ——th Regiment, stationed in Newcastle, would be granted.

Upon returning to Erewile House, he embarked upon the singularly uncomfortable task of apprising his secretary that certain changes in his financial arrangements would be necessary. For the first time in their long association, Darcy saw Hinchcliffe actually start and stare. "Mr. Darcy," he croaked, unable to find his full voice, "you cannot understand what you are saying! To raise that amount above the normal requirements of your interests would involve considerable shifting of assets and inevitable loss. Sir, I respectfully submit that you reconsider! Perhaps there are other ways such a sum—"

Darcy shook his head. "Not in so quickly a manner, I fear, and time is my adversary." Seeing the concern in the older man's eyes, he continued, "Do not fear that I have done something rash or unprincipled, Hinchcliffe. I have not turned gamester, nor am I the victim of blackmail. Rather I have hope that these funds will do some good . . . right a wrong, at least." He stopped and tapped the desk between them. "I put it into your hands, Hinchcliffe," he said to the man who had taught and guided him in all his financial affairs since his father's death, "and have every confidence in your decisions. Proceed with what you think best: I will countersign without requiring explanation or justification."

"As you wish, sir." His secretary rose and looked down upon him, his reserve recovered but his concern still apparent to one who had grown up under his tutelage. "But hope, the kind of which you speak, rarely returns principal, let alone interest, sir."

"Yet, if we have any humanity in us, we must continue to invest; must we not?" He spoke softly but with a sudden, heartfelt conviction.

Hinchcliffe inclined his head and then, for the first time in both their lives, made him a full bow. "Your father would be very proud, sir, *very* proud." So saying, his secretary turned from the surprise and flush of appreciation on Darcy's face and left the room, shoulders set to do financial battle with the world in his master's interest. Hinchcliffe's words, Darcy knew, had not been lightly spoken. Accompanied by his bow, they were the first tokens of a deep and genuine esteem that his secretary had ever offered him. Oh, the man had always been exceedingly polite and patient, even when, at their first meeting, when he was twelve years old, Darcy had bowled over the young, new secretary in the hall outside this very door. *Your father would be very proud.* Darcy's eyes traveled to the small portrait of his sire on the wall and nodded his acceptance. "Yes, thank you, I believe he would."

With the financial pledges he had made Wickham set into motion, it was incumbent upon Darcy that he speak with Wickham again before he could present it all as a fait accompli to Elizabeth's relatives in London. Entering once more into a rough hired cab, he believed himself prepared for any dodges or demands that might arise. Wickham was ever one to surprise his fellows with erratic actions, depending on their sheer audacity to confound his adversaries. But such tricks were become old to as long an acquaintance as lay between them. This time Wickham had ever so much more to lose; and Darcy, a host of allies that could pin him down whichever way he might jump.

Darcy arrived at the inn just before three. Ducking his head to enter the public room, he spied his "shadow" watching for him from the doorway leading to the stairs. With a toss of his head upward and a broad wink, the boy silently informed Darcy that the pair was still to be found above. Casually placing a guinea on a nearby table, Darcy acknowledged with gratitude the urchin's information and was rewarded with a look of surprise that, he imagined, rarely crossed the world-weary child's face.

This time, the place was set into order. Wickham opened the door upon a room where clothing had been packed away, bottles removed, and a sturdier table and chairs had replaced the former hazards. "Darcy," he greeted him awkwardly and motioned for him to enter.

"Miss Lydia Bennet." Darcy bowed to the young woman perched on the windowsill. At a look from Wickham, she scrambled down and offered him a curtsy. "Mr. Darcy," she replied guardedly.

"Lydia, my love, go down to the cook and bespeak something to eat." Wickham took her hand and led her to the door. "Wait for it and bring it up yourself; there's a good girl. Darcy and I have some things to discuss." With a face that clearly indicated her displeasure at such a task, Lydia pulled her hand away and flounced from the room, slamming the door behind her lest there be any doubt of her feelings.

"Disagreeable chit!" Wickham grimaced. "See what you wish to chain me to!"

Darcy would not allow it. "That was determined when, by your own choice, you bundled her into your carriage in Brighton." He sat down on one of the chairs. "She is little more than a girl, George, and you encouraged a girlish fantasy that you have yet to fulfill. It is not to be wondered that she is disappointed and behaves like the child she is."

Wickham granted the possibility with a grunt and took the other chair. He did not look well, even though his clothes were in order and he had shaved. He ran his hand through his hair several times before sitting back into the chair, but even then he did not relax. Noticing Darcy's observation of him, he laughed self-deprecatingly. "Nervous as a cat! Could not sleep last night, and I do not know why, but I feel as if I am being watched. Makes my skin crawl."

" 'Something in the wind . . . ,' " Darcy quoted.

"Yes, that is it exactly! Damned sick of it." He bit his lip. "Yesterday, you agreed to cover my debts no matter the source, yes?"

"Yes, from your time in Meryton until your wedding day, I will cover them all."

"It may take some time to collect them. Except for what is owed the officers, I really have no notion of the amount."

"That shall be yours to accomplish in the next week." Darcy brought forward the leather case he carried and took out paper, ink, and pens. "Write what you can remember and send for those you cannot." At Wickham's alarmed look, he amended, "Have them sent to Erewile House."

"Oh," Wickham breathed out, "that will answer." He looked at the items laid out for him for a moment and raised his gaze back to Darcy's. "And when I have done all this and married the girl, what next? If you will not give me a living in one of your parishes . . ." He paused, but when Darcy did not naysay him, he continued, "Then how am I to support this new style of living you insist upon?"

Here was the second hurdle, and to make it all work, Wickham had to be made to jump it with some degree of willingness. "I have purchased you a lieutenancy in the army," Darcy answered him.

"What!"

"In a regiment that will likely never see action abroad," he assured him.

Wickham fell back against his chair, his face twitching as he absorbed the revelation of his future. Slowly, he appeared to come to some terms with it. He looked at Darcy. "But I shall need—"

"I know what you shall need and shall provide you the credit to purchase it—what is needful and no more. With prudence, you should be able to live comfortably; with advancement, quite well."

"Comfortably!" Wickham laughed derisively as he rose from his chair. "And what is *your* idea of comfort, Darcy? Would you be 'comfortable' living so?" He spread his arms, indicating their current surroundings. "I think not!" He leaned against the frame of the room's one small window and turned his face to the courtyard below.

"There is also your wife's dowry—"

"A trifle!" Wickham spat.

"—and what I will settle on her as well." Darcy offered the inducement without pause. Wickham spun around, his interest rekindled.

"Two thousand pounds!" he demanded, as if the amount were negotiable. Darcy raised an eyebrow. "Fifteen hundred, then, and I'll 'turn Methodist,' if you like, in the bargain."

"I doubt that it would 'take,' George, or that you could sustain it for long." He shook his head. It was time to bring this to a close. "No, I will not bargain with you. One thousand pounds in addition to her dowry, your debts covered, your profession secured, your character reformed, so to speak, and your wife provided for—that is what I offer to enable you to do what is right by this girl and her family."

"As long as I 'behave like a gentleman,' I believe was the condition?" Wickham mocked. He did not seem to require a response, for he turned back to the window to consider what had been laid before him and did not notice Darcy's silence.

. . . had you behaved in a more gentlemanlike manner. Wickham's derisive words merely echoed Elizabeth's charge, but it was close enough. How ironic that Darcy should demand of Wickham what Elizabeth had declared so lacking in himself!

"You have thought of everything, Darcy. I congratulate you." Wickham's voice brought him back to the matter at hand. "Try as I might, I can find no flaw to exploit or contingency to hold over you. Remarkable!" He crossed the room and sat down at the table. "You have hemmed me in quite well, you and Lydia, but in truth, the prospect is not so bad. Much to be preferred to debtors' prison or a court-martial, certainly." He wiped his hands upon his trousers and laid one, palm up, on the table between them. "I believe I must accept your offer, Darcy. Here's my hand on it, one 'gentleman' to another."

"On behalf of the young woman's family," Darcy amended, extending his hand.

"As you wish." Wickham shrugged, and it was done.

Darcy did not allow himself the great sigh of relief that pressed against his chest until he was alone and the hired cab's horse set into motion. His mind cast back to the beginning, to the inn at Lambton and his discovery of Elizabeth in such heartrending distress that it had been all he could do not to hold and comfort her, to dry her tears. He'd had no right, although every feeling in him had urged him toward her in the name of sympathy and love. Her tears had rent him, for he had known instantly where the blame for them lay; but it had been the awful resignation in Elizabeth's voice to the shame and disgrace that lay ahead which had truly devastated him. He had vowed then that it would not be so, and though great patches, dearly bought, had been sown over the tatters of her family's name, he had succeeded, ensured that the weave would hold, and the fabric of her family's honor would once again be whole.

Closing his eyes, he leaned back his head and filled his lungs with air, then let it slowly escape. Elizabeth! Elizabeth was free. No living in the shadow of disgrace—she could be again who she so magnificently was and without apology or blush. Darcy smiled. He had righted a grave wrong caused by his own pride, and it was good. But his vision of Elizabeth restored . . . that was a treasure he would cherish in his heart all his days!

The cab pulled up before the Gardiner residence on Gracechurch Street. As Darcy waited for the cabbie to descend and open the door, he looked about the street curiously. The houses were not grand, but neither were they mean or pretentious, as had been implied by Caroline Bingley's sniggering. Rather, neat and trim residences lined the public way in a row of solid respectability and, occasionally, some grace. One of these was the address before him, and seeing it Darcy better understood the conversation and taste that Elizabeth's relatives had exhibited at Pemberley.

He descended from the cab, mounted the shallow steps beyond

the front gate, and knocked. He wondered how he should begin to explain his visit. His paying a call would be considered highly unusual, even eccentric, especially without having sent his card earlier in the day. But when they heard his reason for calling, how would they regard him?

A servant answered. "Yes, sir?" She appeared rather young for her duties and not at all schooled in the proper etiquette of her position. Likely, she was new to service.

"I have come to see Mr. Gardiner." He handed her his card. "Is he at home to visitors? It is important that I see him."

"I-I dun know, sir."

"Whether he is home, or whether he is home to visitors?" Darcy prodded. Definitely new!

"Oh, he be home, but there's already sum'un wif him. An' the missus ain't back from country yet," she supplied ingenuously. "So, I dun know if he can see *two* visitors. I was hired for the kitchen; never answered door before. Them's what does weren't expectin' to be called back yet."

"I see." Darcy could not help but smile, but he had to see Elizabeth's uncle as soon as possible. "Perhaps I can help you. If you could tell me who the other visitor is, we can determine whether you should announce me. Do you know who it is?"

"The master's brother," she pronounced with conviction, but then doubt crossed her face. "Well, calls him 'brother,' but how can he be with the name Bennet? Brother-in-law, maybe." She appeared satisfied with her reasoning. "He's been here for days, he has, lookin' like thunder and rain." She shook her head at all the trouble in the world. "So, should I let you in?"

"No, I think not." Gently, he tugged his card from between the maid's fingers and sent up thanks that he'd escaped the disaster of stumbling unexpected into the presence of both men.

"Oh." Her face fell, then brightened. "He be leaving tomorrow mornin', sir. Heard it just now. Goin' back home, he is."

"Then I shall call tomorrow, thank you."

"Yer that welcome, sir," she replied, and without asking his name, she shut the door.

"Well!" Darcy snorted in surprise at his summary dismissal. "That is that, and probably just as well!" Climbing back into the cab, he directed the driver to take him to a corner near Grosvenor Square. From that address, he walked home by way of the mews so that he would not be seen by his neighbors. Living secretly in his own house had been necessary for his purposes, but he was finding it rather a blessing as well. Leaving him free from the social obligations that would have interfered with what he had to do, it also freed him to associate with whomever he must to bring all to fruition. "Rather like Dy!" The thought sprang up initially to his amusement, but soon the divergent nature of their purposes sobered him. Where was Dy? There had been no word since he had ridden off hell-for-leather in pursuit of those thought involved in the assassination of the Prime Minister. Was he well, or had it ended badly, far away in America? Darcy wished he knew.

"Oh, Mr. Darcy!" Mrs. Witcher exclaimed, pressing her hand to her heart as he surprised her at the service entrance to the kitchen. "I shall never understand why the master of the house cannot come in through his own front door!"

When Darcy knocked at the Gardiners' door the next morning, the little scullery maid had been replaced by an older woman who knew what she was about. He was ushered into the hall with polite murmurs and curtsies and left for only moments before the master was at the door to his study observing him with astonishment.

"Mr. Darcy!" He stepped forward. "I am honored, sir!"

"Mr. Gardiner." Darcy inclined his head at the older man's bow. "I trust you are well."

"Why, yes . . . as well as may be," he stammered. "But welcome and come in, please!" He motioned to his study. "May I offer you anything? Tea—"

"No, I thank you. Please do not trouble yourself or your staff."

Mr. Gardiner bowed once more and sat down on a settee opposite him. "What may I do for you, Mr. Darcy?" he began. "I must confess my utter astonishment to find you in my hall, but," he hurried on, his eyes bright with curiosity, "that does not mean I am not delighted to return your excellent hospitality during our visit to Derbyshire. How may I serve you, sir?"

Despite the delicacy of that on which he was about to embark, Darcy had thought himself well prepared for this interview; but the open countenance and geniality of the man before him gave him pause. He liked Elizabeth's uncle, he realized suddenly, and did not wish to see his honest, welcoming face harden in displeasure and embarrassment. But it could not be helped. What Elizabeth had confided in despair, he had turned to good use for the man before him and his family, and Elizabeth's relative must have the particulars to complete what he had secured thus far.

"Your niece Miss Elizabeth Bennet must have told you that I happened upon her only minutes after receiving disturbing news from her sister," he began.

Mr. Gardiner's eyes shaded, but he put on a good face. "Yes . . . yes, she did, and I thank you for your understanding . . . and Miss Darcy's, also, I am sure. Lizzy was anxious to rejoin her family, and what can a man do in the face of such entreaty but comply?" He gave a little laugh.

Darcy took a deep breath. "Then, it would appear she did not tell you that, in her distress, she revealed to me the contents of those letters."

"Ah . . ." Mr. Gardiner sat back as if flinching from a blow and closed his eyes. Darcy prepared to allow him his moment, but the man rallied with remarkable speed. "I am sorry that you should have been troubled with our concerns, sir," he said in a firm voice. "Please, excuse my niece for so forgetting herself."

Darcy waved a hand in dismissal. "There is nothing to excuse."

Elizabeth's uncle sighed. "Thank you, sir. You honor us." He shifted forward and continued with some embarrassment. "I know our acquaintance is a tenuous one at best, Mr. Darcy, but I feel that I—that my family—may rely with confidence upon your discretion in this sad affair." Although he'd phrased it as a statement, it was certain he desired assurance.

"My silence on it will be absolute, I assure you," Darcy replied, to Mr. Gardiner's grateful relief. "But for urgent, personal reasons, I could not ignore the situation in which your family finds itself. Frankly, sir, I believe myself to be in great part responsible for it."

Mr. Gardiner's bewilderment could not have been more complete. "You, responsible! I am at a loss, sir, how this could possibly be!"

"George Wickham has long been known to me. He is the son of my late father's steward; therefore, our relationship is from childhood. Sadly, his character was a devious and calculating one from the beginning. Upon my father's death, our connection was severed with the paying over of an amount bequeathed to Wickham by his will. After that, his whereabouts and activities were unknown to me until—"

"My dear sir," Mr. Gardiner protested, "I can find no place for blame! How were you to prevent his arrival in Meryton or predict his seduction of my niece in Brighton? Pardon me, you are very kind; but you take too much upon yourself!"

"I wish it were true," Darcy replied, "that I came here with only a delicate conscience to assuage. To my discredit, it is not so." He breathed in deeply, dreading the confession that had to be made. "Wickham disappeared from my notice for several years until intruding upon it in a way that threatened my own family and name. Mr. Gardiner." He looked him in the eye. "May I return your compliment on my discretion with reliance upon yours?"

"Certainly, sir!" his hearer replied firmly. "Completely!"

"I returned from visiting friends last year just in time to prevent Wickham from accomplishing his designs upon Miss Darcy."

"Good Heavens!" Mr. Gardiner passed a hand through his thinning hair. "Oh, the despicable wretch! Then, no wonder Lydia . . . Why, he is a practiced seducer!"

"Exactly so. He can be very plausible, deceiving most until it is too late."

"What did you do then, upon discovering him?"

"I did not know what to do, except to save my sister's reputation and avert family disgrace. I chose to warn him away and to say nothing, hoping that that would be an end to it. A false hope, an absurd hope." His voice was full of scorn at his folly. "As I should have known! I merely freed him to prey upon others."

"But this is understandable, sir. What could you have done that would not have resulted in pain for Miss Darcy?"

"Perhaps, if I had not been too proud to ask for advice from wiser heads than mine, there might have been something. But I did not, abhorring the thought that my private affairs would become subject to common gossip." Darcy looked away from his listener and sighed. "I fear that I am too long in justifying myself, which is not why I have come." He rose and began to pace about the room. "So, you may imagine my shock when, arriving in Hertfordshire with my friend last autumn, I found Wickham among the favored in Meryton society. As I said, he can be charming and very plausible, especially to females. I, on the other hand, made little effort to make myself agreeable in a society unknown to me. It is a failing of which Miss Elizabeth Bennet has been so kind as to apprise me."

"Oh, dear." Mr. Gardiner shook his head. "Lizzy's wit is not checked by as much discretion as I would wish, but she will be the first to admit her fault . . . once she is convinced of it."

"No, she has done me a kindness; that and many more. To continue—and this is the telling point . . ." Darcy stopped his pacing and stood before his listener, humble. "Because of my reserve and misplaced pride, I did not disclose his character. If it had been known, Wickham could not have gained acceptance into Meryton society. Young women such as your niece would have shunned his company, and fathers would have shielded their daughters. Instead, I chose the course of my own convenience, and your niece and your family have suffered for it. I hold myself entirely to blame and entirely responsible to see that what can be done to make it right is accomplished."

Mr. Gardiner had listened to him with great patience. Even now, he sat in contemplation of all Darcy said without uttering one word of richly deserved condemnation. Darcy waited.

Finally, the man raised his eyes to his face. "There may be some blame in your actions, or inaction, young man, but I cannot find it to the degree that you believe. Others, closer to the events, have more to answer for, I believe, than do you. If you have come to know yourself better, that is to be lauded; but do not, I beg you, take the entirety of this upon your conscience."

Darcy bowed. "You are more kind than I deserve, but I cannot excuse myself. To that end, I left Derbyshire only a day later than yourselves and have been in London with the sole purpose of finding your niece and restoring her to her family."

"As have I, Mr. Darcy. A frustrating business!" Mr. Gardiner sank back into the settee, shaking his head. "It is as if they have been swallowed up. It has so agitated my brother Bennet that I insisted upon his returning to Hertfordshire."

"That is my principal reason for coming to you, sir. I have found them."

"Found them! My dear sir!" Mr. Gardiner bounded from the settee and took him by the arm. "Where? How?"

"It is better you do not know where," Darcy replied earnestly, "and the how is immaterial now. They are found, and I have talked to them both. Your niece is well."

"Truly? I had such fears." He passed a hand over his eyes and turned away to compose himself.

Darcy waited for a few moments before continuing. "She is well but adamant that she will not leave Wickham. He admitted to me privately that he never had any intention of marrying her."

"Black-hearted devil!" Mr. Gardiner cried, turning around.

"Many have said so, and as such he is best dealt with. I have impressed upon him the necessity of doing right by your niece."

"Not by an appeal to conscience, surely!" Mr. Gardiner pressed him. "You have gained the upper hand in some other way—financially, I would guess. Am I correct?"

"I hold all his debts."

"Ah!" Mr. Gardiner responded. "Incentive, to be sure; but I would allow that this would not be enough to induce him. Why, he could promise anything and, when you have paid his creditors, just disappear!" He threw out his hands. "Could he not, even now, be gone?"

"He is being watched, sir, and can make no move without detection. This he knows. He knows, as well, that if he does so he will be disclosed to his colonel for arrest and court-martial. No, he will not bolt."

"Good Heavens, sir!" Overcome with emotion, Mr. Gardiner took his hand and shook it vigorously. "You have done more than anyone . . ." He gulped. "You must disclose all the expense to which you have gone, and I promise it shall be paid back to you."

Darcy drew back. "I will not, sir. The sum goes far beyond Wickham's debts. If your niece's future is to be secure, more must be done, if you will forgive my impertinence, than either you or her father is able."

"No matter," Mr. Gardiner replied sharply. "It is for her relations to retrieve her character and bear the expense of it."

"I understand, sir, and only wish I could bow to your demand." He returned Mr. Gardiner's fierce eye with his own. "But it cannot be."

"Umph!" his host snorted after a time. "We shall see! What is to be done then? I must be of some use!"

Darcy relaxed and resumed his seat. "I leave it to you, sir, to handle your niece's family, for my part in this must never be revealed to anyone beyond your good wife." He paused, then leaned toward his host. "Will you consent to receive your niece and keep her until the wedding day? All must appear as if she was married from your house."

"Of course!" he replied, then added with a small show of indignation, "I believe we are solvent enough to put on a wedding at any rate!"

The warm August light falling softly through the stained-glass windows of St. Clement's could not have been more perfect, Darcy decided as he stood in the sanctuary door two weeks later. It was likely the only perfection he was to witness in the next few minutes, and he paused to allow it some entry into his breast before looking again to the street. The Gardiners were late. It was uncharacteristic of these relatives of Elizabeth whom he had come to esteem during the course of this tawdry drama, and Darcy supposed he could guess where the blame lay. Sighing, he looked over his shoulder to the door that closed upon the groom. The burly form of Tyke Tanner stood against it, his face a study in wry commiseration at the frustrating drag of time toward the moment when their mission could be declared accomplished. With a brief twitch of a grimace, Darcy turned back to the street. "Take her in hand, sir," he advised the absent Mr. Gardiner under his breath. "Take her in hand, and we shall be done!" How he longed for it to be over, to be set free in good conscience to return to Pemberley. As for what was about to take place, he entertained severe doubt that it would redound to his credit. Certainly he could foresee little happiness for the couple involved, but the weight of his duty and the hope of reestablishing Elizabeth's family in the eyes of her society had held him every day to his course. Soon, all that his name and fortune could rectify would be done.

A carriage turned the corner and swayed to a stop at the foot of the church steps. A much harassed-looking gentleman emerged immediately the steps were let down. Mr. Gardiner's complexion was decidedly florid as he looked up to the doorway at Darcy, his relief at the sight of him unmistakable. With a nod, he turned back to the carriage and held out his hand to the ladies within. A flurry of skirts and an impossibly high poked bonnet emerged to be handed down to the curb. The bride was followed by the strained but determined figure of Mrs. Gardiner. Darcy's respect for that lady had grown even more as, during the last weeks, she had worked to impress upon her charge the decorum expected of a respectable young wife.

The small party mounted the steps, Mr. Gardiner reaching out his hand to clasp Darcy's.

"Mr. Gardiner." Darcy inclined his head in respect as well as courtesy. "It is well with you?" He cast his eyes briefly toward the bride. "With all of you?"

"Mr. Darcy," the elder man responded, a slight hitch to his breath from the ascent, "your servant, sir. An unexpected matter detained us, but yes, we are all well and ready to proceed. And on your part, sir?"

"There should be no problem. The groom is prepared. Shall we go in?"

"As soon as may be," returned Mr. Gardiner. "Please God that this business is concluded quickly and duty discharged." Darcy nodded his complete agreement with the sentiments and turned to greet the man's good wife and the prospective bride.

"Where is Wickham?" Lydia Bennet interrupted from under the wide brim of her ridiculous bonnet and strained to look beyond him into the darkness of the church. "Is he within? Should he not be here?"

Mrs. Gardiner looked up in alarm, and Darcy hastened to reassure them. "Yes, he is here. Will you walk in?" He helped the two women through the doorway, stopping only for a quick nod from

Tyke Tanner indicating that Wickham was in position at the front of the sanctuary. He turned to Mrs. Gardiner. "May I escort you, ma'am?" He held out his arm.

"Thank you, Mr. Darcy." She sighed gratefully as she slipped her hand into the crook of his elbow. "Thank you for everything."

"You are very kind, madam," he began, but his companion tapped his arm.

"No, it is you, sir, who are very kind, as well as a great many other good and admirable qualities." She smiled up at him in such a way as to call forth an answering smile from his own lips in spite of the flush that was spreading across his face. Looking before them, Mrs. Gardiner sighed once more. "It is such a lovely day. Lydia does not deserve it, the wretched child, but that is the way of it, is it not!" She looked at their surroundings. "Well, if it were not that it would puff up my wayward niece, I could wish that her family was here, at least Jane and Elizabeth."

They took up a position behind her husband and Lydia and followed them into St. Clement's sanctuary, traversing with slow steps the central aisle, dappled here and there with colored sunlight pouring from the great windows hung above them. It *was* a lovely morning, Darcy thought, slowing even more, and far more than Elizabeth's aunt could imagine did he wish that her desire might have been granted. Would that this were *his* wedding morning and Elizabeth on his arm! The pleasure and pain of it smote him.

They reached the front of the sanctuary. Dropping his arm, Mrs. Gardiner took her place behind her niece as he took his, just to Wickham's right. The crisp newness of the bridegroom's blue coat had lent him a dignity that he assumed with frightening ease there before the minister. The bride blushed and whispered audibly to her aunt, "Is he not handsome?"

"Dearly beloved," the man opened the service. Wickham's shoulders drew back. Darcy looked straight ahead lest the battering wisdom of the words being spoken, breaking upon the charade in which he was playing, should betray his face into revealing his thoughts. In shockingly few minutes, it was done. He bent to record himself as witness in the register while Mrs. Gardiner embraced her niece and tepidly shook her new nephew's hand. Mr. Gardiner bestowed a quick kiss upon the bride's forehead.

"Well, then," Mr. Gardiner said, ignoring Wickham's move to clasp his hand, "I believe all is in readiness at home. Will you share in the wedding breakfast, sir?" he addressed the minister, who politely declined. He turned to Darcy. "I know that you must be away and will not join us save for dinner tomorrow, when this pair are gone." He extended his hand, and each shook the other's with a firmness that testified to their mutual regard. "You are very good, Mr. Darcy. It is an honor." Mr. Gardiner bowed and, calling his wife to his side, descended to the waiting carriage.

"Darcy." Wickham addressed him.

"Wickham . . . Mrs. Wickham," he acknowledged them. Mrs. Wickham curtsied and giggled.

"When will—?" Wickham asked, stepping closer.

"As soon as I arrive home, all will be set into motion," he murmured. "See to your wife, and it will be well."

"Of course!" Wickham stepped back and clasped his new wife to his side. "She is worth a great deal to me, is she not?" A new cascade of giggles fell.

"Mrs. Wickham." Wanting nothing more than to be gone from them both, Darcy bowed quickly to the bride and strode down the stairs to his carriage.

"Home," he directed his driver.

"Yes, sir," his coachman answered him as he gathered the reins. Folding up the stairs, the groomsman shut the door, and Darcy's view of the newly married couple was obscured. Dropping his hat onto the seat, he closed his eyes and stretched, releasing tension in muscles cramped by a tight grip on decorum. Ah, it was good to be in his own carriage again! Traveling about anonymously in noisome hired cabs had held some adventure, but it was over; and he was glad of it. Such intrigue was better left to others who by nature enjoyed it. He must be for Pemberley as soon as possible . . . as soon as possible. He relaxed into the thought. Pemberley. How he needed to be home!

CHAPTER 10

Full Circle

$\mathcal{D}$arcy examined the knot of colorful silk that was his driving club's signature neckcloth, observing in particular the series of knots cascading with deceptive ease into the top of his waistcoat. Club rules decreed that it be arranged precisely so, and no member would be granted entrée to the dinner if it deviated in the slightest degree. Never one to abide such nonsense, Darcy had not attended the Four-and-Go Club's annual dinner since his induction a number of years before, but tonight was Bingley's night. Therefore, not only Fletcher's skill but his memory also had been called upon to produce the required entrance ticket.

"Well done, Fletcher!"

"Thank you, sir." The valet lowered the hand mirror and placed it carefully on the dressing table. "I only hope that Mr. Bingley's man can achieve the same result. His last attempt was merely passable."

"That is why Mr. Bingley will come to Erewile House for your inspection before going to dinner." Darcy shrugged into the frock coat his valet held up.

"Indeed, sir!" Fletcher replied as he smoothed the shoulders. Darcy could hear the smile of satisfaction in his voice. "I shall await your summons."

Nodding, Darcy gathered his fob and pocket watch, left his rooms, and proceeded down the stairs to the Small Parlor. The much-longed-for retreat to Pemberley after the Wickham affair had lasted only a week. His Matlock relations had arrived hard upon his return, and most of his time had been spent in their service. Lord and Lady Matlock were not unwelcome guests, and the introduction of his cousin D'Arcy's new fiancée, a lovely and modest young woman suggested by Her Ladyship, was a pleasure, especially for Georgiana. Darcy managed a few private moments with his sister in which to confide his discovery of Wickham and relate in general terms that the affair had been brought to a successful conclusion. She listened with sympathy and accepted his abbreviated account with a sincere joy that all had ended well for the family of her newest acquaintance. "Might Miss Elizabeth Bennet visit us again?" she asked, but he held out only a weak "Perhaps" as a possibility.

Georgiana's desire to see Elizabeth again echoed strongly in his own heart. How he longed to know her thoughts, her feelings about all that had transpired! Was she recovered from her pain? Had she returned to her former liveliness, or had the whole affair changed her irrevocably? The frustration of his desire was an ache in his chest. She could never know of his involvement beyond her desperate confession to him that day in Lambton. He had expressed to the Gardiners in the strongest terms that his involvement be kept secret and that Lydia be sworn to silence. The Bennet family was to know nothing. He had, in short, no reasonable expectation of *ever* seeing her again. It was entirely possible that he would never witness the least result of his efforts. But had he not known that from the first?

"Show him in, Witcher," Darcy instructed his butler upon Bingley's announcement at the parlor door. With quick strides, his friend came and, in some perturbation, stood before him and demanded Darcy's opinion of "this blasted knot."

"Driving the course under the critique of the country's most noted horsemen and whips was not half so unnerving as my man's fiddling with this thing." He flipped the ends of his silks with contempt.

Darcy laughed. "I have already put Fletcher on notice, Charles. Come, let him set you to rights before the others have at you."

"I feel at such sixes and sevens," Bingley confided to him later as Darcy's carriage pulled away from the curb. "It is not just this." He motioned to his neckcloth. "Or the scrutiny of the club on my every word until my induction this evening. It is my whole life!" he ended in exasperation.

"How do you mean? Has something happened?" Darcy turned to him in concern.

"Nothing in particular, but that is part and parcel of the problem. I have no goal, no direction. Nothing to strive for or against," he answered. "Yet, there are decisions which I must make that could very well determine my future."

"The stuff of life," Darcy commiserated lightly, but his companion was not deterred.

"For instance," Bingley continued, "I determined last year that I simply *must* have my own country house. My social obligations demand it. I had hoped to have that settled by now, but deuce take it, I cannot make up my mind. Only last week, I received an inquiry from the agent for Netherfield Hall asking if I intend to purchase it or not. Caroline is against it . . ."

Netherfield! Darcy's mind set to racing. He had forgotten about Netherfield, assuming that Bingley had terminated his lease months ago. Netherfield! And only three miles distant—Elizabeth!

"Perhaps," he delicately interrupted his friend's musings, "another visit might help you to make your decision."

"You advise it?" Bingley drew back. "That was my own feeling, but . . . So, you do! Well!" He shook his head as if in wonder. "Would you, then, possibly consider—?"

"Accompanying you?" Darcy finished for him, then wished he had bitten his tongue rather than betray his eagerness.

Bingley did not appear to notice, for his next words were a rush of gratitude that spilled on into dates and plans until the carriage pulled up to the site of the club's dinner. "This is so good of you, Darcy!" he exclaimed, descending to the curb.

Good of you? Darcy thought to himself as he followed Bingley into the hotel, or was it merely selfish opportunism? Upon reflection, he decided that it was a mixture of both. He had interfered last autumn with such harmful results that, whether Jane Bennet received Bingley or not on this second foray into Hertfordshire, Darcy was forced to acknowledge he owed his friend a full account of his conspiracy to part them on the first. It would be uncomfortable and embarrassing—eventualities he richly deserved—but worse, it might very well cost him the friendship of this decent man. That, he owned with a deep pang, he would deserve as well.

"You are arrived at last!" Bingley's great smile and hearty clap on his shoulder attested to Darcy's welcome one week later on the very doorstep of Netherfield Hall. "I thought I would be driven mad awaiting you these several days, but there is such a great deal to be done opening a house! Dawn to dusk!"

"Really?" Darcy raised an eyebrow. "I had no notion!" he teased.

Bingley laughed. "Come in, come in!" Darcy followed behind as his friend led him to the library. Their progress was slowed somewhat as Bingley confidently nodded directions to a servant here or answered a question from another one there until at last they were alone within their old haunt awaiting the arrival of a tray. Had it taken but two days as master of Netherfield to effect such a difference in attitude? From whence had come this ease?

Darcy teased his friend. Coloring at his praise, Bingley quickly placed its origin in the warmth of his reception. A number of the county's landowners had paid him visits within hours of his arrival, welcoming him back into the neighborhood and pressing upon him all manner of invitation. Then there were the servants, largely the same as those he'd had the previous year, who showed every indication that they were, indeed, glad to see him returned to Netherfield. "It is truly above everything," Bingley concluded with obvious pleasure, "more than ever I expected!"

Darcy smiled and murmured his agreement, pleased with his friend's doubly good news. The neighborhood, it appeared, had not held the events of last year against Bingley but was, in fact, eager to renew its acquaintance. That the servants were glad for his return also boded well. Bingley's increased confidence and ease in his role were undoubted testimony of their efforts to encourage him to stay. There remained but the question of Miss Bennet. Had he tried to see her?

The ordered tray arrived, and after the servant closed the library door behind him, Darcy inquired whether his friend had paid any visits since his arrival. He had been far too busy to do any more than pay a call on Squire Justin, Bingley replied and shook his head, and that only because he had encountered his carriage on the road and been strongly importuned to follow him home for a welcoming cup. "But yesterday, I determined to remedy that." He looked at Darcy, a mixture of anxiety and excitement in his eyes. "I intend to visit the Bennet family tomorrow."

"Indeed?" Darcy accepted Bingley's statement with no show of his surprise, but his heart pounded in expectation.

"I know that the company of the Bennets is not what you prefer," Bingley continued, sitting back in the chair, "and the younger girls can be rather tiresome. I could put it off—"

"My dear Bingley," Darcy remonstrated with mock severity, "you are not to neglect your social obligations to as prominent a family as the Bennets on my account!"

His friend laughed, then sobered only a little before asking, "You have no objection, then?"

"None." Darcy rose from his chair, the rapidity of his immersion into Elizabeth's society exciting both a joy and a fear he was not certain he could disguise, and approached a window that looked out onto the fields and wood of the hall. "Shall we see how the land has fared in the year you have been absent?"

Rather than send his card in announcement of their visit, Bingley decided over their evening port that they should give their prospective hosts the joy of it in person. Torn between an engulfing desire to see Elizabeth and an innate caution that his appearance might not give her or her family as much pleasure as Bingley predicted, Darcy could only nod approval to his friend's plan before steering the conversation elsewhere. Yes, he had come to Netherfield with Bingley's welfare as his prime motivation and, if he had made a terrible mistake in his assessment of Jane Bennet's affections, rectifying his misdeed. The sooner he determined the yea or nay of the matter, the better—not only for Bingley but for his own conscience. But he had come, too, nurturing the hope of discovering what remained of the beginning he and Elizabeth had made at Pemberley. He had pondered how to achieve these ends during the greater part of his journey to Hertfordshire, but miraculously, the opportunity for seeing to both was set before him without effort on his part! Nevertheless, the speed at which his hopes and fears were distilling into irretrievable action was breathtaking, beyond anything he could have planned or, truth be told, even wished!

Despite what he wished, there was no denying the material fact that tomorrow would bring him face-to-face with Elizabeth. How should they meet? How should they go on? It was certainly quite paradoxical, he wryly observed as he lay in bed that night, how an event for which one had longed could, upon the eve of its occurrence, so handily transform itself into a thing fraught with the most wrenching apprehension. An unquiet night followed, but when morning finally dawned, with it came the conviction that, in order to accomplish what he had come to do, it was not Elizabeth but Jane Bennet he must learn of and toward whom the greater part of his powers of discernment must bend.

They rode slowly. When Darcy had met his friend at the mounting block, Bingley greeted him with his usual smiling exuberance and chatter, which had lasted until they met the road to Longbourn. Then, his conversation lagged. Now Bingley was almost silent, the gait of their horses reduced to no more than an amble. Darcy looked sideways at his friend, searching for some revival of his liveliness, but Bingley continued gripped by a pensive mood Darcy knew not how to brook.

They had just turned in to the lane leading up to Longbourn when Bingley reined in his horse. "It *is* better to be certain of the truth of a matter, is it not?" he demanded of Darcy. "One should not go on without having resolved the past."

Darcy nodded slowly, his eyes trained on Bingley's countenance. "That is usually the wisest policy."

Bingley nodded back. "Well then." He turned and, setting his shoulders, nudged his mount forward. Following a moment later, Darcy observed the set of his friend's shoulders with dismay and no little sting of guilt. If, as he suspected, Bingley had sunk into self-doubt and a wariness of his reception as they rode toward Longbourn, it could be laid entirely at Darcy's door. He had exposed Bingley to the censure of the world for caprice and instability—that was how Elizabeth had put it. Thank heavens the "world" in the environs of Meryton seemed to have forgiven Charles the events of last year. Would those at Longbourn be as kind?

Bingley's doubt of his welcome must have been swept away as

soon as he dismounted from his horse. The stable boy who ran up
to them, the maidservant who opened the door to them, and the
housekeeper who announced them—all did so with the infectious
sort of enthusiasm that portended a unanimous welcome within.
Darcy hoped that the pleasure at Bingley's coming might spill over
to include him in a general way and lessen the awkwardness his
presence must provoke. The door to the Bennets' parlor opened
under the housekeeper's hand, allowing a shaft of sunlight to
pierce Longbourn's hall. Darcy drew a breath against the sensation
that time and space were careening wildly beyond his grasp.

"Mr. Bingley! How delightful that you have called!" Mrs. Bennet's ample form blocked the doorway. "We were just remarking,
were we not, girls, how wonderful it would be if you were to call
today; and here you are! Is it not marvelous?"

"Ladies!" Bingley bowed immediately upon entering the parlor, Darcy following him. When they rose, Kitty was smiling at
Bingley. She quickly curtsied at his bow, then returned to a pile of
ribbons on the table. Mary dropped a perfunctory curtsy and
walked away to resume her book at the far side of the room. Darcy
and Bingley turned to the last two. Miss Bennet and Elizabeth
stood together, the color in their faces rising ever so slightly as they
offered their curtsies. The picture of grace and modesty Elizabeth
presented sent Darcy's heart thudding so loudly against his ribs
that it hurt. He allowed himself the luxury of a few moments' gaze,
searching for a look, a smile that might indicate the state of her
heart, but Elizabeth seemed distracted. He forced his eyes away
and commanded his heart to be still.

"Please, be seated," Mrs. Bennet spoke again. "Mr. Bingley, you
must sit here out of the sun." She guided him to quite the most
comfortable chair in the room. "There, is that not pleasant? And so
convenient for conversing. Should you like some refreshment?" It
was only after Bingley had murmured a denial that she finally
turned to Darcy. "And Mr. Darcy." She waved her hand vaguely
about the room before seating herself close to her preferred guest.

Free to see to himself, Darcy found a chair that was admirably situated for his purposes yet close enough to Elizabeth to allow some conversation without demanding it. He sank gratefully into its contours and waited a few ceremonious moments before leaning in Elizabeth's direction with what he considered must be a safe topic. "May I inquire after your aunt and uncle, Mr. and Mrs. Gardiner? Are they well?"

Elizabeth started and colored before informing him breathlessly that yes, her relatives were well and would desire her to thank him once again for his courtesies to them at Pemberley.

"It was my pleasure," he assured her, then looked away, puzzled that she should be disconcerted by a question so customary as to be trite. He looked down at the floor even as all his inclinations yearned to discover what she was thinking. Steeling himself against them, he turned back to Bingley only to be surprised by a question from Elizabeth in turn.

"And Miss Darcy? Is she well?"

"Thank you, she is very well," he answered, "and sends her greeting with a wish that you might visit again someday."

"Oh, she is very kind." She may have intended to say more, but he was not to know.

"It is a long time, Mr. Bingley, since you went away," Mrs. Bennet declared, overriding all conversation. "I began to be afraid you would never come back again. People *did* say, you meant to quit the place entirely at Michaelmas; but, however, I hope it is not true." She looked at him slyly. "A great many changes have happened in the neighborhood since you went away. Miss Lucas is married and settled. And one of my own daughters. I suppose you have heard of it; indeed, you must have seen it in the papers." Bingley could offer no comment on this assertion, for she gave him no opportunity. "It was in *The Times* and the *Courier*, I know; though it was not put in as it ought to be. It was only said, 'Lately, George Wickham, Esq., to Miss Lydia Bennet,' without there being a syllable said of her father, or the place where she lived, or anything."

She leaned toward him, shaking her head pettishly. "It was my brother Gardiner's drawing up too, and I wonder how he came to make such an awkward business of it. Did you see it?"

While Bingley replied that he had and made his congratulations, Darcy could only sit, struggling that his astonishment should not show in any part of his person. He had anticipated a discreet mention of Lydia's marriage in explanation of her absence, delivered, of course, with a painfully acquired circumspection of manner. But, no, there was to be none of that! A glance at Elizabeth showed her struggling with embarrassment at her mother's words. She glanced at him briefly and then quickly returned to her needlework.

"It is a delightful thing, to be sure, to have a daughter well married," Mrs. Bennet continued with not the slightest indication of prudence, "but at the same time, Mr. Bingley, it is very hard to have her taken away from me." They were gone to Newcastle, she informed them, where his new regiment would be for some time. "I suppose you have heard of his leaving the ——shire, and of his being gone into the Regulars. Thank Heaven, he has *some* friends, though, perhaps, not so many as he deserves." Her eyes traveled past Bingley to scour Darcy's stony face.

Disbelief warring with indignation, Darcy stood and moved to a window as he labored to retain his self-possession under her condemning eye. As his gaze traveled over the last flowers of the season in Longbourn's garden, it struck Darcy how extraordinary it was that this woman could be Elizabeth's mother! Mrs. Bennet's self-delusion was complete, her experience of the last weeks incapable of reforming her opinions or teaching her prudence. His pique cooled; its place was taken by a compassion for what Elizabeth and her sisters must always suffer because of their mother.

"Mr. Bingley." Elizabeth's tremulous voice recalled him, and he looked up at her profile. "Do you mean to make any stay in the country at present?"

"I believe we shall stay a few weeks. The hunting season, you understand." He looked at Miss Bennet during his reply and might have said more, but her mother pounced upon his words.

"When you have killed all your own birds, Mr. Bingley, I beg you will come here and shoot as many as you please on Mr. Bennet's manor. I am sure he will be vastly happy to oblige you, and will save all the best of the covies for you."

"You are very kind, madam." Bingley responded to her absurd speech with remarkable grace. He turned to the sisters. "But I do not anticipate being forever in the field. Is there anything, Miss Bennet, that will call *all* the countryside together?"

Ah, here at last was what he had come to observe! As Bingley engaged Jane Bennet in conversation, Darcy considered them both. Bingley was flushed, his eyes cautiously hopeful as he carefully drew her out from her mother's shadow. His feelings were unmistakable. Miss Bennet's responses were, by contrast, measured but gracious. Bingley persisted. Her eyes warmed a little as he teased her on some point, then she laughed. A smile spread across Bingley's face and his shoulders straightened, at which Miss Bennet blushed and looked down, but not before Darcy saw the shining eyes and gentle smile that accompanied it. A beginning that held promise, he decided and wondered how he ever could have imagined Jane Bennet scheming to trap his friend into a socially advantageous marriage.

What, then, of Elizabeth? He looked at her quickly, then back to Bingley, his heart sinking. She was so quiet! Tension emanated from her in waves. Did she wish him gone, or did she wish him to speak? Should he allude to their time at Pemberley? Dare he attempt to continue as they had during her visit, before the arrival of the letter bearing news of Wickham's treachery? He looked again out the window as conflicting explanations for her behavior racked his brain.

A scraping of chairs alerted Darcy that their call was drawing to a close, and he rose to make his good-byes, eager to put an end to both their suffering. But he and Bingley were not to make an immediate escape.

"You are quite a visit in my debt, Mr. Bingley," Mrs. Bennet accused playfully as they made their way to the door, "for when you went to Town last winter, you promised to take a family dinner with us as soon as you returned. I have not forgot, you see; and I assure you I was very much disappointed that you did not come back and keep your engagement. You must dine with us this very week, sir! Is Tuesday agreeable?"

Bingley's eyes flew to Darcy's, a flush creeping above his neck-cloth, before he turned to his hostess and stammered an apology. With a glance at Miss Bennet, whose color had also risen, he accepted the inelegant invitation on behalf of them both. "Mrs. Bennet." He and Darcy bowed in farewell. "Miss Bennet, Miss Elizabeth . . ." Bingley continued taking leave of them all, Darcy repeating the compliment after him. Miss Bennet's answering farewell to Darcy was all that was composed, and he was quite able to meet her eyes; but Elizabeth's he feared to pursue for the relief he might see in them.

They were to meet again, dine together at Longbourn, in two days' time. He was glad for Bingley's sake. "What do you think, Charles?" he asked when they reached the end of the lane and turned in to the road. "Would you say it went well?"

"As well as can be expected after so lengthy an absence," he replied thoughtfully, then launched suddenly into a veritable paean. "Is she not beautiful? As beautiful as I— No, *more* beautiful than I remember! Oh, Darcy, the way she smiled at me!"

As they wended their way to their next morning call, Darcy listened with sympathy to all his friend's expressions of renewed hope, but his own hopes he considered as gravely in doubt. If, as it appeared, he only caused Elizabeth pain or his presence confused her into silence, he would not give her cause for more by imposing himself upon her notice any more than necessary. He would place himself even more firmly at Bingley's disposal and continue to observe Miss Bennet, his eyes this time attuned to the more subtle signs of affection which resided in that Bennet sister. As for Elizabeth, he decided as they rode to the squire's, he would need a sign from her or he was for London as soon as possible.

Their visit with Squire Justin was conducted along such familiar lines as to deny they had been absent from Hertfordshire for more than a fortnight. Under the squire's hearty ministrations, it occurred again to Darcy that, should his friend become a fixture in the neighborhood, he would do quite well among them. The squire, Darcy noted, might be just the sort of older, wiser head toward whom Bingley would do well to turn as Darcy eased himself out of a role he felt less and less qualified to play. He would mention it to Bingley, should his friend find that all he desired did, indeed, reside in Hertfordshire.

It was decided. He would leave on the following day. Darcy looked up at the ceiling above his bed, then flung an arm over his eyes. The dinner at Longbourn the previous evening had provided every reason to believe Bingley's feet upon the path to happiness. He had watched the pair, their delight in each other patently obvious, with growing certainty. With the confession Darcy must make to him today, Charles would soon be well down the road to matrimony. It was time to cut him loose and leave him to make his future. As for his own . . .

The company at Longbourn had proved to be large in number. Of this fact, Mrs. Bennet had not hesitated to remind him several times, harking back, Darcy supposed, to his utterance last autumn about the confining nature of country life. Other than those commonplaces required of a hostess, she had ignored him most of the evening, and he had kept his distance from her. Only at dinner had he been forced to sit near her and partake of a meal replete with the reiteration of all the vulgar speculations of the dinner ball at

Netherfield, now generously seasoned with raptures over her recently married daughter and son-in-law.

After being greeted in the hall by his hosts, he had come to Miss Bennet, who had greeted him with the kind smile she was wont to bestow on every creature. Making his bow, he had moved on. Elizabeth. His heart had turned over as he looked down on her glossy curls and creamy brow. How could she always surprise him with more loveliness than he remembered when he remembered and cherished every moment between them?

"Mr. Darcy." Elizabeth had looked up at him, her glorious eyes uncertain as she briefly explored his face, then looked down in her curtsy. "So good of you to come."

"Not at all," he had replied upon rising from his bow. "It is you who are good to invite us." And that had been the sum of their conversation until the evening was almost over. When he had taken the opportunity to stand by her, she had asked about Georgiana. He had answered her and then waited, standing there awkwardly, his tongue tied against the riot of questions he longed to ask, but she had said no more and he had walked away when another young woman required her attention. Not once that evening had she approached him! Neither had the vivacious Elizabeth, full of life and wit and challenge, ever made an appearance.

Soon after, he had found himself planted at a table of whist players whose fiendish affinity for the game fortunately required his unwavering attention. Between hands, he had stolen glances across the room to Elizabeth's table. The look upon her face had indicated little pleasure with her cards. Perhaps it had indicated little pleasure with the whole of the evening. He could not tell. What had pleased her was the renewal of Bingley's attentions to her sister. The soft look he so coveted for himself she had bestowed often on the pair as they walked about the room together or sat and conversed with other guests.

Well, so it must be, he thought to himself with something like despair and threw off the covers. He had wished for a sign, and though he had not received a negative reception, there was in no-wise enough positive in their exchanges to constitute any encour-agement to stay. So, he was for London. Darcy rose and threw open the curtains. One last day . . . one last day that must end in either strengthening or destroying a friendship. His eyes traced the distance over the fields from Netherfield to Longbourn. Eliza-beth . . . Elizabeth.

"What good fellows they are!" Bingley turned a bright, satisfied countenance upon Darcy when the last of his guests had called for his carriage or horse and departed into the cool of the autumn night. "I like them quite as well as—better than—I did last au-tumn." An impromptu gathering of gentlemen for cards had been announced by Bingley the night before at Longbourn, and many had come, glad for an evening away from the eyes of mother, wife, or sister.

"A good sort on all counts," Darcy agreed as they returned to the drawing room and a last glass of port. "It is gratifying to know that I leave you in such good company. You shall want for nothing to keep you occupied during my absence." He observed Bingley carefully as he poured out their drinks. His friend was in the best of humors. The visits to Longbourn and the welcome of his return by the neighboring gentry were doing his friend great good, and for this, Darcy was exceedingly thankful. Now, the night before he was to leave Hertfordshire for London, was the time to tell him. His stomach tightened even as he accepted a glass from his friend.

"I wish you would not leave so soon, but since you must, here is to those fellows who just departed, and to your speedy return." Bingley raised his glass, smiling at him. A swift pang smote Darcy at the sight. When he had done with what he must tell him, would Bingley still wish for his return? Darcy tipped his glass to Bingley's, and each downed a portion of his liquor. *Go to!* Darcy's conscience badgered him.

"Charles, there is something that I must tell you before I leave."

"Tell away, Darcy!" Bingley set his glass down, flung himself with a bounce into the large stuffed chair, and motioned to its mate before the fire.

"No, thank you, I think I will stand." Darcy took another sip of the port and stared into the flames.

Bingley looked up at him in concern. "Are you quite the thing, Darcy? I did notice that you have been more quiet than usual this evening."

"A sore conscience tends to subdue the spirits, my friend, and that is the reason for my behavior tonight. I knew that I must speak, and the prospect of confession, however necessary, is never pleasant."

"I say, you are sounding frightfully somber, Darcy. Confession! What can you have to confess to me?"

"I have interfered in your life, Charles, in such a manner that I can only regard as the most absurd piece of impertinence that I have ever committed." Darcy looked down into his friend's confused but trusting countenance, and regret washed over him as a tide. "My only excuse, if I may be allowed one, is that at the time I had convinced myself I was acting entirely for your good. I have come to see that I was wrong, very wrong, on every side."

"Darcy! Come, my friend—"

"Charles." He forestalled Bingley's denial of his guilt with an upraised palm. "You must understand my offense." He bit his lip as a sigh escaped him and then took a deep breath. "Without any regard for your feelings or hers, I made it my aim to do everything that was within my power to separate you from Miss Bennet last autumn."

"What?" Bingley stared uncomprehendingly at him.

"I worked to prevent you from pursuing the connection despite the evidence of your attachment. I had convinced myself of Miss Bennet's indifference to you and then made it my business to cast doubt upon her character and dissuade you from trusting your own mind and heart." He stared down into the glass in his hand, unable to look at his companion. "My temerity so astounds me, even as I tell you, that I should not complain should you order me from your house this instant."

Bingley's face had gone pale. His hand shook as he set down his glass. "All this time? Do you mean to say that all this time she . . . But Caroline and Louisa both said the same!"

"Your sisters did not desire the connection, Charles. They have more exalted hopes where your marriage is concerned. Frankly, and to my shame, I conspired with them in this."

"Good God, Darcy! I cannot believe it of you!" Bingley jumped up and walked away from him, raking his hand through his hair.

"It was in every way reprehensible." Darcy watched in concern and not a little pain as Bingley paced to and fro. If only he could end it here, but of course, there was more. "My dishonor does not end there, Charles. I must also confess that Miss Bennet was in London above three months last winter, and I directed that her presence be hidden from you."

"Darcy!"

"I should also tell you that Miss Bennet called on Miss Bingley and waited weeks for her notice, which when it came, was made only to cut the acquaintance. That, also, was under my direction." The look on Bingley's face was terrible to see, and Darcy's heart sank. He closed his eyes, searching for the words for a proper apology.

"I am sorry for the pain I have caused you and Miss Bennet. Heartily sorry, Charles. The only amends I can offer are my assurances that I was very wrong about Miss Bennet and that she, indeed, loves you and would yet make you a very happy man."

Bingley rounded on him. "Your assurances! You tell me that you deceived me, defrauded me of the love of the sweetest of women, encouraged me to doubt my own heart; and I am to accept your assurances?"

"You are right not to depend upon me, Charles. I have proved a poor friend. Leave me out of it. What is your *own* view of Miss Bennet?" Darcy asked quietly.

A variety of emotions played across Bingley's face as he wrestled with what he had learned. Turning away and taking a seat, Darcy allowed him the dignity of silence. He sipped at the last of his port and waited, the hearth fire snapping against the irons.

"That my dear Jane suffered all those weeks in London, Darcy! What she must have thought of me! What *all* the Bennets must think of me! I cannot understand why they received me with such civility when I returned!"

"Charles, the fact that you were so warmly welcomed by them is further proof that Miss Bennet's affections are very much in your favor."

"Yes," Bingley mused aloud, "that seems reasonable. I *was* welcomed! Although it is true that Miss Bennet and I are not on quite as easy terms as before, I *have* only just returned."

"If I may be allowed an opinion, I believe a proposal on your part will be answered in a manner that will afford great happiness to you both."

"Do you, Darcy?" Bingley flushed. Drawing back a little, he cleared his throat. "Truly?"

"I have no doubt; do you?"

"I don't know!" Bingley resumed his pacing. "I *think* . . . Last night she . . . Oh, if I dared to ask! Darcy!" he pled, coming to stand before him.

"Wait if you wish, but it will end the same, Charles, and with that I am silent now on the subject!"

With a shout, Bingley grabbed his hand in a crushing grip. Thereafter such a flood of words poured from that gentleman as went far to assure Darcy that, though he had behaved abominably, he had not lost a friend and that that friend forgave him everything in light of his future happiness.

CHAPTER 11

The Course of True Love

*L*ondon was yet thin of company, most of its exalted inhabitants remaining at their hunting boxes as long as possible before Parliament and the Season called them back to the frantic activities of Town. The normal dizzying round would be greatly exacerbated, Colonel Fitzwilliam told his cousin over a glass at Boodle's, when they heard the news that Bonaparte had been denied Moscow, albeit at a terrible price. Darcy shook his head. What could one say to desperation so great that it drove men to burn their own homes—an entire capital city!—to the ground rather than leave them to that rapacious monster.

"What are you tsking at now, Darcy! Good Lord, you look like two old men!"

Darcy twisted around at the voice but gave up trying to see its owner and bounded from his chair to pound him unmercifully on the back. "Dy! My God, when did you get back? Why did you not write?"

Lord Dyfed Brougham held up carefully manicured hands in protest at such a greeting and took a step away when Fitzwilliam rose as well. "Write? Too fatiguing by half, old friend! And you,

Fitzwilliam, may shake my hand but no more. Yes, that will do." He grinned at the two of them in fatuous triumph and then helped himself to a nearby chair and motioned for them to sit down. "Write? No, no . . . thought to surprise you, which I have, quite handily it seems." Darcy resumed his seat, the absurdity of Dy's words a signal of the persona he wished to play.

"And how was America, Brougham?" Fitzwilliam sat, stretching out his lanky frame. "You don't look like it agreed with you." Looking closely at his friend now, Darcy had to agree, and the closer he looked, the more alarming were his conclusions. Dy was dressed elegantly as always, but his clothes hung about him in an odd manner. His face, neither broad nor fleshy to begin with, was now grown very thin, his cheeks almost sunken. It could not have gone well with him over the sea.

"Do not, I beg you, mention that place in my presence!" Dy laid a dramatic hand over his brow. "How I ever allowed myself to be talked into going, I shall never know. The voyage was brutal, Fitzwilliam, absolutely brutal! The natives are completely without culture or the least morsel of sensibility. It was ghastly!"

Richard hooted at Dy's description, then asked, "Which natives were these, Brougham? The Algonquian, the Iroquois?" He looked at Darcy for help, but Darcy could only shrug his shoulders.

"No, no, old man." Dy looked at him as if he had taken leave of his senses. "The natives of Boston and New York!" He removed a handkerchief from his coat pocket and dabbed at his temples. "Dreadful, simply dreadful."

Richard rolled his eyes at Darcy and stood up. "Well, I shall leave you to my cousin, who will be of more help to you than I in your recovery, I am sure. Fitz." He turned and addressed Darcy. "I must get back to post. Remember, His Lordship and Mater expect us for supper tonight, nine sharp!" He bowed to Brougham. "Rather face red Indians myself than delay His Lordship's supper. Your servant, Brougham." Dy nodded and graciously waved him away.

Both Brougham and Darcy remained silent as they watched

Fitzwilliam make his way to the door through the knots of club members and servants.

Darcy turned back to his friend. "My God, Dy, you look terrible!"

"That bad, then?" His Lordship responded, straightening in his chair, motioning a servant over, and ordering something to drink. "I had not wished to show my face in Town until I had put more flesh back on my bones"—he sighed—"but I had been gone so long as it is that the Home Office was afraid I would lose my footing if I stayed away longer. So, here I am." He raised his arms. "I look like a scarecrow!"

"What happened?" Darcy leaned across the table.

"I cannot tell you, my friend." Dy smiled sadly. "Except to say that she eluded me."

"And Beverly Trenholme, did you find him?"

"He never set foot on that ship you provided passage upon. He, in fact, never left England. Someone else believed she was more needful than Trenholme."

"Sylvanie! But, no one has seen Bev— Good God, you do not mean . . . !" Dy nodded, and both men fell silent. The buzz of conversation and laughter of the crowd continued unabated as they sat. Somewhere a glass hit the floor, accompanied by sounds of an argument.

"Tell me," Dy asked finally, breaking the shocked quiet that had settled between them, "how is Miss Darcy?"

"She is well." Darcy spoke slowly. "Quite well, actually, although she does miss your company." Another sort of foolish grin spread across Brougham's face, this time a sincere one. Darcy sat back and arranged his face and frame in as disinterested an attitude as possible in order to deliver his news. "She has made a new friend since you have been gone."

Dy's grin dissolved instantly. "A 'new friend,' you say?" He traced the rim of his glass with a finger once, twice, then tapped it. "Might one inquire the name of this 'new friend'?"

"One might, and I see what you are thinking. No, that is not what I meant." His friend's shoulders relaxed. The tight cast of his jaw softened. "Her new friend is Elizabeth Bennet."

"Elizabeth Bennet!" Dy was all attention. "*Your* Elizabeth? How on earth did that come to pass?"

Maintaining his pose, Darcy told Dy of their meeting by chance at Pemberley in August. Brougham raised a brow at the word *chance* but did not interrupt his recital. "Unfortunately, a letter from home required that she return posthaste, so Georgiana was deprived of her company sooner than she wished."

"Georgiana," Dy echoed dubiously, "hmm." He looked at Darcy compassionately. "It would seem that Miss Bennet is not so ill disposed toward you as you feared. What a shame that she was called away! Have you seen her since, or heard of her?"

Darcy nodded and shifted uneasily. "A little over a week ago I went down to see my friend Bingley—you remember Bingley, the Melbourne ball?" Dy nodded. "I visited him at Netherfield, the property he is thinking of purchasing in Hertfordshire. We called on the Bennets the day after my arrival. It did not go well."

Dy shot him a questioning look. "How?"

"She scarcely looked at me, barely spoke, although we were in each other's company several hours."

"That seems odd!" Dy replied thoughtfully. "Do you mean to say that she refused to answer when you spoke to her, gave you the cut direct?"

"No, certainly not!" Darcy grew defensive. "She was . . . she was not herself and I . . ." He looked down at his hands. "I did not know what to think, what to say."

"Ah, so neither of you could say much to the other," Dy concluded. "Well, that does make it rather difficult to conduct a conversation or pursue an acquaintance of any sort. Yet you both had less difficulty when she was at Pemberley. Can you think of a reason?"

Darcy eyed his friend. "You *are* persistent, aren't you?" Dy merely shrugged and smiled back at him. "Yes, there had been some family difficulties of which I was more aware than a passing acquaintance should be."

"The letter from home!" Dy smacked the table. "Yes, it is coming together. She was embarrassed for what you knew of her family! Quite a predicament for her after she had criticized *your* behavior so severely." He settled back into his chair and after a few moments had passed asked, "Did Miss Darcy truly like her?"

"Yes, she did, in what time they were together. Georgiana expressed a most sincere wish that they meet again."

"So," Dy probed gently, "do you desire some advice, my friend?" Darcy considered and then breathed out an assent. "Then, my advice is to have faith and wait. Your friend is admirably placed to give you reason to visit the neighborhood. Allow time to pass, and try again when the tides of discomfiture run farther from the surface. If she is worth the having, she is worth the time and effort it will take to win her. 'For aught ever I could read,' " he quoted. "But I suppose you know *that* already!" He rose and looked down at his good friend. "I must be off! Recommend me to Miss Darcy with as much affection as you deem appropriate, and tell her I hope I shall see you both again soon." He bowed then with a flourish and took himself to the other side of the club's dining room and a group of younger gentlemen known for their flash and dash.

As an inquiry concerning a cockfight drifted back to him, Darcy shook his head and smiled ruefully at the life his friend had chosen or, perhaps, had had thrust upon him. *Wait* had been Dy's advice, *wait* and *hope*. He could do that, painful as it might be.

For aught that ever I could read. Darcy struggled to recall the Bard's words as he rose to leave. *Could ever hear by tale or history, the course of true love never did run smooth.* He had just received his hat and walking stick from one of Boodle's ubiquitous servants when another addressed him, thrusting under his nose a note upon a silver servier .

Darcy mounted the steps of Erewile House with barely a look at his Aunt Catherine's traveling coach pulled up at the curb. Singular enough that she had not written of her intention to visit, but it must have been urgent indeed if she had come straight to his door. What her reason could be he could not imagine save if it were in some way connected with Anne's health. The door opened before he reached the top step, revealing a somber-faced Witcher, who reached for his hat and walking stick.

"Where is she?" Darcy asked, stripping off his gloves as he crossed the hall.

"In the drawing room, sir." Witcher bowed as he received the gloves. "I beg your pardon, Mr. Darcy, but she insisted you be summoned."

"She gave you little choice, I am sure," Darcy assured his butler. "You did well. Has Her Ladyship been offered refreshment?"

"Yes, sir, but refused it. Perhaps now that you are here . . . ?"

"Bring up some tea, Witcher. There's a good man." Darcy strode up the stairs and to the drawing room doors. Whatever it was that had occasioned this appearance of his aunt, he would soon know more than he wished, of that he had no doubt. Let it not be bad news of his cousin!

"Darcy! At last, you are here!" Lady Catherine stood in command of the room, her posture as straight and stiff as the silver-tipped walking stick she held before her. "Come!" She held out her hand to him urgently. He quickly took it and, giving her the support of his arm, led her to a seat.

"My dear aunt!" he exclaimed at her worn countenance as she sank onto the settee. "What can be the matter!"

"Never, *never* in my life have I been subject to the sort of ill usage and ingratitude I have encountered today. I cannot think to what the world is coming!" Her Ladyship pronounced these words forcefully. "I was never put to such pains and trouble only to be so insulted!"

"Aunt!" Darcy looked down at her with a mixture of relief and consternation. If it was not news of Anne, what could have set her off so and then sent her here?

She fixed her gaze upon him. "It was on your behalf, Nephew, that I exhausted myself. Yes," she replied to his expression of surprise. "And on behalf of the entire family! Someone must see to these things before it is too late, and as I have always been attentive to the demands of propriety and decorum, the disagreeable task fell to me. If all of the family stands together, we may yet contrive to stop this vicious and scandalous falsehood from spreading further."

A knock sounded at the door, interrupting for the moment his aunt's astonishing charge. At Darcy's call to enter, Witcher and a footman walked into the room with the tea. As it was being laid out, Darcy rose from his seat to escape his aunt's sharp eye and afford himself an opportunity to think. A scandalous falsehood? His thoughts had immediately gone to Georgiana at the words, but then his aunt had laid it at his door. Could it be something to do with the business at Norwycke or Lady Monmouth? It seemed improbable, but what else was there?

Their tasks completed, the servants withdrew, and Darcy turned back to his aunt. "I do not take your meaning, Ma'am. What falsehood is this?"

"You have not heard it?" A small smile escaped Lady Catherine's pursed lips and then was briskly packed away. "But then, it is too incredible for anyone of sense to repeat." She leveled a censorious countenance upon him. "Nevertheless, Nephew, it must be vigorously denied, especially on your part, and its originator proved a fraud."

Never one to leap at his aunt's willful commands, Darcy felt his patience with her odd reluctance to come to the point vanish. "Perhaps, Ma'am, I could more easily put this and your mind to rest if I knew what it is that has excited your apprehension."

Lady Catherine's eyes widened disapprovingly at his tone, but he could see she was not checked. Rather, she appeared on the verge of apoplexy. "That young person . . . toward whom I extended my interest last spring . . . the friend of my rector's new wife—"

"Miss Elizabeth Bennet?" Darcy was incredulous. Good Lord, had his assistance on behalf of Lydia Bennet been made public?

"The same! She has shown herself to be in every way undeserving of the notice she received from me. That woman has industriously set about the rumor that *she* is shortly to become Mrs. Fitzwilliam Darcy!" At the last, Lady Catherine pounded the tip of her walking stick on the floor and sat back, her eyes trained upon his face.

The shock of her words could in nowise excuse the need to maintain the utmost self-control, Darcy knew, as his heart jumped faster, blood and ice running crazily through his veins. "I see," he managed to reply in an even tone and quickly turned away to the settee across the low table from the one his aunt occupied. He sat down.

"Do you, indeed, Darcy? The tale is already spread in Hertfordshire and came to me in Kent not three days ago. I acted upon it immediately, of course, and have done what could be done." What had his aunt done? Elizabeth . . . oh, he was wild to know! Yet if he hoped to wrest all he needed from his aunt's iron grasp on these events, he must disguise his own emotions and play upon her prejudices with care.

"What I see," he enlightened her, "is that you are quite overset by a report concerning Miss Elizabeth Bennet. From whence has it come? Is the source reliable?"

His aunt relaxed her grip on her walking stick and then set it aside. "Upon two counts, it is from the best authority. My rector,

Mr. Collins, brought it to my attention, and besides being my clergyman, he is related to the woman. Also, she is his wife's intimate friend. There can be no mistake, Nephew."

"Perhaps." Darcy drew out the word as he leaned forward to avail himself of the shield of a cup of tea. From Collins, was it? In truth, it must have been from his wife. A letter from Elizabeth? Or from Lucas Lodge? "In what form did the report arrive, Ma'am?"

"In what form? I had it from Collins's own lips, Darcy!" She bridled a little at his raised brow but then relented. "A letter, evidently, from his wife's family imparting the news of the engagement of the eldest Bennet daughter to your friend." Her voice rose. "Soon to be followed, it was supposed, by your own nuptials with the next daughter. This vicious rumormongering is not to be borne!" The walking stick she'd picked up in her passion came down again with a resounding thud.

Darcy shook his head. "My dear aunt, my name has been coupled with those of any number of young ladies over the years. Rumors all. Complete fabrications. Why should you be distressed by this latest?"

"Because," she retorted, "you . . . or rather, she" her mouth snapped shut, and for a moment she could only glare at him. He returned the favor with as much innocence as he could contrive, but in fact her answer to his question was essential. There had to be something more than an idle report to have put Her Ladyship in such a state.

"Please, continue, Ma'am."

"Oh!" she burst forth. "If you would just have allowed your engagement to your cousin to be published, this could not have happened! The girl could not have presumed to begin with, or lacking that, I would have her promise—"

"Her promise!" Darcy shot to his feet. "What have you done? Have you communicated with Miss Elizabeth Bennet?"

"Do not imagine, Darcy, that a letter is sufficient to put an end to matters such as this. I confronted that person to her face with her—"

Everything in Darcy went cold. "When?" he demanded, "when did you speak with her? What did you say?"

"This very morning, sir, and was met with an obscene impertinence and ingratitude the like of which I pray I never encounter again!"

Darcy walked slowly away to the window, the better to overcome the horror her words had engendered. Horror soon gave way to a caldron of indignation for himself, but more so for Elizabeth. By the time he faced his aunt again, his rioting emotions had coalesced into a rigid anger that could not be hidden. "Am I to understand," he began in a precise, demanding tone, "that you traveled to Hertfordshire to tax Miss Elizabeth Bennet with this rumor and then required some sort of promise of her? Good God, Madam! To what purpose and by what right do you interfere in a matter that is properly mine to resolve?"

A martial light glinted in Lady Catherine's eye. She straightened and, grasping her walking stick, stamped it again on the floor. "By right of your closest relative and in your best interest!" She rose and addressed him scathingly. "Yes, *your* interest! Oh, I saw your weakness when she was about Rosings last spring, but I could not credit that you would so lose yourself to her arts and allurements—and under my own roof!—as to encourage any pretensions! Should I have put this into your hands, what might have come of it? If she will not be moved by claims of duty, honor, and gratitude, how else shall she be worked on save by the truth of what would await her presumption? And that I am entirely within my right to tell her! She shall not stand in the way of your duty to your family or my daughter's rightful happiness!"

Darcy rounded the table, returning her hawkish eye with all the cold anger her words and actions had birthed. "You have far overreached yourself, madam. There can be no excuse sufficient to pardon your interference in so personal an affair as you describe or to harangue one so wholly unrelated to you yet subject to your whims by your advantage of rank."

"If I had brought it to you, you would only have denied it! Then where should we be? She, at least, did not deny—"

"Deny what?" Darcy's hands itched to shake the woman before him, aunt or no. "How did you leave it with her?"

"She would promise me nothing! Though I plied her with every disadvantage attendant upon such a marriage, she would have none of it! She refused to promise not to enter into an engagement if such were offered. Obstinate, headstrong girl! And so I told her! She is determined to ruin you! She is set upon making you the joke of the world."

Something like hope broke through the ice that had encased Darcy's heart. She would not promise! She had suffered the most outrageous invasion of her privacy and inquisition of her character, yet she would not promise! Elizabeth . . . A warm feeling arose in his chest which he longed to nurture. If it were ever to become more, he must clear its path, a task that he must begin immediately.

"Your Ladyship." Darcy stepped back and bowed. "I must be clear. Your actions in regard to Miss Elizabeth Bennet I can never approve or condone. Perhaps, however, I am somewhat at fault."

"Humph!" his aunt snorted, a glimmer of triumph in her aspect. "That I should have to remind George Darcy's son what he owes to himself and his family!"

"No, Madam, my fault lies in another direction entirely. A nuptial between Anne and me is something neither of us desires and never has." Her Ladyship gasped, but Darcy cut her off. "I should have made that quite clear years ago, but instead, I took the easier path of silence at your hints and maneuverings in the hope that you yourself might see how impossible it would be. I must humbly beg your pardon for what I see now was not only cowardly but cruel."

"Darcy, you cannot . . . Anne expects—"

"My cousin does not expect marriage from me. We have spoken of this and are agreed. My cruelty lies in allowing you to labor under a hopeless delusion rather than be forthright concerning the truth of our situation. For that, I beg pardon, Ma'am." He bowed again.

His aunt for once was speechless. Her face contorted with the effort to assimilate what she had heard. She turned away, turned back as if to speak, and turned away again. Finally, with agonizing effort, her disappointment was cast aside and she rallied her other flank. "Be that as it may, Nephew, you will never impose that . . . that . . . *woman* upon your family! You cannot possibly mean to do so against all their wishes and expectations!"

"Madam!" Darcy warned.

"Such an alliance lies in opposition to all interest! She will not be received, have no doubt of that! Who is her family? They can claim no connections or standing save being the subject of the vilest scandal! The youngest daughter—surely you have heard of that!—run off with an officer to London! A patched-up, tawdry affair!"

"Madam, no more!" Darcy thundered, and for a moment his aunt quailed.

Hastily, she cast about for her shawls and hat. Clutching them to her, she turned upon him in such wrath as he had never seen. "I will *not* be silent! I am your nearest relation and must stand in the place of your parents. It is for their sakes and yours that I tell you marriage to that woman would be a disgrace!" Darcy stared at her in stony silence.

"If you persist in this folly," she railed at him, "Rosings will be closed to you, your name will never be mentioned in my hearing, and I will forswear you as any relation of mine!"

"So be it, Madam; as you wish." Darcy bowed to her once more and then strode to the door. "Lady Catherine's carriage," he called down the hall and, turning, held the door open for her. "Your Ladyship."

"Do not think that I shall be the only one to object to such a misalliance!" Lady Catherine continued as she swept past him and down the stairs. "I shall write your uncle, Lord Matlock, immediately! He will make you see sense. He will cause you to know . . ."

Only when the door was closed behind her could Darcy release the breath that he'd held in anger against his aunt's innumerable insults. Stepping to the window, he observed her storm out into the street below. Her carriage swaying under her fury, her driver pulled swiftly away from the curb and set the horses to a hurried trot. Well might she hurry, he thought, as he took up the decanter and poured himself a drink. Good God! He had never been so close to . . . ! He picked up the glass and tossed down a portion. Then setting it down, he strode to the door, then back again. That impossible woman! He took another drink. What had she done! Standing in the middle of the room, his breath coming in chuffs, he raked his hand through his hair. Elizabeth so accosted! He shook his head. What could his aunt have heard that would send her posthaste to Hertfordshire? A mere rumor? No, he decided. There must have been more. He held his breath, attempting to calm himself enough to think rationally. What *had* his aunt done? What had been the actual result of her outrageous presumption?

Sitting down on the settee, he returned to the material truths of the entire extraordinary interview. Elizabeth would not promise *not* to accept him. That was what had so infuriated his aunt. Did he dare believe the converse? Would she accept him? Her manner during his last visit would never have tempted him to believe that she would. Why had she not said as much and been spared such insults? Was it her heart or her anger that had turned back Lady Catherine's every demand? How was he ever to know unless he returned to Hertfordshire?

"Witcher!" he bellowed down the stairs. "Witcher!"

"Sir?" The old butler appeared, a look of apprehension on his face at such goings-on in the usually sedate confines of Erewile House.

"Order my traveling coach and send Fletcher up to pack. I wish to be gone in the morning!"

"Yes, sir!" the butler replied and scuttled off belowstairs as quickly as his old legs could carry him to deliver the master's extraordinary demands to an already scandalized household.

"Have faith and wait," Dy had counseled. Now, as he looked out the coach's window at the passing scenery of a Hertfordshire afternoon, he could easily imagine the scene that had taken place. How imperious and insufferable his Aunt Catherine could be under the most modest of irritations, he knew very well; but in this, her passion had been thoroughly roused. It must have been terrible for Elizabeth to have been its object, yet she had withstood it and refused to bow to demands easily met had she decided against him. For the hundredth time since yesterday, he wondered what was her mind and whether by returning to Hertfordshire he was committing folly enough to match all he had ever committed in his life.

In less time by the watch than his anxious thoughts could credit, his coach was rolling up Netherfield's drive, and the house came into view. He had sent no letter announcing his return, and Bingley's expectations of it were vague, as Darcy had wanted them to be in case he decided against it. His friend might not be home. But as the coach drew up to the house, the door opened, and Bingley stood at the entrance with a look of pure delight upon his open countenance.

"Darcy! I say, Darcy!" he exclaimed as he came down the steps to meet him. "This is above everything!" He grabbed his friend's hand as soon as Darcy descended from the coach.

"Charles," he began, "I apologize for giving you no warning—"

"Nonsense," Bingley replied. "I am that glad that you are here. I am about to run mad with no one with whom to share my good fortune. Here, you must come in. I have so much to tell you!" Refreshment was ordered as Bingley pulled him into the library and begged him to be seated.

"But, Charles, my dirt!" Darcy indicated the traveling dust that had settled on his arms and shoulders.

"Dirt be hanged, Darcy!" Bingley laughed. A servant knocked and entered with the tray, but almost before the door shut behind him Bingley burst forth. "I am engaged! . . . Engaged to the loveliest angel in the world! My beautiful Jane has consented, and her father agreed. We are to be married, Darcy, married!" He laughed again. "Can you believe it, for I cannot! It is too wonderful!"

"Not at all, Charles!" Darcy took him by the shoulders. "I can think of no other man who deserves such happiness, truly I cannot. Did you think she might refuse you? What nonsense! I wish you joy, my friend, you and your future wife." At his words, tears stung at Bingley's eyes. Darcy clapped his shoulders roughly and turned away.

"Thank you, Darcy." Bingley cleared his throat. "Thank you. Now, how may I serve you?"

"I can hardly say, except that I hope you will allow me to stay. It may be only a day, it may be more; I do not yet know."

Bingley regarded him curiously. "My home is at your disposal, you must know that. Can you tell me no more?"

"Unfortunately, no," Darcy replied. "It is business of a personal nature. Perhaps it is all folly, I do not know. But," he continued with a smile, "it is nothing that will diminish your own joy however it falls out. All I ask is that you allow me to come with you when next you visit the home of your fiancée."

"Certainly," Bingley answered him. "I am to visit tomorrow. Since Jane and I are engaged, there is no time I am not welcome. We can go as early or as late as you please." Bingley continued to look at him curiously.

"What do you say to a game of billiards before dinner?" Darcy proposed a distraction that had always worked with his cousin.

"Certainly!" Bingley pursed his lips. "Shall we wager on the outcome?"

Early the following day, Darcy and Bingley set out for Longbourn with a fresh autumn breeze at their backs. The leaves were turning, the multihued trees framing the harvested fields and golden pastures. Although Bingley had caught Darcy up on all the events since his departure two weeks before, there still seemed to be minutiae yet to be imparted; and so the ride was filled with the overflow of Bingley's enthusiasm for his soon-to-be in-laws. Far from being bored, Darcy listened carefully for any clue that might lend him insight into the tenor of the Bennet household in general and Elizabeth in particular. From Bingley's descriptions, it seemed that all there were in a flurry of goodwill and excitement over the coming nuptials. Of Elizabeth, he heard only how good she was to her sister and how often she had turned her mother aside to some task in order to allow Bingley some precious moments alone with his bride to be.

Their arrival was greeted with all the happiness that Bingley had described, although several curious glances were thrown Darcy's way. Not a little fearful of what this day would bring, he could hardly look at Elizabeth. When they had dismounted and made their bows, Bingley immediately advocated that, on this beautiful day, they should all walk out and enjoy it. His proposal was readily agreed to, and while Jane, Elizabeth, and Kitty sought their bonnets and wraps, Mrs. Bennet took her prospective son-in-law by the arm and advised him with authority that the paths to and from Longbourn were the prettiest to be had in the area, although, she confided, she herself was not in the habit of walking.

While Bingley was thus engaged, Darcy stepped away and looked out over the garden. Most of it had been raked and over-turned, but some hardy blooms still waved their colorful heads in the light breeze. He breathed in the musty scent, holding it for a moment in an attempt to soothe the racing of his heart. Again, time seemed to be plunging headlong into the future, his future, consuming and discarding the precious present in the most wanton manner. At one and the same moment, he longed for Elizabeth to appear and devoutly wished that she would delay, at least until he could achieve some semblance of control over his heart.

A noise from the doorway told him that the young ladies were ready, and he turned back to see Bingley holding out his hand to Jane. Elizabeth stepped lightly from the house, the sunlight dappling dark and light over her rusty brown spencer and green muslin dress. There was nothing elegant about her appearance. She was dressed for a walk. Yet her every expression and movement inspired his admiration.

Bingley secured his Jane's hand, and as the pair set off, Elizabeth turned away from them with a smile and then—oh, it took his breath away to see it—lifted her eyes to him. It required no exercise of will or command of his limbs to take him to her side. He was suddenly there, and they were turning down the path after Bingley and Jane, the younger sister somewhere behind them. After a brief discussion of their route, in which Darcy took no part or interest, it was decided that they would walk toward Lucas Lodge, where Kitty would leave them in favor of a visit with Miss Maria Lucas. The arrangement could not have fallen out more favorably. It remained only to put some distance between themselves and the newly engaged pair, and he would have no excuse, nothing save his own fears, to hinder him from knowing his fate.

The group moved forward down the lane between fields and through a small wood. Sooner than he had expected, Bingley and Jane were well behind them, walking slower and slower as the privacy of their surroundings increased. "Mr. Bingley has chosen a fine day for a walk," Elizabeth ventured, "although I do not think he notices where he is going."

"Yes, it is a fine day." Darcy looked behind them. "And I believe you are correct about Bingley. Your sister also, perhaps?"

"Very likely." They walked on, leaves crunching and sliding beneath their feet, a renewed silence between them. Several excruciating minutes passed before he asked whether this was her favorite walk.

"Only when Charlotte is home, for there—do you see it?" She pointed ahead to a divergence among the trees. "That is the way to Lucas Lodge. I suppose I could walk it blindfolded." He nodded that, yes, he saw where the way divided, and as he did so, Kitty brushed past them.

"May I go, then, Elizabeth?" she asked, studiously avoiding Darcy's eyes. He could see that she wanted nothing better than to be away from such dull company as he provided.

"Yes, you may go, but return before dusk, and do not ask Sir William to drive you home," she admonished her younger sister. With a roll of her eyes, Kitty left them, hurrying down the path to her friend. Darcy looked back the way they had come, but Bingley and Jane were not to be seen. They were now quite alone. He waited to see which direction Elizabeth would go. With a quick glance up at him, she stepped forward, continuing down the path. He struck out after her. It must be now, he told himself.

He drew abreast of her and began to reach for her arm to arrest her stride when she slowed of her own accord and looked up at him with a troubled countenance. "Mr. Darcy, I am a very selfish creature," she began, "and for the sake of giving relief to my own feelings care not how much I may be wounding yours." Surprised by such a speech, Darcy stopped short and regarded her with concern. "I can no longer help thanking you for your unexampled kindness to my poor sister." Elizabeth's words rushed on although she could hardly meet his eye. "Ever since I have known it I have been most anxious to acknowledge to you how gratefully I feel it. Were it known to the rest of my family I should not have merely my own gratitude to express."

She knew! Darcy's heart twisted into an icy knot around this revelation, which changed everything, perhaps damaging every possibility between them. The reasons for her actions on his last visit were now only too explicable. "I am sorry," he managed to reply, "exceedingly sorry that you have ever been informed of what may, in a mistaken light, have given you uneasiness." He looked past her and exhaled a pained chuff of air before saying, "I did not think Mrs. Gardiner was so little to be trusted."

"You must not blame my aunt." Elizabeth's voice was pleading. "Lydia's thoughtlessness first betrayed to me that you had been concerned in the matter; and, of course," she confessed, "I could not rest till I knew the particulars." She took a deep breath. "Let me thank you again and again, in the name of all my family, for that generous compassion which induced you to take so much trouble, and bear so many mortifications, for the sake of discovering them."

Darcy listened, his heart released from his initial fears as he heard Elizabeth describe his actions in the most benevolent of terms. She did not blame him for interfering. She was grateful, that was clear. But gratitude alone could be devastating to his hopes. He wanted more than her gratitude or an alliance founded on such an inequality. He wanted her heart, fully and freely given, or not at all.

"If you *will* thank me, let it be for yourself alone," he responded to her firmly. "That the wish of giving happiness to you might add force to the other inducements which led me on I shall not attempt to deny. But your *family* owe me nothing. Much as I respect them, I believe I thought only of *you*." He waited, anxious as well as fearful that she understood his meaning, but Elizabeth said nothing.

Her face was partially hidden by her bonnet but the pink tinge upon what he could see was unmistakable. Then, something inside him moved with such powerful emotion that he had to know all . . . here . . . now.

"You are too generous to trifle with me," he began, putting his future in her hands. "If your feelings are still what they were last

April, tell me so at once. *My* affections and wishes are unchanged; but one word from you will silence me on this subject forever."

"Mr. Darcy." His name came haltingly to her lips as she brought her face up. "Please . . . my feelings . . ." She seemed to be struggling to catch her breath, but the glow of her eyes told him that she was not in danger. "My feelings have undergone so material a change since that unfortunate day last spring that I can only receive with sincere gratitude and the most profound pleasure your assurances that yours continue the same."

"Elizabeth." He whispered her name lest the spell he knew himself to be under shatter and fall to the earth around him. "Elizabeth," he repeated, gently enfolding her hands in his as he reveled in her sweet smile and shining eyes. Bringing her hands to his lips, he kissed one gently, then the other, then held them close against his heart as he told her, at last, all that resided there in terms of his deepest love, gratitude, and hope for the future.

He did not know how it happened, his heart was too full, but they were moving, walking he knew not where. There was so much to feel, so much to say, so much happiness that begged to be examined. Darcy told of his aunt's visit, of his painful confrontation with her, and yet how it had taught him to hope. He spoke of his struggle to mend his ways and how he had studied to show her at Pemberley that her complaint of his character had been heeded. Elizabeth expressed her surprise at the manner in which he had taken to heart all her harsh words and blushed to recall them. His letter he forswore, but she cherished it, advising him to think of the past only as its remembrance gave him pleasure.

"I cannot give you credit for any philosophy of the kind," he replied, kissing once again the hand he held. "*Your* retrospections must be so totally void of reproach, that the contentment arising from them is not of philosophy, but, what is much better, of ignorance." He tucked her hand against his side. "But with *me,* it is not so. Painful recollections will intrude, which cannot, which ought not to be repelled." He stopped their progress and, tracing her cheek, sighed. "I have been a selfish being all my life, in practice, though not in principle. As a child, I was taught what was *right;* but I was not taught to correct my temper. I was given good principles, but left to follow them in pride and conceit, allowed, encouraged, almost taught to be selfish and overbearing—to care for none beyond my own family circle, to think meanly of all the rest of the world, to *wish* at least to think meanly of their sense and worth compared with my own."

He dropped his hand and gathered hers to him again as he spoke his soul into her beautiful eyes. "Such I was, from eight to eight-and-twenty; and such I might still have been but for you, dearest, loveliest Elizabeth! What do I not owe you! You taught me a lesson, hard indeed at first, but most advantageous. By you, I was properly humbled. I came to you without a doubt of my reception. You showed me how insufficient were all my pretensions to please a woman worthy of being pleased."

They walked several miles, Elizabeth telling him of her apprehensions on his discovery of her at Pemberley, Darcy assuring her that his only thought had been of earning her forgiveness. He told of Georgiana's pleasure in her acquaintance and her disappointment at its sudden end and that his gravity at the inn had been caused by the measures he was already planning in rescue of her sister. She thanked him again, but of that painful affair neither desired to speak more.

"What could have become of Mr. Bingley and Jane!" Elizabeth glanced at her watch and then down the path behind them. "We should be returning home, and they are nowhere to be seen!" They turned back, Darcy holding her hand and placing it within the crook of his arm. "I must ask," Elizabeth addressed him, "whether you were surprised to learn of their engagement."

"Not at all. When I went away, I felt that it would soon happen."

"That is to say, you had given your permission. I guessed as much."

"My permission!" Darcy exclaimed. "No, no, that would be heights of presumption I would never dare scale, my dear girl! I hope I have learned better!" She smiled. He told her of his confession to Bingley the night before he left for London, how he had been mistaken in so much of what had occurred the previous autumn. "I could easily perceive his attachment to her, I told him, and was convinced of her affection. Then, I was obliged to confess that I had known your sister to be in Town last winter and conspired to keep it from him. He was rightly angry. But his anger, I am persuaded, lasted no longer than he remained in any doubt of your sister's sentiments. He has heartily forgiven me now."

They walked on, and if he had ever been speechless in her presence, it was ended now; for he knew her to be sympathetic to all his visions and plans for their shared future. In this vein, he continued till they reached her home, parting only just before entering the dining room at Longbourn.

CHAPTER 12

Love's Fine Wit

They were abominably late. Everyone, including Bingley and Miss Bennet, was already at table when they came in the door. "My dear Lizzy, where can you have been walking to?" came a chorus of inquiries led by Elizabeth's˙ elder sister as they entered. Darcy resolved to bear the blame, but Elizabeth's answer—that they had wandered about till she was quite beyond her own knowledge of where they had been—was enough to satisfy their curiosity.

Darcy looked down the table. Elizabeth had taken a seat removed from him lest they arouse any premature speculation, but she was the only one whose conversation he desired, whose smile he coveted. He looked on with some envy at Bingley and Jane. The acknowledged lovers were under no constraints of convention and could talk together in a semiprivacy denied to the rest of the company. With growing resignation, Darcy looked to Elizabeth's parents and ruefully acknowledged that it was toward them he should direct his attention. He had experienced rather more of Mrs. Bennet than he could wish over his recent visits to Longbourn, but of Mr. Bennet, he knew little. Where should he begin with this man from whom he would soon be requesting Elizabeth's hand?

The meal ended. They rose and repaired to the sitting room, where the smallness of the company urged upon Darcy the necessity of engaging Elizabeth's father. Accepting a cup of coffee from Mrs. Bennet's hands, he stepped over to his host. "Mr. Bennet," he addressed him, lifting his cup slightly in salute.

"Mr. Darcy," he replied, and then with a quirk of his chin, he motioned to Bingley and Jane, who were now snugly alone in a corner of the room. "A likely pair, are they not, Mr. Darcy? Although all of these smiles and whispers are rather tiresome for the rest of the world, Mrs. Bennet assures me that it is to be expected."

Darcy set down his cup and turned to him. "I believe Bingley will make her a very good husband," he offered thoughtfully. "I have known him well for several years now. He is one of the finest men I know."

"Oh, I have no doubt of it!" Mr. Bennet replied. "They are very well suited, he and Jane. Their children will never hear an angry word from either and may even allow their parents a say, on occasion. Still, I am happy for her." He sipped at his cup. "And what of you, sir? Shall you remain long in Hertfordshire, or does London demand your presence?"

"My plans are unfixed at present, but I should not wonder that I will remain awhile longer."

"Indeed!" Mr. Bennet seemed surprised. "Indeed," he repeated. "Well, you are welcome to visit Longbourn at any time, Mr. Darcy. As you can see, I have any number of daughters who can provide an educated man with stimulating conversation." He nodded at Mary, deep in a book, and Kitty, fixing ribbons on a large-brimmed bonnet. Then setting down his cup with an amused air, Mr. Bennet excused himself and announced to his wife, "I will be in my study should anybody need me, my dear."

Darcy looked to Elizabeth, surprised that his host would abandon his guests so abruptly and wondering if this was a signal that he and Bingley should leave. But no one else seemed to take notice of their host's odd behavior or move to conclude the evening, save to bid Mr. Bennet good night. Still, they did not stay long, and when he and Bingley rose to leave, Elizabeth followed him to the door and then outside, as had Jane with Bingley. With her arms wrapped about her against the chill, she watched him mount his horse. Looking down at her, her face turned up to him in the starlight, he was reminded of an evening a year ago outside the assembly hall in Meryton. So much had happened since that night that today had been resolved toward making him glad of the future. Yet in that same moment, he was restless as well. Elizabeth was his and not his, the companion of his heart but not yet at his side.

He leaned down to her. "Tomorrow," he whispered. She nodded. "Tomorrow," she mouthed and stepped away to her sister's side, watching after them as their horses moved into the darkness.

Bingley was humming when, after urging his horse on, Darcy caught up to him. Tuneless, as usual, and progressing in fits and starts, the song drifted into the night. Darcy could only smile at his friend's distraction and consider how light his own heart was. "And what creature are you summoning at this hour, Charles?" he teased him. "I believe all decent animals are tucked away in their barns."

"Darcy, I am the most fortunate of men!" Bingley ignored his jab. "What a marvelous day it has been!"

"Quite," Darcy murmured in agreement.

Bingley turned to him. "I say, it may not have been so marvelous for you to spend an entire evening with the Bennets. You have been a good friend to bear with it, Darcy, and I thank you."

"Not at all, Charles." Darcy dismissed it. "It is only natural that you should wish to be in the company of your fiancée as much as possible. I am, after all, here at my own invitation and can take myself away at any time."

"You are very kind," Bingley replied. He paused a little before adding in quite another tone, "And so *very* obliging as to lose Jane and me in the wood. How *did* that come about? We never saw you after the first half hour."

"You did not wish to be so long alone then?"

"That is not what I meant." Bingley laughed. "Well, I was not so concerned, not as concerned as Jane, certainly; for she had not seen how well you and her sister got along together at Pemberley. It was my thought that you lost us apurpose, for our sakes, and did not mind keeping Miss Elizabeth company while you did so."

"Did you say as much to Miss Bennet?"

"Something to that effect. Should I not have?"

Darcy did not answer him immediately. Was there any purpose to keeping his joy to himself? Soon it would be public knowledge, and Bingley was his close friend. In any event, he was desirous to hear himself say the words that would give substance to the events of the afternoon. And he was curious to behold Charles's reaction. He brought his horse up close to Bingley's until they were knee to knee. "You are only partially correct, my friend. I confess I had little thought for you and Miss Bennet this afternoon. My intent, upon your happy suggestion of a walk, was to devise a way to speak with Miss Elizabeth privately."

"Speak privately!" Bingley pulled back on his reins and stared at Darcy in the moonlight. "What about, I wonder?"

"A private matter." Darcy's smile widened.

"Of course." Bingley was not put off. "A private matter concerning what, might I ask?"

"Well might you ask——"

"Darcy!" Bingley's voice grew menacing.

Darcy relented with a laugh. "Concerning the fact—and this may surprise you or not; for I can trust my own perception of myself no longer—that I have admired . . . nay, more than admired Miss Elizabeth almost since our first meeting."

"Good Lord!" Bingley breathed out, astonished. "I suspected affection this summer at Pemberley, but since last autumn? You did nothing but spar with her!"

"Yes, that is true. We did not get on well last autumn. I blame my own behavior for her poor opinion of me at the start. But then there were also pernicious rumors concerning me set about by Wickham that fixed this opinion."

"That rogue! And to think I must be his—" Bingley's jaw snapped shut on that subject in favor of a more immediate one. "Go on, Darcy! You have loved her all this time! Well . . ." He drew in a breath. "This is *truly* marvelous! Rather like a play . . . that Shakespeare one. Oh, what was it . . . about that fellow . . . Benedick?"

Darcy laughed. "Yes, very like!"

"But what happened between then and Pemberley?"

"We met again last spring, when she visited friends in Kent near the estate of my aunt, Lady Catherine de Bourgh. There was more misunderstanding and more abominable behavior on my part, I am sorry to say, but the nature of the problems that lay between us was finally revealed. When next we met at Pemberley, we found each other's company much more agreeable."

"Pray, continue!" Bingley urged as they set their horses into motion but slowly.

"We made a beginning, but that was all. When she was unexpectedly called home, it seemed unlikely that an occasion might arise when we might speak further."

"A devil of a fix, that!" Bingley shook his head. "But then I spoke to you about Netherfield. No wonder you were so keen upon my coming back!"

"I remain forever indebted to you, my friend," Darcy replied with a broad grin, "for your lamentable inability to come to a decision." Bingley acknowledged his flaw with a hoot of mirth. "It provided exactly the circumstance to allow me to bring two vital matters to a conclusion," Darcy continued. "First, to correct my inexcusable interference in your affairs, and second, to determine Miss Elizabeth's inclination and whether a proposal might have any chance of acceptance."

"A proposal! This is wonderful, Darcy! Why, of course she will accept you . . . what woman in England would not?"

"Oh, such a one exists, I assure you. This was not my first proposal." Darcy looked at his friend's surprised countenance. "The 'misunderstanding' I spoke of last spring . . ."

Bingley sucked in his breath. "Incredible! Elizabeth?"

"Is she not?" A note of pleasure sounded in his voice. They rode in silence as the lights of Netherfield Hall appeared through the trees. Darcy continued, more thoughtful now. "She sent me packing without ceremony, Charles. And I am forever indebted to her for that. I was bitter. I was angry for a time. But she humbled me and let me to know that all my pretensions mattered not a whit to a woman of worth and substance."

"But this second proposal? She *did* say yes?" There was a worried, uncertain tone in Bingley's question.

Darcy smiled. "She said yes."

Rising in his stirrups, Bingley gave a shout, which was greeted with answering howls from the Netherfield kennels. His horse danced at the unusual activity, and Darcy's shied. "Darcy, this is above everything!" he continued after regaining his seat. "Do you realize? We are to be brothers! Oh, Jane and I talked of this, wished for it, but thought it to be impossible. How surprised she will be!"

"Charles, I beg you will not speak of this until a formal announcement is made." Darcy interrupted his exuberance. "I have yet to speak to Mr. Bennet, and there is some awkwardness . . ."

"Say no more." Bingley laughed ruefully. "I understand and shall not speak, but oh, it shall be exceedingly hard!" After a few minutes of silence, he turned back to Darcy. "Shall we get lost again tomorrow?"

"The paths of Hertfordshire *are* largely unknown to us," Darcy offered.

"Indeed!" Bingley agreed. "Damned tricky place!"

After dinner the following evening, Darcy approached Long-bourn's library door. A pool of candlelight seeped weakly from under it, but there was nothing to be heard. A quiet knock brought him a muffled "Yes?" from within. Softly, he turned the knob and opened the door. "Your pardon, sir. May I have a word with you?"

"Mr. Darcy!" Mr. Bennet's eyebrows were raised in frank surprise to see him in the doorway. Recovering himself, he rose from a desk of scattered papers and books, bade him enter, and motioned him to a chair beside the desk. "Would you like something to drink? No?" He set down the decanter he had raised. "Well then." He resumed his seat. "Well then, how can I be of service to you? I believe my wife has already offered you all of the birds on my lands. I will not gainsay her if that is what concerns you."

"No, sir. That is most generous of you, but I have come about quite another matter." He paused. There was nothing for it but to launch into the matter directly.

"It is my honor to inform you, sir, that I have asked for your daughter Elizabeth's hand in marriage. She has consented, upon your approval, to make me the happiest of men."

"Elizabeth?" Mr. Bennet sat up straight, his face gone pale, and with an unsteady hand he put down his glass of wine. "You must be—" His mouth shut down on what he had been about to say. After a moment, he continued in another vein. "Elizabeth . . . Elizabeth is of a lively mind and disposition. I hope you will not take offense, but are you sure you are not mistaken? She may have said something in jest."

"No, sir, I am not mistaken," Darcy replied, surprised by such a response. "I am well acquainted with her temperament, and I assure you, she has consented."

From the look of him, Mr. Bennet was in no way reassured. "Mr. Darcy, you astonish me!" He fell back, shaking his head. "How has this come about? I have seen no evidence of affection between the two of you. I have heard nothing."

"No doubt you have not expected this." Darcy drew himself up. "I can easily imagine your dismay that my suit has come upon you without warning. It appears sudden, I know, but it is not without foundation. My admiration for Elizabeth has grown over the months I have known her. In truth, sir, it began when I first met her last year."

Mr. Bennet's brow furrowed. "That is as may be; you have said it is so. But my concern is for my daughter. You seek my blessing." He looked across his desk at Darcy. "But are you certain that there exists a true and abiding affection between you?"

"My attentions to your daughter were not always reciprocated—this I admit, and acknowledge my many faults." Darcy rose from his seat. "But I *have* won Elizabeth's heart in spite of everything! I tell you, sir, I love her; and I vow to you that her happiness and welfare is and will always be my first concern." He stopped, then continued in a lowered voice that was no less direct. "I do ask you, Mr. Bennet, for your blessing."

A sigh escaped his listener, and Mr. Bennet appeared to shrink into his chair. Moments passed. Then the man's chin rose slightly as he broke the silence. "It is no secret that my Lizzy is the child of my heart, Mr. Darcy. I have had a special fondness for her since she was a babe. I believe I always shall. Her happiness concerns me deeply, for I know what she, more than her sisters, will suffer in a marriage that is indifferent to her character and unequal to her mind. You seem to be a sincere and honorable man. If you have won Elizabeth's heart, I will not withhold my consent."

"Thank you—"

Mr. Bennet held up his hand, restraining his words of gratitude. "You stand to gain an uncommon treasure, Mr. Darcy," he continued, "but I caution you, sir, it will be yours only if you are wiser than most men."

"Indeed, sir." Darcy bowed to the sagacity of his warning. "I love Elizabeth above all things. I will not disappoint you."

"Then you will be the most blessed of men, Mr. Darcy." He raised tired eyes to Darcy's. "You have my consent."

"Thank you, sir." Darcy bowed again. But instead of offering a shake of his hand or a request for the figures he meant to settle upon Elizabeth, his future father-in-law went to his library door and opened it to the hall.

"Please," Mr. Bennet directed him, "send Elizabeth to me."

"Woolgathering, Mr. Darcy?" He turned at the beloved voice. For the third time in as many days since their engagement he had been sent out of doors to await her retrieval of her bonnet for what had become daily walks and had fallen into a sort of reverie in which how undeserving he was of his very good fortune was the primary subject. Now, there she was, her face wreathed in smiles and her eyes alight with mischief under her impertinent bonnet.

"Come!" he commanded with a grin and pointed his chin toward a path that led quickly away from the house. Once out of sight, he reached out his hand and discovered that Elizabeth was of the same mind. As he clasped her hand to him, they started out. Their strides at first were rapid and punctuated with laughter in their eagerness to be away from the notice of others, but when their aim was accomplished, they slowed; and the truth of their new understanding cast a warmly intimate sobriety over their spirits. The contentment Darcy felt was like nothing he had ever known, and he searched for a way to speak of it to her apart from the simple words that most readily came to mind. She deserved a sonnet, but he was no poet. He had just decided that those simply phrased sentiments might serve better than silence when Elizabeth swept all before them with a question.

"When did you begin to fall in love with me?" she asked, her brow arched provocatively. Darcy looked down into her face and smiled. "I can comprehend your going on charmingly, when you had once made a beginning," she continued airily, "but what could set you off in the first place?"

"I cannot fix on the hour or the spot . . ." He listed and then laughed at her expression of impatience with his indecision. Stopping their progress, he bent and captured her eyes with his. "Or the look, or the words, which laid the foundation. It is too long ago. I was in the middle before I knew that I *had* begun."

"Where was your middle, I wonder?" She pursed her lips at him.

"Of that I am not entirely sure, lady." He paused and looked at her speculatively. "But most probably it was the day I became a thief."

"A thief!" Elizabeth laughed. "A man who has everything! Why would *you* turn thief, sir?"

"I was a man who *thought* he had everything," Darcy corrected her. "But one thing I lacked—the love of an exceptional woman."

She blushed at his compliment but did not allow it to deter her. "And this theft?"

"You will not think ill of me if I confess it?" He feigned an anxious countenance, delighting in their play.

"Even better, I shall act as your confessor!" Elizabeth fell in with his conceit. "Confess then, and I shall absolve you!"

Darcy laughed again. "Do you remember what volume enthralled you in Netherfield's library during your sister's illness?"

She shook her head. "Such a wealth of books, who can remember? I was there only a few minutes."

"You were there long enough to drive me to distraction! I believe it took me three attempts to get the sense of every page! No, you were there quite long enough, and left a token to mark your place."

The memory lit her face. "A few threads . . . in a volume of Milton. I remember!" Her brow wrinkled. "I returned for the book but could not find my place."

"That was because of my theft. I took them . . . and kept them for months afterward . . . here." He patted the pocket of his waistcoat. "Rolled about my finger and tucked in my pocket when I was not using them as a mark myself."

"And where are they now?" She looked up at him, her smile gentle.

"Providing some fledglings a nest, I hope. When I could stand to tease myself with them no longer, I left them to the wind last spring on my way to Kent." He laughed ruefully. "I had finally determined to forget you. Putting away those threads was to be the beginning. Much good it did me." He raised her hand to his lips and kissed it reverently. "For there you were, dearest Elizabeth, the reality behind those threads, and I was completely and utterly lost."

"Here now, Fletcher, the man must breathe!" Colonel Fitzwilliam came languidly to his cousin's rescue from the safe distance of a chair across Darcy's Netherfield dressing room.

"My dear Colonel, I assure you he can!" Fletcher protested. "There now, sir," he directed his master, "one more twist of the cloth and you may bring down your chin, but slowly, sir, slowly!" Darcy groaned but complied. "There now, sir. Yes! Behold, sir!" Fletcher held up a mirror to reveal an exquisite array of folds, knots, and twists gracing Darcy's neck and falling elegantly upon his waistcoat.

"What do you call it, my good man?" Dy inquired, his lorgnette held superciliously to one eye as he looked over the new masterpiece with interest.

"The *Bonheur,* my lord." Fletcher inclined his head.

"Happiness? That *is* bold, but then so was the *Roquet.*" Dy tucked his eyepiece into a waistcoat pocket. "Fletcher, I congratulate you." His Lordship turned to his friend and tapped him on the shoulder. "You must promise to lend him to me, Fitz, when it is *my* turn for leg shackles, or I shan't invite you."

"Done!" the bridegroom replied and turned back to the mirror. For all the annoyance, it looked rather well; and it was, after all, his wedding day. He turned his head this way and then the other, testing the restriction. It was bearable. "Richard, what do you say?" he called over his shoulder.

Colonel Fitzwilliam unwound from his comfortable observation post and cautiously approached. Crossing his arms, he studied his cousin thoughtfully. "It's not a uniform"—the men hooted at the jibe—"but Fletcher *is* a genius, as everyone knows." He grinned and laughed. "You look quite well, Cousin. Miss Elizabeth shall say 'I will' on the basis of your neckcloth alone!" Darcy threw a towel at him.

"Thank you, *dear* Richard." Darcy looked up to his valet. "Fletcher, excellent work." He rose from the seat, checked the clock on the mantel, and motioned to his new blue frock coat. "Are we ready for that now?"

"Yes, sir." Fletcher went to the wardrobe and retrieved the coat, handling it with the utmost care.

"So, tell us old bachelors," Dy addressed the valet, "how *is* married life, Fletcher?"

The valet colored, but his chest puffed out and his shoulders straightened. "Very fine, my lord, very fine indeed, I thank you." He held the frock coat out to his master. "Mr. Darcy?" Slipping the sleeves up his arms, he came around him, bringing the front down snugly over his shoulders and waistcoat and buttoning it.

"And Mrs. Fletcher is waiting upon the bride, I understand."

"Yes, my lord, and very happy to have the honor." Fletcher smoothed the back and twitched at one of the coattails before beginning his examination for stray threads or lint. When he had finished, Darcy went to his dresser and opened a book that lay atop it, turning the pages until he came to what he was looking for. There, from between the pages and lying next to the note in Elizabeth's hand, he retrieved her first wedding gift to him. Smiling down at the knot of threads in his hand—three green, two yellow, and one each of blue, rose, and lavender—he stroked them once, then wound them about his finger and secured them in his waistcoat pocket.

The clock struck, and Darcy's companions straightened from the lax stances they had adopted. "It is time, Fitz." Richard's voice shook slightly. He cleared his throat. "Damn me if you are not the most fortunate of men! You know I would knock you over the head if I thought otherwise." They all laughed at that but sobered quickly as Richard took his cousin's hand in a tight grip. "I have never seen a couple more suited in the usual respects, but the depth of emotion you share . . ." He paused. "Well, it gives me hope." He released Darcy's hand and added with a grin, "And now that *you* are off the marriage mart . . ."

"Move along, there, you!" His Lordship shouldered Richard roughly aside with a laugh and offered Darcy his hand as well. "My good friend." Dy's smile turned into a solemn yet affectionate regard as he looked him squarely in the eye. "I cannot begin to tell you how happy I am for this day."

"Dy . . ." Deeply moved, Darcy began to thank him; but Brougham cut him off.

"No, allow me to finish." Dy breathed in deeply. "Fitz, I have valued your friendship, envied you your good family, and generally admired you since we first met, you know. But this last year I have watched as you were shaken to your very core. I love you, Fitz, but you were in great need of *something* that would shake you out of your damned cool complacency. Thank God, it was love"— Dy swallowed hard—"and the love of an extraordinary woman that did so."

Darcy gripped his shoulder. "If you had not confronted me . . ."

"For what other use is a friend?" Dy whispered and, stepping back, glanced at the mantel clock. "Now, it truly *is* time." He gripped Darcy's hand even tighter. "There were moments when I almost despaired, but you, my friend, faced the worst a man's mirror can reflect and have shown yourself one of the best men I have the privilege of knowing." He then smiled broadly and with a wave of an elegant hand commanded, "Off with you now! Claim your bride, for you have won her heart in the best possible manner."

"Dearly beloved, we are gathered together here in the sight of God, and in the face of this congregation, to join together this man and this woman in holy matrimony; which is an honorable estate, instituted of God in the time of man's innocency, signifying unto us the mystical union that is betwixt Christ and his Church . . ."

They were all there: those who loved him and those whom he loved in turn: Georgiana, his Matlock relations, Dy; and those whose coming was politic: members of his various clubs, university friends, the Bennets' neighbors, and Bingley's relations. All together. Yet he could look nowhere but into Elizabeth's eyes as she stood beside him. Her calm beauty worked on him, soothing his own racing heart as the words of the wedding service flowed over and around them, filling him with wonder. *"This man,"* he thought, he, himself, and *"this woman,"* this amazing, precious woman! Light streamed through the stained-glass windows there at the front of Meryton Church, illuminating their small circle in a benediction of softly colored glory. It lit Elizabeth's hair, her eyes, her whole being, so that when the minister spoke of "mystical union," Darcy felt the words swiftly and keenly pierce him to the heart.

His first sight of Elizabeth at the door of the sanctuary had left him in a perilous state. Such loveliness! The smile that graced her lips and the flash of her eyes as she and her sister Jane neared him and Charles, showed her joy and confidence in him. He must have stepped back or swayed, he knew not which, but he had felt Richard's hand briefly on his arm. Elizabeth, Jane, and her father took their places and Darcy turned to face the minister, devoting those faculties he could spare to absorbing the words that would unite him to Elizabeth in truth as they were already in heart.

"Wilt thou have this woman to thy wedded wife," the Reverend Stanley addressed him solemnly, "to live together after God's ordinance in the holy estate of matrimony? Wilt thou love her . . ."

Yes, Elizabeth, his heart sang.

". . . comfort her, honor, and keep her in sickness and in health . . ."

Yes, my love.

". . . and, forsaking all other, keep thee only unto her, so long as ye both shall live?"

"I will," he responded, his vow strong and resonant. *Gladly, completely, always.*

The priest now turned to Elizabeth. Her eyelashes fluttered down, but Darcy could sense her happiness. "Wilt thou have this man to thy wedded husband, to live together after God's ordinance in the holy estate of matrimony? Wilt thou obey him, and serve him, love, honor, and keep him in sickness and in health; and, forsaking all other, keep thee only unto him, so long as ye both shall live?"

"I will."

"Who giveth these women to be married to these men?"

"I do." Mr. Bennet turned to his daughters and slowly brushed their cheeks. Darcy could see tears forming in Elizabeth's eyes as her father took up her right hand and, stepping back, placed it in the minister's. At the reverend's nod, Darcy came to Elizabeth's side. Gently, the priest placed her hand in his. The words flowed on . . . *to have and to hold . . . for better for worse. . . .* His heart swelled with love and pride—proper pride, now—as he spoke each line, looking deeply into her eyes. ". . . to love and to cherish, till death us do part, according to God's holy ordinance; and thereto I plight thee my troth."

Slowly, he unwound his fingers from hers. Elizabeth took his right hand. "I, Elizabeth Bennet, take thee, Fitzwilliam George Alexander Darcy, to my wedded husband . . ." The import of her whispered vows, that it was in him she placed her trust for all her future days, threatened to undo him. Richard leaned toward the minister and placed Elizabeth's ring upon the book he held. Darcy took it up.

"With this ring I thee wed," he promised, vowing into her keeping all he was or ever would become, "with my body I thee worship, and with all my worldly goods I thee endow." He slipped the ruby-crowned band up her fourth finger, seating it gently before bringing her hand to his lips, his eyes never leaving her face. The pain of the past—the rejection and revelation, the self-conceit and self-pity, his consuming loneliness—was finished! And upon that blessing, compounding all others, was the trust and devotion of this woman. For all their tomorrows, they would be one in body and spirit. It lacked only one last benediction. They both turned back to the minister.

"Forasmuch as Fitzwilliam Darcy and Elizabeth Bennet and Charles Bingley and Jane Bennet have consented together in holy wedlock, and have witnessed the same before God and this company . . ." The Reverend Stanley had read through each line of the service, but coming now to the close, he paused and encompassed them in a warm smile of blessing. "I pronounce that each couple be man and wife together, In the Name of the Father, and of the Son, and of the Holy Ghost. Amen."

"Amen," the assembly responded.

Sweeping up her other hand, Darcy brought both to his heart. She was his; he was hers. He was in want of nothing more. "Elizabeth," he whispered. She looked up into his eyes. "Dearest, loveliest Elizabeth."

Acknowledgments

The publishing of this volume brings to a close an eight-year labor of love that began as an experiment, became an education, progressed into a vocation, and finally transformed my life. It has brought me innumerable new friends and associates, and best and most wonderful of all, my husband, Michael.

An immense debt of gratitude goes to my friends Susan Kaye and Laura Lyons, fellow writers who encouraged and supported me every step of the way.

Finally, I must mention my readers. Your letters and notes through these many years have encouraged and humbled me more than you could ever imagine.

Bless you all!
Pamela Aidan

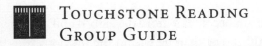
THESE THREE REMAIN

SUMMARY

These Three Remain, the thrilling conclusion of Pamela Aidan's *Fitzwilliam Darcy, Gentleman* trilogy, takes readers through the climactic final events of Jane Austen's *Pride and Prejudice*. His proposal of marriage to Elizabeth Bennet thoroughly rejected, Darcy must come to terms with her evaluation of his character and a future without her. *These Three Remain* recounts Darcy's painful journey of self-discovery in his quest to become the gentleman he always hoped he would be, and the kind of man of whom Elizabeth Bennet would approve. A chance meeting with her during a tour of his estate in Derbyshire offers Darcy an opportunity to prove his changing character to Elizabeth, but the activities of his nemesis, George Wickham, interfere once more in a way that may ruin everyone's hopes for happiness—unless Darcy succeeds in putting his newfound strengths to the test.

Set vividly against the colorful historical and political background of the time of the Regency, Aidan revisits the events of *Pride and Prejudice*, remaining faithful to Jane Austen's beloved characters while introducing her own fascinating cast as she weaves a rich tapestry from Darcy's past and present.

Discussion Points

1. What first led you to suspect that Lord Brougham's feelings for Georgiana Darcy went beyond protectiveness on behalf of her brother?

2. Dyfed Brougham becomes a more developed and complicated character in this novel than he was in the previous two. How do you feel about the spy plot twist? What kind of foil does Dy serve for Darcy?

3. Compare and contrast the formality and tradition-drenched ambience of Rosings to the atmosphere at the Collins' Hunsford home and the scenes that unfold there.

4. Lady Catherine seems symbolic of a bygone era as far as "decorum" goes. Do you think the clash between her value system and what she sees as the "lack of propriety" in Darcy's generation is similar to the recurring "generation gap" that still persists in our culture today?

5. Is it merely a moment of drunkenness or something else that pushes Darcy to confess his torment to Brougham? Why do you think, of all his acquaintances, it is Brougham to whom he finally opens his heart?

6. In this novel, Darcy continues to carefully shield and guide his younger sister, Georgiana. Why is it so difficult for Darcy to see Georgiana as the incredible young woman, by Lord Brougham's account, she has already become? What finally opens his eyes?

7. What did you suspect were Lady Sylvanie's motives for visiting Georgiana? Were you surprised when Dy appeared, incognito, to whisk Darcy away? Why or why not?

8. Darcy often finds himself interpreting "messages" from Elizabeth, both verbal and physical. Do you think he misreads her during their walks alone together at Rosings?

9. Discuss the ways in which duty and desire are at war with each other in this novel.

10. Darcy holds himself responsible for Lydia's entanglement with Wickham because pride caused him to remain silent about Wickham's character to those in Meryton. Do you agree that he is responsible for what happens?

11. Though it takes liberties, there are carefully designed moments of intersection between *These Three Remain* and Austen's *Pride and Prejudice*—more importantly, Aidan's novel gives readers a behind-the-scenes look at certain events, such as Darcy's intervention regarding Lydia Bennet and Wickham. How do these connections contribute or detract from your reading experience?

12. With a wider cast of characters than Austen's novel, *These Three Remain* serves to tie up far more loose ends. When all is finally revealed, do you believe that everyone has received his or her "just desserts?"

13. Now that you have seen the world through Darcy's eyes, is Elizabeth's estimation of his character accurate?

14. What does each of the titles in the trilogy reveal about the Darcy within it?

15. Since the trilogy is now complete, what would you like to see Pamela Aidan tackle next?

ENHANCE YOUR BOOK CLUB EXPERIENCE

1. The renowned poet, Lord Byron, is mentioned in the novel as a somewhat scandalous introduction to the drawing rooms of high society. Shakespeare and Milton are quoted often in the novel as well. For your next meeting, bring a poem or sonnet you feel one of Pamela Aidan's characters would enjoy and discuss the reasons behind your selection. Or if you really want a

challenge, write an original piece in the voice of Mr. Darcy or the other characters!

2. As one of the world's most celebrated writers, Shakespeare's plays are performed with regularity throughout the United States. Find a local performance of *Much Ado About Nothing*, or rent Kenneth Branagh's 1993 film rendition, to watch a couple who spar with as much wit as Elizabeth and Darcy. You can even make a night of it with members of your Book Club!

Q&A WITH PAMELA AIDAN

With such beloved characters, the pressure to write a fantastic climax to the **Fitzwilliam Darcy, Gentleman** *trilogy must have been great. Can you tell us a little about your process for writing* **These Three Remain?**

This book was far and away the most difficult to write. That it was finished at all is due in great part to the encouraging yet critical help of my husband.

As I wrote a section, he would read and critique it with an honesty that sometimes smarted but was always with the goals of keeping me on target with Austen and the characters as I had drawn them and challenging me to become a better writer.

The details of Rosings Park truly make the magnificence of the garden come alive for readers. Did you visit any such estates or parks for inspiration?

I've been to Europe several times and toured gardens in France and Italy as well as paged through books about gardening and its history. Gardens were a deeply integral part of European homes, whether wealthy or not. Great changes in gardening philosophy had occurred during the fifty years before and during this time period that relate to how people of the time regarded nature and their place in it.

The scene at Lord and Lady Monmouth's soiree introduces the historical conflict between the Irish and the English. Can you elaborate a little on the state of affairs between these two peoples at that point in history, and on why you chose this subplot?

Ireland was a conquered land and all the worst excesses of occupation that accompany that fact had and were being visited upon its people. The other factor in its oppression was Ireland's Catholicism. Since the time of Henry VIII—excluding the reign of his daughter Mary—Catholics had not been allowed to vote for fear that the Pope would then be able to reinsert himself into British politics. During the Regency, the loyalty of the Irish troops in the war with Napoleon became a serious issue, as was the loyalty of Irish peers, so "The Catholic Question" (i.e. their enfranchisement) was taken up by Parliament. Prince George had previously let it be known that he was in favor of giving Catholics, and therefore the Irish, the vote and full citizenship in the Empire; but when he became Regent, he disavowed it and the upheaval of a war-time political scene pushed it back out onto the fringe of consideration. Ireland had long been sympathetic to France due to their shared Catholicism and lately their overthrow of a hated aristocracy. Some British Whigs were also sympathetic to "republican" ideas. Then, there was the assassination of the prime minister in 1812, when *Pride and Prejudice* is generally allowed to have taken place. It seemed hard to ignore.

Its usefulness as a subplot only occurred to me when I decided to bring Lady Sylvanie back into the story. In her, I had a half-Irish villainess who had disappeared, only to marry an old classmate of Darcy's. Characters and events began to fall into place in my mind, and I decided to use Sylvanie and her new quest for power through politics to bring Darcy to a situation in which he finally was forced to admit that he no longer could trust his own judgment or perception.

The twist of Lord Brougham's being a spy was surprising! What inspired you to shape this character into a man of intrigue?

Dy Brougham was a surprise from the beginning and was another one of those characters that appeared full-blown almost out of nowhere and told his own story whether I liked it or not! Of course, Sir Percy Blakney—the Scarlet Pimpernel—was a model in some ways. I wanted Darcy's friend to be a character of great wit and yet a mystery. But any true friend of Darcy's would have to be much more complex than a public clown. By creating him as a domestic spy, he immediately became someone who could appear and disappear from the storyline and yet be incredibly well-informed and capable when he was needed. As the story progressed, the usefulness of his "occupation" dovetailed so well with his friendship with Darcy, that it became integral to the plot.

You've added quite a bit of material to the story, including new scenes, characters, and significant events that never graced Austen's pages. Did you feel like you were "filling in the blanks" of Pride and Prejudice, *or did the story take on a life of its own?*

Both of your surmises are true. The trilogy was always meant to be more than merely a converse look at *Pride and Prejudice.* Its beginning was the intriguing question: how did Fitzwilliam Darcy change so dramatically between the opening pages of the book and his reacquaintance with Elizabeth at Pemberley, a change not only in his inner man, but one that carries him to great personal acts of charity involving a man he has every reason to hate? To discover this, there had to be a significant "filling in" because it was an entire blank! That is why Elizabeth is not in every scene, why the events of *Duty and Desire,* why the new characters and scenes. How else can we get to know Darcy and see him change than by observing him in *his* world and plunging him into challenging situations? Then, also, the story quite often took on a life of its own.

There were times I felt more like a secretary taking down dictation from all my characters than their creator!

This gives a "behind-the-scenes" look at some of the most exciting plot points in the conclusive chapters of Pride and Prejudice. How did you choose which events to highlight?

I chose the ones that seemed to me to be the most difficult for Darcy to deal with: challenging his long-held assumptions, demanding he make a choice, or sorely testing his new growth, understanding, and character. Some of them were great fun to write, almost writing themselves, and others were very difficult. And, frankly, some just offered delicious moments of high drama!

Will you explain the significance of the title, These Three Remain?

These Three Remain is a portion of the New International Version's translation of I Corinthians 13, the famous chapter on love written by the apostle Paul that is often heard at weddings. There he lists admirable character qualities and actions, but states that without these things arising from love, they mean nothing and will not, in the end, last beyond the grave. But (in verse 13) "These three remain: faith, hope, and love (charity, in the King James Version), and the greatest of these is love." Throughout the trilogy, these three concepts—along with the related one of mercy—have challenged duty and desire as the keys to character and living a worthy life.

The primary male characters in this novel—Richard, Darcy, Brougham, and Bingley—are all more sentimental and romantic than readers may be used to when it comes to reading about men and love. How would you compare them to the heroes of today's romance novels?

That is a question I'd like to hear answered by my readers! I don't read much Romance nor do I write by formula. So, please, let me know!

There are new Jane Austen spin-off novels and movies being made every year. Do you have any favorites you'd like to share with your readers?

I don't read other Austen spin-offs that have to do with *Pride and Prejudice* because I don't want to be influenced by them. A friend of mine is publishing her take on *Persuasion: Fredrick Wentworth, Captain* in late 2006 that is great fun to read. My favorite movies besides the 1995 *Pride and Prejudice* are the version of *Emma* with Kate Beckinsale and Mark Strong and *Persuasion* with Amanda Root and Ciarin Hinds, as well as the wonderful rendition of *Sense and Sensibility* with Emma Thompson, etc.

Is it safe to assume Mr. Darcy is your favorite Austen character? Do you have other favorite romantic literary heroes?

Yes, you are perfectly safe in that assumption! Sir Percy Blakney, the Scarlet Pimpernel, mentioned previously would be another.

Now that the trilogy is complete, what's next?

I want to write a follow-up book on the Darcys and tie up some deliberately left loose ends. Principally, I want to write Dy Brougham's story and intersect it with Darcy and Elizabeth and their young family and an "of age" Georgiana Darcy during the years shortly after the war with Napoleon ends.